THE SECOND MEONBRIDGE CHRONICLE

A WOMAN'S LOT

SilverWood

Published in 2018 by SilverWood Books

SilverWood Books Ltd
14 Small Street, Bristol, BS1 1DE, United Kingdom
www.silverwoodbooks.co.uk

ISBN 978-1-78132-788-3 (paperback)
ISBN 978-1-78132-789-0 (ebook)

British Library Cataloguing in Publication Data
A CIP catalogue record for this book is available from the British Library

Page design and typesetting by SilverWood Books
Printed on responsibly sourced paper

CAROLYN HUGHES was born in London, but has lived most of her life in Hampshire. After completing a degree in Classics and English, she started her working life as a computer programmer, in those days a very new profession. But it was when she discovered technical authoring that she knew she had found her vocation. She spent the next few decades writing and editing all sorts of material, some fascinating, some dull, for a wide variety of clients, including an international hotel group, medical instrument manufacturers and the government.

She has written creatively for most of her adult life, but it was not until her children grew up and flew the nest several years ago that writing historical fiction, took centre stage in her life. She has a Master's in Creative Writing from Portsmouth University and a PhD from the University of Southampton.

*A Woman's Lot* is the second novel in the MEONBRIDGE CHRONICLES series. The first, *Fortune's Wheel*, was published in 2016. A third novel is under way.

Also by Carolyn Hughes

*Fortune's Wheel*

A WOMAN'S LOT

# CAST OF CHARACTERS

## PRINCIPAL CHARACTERS ARE IN BOLD; NAMES IN ITALICS HAVE NO VOICE IN THIS NOVEL

**Eleanor Titherige, inheritor of her father's flock of sheep**
Roger Stronge, her stepbrother
Nathan and Hawisa, her servants
Walter Nash, her shepherd
Cecily, Walter's aunt, a healer
Will Cole, a cottar, works for Eleanor

**Emma Ward, labourer, works for Eleanor**
Ralph, her husband
Beatrix and Amice, Emma's children by her first husband Bart, and *Bartholomew*, her son by Ralph
Alys, Ralph's mother, a sharp-tongued besom
Ann Webb, Alys's friend, also a cottar

**Agnes Sawyer, carpenter's wife, mother of the de Bohuns' grandson**
Jack Sawyer, her husband
Alice atte Wode, her mother
John atte Wode, her brother, the Meonbridge reeve
Dickon, Agnes's son by Sir Philip de Bohun, and *Stephen* and *Geoffrey*, Agnes's sons by Jack
Marye, nursemaid to the Sawyer children
Christopher, Jack's apprentice

**Susanna Miller, the miller's wife**
Henry Miller, the current miller
*Francis* and *Joan*, their children, and Tom, Henry's son by his first wife
Maud, Thomas's last surviving child, living with Henry and Susanna
Thomas, Henry's older brother and former miller

Lady Margaret de Bohun of Meonbridge
Sir Richard de Bohun, lord of Meonbridge
*Matilda Fletcher, Lady de Bohun's companion, and Libby, her daughter*

Geoffrey Dyer, the Meonbridge constable
Simon Hogge, the barber-surgeon
Master Hugo Garret, priest
Godfrey Cuylter, aged curate
Adam Wragge, the Meonbridge bailiff
Nicholas Ashdown, an incomer from Winchester

Matthew Ward, cousin to Ralph
Luke, his son
John Ward, Matthew's brother
Arthur, his son
William Mannering and his young son, Harry
Fulke and Warin Collyere, incomers from Upper Brooking
Kit Chapman, itinerant pedlar

The Sheriff of Hampshire
The Hampshire coroner, Hubert Gastingthrop
The Winchester gaoler
Edith Wyteby, a kindly Winchester matron
Sir Anthony Appylton, chief justice on the King's Bench

# PROLOGUE

## SPRING 1352

Luke blasphemed and Arthur whimpered as they tripped and stumbled over jutting roots and fallen branches, or lost their footing in the dips and hollows of the woodland floor. It was so dark, with not a single shaft of moonlight piercing the canopy of leaves, the lads were forced to feel their way through the dense-packed beeches, tree trunk by tree trunk.

They'd only come this way to avoid the risk of being caught. Luke thought he'd not bother next time.

But at last they reached a stand of oaks at the woodland's edge, where the downland opened out beyond. Arthur was snivelling, complaining that he'd torn his hose on a holly's spiky leaves and grazed his leg when he tripped over a protruding root. Luke scorned his cousin's moaning, and told him to shut up. He came to an abrupt halt and thrust out his arm, catching Arthur across the chest as he came up behind him.

Arthur gasped out a wheezing cry and Luke clapped his big hand across the boy's mouth. 'Keep quiet, I said.'

It was lighter here, bright enough to make out each other, but not yet to see the sheep clearly. Luke pushed his cousin back, signalling him to keep hidden behind a tree. Then he pointed to the sky, and held up two fingers. Arthur nodded. And, before long, the slow-moving clouds drifted past and the moon's light revealed the flock, spread out before them across the down.

Several sheep were grazing close to the trees. The soft rasp of sharp teeth cropping grass travelled clearly on the quiet night air. It would be easiest to catch one there. But grazing sheep were not their target. They scanned the flock for those with droopy heads.

'Can you see a dozy one?' Luke said, keeping his voice low. He scratched at his tangled thatch of strawy hair then, putting his fingers to his mouth, chewed at his grimy nails.

Arthur shook his curly head. 'I thought they'd *all* be sleeping.'

9

'Don't be daft.' Luke sneered. 'Don't you know aught about sheep? They sleep in the day. It's too dangerous at night, with wild beasts a-prowl, wanting to snatch 'em.'

'Like us,' said Arthur, sniggering. 'So why we looking for sleepers, if there ain't none?'

Luke snorted. 'Well, o' course, *some* of 'em sleep, and some keep watch.'

Arthur stared into the gloom. 'They *all* seem to be watching now.'

'Nah. There'll be 'least one dozy one. We just have to wait.'

Arthur didn't much want to wait. He'd thought they'd just come up here, take a sheep, and go. It hadn't occurred to him they might have to hang around. And he'd not thought either it'd be so scary.

As they hunkered down between the roots of the towering trees, the moon passed in and out of the clouds, casting them alternately into blessed light and fearful dark. And, in the dark, Arthur realised how full of noise the night was – the whisper of leaves, the creak of branches, the rustlings in the undergrowth, the screams and barks that kept shattering the silence, sounding like the howls of demons or of evil spirits.

'Whassat?' Arthur gripped Luke's arm when, close by, a long, piercing screech rent the air. 'I don't like it,' he wailed, all for abandoning their adventure and going home.

Luke shook him off. 'You milksop! It's just *animals*.' Though even he was a bit unnerved. He thought that scream sounded just like someone being murdered, but he would never admit to being scared.

Then, again quite close, they heard a bark, more that of a dog than a demon. And, as the clouds scudded across the moon and left it beaming down once more onto the pasture, they saw, not very far distant, towards where the downland fell away, a running fox.

Luke fleered, and poked his cousin in the ribs. 'I coulda told you it were a fox.'

Arthur blew out a huge breath. 'Thank Jesu!'

But the sheep must have spotted the fox too, for they became restless, bleating and trotting back and forth. Then a few turned decisively and ran in the opposite direction. The fox stopped, one foot raised, its head alert, and watched them for a few moments. But there were as yet no lambs to take, and it scampered off down the hill, perhaps in search of other prey.

The sheep settled down again, those that had run away trotting back towards their sisters and the shelter of the woodland edge. But none seemed to want to sleep.

The lads just had to wait.

A slight wind got up and the trees rustled more vigorously overhead. Arthur was shaking, and Luke noticed.

'What's up wi' you?' he said, scratching at his hair again.

'Cold,' said Arthur, not willing to admit he was still scared. He wrapped his arms around his scrawny chest and wedged his body into the space between the roots of the tall, broad oak, trying to find some comfort in the tree's rough embrace.

But, moments later, he was shrieking.

For a great shape, its underside bright white, had loomed above them, speeding out from between the trees and out across the down, skimming so low over their heads the draught had ruffled Arthur's hair.

Luke thumped his cousin hard upon the shoulder. 'Shuddup, you idiot. You'll scare the sheep.' And many were taking to their heels again, running from where the boys were hiding. 'Why d'you have to scream, you half-wit? It were an *owl*, not a demon.'

Arthur sniffled. 'I were took by surprise.'

'So now we'll just have to wait some more.'

Arthur was quivering like a lamb's tail by the time the sheep were quiet once more, but Luke thought they might risk inspecting them at closer quarters.

'Keep your mouth *shut*,' he warned his cousin. 'Just have the sack good an' ready.'

At that moment, clouds veiled the moon once more, leaving just enough light for them to see each other's outlines and those of the sheep, as they crept forward from the cover of the trees.

Their luck was in, for they found a small ewe sleeping a short distance from the main flock.

Luke nudged Arthur's arm with his elbow and pointed. Arthur nodded, and they padded forward, approaching the dozing animal from behind. Luke made a sudden lunge at the sheep's rear end and, as it staggered to its feet, he grabbed at its back legs. He was a strong lad, not tall but firm muscled, and his hands were unusually large yet, even so, the beast's struggles were so violent he found it hard to keep a hold.

The animal was bleating piteously, but Luke held on tight and nodded to Arthur, who knew what he had to do. Running forward, he threw his sack over the sheep's head, while Luke heaved its back end up and shoved it bodily inside the bag. Then Arthur took a piece of twine from the small pouch at his waist and tied it around the top.

Luke hefted the struggling, bleating sack to his shoulder and staggered towards the downhill track, with Arthur running after him. There was a good chance now of being caught. The sack was heavy, and Luke, for all his bluster, was finding it hard to run. And the whole flock seemed to be bleating in alarm, some following the boys, on a track that would take the mayhem only yards from the shepherd's cottage.

But again the lads were lucky, for the sheep stayed on the ridge and the shepherd did not appear. After numerous stops for Luke to put down his load, at last they made it back to Meonvale, the area of Meonbridge where the cottar hovels were clustered together. They headed for an abandoned croft, its former occupiers all lost in the Death. A large decrepit barn stood at the croft's far end, well hidden behind an unchecked thicket of brambles and ivy. It was where they planned to hide the sheep. But, when they arrived, out of breath and gasping, the captured sheep had become so quiet and still, they feared it might have died of shock.

It was dark inside the barn, despite the broken timbers of the roof letting through a narrow shaft of moonlight. Yet each lad saw the other's eyes were scared, as Luke untied the sack.

'D'you think it's dead?' said Arthur in a whisper.

''Ope not, after all we've been through.'

But when Luke loosed the twine and opened the sack, the sheep tumbled out and scrambled to its feet. It shook itself and gave a solitary bleat, and the boys shoved it into one of the pens the family had probably once used for pigs, and shut the gate.

A few days before, in the rundown ale-house in cottar Meonvale, Luke's father, Matthew, had been holding court, as usual, complaining in a raucous, bitter voice of how badly Meonvale folk were treated. His brother John sat hunched beside him, silent as ever, his hands gripping his pot of ale. Since both men had lost their wives in the Death, and all their children apart from a son apiece, they invariably shared their evenings. Though each still returned to the allotted tiny hovel and meagre croft, in return for which they paid a modest rent and provided some menial labouring tasks on the lord's demesne.

Men like John and Matthew stood on the bottom rung of Meonbridge manor society. They might struggle to earn enough even for their rent, let alone to feed their families. Yet, some cottars were well-respected for their diligence and skill, turning their hand to any one of a dozen labouring tasks around the manor. John was such a man, as was his cousin, Ralph, and both were never without employment. But Matthew was quite a different sort, well-known for his unreliability, as well as being lazy, invariably drunk and often violent. Scarcely ever finding work beyond his manorial obligations, he relied on the generosity of his brother and his only son for his scant subsistence. Neither Adam the bailiff nor any of Meonbridge's wealthier tenants or freemen would waste their money on employing him.

And neither would Eleanor Titherige.

Indeed her spurning Matthew that very morning was the reason for his rage.

''Aughty cow,' he said, thumping his ale down upon the table, ''oo do she think she is?'

Matthew's cousin, Ralph, chuckled. 'A successful farmer, mebbe?' he said. 'And less of the "cow", if you don't mind. Mistress Eleanor's a respectable woman.'

Matthew spat into the filthy rushes on the floor. 'Farmer?' he snorted. 'Her's just a wench. What's she know 'bout farming?'

'A good deal more 'n you,' said William Mannering, taking a deep draught of his ale. 'I daresay she felt she couldn't trust you wi' her precious sheep.'

Everyone laughed at that, except Matthew. He had thought he could cajole the "haughty cow". Since he had lost his wife, he had been courting every available woman in Meonbridge and beyond, though none had taken him up because, no doubt, however strong-looking and, at times, silver-tongued he was, he had nothing at all to offer, save a dilapidated hovel and an overgrown, neglected croft.

Eleanor had not been taken in at all, and Matthew would have to stay dependent on handouts from his brother and son who, at sixteen, was being given a chance by Adam the bailiff to prove himself more reliable than his father. Some thought it noble of the bailiff not to dismiss the lad as merely his father's son. Perhaps he hoped the boy might follow the example set him by the other men in his family?

But most thought Adam's confidence misplaced.

That evening, Luke, with Arthur, was lurking in a corner of the ale-house, not drinking but playing nine men's morris with some other lads, and listening in on Matthew's heated diatribe. They overheard the man's complaints and, later, Arthur agreed with Luke to somehow put the "haughty" Mistress Titherige in her place.

'Half a dozen'd be enough,' said Luke.

Arthur agreed, though the thought of stealing sheep was frightening. 'Six'd make a fair few pennies.'

Luke grinned. 'We'd have to take 'em one at a time. We couldn't get away with more 'n one without a cart.'

'An' her's got so many,' said Arthur, 'she'll not miss 'em if we take 'em one by one.'

After the first, they went back and stole two more, penning them all up inside the ramshackle barn. But, after three, they had had enough.

'It's too much like 'ard work,' said Luke, and Arthur agreed, relieved he'd not have to spend any more nights up in those noisy woods.

But they could not stop themselves grinning like fools. 'We got *three* sheep!' said Arthur, crowing, and Luke laughed and thumped him on the back.

One evening after that, Luke acquired a flagon of strong ale from the girl who helped out in the cottar ale-house. She stole it for him in return for the promise of a kiss and cuddle later. Luke was as much of an occasional charmer as his father, and she was flattered by his attentions, not being the comeliest of maids.

Luke and Arthur hunkered down in the ale-house lean-to with a couple of their friends, and all took turns to slurp the ale from the flagon. But unaccustomed to drinking such strong ale, Arthur soon became quite drunk.

'You'll ne'er guess wha' we got,' he said to the friends, slurring his words a little, 'pen' up in an ol' barn.'

Luke might not have said aught of it himself, but he was so pleased with how clever he'd been, he could scarcely bear not to brag about it too. 'Sheep!' he said. 'Three of 'em.'

Then he boasted about how easy it had been, and his friends were much impressed.

But Luke and Arthur didn't know that, listening outside, was William Mannering's young son, Harry. He'd been with his father in the ale-house, and had come outside for a piss in the long grass just beyond the lean-to. Hearing laughter coming from inside, he stayed to listen. Then, going back into the ale-house, he told his father what he'd heard. And his father told Will Cole, who was eating his supper there, as he often did, after a long day up on Riverdown with Mistress Titherige's sheep.

Will thought well of his employer, admiring the success she had made already of her flock. He leapt to his feet, knocking the table in his haste, so his ale spilled from its pot and some of the stew he had been spooning up spurted from the bowl and landed in a lumpy puddle on the table.

Will marched outside, with Ralph and William close behind him. And, at that moment, John and Matthew got wind of something afoot, and ran outside to find out what. They arrived to see Will looming at the lean-to's entrance, Ralph and William backing him up on either side.

'What's this I just heard,' roared Will, "bout you stealing Missus Titherige's sheep?' A stabbing finger was levelled at Luke and Arthur.

Then Matthew shouted, 'Lemme pass!' and pushed inside past Will. 'What you saying 'bout my lad?' he said, jabbing at Will's shoulder.

Will swung round and faced him. 'That he's been stealing sheep, that's what.' He glared at Matthew. 'That's an 'anging offence.'

Matthew lunged over to his son and hauled him to his feet by the front of his shirt. 'Is he right?' he yelled, cocking his head in Will's direction.

Luke shook. ''Course not, Da.'

'So what was you saying in here?' said Will.

'We was just joking. Pretending. We done nothing.'

But John saw his boy was terrified and, coming forward too, knelt down beside him. 'Well, son?' he said, and Arthur burst into tears and blurted out the truth of what he and Luke had done.

And now Ralph too came forward into the little shed. 'We must raise the hue and cry,' he said. 'It's our tithing duty, John.'

John raked his fingers through his hair. Then he took Arthur's hand and, pulling him to his feet, put his arm around his shoulders.

But Matthew was already laying into Luke, with slaps about his ears and punches to his chest. 'You bloody fool,' he yelled, tears starting from his eyes. 'What d'you do it for?'

Luke was crying too. 'For you, Da,' he whispered. 'To get back at Missus Titherige—'

But Matthew seemed not to hear.

Ralph and the two Wills left the lean-to to call up their neighbours, members of the cottar tithing, to bring evidence against the two young thieves. Matthew shoved his son away from him with a final thump, and ran after them.

'Ralph,' he cried, grabbing at the sleeve of his cousin's tunic. Ralph faced him, shaking his head. 'Please, Ralph.' Then Matthew turned to Will. 'Don't raise the hue an' cry. You know what it'll mean. My lad'll lose his life, or 'least his hand.'

'It's the law, cousin,' said Ralph. 'You know that.'

Matthew sobbed, but Will was unmoved. 'Sheep-stealing's a serious crime. Your boys knew what they was doing. They should face justice.'

Then John was also at their side. In the faint light coming from the tiny unshuttered windows of the ale-house, the other men saw the terror on his face. 'They'll give the sheep back,' he said.

'Yeah, tonight,' said Matthew, his head bobbing up and down. 'She'll never know they're gone if we give 'em back tonight.'

'Too late,' said Will, shrugging. 'She's already noticed three are missing.'

Matthew clasped his brother to his chest.

But Ralph rubbed his hand across his face, then patted John's shoulder. 'Mebbe the lads've been scared enough. Mebbe we can hold off the hue an' cry, if you promise to take the beasts back up to Riverdown tonight.'

Will's brow wrinkled at that. 'You're the tithing-man, Ralph. You know we must turn them in.' Then his mouth twisted. 'An', if Mistress Titherige hears of it, I'll lose my job,' he whispered.

'But for the sake of cottar fellowship?' said Ralph, and at length Will tightened his lips and shrugged.

# 1

## SPRING 1352

It was such a clear, bright morning that Eleanor rose earlier than usual and reached the crest of Riverdown before her shepherd, Walter, had even emerged from the two-room cottage that nestled against a stand of tall beech trees with a good view of the pastureland where Eleanor ran her flock.

She was surprised to find Will already up there, moving amongst the flock of ewes, lifting heads and inspecting faces.

She waved at him, and ran over. 'Will? What are you doing here so early?'

He took off his cap and nodded in greeting. 'Just checking if the missing dams are back.'

'And are they?' said Eleanor, wondering quite how Will would know which ones they were. She had discovered two days past, when they did a head count, that three of her ewes seemed to have disappeared, but she was not sure she would recognise them amidst the flock even if they had returned. It was a blessing both Will and Walter seemed to know each animal as an individual.

But Will shook his head. 'No, missus, they're not.' He scratched at his head.

'So what do you think has happened to them?' said Eleanor. 'Just wandered off, or taken by a fox?'

'Too big for a fox.' He shuffled his feet, then carried on inspecting faces.

Eleanor thought Will looked unsettled, and said so. When he looked up at her again, the skin on his face was taut, and his brow was creased.

'Do you know something, Will?' she said.

He pushed out his lips and came forward, his cap still in his hand. 'I got summat to tell you, missus.'

Eleanor felt a quickening in her breast, thinking that, perhaps, he knew her ewes were dead.

She let out a long breath when he denied it. 'But I do know who took them, missus, an' why.' And he told her all he had learned in the ale-house.

17

'They promised to bring them back last night,' he said, then knit his brow. 'But they 'aven't.'

Eleanor's heart was thumping now, her fists clenched so tight her fingernails were digging into her palms.

'Losing sheep's a serious matter, Will, especially when we're trying to build a purebred flock.' She wanted to march right back down the hill and beat on Matthew's door, demanding that he and his errant son give back her sheep.

'I know that, missus.' Will passed his cap through twitchy fingers. 'But it's tricky now—'

'Why?'

''Cause Ralph agreed with the lads' fathers not to raise the hue an' cry, and let them go on the understanding they brought back the sheep—'

Eleanor gasped. 'But Ralph had no right to do that. Boys or not, they *must* be brought to justice—'

'I said that, missus. But little Arthur's 'specially sorry for what he done, and it'd be a shame for the lad to lose his hand, if the beasts can be returned wi' no harm done.'

Eleanor lifted her eyes to Will's. 'Do you truly think that, Will?'

He pursed his lips. 'I didn't last night. An' now the sheep aren't back, I'm still of a mind to bring the lads to justice. But then...'

'Then what?'

'Arthur's still a lad, missus, as well as simple. I warrant he were led astray by Luke. And John's a good man. He don't deserve to lose his only son, or have him maimed.'

Eleanor was angry, of course she was, but retribution would not have been her father's way, and she knew it should not be hers. Better to be generous to those less well-off than herself. Especially when they were children.

'But what of Luke?' she said. 'He's hardly a child.'

'True enough. But Matthew's got problems enough wi'out him losing his livelihood.'

Eleanor opened her mouth, about to say that Matthew Ward was well-known as a drunk and a wastrel, and hardly deserved consideration. But she stopped herself, remembering another drunken wastrel who, like Matthew, had been lazy and work-shy, yet was loved – if not respected – by most folk in Meonbridge, and adored by the woman who would shortly be climbing up the hill to Riverdown to bring her lambing skills to Eleanor's aid. Eleanor admired Emma for the way she had stuck by her handsome, idle Bart. It may be true that no one loved Matthew the way Emma had loved Bart, but, surely, even *he* was not an evil man? If she had it in her power to give him – or at least his son, and certainly young Arthur – another chance, then should she not do so?

'I agree,' she said at last. 'Let's wait another night, to see if they come back.'

Walter did not agree with Eleanor's decision.

'Would you see a boy of eleven hanged, or lose his hand?' she said, her head held high, when he declared the Ward cousins should be taught a lesson.

'No,' said Walter, 'but if *they* get away with theft, who else'll think they can just walk off with other people's property?'

In truth, Eleanor thought that too, yet she wanted to be kind, but doubted Walter would understand. So she changed the subject. 'Anyway, how was it that the sheep were stolen? Surely they should be safe enough up here?'

Out of the corner of her eye, she saw Will strolling off down the hill with Meg, one of Walter's dogs, trotting along behind. Perhaps he'd noticed her and Walter arguing and had decided to leave them to it?

Walter crossed his arms, and his index finger tapped against his sleeve. 'Sheep are never *safe*, even if they're kept in cotes. But out here on the downs, they're free to wander. That's what sheep do. And if they wander, they might get taken, not just by boys, but foxes.'

He was right, of course, but surely it was *his* job to protect them. 'Can we not guard them better?' said Eleanor.

He lifted his shoulders. 'We could bring them in at night, to cotes or holding pens – but, as the flock grows bigger, it'll become all the harder to do that.'

'So guard them better outside?' she said, knowing the idea was probably preposterous.

He gave a half sort of laugh. 'All day *and* all night?' His eyebrows arched. 'We'd need far more men, and all of them full-time.'

'How can I afford that?'

He uncrossed his arms, and spread his hands. 'If that's what you wanted, Mistress, you'd just have to.'

She flinched. He had not called her "Mistress" in a long while. She knew this argument was getting silly, yet somehow she could not back down. 'Then, find a way,' she said, not meaning for her voice to sound so shrill, and turned and followed Will down the hill towards the flock.

Or rather, she did not catch up with Will but, once out of Walter's sight, slipped across the pasture to the patch of woodland bordering the crest of Riverdown, and stomped back and forth amidst the trees, kicking at the leaves that had fallen last autumn and were still lying thickly there, soft and rather sodden.

Eleanor waited two nights for her sheep to be returned but when, on the third morning, Will told her they were still not home, she decided her generosity was being over-stretched.

'I am going to see the bailiff,' she said, 'to demand my sheep are found.'

'There's naught else you can do, missus.'

'You should've done it sooner,' said Walter, his tone sharp, but then he shuffled his feet. 'Shall I come with you?'

But Eleanor, already bridling at his censure, refused his offer. 'I'm quite capable, thank you, of talking to the bailiff on my own.' She knew she sounded tetchy, and noticed the hurt in Walter's eyes before she ran back down the hill.

Eleanor was careful what she said to Adam, not wanting either to get Ralph into trouble for going against legal ordinance and custom, or to make the cottar boys seem more wicked than they were.

Adam knit his brows. 'When the sheep first went missing, why didn't Ralph raise the hue and cry?'

'Because they were lads, I think. Not wanting to get them into trouble. After all, I'm sure it was just a silly prank. You know how mischievous lads can be...'

Adam pulled on his beard. 'Lads can indeed be wayward, but Luke's hardly a child, and taking sheep is, as you know, Mistress Titherige, deserving of the rope.'

She feigned a gasp of horror. 'Surely not in *this* case, master bailiff?'

'Sir Richard'll not be pleased the tithing-men failed in their duty.' He frowned. 'If the sheep are found, and returned to you unharmed, his lordship *might* be willing to consider the theft a childish prank, and impose some lesser penalty.'

'*Much* lesser, I trust,' said Eleanor, fixing Adam's eyes with hers. 'I'd not want to lay charges against the boys.'

'I'll do my best, but I'd not rely on Sir Richard being generous. A pity about young Luke. I'd thought better of him...'

He seemed to drift off into a reverie and Eleanor coughed. 'My ewes, Master Wragge?'

'Ah, yes,' said Adam, smiling. 'Let's call out the constable and his men.'

But when, later that morning, Eleanor accompanied Geoffrey, the constable, and his men, to the cottar cottages, in the hope of apprehending Luke and Arthur, the boys were nowhere to be found. Men were sent off in all directions to search for them, but they seemed to have disappeared.

'Tipped off, I warrant,' said the constable to Eleanor, shaking his head, and she agreed that seemed quite likely.

'But I'm more concerned to find my sheep, master constable,' she went on. 'You can surely catch the boys later, but if my sheep are being neglected, I must save them.'

Geoffrey agreed, but it was well into the afternoon before they all regrouped and went back to Matthew's wretched home, the constable bearing the bailiff's writ to search his entire premises. Will had told Eleanor he thought the sheep were more likely being kept on Matthew's croft than his brother's. 'John's not the sort o' man to let stolen goods be hid on his property,' he said.

But neither, it turned out, was Matthew.

When Geoffrey asked him where his son had hidden the stolen sheep, it was plain that Matthew had truly no idea. And he was affronted when, despite his pleadings, the constable's men as good as ransacked his meagre home and croft in their search for the missing beasts. Yet the sheep could not be found.

'So where are they?' Eleanor pleaded with a now indignant Matthew. But, recalling the way his face had crumpled this morning, when the constable had demanded to know the whereabouts of his son, Eleanor believed him when he said he did not know. In truth, he seemed quite shocked to find that his son, and nephew, had completely vanished.

'So where *are* the sheep your son stole from Mistress Titherige?' demanded Geoffrey once again, but Matthew just shook his head, and the constable had to cast his search net wider, and commandeer the services of a larger group of men.

It was almost dark by the time Eleanor's sheep were at last discovered in a derelict barn at the far end of an abandoned cottar croft. At first, Eleanor had joined in the search, but fatigue and distress had soon worn her down and at length she knocked on Emma's door and asked if she might rest.

Emma seemed pleased to welcome her into her home. 'You poor thing, you look exhausted,' she said, fussing over her. 'Sit down by the fire and I'll bring you a pot of ale and a bite to eat.'

Eleanor noticed how neatly Emma kept her tiny cottage, so very different from Matthew's, a hovel by comparison, yet only a few steps along the lane. But Emma was ashamed that all this upset was the fault of cousins of her husband Ralph.

'I scarce know Matthew, or his son,' she said, 'but John's truly a good man, and young Arthur's a simple, gentle boy who I'm sure might be led easily into mischief.'

'I suspect the theft was Luke's idea,' said Eleanor. 'Though I still do not know *why*.'

'A prank? Or a chance to make some money?'

'Or both? But a very dangerous prank, given the penalty for theft.'

Emma's eyes were wide. 'D'you think Sir Richard'll demand it?'

'I hope not. But the lads have vanished, so we may never know.'

At that moment, the constable knocked on Emma's door. 'Is Mistress Titherige with you, Mistress Ward?'

Emma invited him inside and he bowed to Eleanor. 'Your sheep are found, mistress.'

She blanched at the gloomy expression on the constable's face. 'Are they dead?' she asked, in a whisper.

He shuffled his feet and, when he spoke, his voice was quiet too. 'Two dead, mistress. The third, nearly so—'

Eleanor cried out. 'Dead! My lovely ewes. And their unborn lambs.'

Emma put her arm around Eleanor's shoulders. 'It's wicked, that's what it is. Those poor innocent creatures...'

Eleanor got to her feet. 'Take me to them, master constable.'

But Geoffrey demurred. 'No, no, Mistress Titherige, there's no need—'

She tossed her head. 'Yes, there is. I want to see them. Please lead me, Master Dyer.' And she swept from Emma's house and strode down the lane behind Geoffrey, who was still trying, but failing, to dissuade her from her mission.

But if Eleanor had been determined to see what had happened to her sheep, when she did so, she wished she had not come after all.

The derelict barn was cold and damp, its roof partly fallen in, and the ancient hay piled up in the stall where her sheep were penned was giving off a foul and musty stink. As Geoffrey had already said, two of the sheep were dead, lying close together in the rotten hay, their tongues lolling from their mouths, their lovely fleeces all filthy and reeking. One had dried blood around her tail and, when she saw it, Eleanor's hand flew to her mouth.

'Had she already birthed?' she said, a choke rising in her throat. She cast about her, looking for a lamb. Then Geoffrey hurried forward and scrabbled in the hay, one of his men holding a lantern high.

Shortly, Geoffrey stood up. 'It's here, mistress. Don't look—'

But, refusing his advice, Eleanor went forward too. He pointed, and she pressed both hands to her face, as she stared down on the pitiful little body, dark and bloodied, nestled in the foul hay a short distance from its dam.

'Where's the third?' she said, her voice a whisper.

'Over 'ere, missus,' said the constable's man.

The third sheep lay apart from the others, on its side, panting, its eyes sunken.

'She's been deprived of water,' said Eleanor, kneeling by the animal's side. 'How cruel...'

'Or mebbe just ignorant?' said the constable. He bent down and picked up some hay. 'The hay's all rotten, mistress. It's been here years. Won't 'ave done them no good.'

She looked up at him. 'Bad hay *and* no water?' She stroked the sheep's muzzle, and tears filled her eyes. 'The poor, poor creatures.'

Eleanor wiped away the tears on the sleeve of her kirtle. 'Anyway, she's past saving. So please, master constable, arrange for her to be freed from her suffering.'

Geoffrey bowed his head. 'Will Cole'll do it.'

Eleanor returned to Emma's and let herself be solaced for the loss of her sheep. By the time she realised she should be going home, the sky had become quite black, with thick clouds obscuring what light the moon might offer.

'I'll walk with you, Mistress Eleanor,' said Ralph, returned now from his part in the search.

'No need, Master Ward.'

Ralph cleared his throat. 'It's not safe for a young lady to walk alone at night,' he said gently.

So she accepted, and in truth was grateful for his company.

'What'll you do now, Mistress Eleanor?' Ralph said, as they picked their way along the uneven, rutted road that ran between the cottar cottages, back towards the middle of the village. 'Now the beasts're dead, your case against my cousins' sons is stronger.'

Eleanor nodded in the dark. 'You're right, Ralph. Yet I'm still loath to bring an accusation against the boys, especially Arthur.'

From the village green, they took the slightly better road that led out towards the manor and the area where Eleanor had her house.

'I'm grateful for your kindness, mistress.'

'Yet I do feel entitled to some recompense. Though I suppose the boys' fathers are hardly in a position to repay the full value of the ewes and unborn lambs.'

'An' I think Matt'll take it hard if you pursue it.'

'I daresay he would, but in truth I can't afford just to let it go. Yet I'm sorry your cousin John would also be obliged to pay.'

When Ralph had bidden her goodnight, Eleanor climbed the narrow stairs up to the small solar that her father Edward had built many years ago, making his house then one of Meonbridge's finest. She lay down on her bed, craving sleep. But, although she closed her eyes, slumber would not come. Instead, she argued back and forth with herself about whether or not she should demand justice for the loss of her sheep. Yet the decision might not be hers to take. For Sir Richard might think he could not permit such lawlessness on his manor without the perpetrators being punished.

And when, in the morning, Eleanor went to see Sir Richard, she found that was indeed his view.

'I understand your generous attitude towards the cottar boys,' he said, 'but what they have done is a criminal offence. I cannot just ignore it.'

'Though of course the boys are missing.'

'So they cannot *yet* be brought to justice. But, at the very least, their fathers can be held to account. One way or another, Mistress Titherige, you will be compensated for your losses.'

Eleanor was grateful for his lordship's support, yet she remained fearful of what might happen to the boys if they ever returned home. Even though, in some ways, she hoped they might, worrying about how young Arthur was faring, away from the comfort of his father's love.

# 2

Susanna looked around with satisfaction at the mill cottage, the home she'd nurtured for Henry and their children, now a model of cleanliness and comfort compared to how she remembered seeing it three years ago, when Henry's brother, Thomas, was still the miller. She'd never forget that dreadful day, a few months after it was clear the Death had finally left Meonbridge, when she and Eleanor had come to see how the Millers' new baby was faring, and had been so shocked by what they found.

The Death had taken five of the Millers' six children, then little Peter lost his life in a needless accident in the mill, for which Thomas blamed himself. The poor man had sunk into the deepest melancholy and his wife, Joan, had fallen into the most desperate state. Their baby, Maud, was a tiny bag of bones, her sweet face disfigured by her reddened, vacant eyes. The child had seemed barely human, her fitful cries more like those of a wild creature than a baby girl.

Susanna had once been Joan's closest friend. But, after the pain and horror of the Death, when both women lost so many loved ones, she thought it had been *she* who'd let their friendship slide. Although, Susanna thought she could forgive herself for neglecting friendship when her husband and children had all been taken from her on the very same day. But perhaps, after all, it had been Joan who'd given up on it, overwhelmed with grief at losing little Peter, so soon after the Death had wrested all her older children from her?

Either way, Susanna had felt somehow responsible for her best friend's melancholy. She'd tried to help Joan recover her good spirits. But her efforts came to naught and, only a few weeks later, Joan died, drowned in the millrace, leaving baby Maud hidden like Moses amongst the reeds. It had been sheer good fortune that she and Eleanor had found the child in time, and now she was mother to the little girl she helped save from death, and to Henry's first son, Tom, as well as their own two babies.

It was after Joan's death that Thomas seemed to lose his wits completely and Henry had taken over as the miller. Shocking as it was to think it, Susanna was certain Joan had robbed herself of life, unable at last to bear the loss of so many children. And she was sure everyone in Meonbridge knew it too, for rumours had spread that Joan's despair had been inspired by the Devil. But the rumours were soon quashed and no one spoke of it now.

If the priest believed Joan a sinner and not fit for consecrated ground – as Susanna had suspected – he didn't say so. Indeed, his words were almost kind. And when little Peter's body was lifted from his grave and brought to lie with his mother, tears sprang to the eyes of many there who saw it, and all wished Joan Miller might now rest in peace.

But, despite the passing of the years, Susanna still thought of herself – as wife of the present miller – as somehow *usurping* Joan's rightful place. And, when she herself was feeling melancholy, it still troubled her that she might have failed her friend.

Yet Eleanor had urged her to conquer her sense of guilt. 'You tried so hard to help her, Susy. Joan's death was not your fault.'

'Perhaps the Devil whispered too loudly in Joan's ear?'

'Don't think that, Susy. We must hope Joan's now with God.'

Susanna had nodded, though she didn't know whether she believed that likely.

She'd been glad of Eleanor's friendship then: since their shared discovery of the drowned Joan and still breathing Maud, they'd become close, their ordeal forging what she'd thought would be a lasting bond. Eleanor had even agreed to stand for Maud as godmother.

She thought of Eleanor often but, these days, Susanna saw little of her friend, ever busy, she supposed, building up her flock. News of the theft of Eleanor's sheep was all around the village and Susanna was sure she'd be much distressed about it. Yet Eleanor never visited, or shared her concerns with her any more, as she so often used to do.

Susanna sat down heavily on a stool and rested her elbows on the table. Then she cupped her chin in her upturned hands and let out a deep sigh. Perhaps Eleanor no longer thought of her as her friend?

Eleanor was now a woman with ambition, more so than any other woman Susanna knew. And, in all this time – three years since the Death! – she'd not yet got herself a husband. Surely Nicholas Ashdown would be a suitable choice? Good-looking, prosperous and a freeman! Susanna sighed again and frowned.

She worried about her friend. Was Eleanor *wilfully* forswearing a woman's natural lot in life for the sake of achieving prowess and prosperity?

Susanna thought, nowadays, that would be Henry's scathing view.

Henry no longer kissed her when he came home from work. In the first few heady months of their marriage, they exchanged a playful kiss every time they saw each other, and often Henry would pick Susanna up and whirl her round as if she was a girl, laughing with the sheer joy of being wed to her.

But that was years past – well, only three. Henry now seemed quite a different man from the one she'd married. He was no longer "Harry". Somehow the joyful, boyish "Harryness" had left him, leaving behind the gloomy, long-faced, mostly humourless Henry, who seemed much older than his years.

Nothing much, it seemed, could give him pleasure. Not even – and Susanna found this a worry – the children. Maud, now three, was the most delightful, funny little poppet, but she was, of course, not Henry's child, which was perhaps the reason he never let himself be won over by her charm. Yet neither did he pay much attention these days to his own children, Francis and Joan. Yet, it wasn't so very long past when he enjoyed playing with Tom and Maud, and even little Francis.

But, now, he and Tom seemed always to be arguing. Not that Tom was helping, doing little to win his Pa's affections. Rather, he aggravated his lack of humour by pressing him to let him work with him in the mill. Susanna knew Tom kept asking for the best of reasons, but Henry refused to see it, and the boy's goading simply made him angry.

'How many times do I have to tell you, boy?' Henry said, his hand coming down hard upon the table. 'Not until you're twelve!'

Susanna rested her hand lightly upon Tom's shoulder. 'Pa's told you oft enough, the mill's not safe for a lad as young as you.'

Tom shrugged away her hand. 'But it's not fair,' he cried. 'Other boys help their fathers—' And he named several Meonbridge boys who did so – the baker's son, one of the potter's boys, the sons of a man who'd come from Winchester two years past and set up as a tailor.

Henry growled and banged down his hand again, but Susanna, returning to the fire to give the supper stew a stir, gave the answer she always did.

'But *their* work isn't dangerous, Tom, whereas in the mill—'

She didn't need to spell it out. And almost all work *could* be dangerous: bakers' ovens were hot, some said potters' clay was poisonous, and she remembered how, last year, one of the tailor's boys died after falling onto his father's shears. But she didn't mention any of these hazards. Tom had to understand that the reason his father refused to let him work in the mill was because he loved him and was not willing to risk his life.

Tom knew that well enough, but was as stubborn as his father and, flouncing away, threw open the cottage door and marched out into the garden.

Susanna ran to the door and called after him, 'Supper's soon, Tom', but he didn't look back and she thought he might just forego his supper for the sake of proving to his father how miserable he was.

She closed the door. 'You know he only wants to help you.'

'But I won't allow it, and let that be an end to it.'

Supper was a silent meal. Tom did not return to eat it, and Henry wouldn't let Susanna go and bring him home. 'It's his own fault if he's hungry,' he said, and her heart ached at the boy's estrangement from his father. But she thought it safer to say nothing.

As she cleared away the supper bowls, Henry left the cottage, saying he'd go and look for his son. It was almost dark when he returned, Tom riding on his shoulders. Susanna's heart skipped to hear them laughing, glad they'd mended the rift between them, even if just for now.

It wasn't long before Tom and Maud were sleeping soundly on their pallets by the covered fire. Susanna picked up the baby from her cradle and followed Henry, carrying little Francis in his arms, into the tiny chamber that had once been a storeroom but was now where they had their bed. Although both she and Henry were always tired by bedtime, it was the one chance they had to talk, as the little ones fell asleep.

When they'd first married, this was the time of day Susanna looked forward to the most. Not because she'd be nestling up to her adoring Harry underneath the blanket – though that too was, of course, a great delight – but because the Harry of those lovely long-ago days had been a wonderful source of stories, gathered during his days spent at the mill. For the mill was then a place where laughter was heard daily, and where gossip abounded, of betrothals, and rumours of scandal, and news from abroad. And the "old Harry", as she thought of him, would make her giggle and even laugh out loud at what he told her, until at last each clasped the other close, and quietly sealed their contentment with one another.

But those funny, happy times seemed to have gone. Henry still occasionally took his pleasure from her body, though Susanna no longer much enjoyed it. Yet she did sometimes still enjoy the talking, even if it was rarely as amusing as it once had been. She wondered if the mill was still a place of laughter, or if Henry's melancholy had driven it away.

Tonight Susanna had something to tell him, for she thought he might not have heard of the discovery of Eleanor's sheep. She was right, but was disappointed by his reaction to the news. She might have expected his sympathy for the loss of the poor beasts – the old Harry would surely have offered words of solace – but the present Henry snorted.

'Perhaps she's not as good a shepherd as she thinks she is, if she can't even keep her sheep safe from a couple of cottar lads.'

Susanna protested. 'But surely it's impossible to prevent a thief taking a sheep if he's intent on it, when they're grazing in the open?'

But Henry snorted again. 'Maybe the beasts shouldn't be out at night?'

Susanna didn't answer, thinking he was being silly. Whoever heard of keeping sheep indoors? But, not wanting to get into an argument, she was about to change the subject, when Henry let out what sounded, in the dark, like a scornful sneer.

'Maybe it's God's way,' he said, 'of showing her she shouldn't be trying to raise the so-called "best flock in Hampshire"?' The last few words were spoken in a mocking tone.

Susanna bit her lip. 'But why shouldn't she try?' she said, keeping her tone light and even.

'You know why, Susanna. It's not a woman's place.'

Despite her own worries about Eleanor, Susanna was nonetheless determined to speak up for her. 'But since the Death—' she began, but knew she'd not be allowed to finish.

'Women've taken it into their heads they're as good as men in matters that shouldn't concern them – like rearing great flocks of sheep.' He grunted. 'It's not natural. A woman like Eleanor Titherige should be married and having babies. To help Meonbridge recover. Like you are.'

'She's only twenty-two, Harry, four years younger than me.'

'But you were wed and having babes a lot younger than that. That's what women are supposed to do. Not run about the hillsides thinking they're in charge.'

Susanna truly didn't understand where this woman-scorning Henry had come from. Even if most men held women in contempt, surely Henry didn't? Or perhaps he did, and she just hadn't noticed?

She was relieved when Henry gave a final snort and rolled away from her. Only moments later his breath was coming in regular noisy rattles, and Susanna closed her eyes, wishing, as she always did, she hadn't after all said anything to irk her tetchy husband.

Come morning, it was hard to tell whether or not Henry had forgotten their disagreement. He ate the small piece of coarse bread and drank the weak ale Susanna put before him. Then, standing up so abruptly his stool toppled over, he made a lunge for the door and hurried out and down the path towards the mill without another word.

Susanna stared after him, wondering, as she did most days, why Henry no longer seemed to think it necessary to bid her fare well, let alone give her a kiss, as he always used to do. It was vexing but, even more so, it was disappointing.

Later, Tom was pouting as he came indoors and sat down at the table to help Susanna chop vegetables for their dinner stew. She knew how much he hated doing what he dismissed as "girls' chores", and she tried to give him more manly tasks, tasks that she found hard to do, like digging in the garden, and carrying heavy pails of water from the well. He might have been only ten, but Tom was a big lad and strong. Which was mostly why he was so aggrieved that his father refused to let him work with him in the mill.

He slumped down on a stool and picked up a leek. He stared at it a moment before expertly stripping off the dirty outer layers and swishing what was left in a bowl of water. Then he picked up Susanna's chopping knife and sliced the leek into rounds.

'Thank you for helping, Tom dear,' said Susanna. 'Dinner'll be all the quicker if you slice the rest whilst I feed the baby.'

She knew Tom was happy enough to help her. He just wished it was his Pa who needed him. After he'd sliced the leeks, he waved the knife about. 'Why's Pa so nasty to me, Ma?'

Susanna was bending over the baby's cot, and stood up again with Joan in her arms. 'He's not *nasty*, Tom. He's, well… Well, you're just like him. Stubborn.'

'What's stubborn?'

Susanna laughed. 'When you get an idea into your head and won't let it go.'

Tom's eyes crinkled. 'Is that what I'm like?'

'And so's your Pa. And, in his case, he's stubborn because he loves you.'

Tom grunted. 'But I'm big enough to help. I'm bigger 'n lots of boys my age, bigger 'n boys of *twelve*.' He pulled a face. 'It's not *fair*.' Something Susanna thought the poor lad said at least a dozen times a day.

'Pa just wants to keep you safe.'

'But he can't keep me safe forever. Even when I'm twelve? Even when I'm a man?'

It was true enough. Accidents could – and did – happen to folk of any age. But Henry had got it into his head that twelve was the age he'd permit Tom to start work, and there seemed to be no shifting him. Yet Susanna did sometimes wonder if, having made a decision, Henry was reluctant to be seen to yield, and was digging in his heels out of pig-headedness, rather than in confidence that he was right. And perhaps it was the same with his employees?

When he first took over the mill from Thomas, Henry employed a journeyman to help him. Since then he'd had another two, but the last one left under a cloud and Henry refused even to seek another one, claiming he couldn't afford it. He still had casual help from a couple of cottars, who did the heavy lifting and cleaned the mill machinery. But, without a journeyman, Henry did the work of at least two men – work that, three years ago, he used to share with his brother, when Thomas was the miller and Henry his assistant. Susanna found it all very troubling, but Henry didn't like her asking him about it.

Henry didn't often come home for dinner. He was invariably so busy Susanna would wrap up a small dark loaf and a piece of cheese in a cloth, and give it to him each morning along with a flask of ale. She shuddered to think of him eating his meagre dinner crouched amidst the mill machinery, the dust rising from the floury floor, the turning of the wheel and the grinding of the stones giving him not a moment's respite from the din. She thought a break away from the mill house to have a bit of dinner would do him good, but had stopped suggesting it.

The church bells had rung Sext, the time when most folk in Meonbridge did interrupt their work for dinner, either at home or out in the fields. Susanna was hurrying back along the narrow path from the vegetable plot to the house, bearing the last of the winter kale, which she intended to add to the beans and onions already in the pottage on the fire. But, hearing the sound of footsteps a short distance away, she turned and saw her husband trudging along the path that led up from the mill.

She called out to him. 'Harry, are you come home for dinner?'

'Went without my pack.'

Susanna's hand flew to her mouth. 'Oh, I quite forgot it. How foolish of me—'

But Henry didn't seem angry at her negligence. 'No matter. It'll be good to eat a hot dinner for a change.' As he came closer, he glanced asquint at her. 'I assume you have *made* a hot dinner?'

She giggled a little, for the way he said it was just like the old Harry would've done, teasing. 'Of course, Harry dear. I always make a hot meal for the children.'

'And there's enough for me?'

Susanna pushed her free hand through Henry's bent arm, and they strolled the last few steps up to the house together. How she wished he could always be like this.

But his seeming good humour didn't last much beyond the meal. Unusually, Henry praised her for her cooking but, the moment he'd scraped up the leavings of the pottage with some bread, he eased himself up from his stool and took a couple of steps towards the door, scuffing the toes of his boots in the rushes Susanna had strewn fresh that morning.

'Back to work?' she said, keeping her voice light.

But he shook his head. His long mouse-brown hair was uncovered and flapped listlessly against his face. 'I'll sit a while, in the sunshine.'

'Shall I join you?'

His mouth stretched into a small grin. 'Why not?'

When they first married, Henry had made a sturdy bench from the timber of a fallen apple tree, and placed it close to the front wall of the house, where a fine view took in the millrace, and the trees beyond, towards the high walls and glinting windows of Meonbridge manor. They'd often sit there together on warm evenings, taking pleasure in the landscape and each other's company.

Leaving Maud and Francis in Tom's rather disgruntled care, Susanna picked up baby Joan from her cradle and went to sit next to Henry on the bench. He gazed into the distance, as she let the baby suckle for a while, rocking her back and forth, until her mouth slipped off the breast and she fell asleep.

Henry gently stroked the baby's head with his fingers. 'Mothers and babes,' he said, his eyes slightly moist.

Susanna knew what was in his mind.

Henry scanned the view ahead of him again, then grunted. 'Agnes Sawyer stopped by earlier.'

'Truly? I'd not imagined Agnes making her own dough.'

He grunted again. 'Perhaps the master carpenter's taking control in his own house at last?'

'Whatever d'you mean, Harry?'

He leaned forward, his elbows on his knees, and rested his chin in his upturned hands. 'Agnes has not been the most dutiful wife and mother the past couple o' years. Jack's beginning to understand his error, letting her into that workshop of his.'

'*Their* workshop,' said Susanna, then bit her lip, for Henry frowned and shook his head.

'No, Susanna, *Jack's* the craftsman. A workshop's no place for a woman.'

She wanted to say Agnes was a craftsman too, but decided not to.

'He should've never let her do it in the first place, pretending to be a carpenter. It's men's work.' He grimaced. 'I told him, he should be training up a couple of young lads rather than using his wife as unpaid labour.'

Susanna had to suppress a gasp. As if Henry had any right to preach to Jack about apprentices, when he refused to have one himself. But she didn't say so. Instead, she feigned a giggle. 'You make it sound like Jack's wronging Agnes, when it was a decision they made together when they first came back to Meonbridge.'

'That's as maybe. But it was a bad decision.' Henry eased himself upright. 'Jack can see that now. I think he's met disapproval from his fellow craftsmen, who think the same as me.'

'Truly?' said Susanna. How could he know?

'Indeed,' he said. 'It'd be different if she were a widow, continuing her husband's business. Though, even then, not as a craftsman... But married women belong at home. It's not as if there isn't plenty to do, with children to look after, the house to manage, food to prepare, animals to tend, the garden to work. How can a woman have time for aught else? You don't, do you?'

Susanna agreed her time did seem fully occupied. Yet she knew lots of women in Meonbridge, certainly all the cottars and many villein wives, who worked alongside their husbands in the fields as well as their domestic duties. Some had a separate occupation, like spinning or brewing, to bring extra income into the family. It'd always been that way. Didn't Henry know that?

But she decided against questioning his opinion and, at length, he stood up, declaring it was time he went back to the mill.

Susanna found these conversations baffling, and wearying. Surely most men these days were *not* so narrow-minded? It made no sense for them to ignore the realities of life. So why did Henry? After he'd disappeared down the path to the mill, she sat on the bench a while longer, rocking Joan back and forth, though the child was still asleep.

Susanna was disappointed that the good, kind man she'd married seemed to have changed. At first, she hadn't *loved* him. She married him because he seemed to love her, and wanted her to be a mother to his son and niece. She had once confessed to Eleanor how guilty she felt that she didn't love him back, but her friend had dismissed her fears.

And it was true she did find happiness quite soon after their marriage, looking after Henry's house and croft, and the two children. Then, when Francis came along, and little Joan, she thought her life was perfect.

So when was it he'd begun to change? Only months ago perhaps, soon after that last journeyman left the mill? Long before, she'd come to love him, only to find him less loving towards her. But the change in him did frighten her a little, for, where once he'd been a merry, easy-going man, now he seemed more often like an angry bull, snorting and pawing at the ground.

# 3

Emma was approaching the broad green heart of Meonbridge. After a morning up on Riverdown, helping Eleanor with the first of the newborn lambs, she'd dropped off her work bag at the cottage, before walking the short distance to the village to collect her bread from the bakehouse.

As she came closer, she saw a cluster of people, women mostly, gathered beneath the huge and ancient oak that dominated the green. Curious, she skirted the bakehouse and skipped across the springy grass, the newly growing blades now mostly keeping the winter mud in check. She was almost excited to find the women were gathered around the old pedlar, Kit Chapman, who had a tray of trinkets hanging on the strap slung about his skinny, grimy neck.

Emma pushed through the group to see better what he had for sale. She saw at once that most of it was rubbish, but she picked up a circular tin brooch and turned it over in her hand.

'How much?' she said.

Kit grinned, showing a mouthful of damaged and missing teeth. 'To you, missus, tuppence.'

She huffed. 'That's scandalous. It's just a bit o' tin.'

'Up to ye, missus.' He turned away, pressing another piece of rubbish on a customer.

Emma was disappointed. She quite liked the brooch and needed a new one for her cloak. But tuppence was absurd – as much as she earned in a day. The pedlar had cheaper brooches in his tray, but they looked it, and Emma didn't want them. She'd just go without.

Her regret made her downhearted, but some of the other women were chatting merrily to the pedlar and, as she listened, her heart lifted a little. For Kit had come recently from Winchester and, when someone asked what it was like there, his eyes crinkled at the corners.

'Ah, well, missus,' he said, tapping his nose. ''Tis a fine city, Winch'ster, with her grand houses and streets all paved wi' stone.' The picture he painted was of a prosperous town, the miseries of the Death already put behind it, and work available for all.

Emma was by nature distrustful of anyone making wondrous claims, but she couldn't help feeling gladdened by his words and, later that afternoon, when Ralph was home, she spilled over with excitement at the possibility of a new life in the city.

But Ralph scoffed. 'Kit's a rogue. You'd surely not believe a word *he* said.'

'But mightn't there be a tittle o' truth in it?'

Ralph put his arm around her. 'You might *want* it to be true, but it don't make it so.'

'But suppose we *could* find new work, an' a master who pays proper wages?'

'Leave Meonbridge? Us?' Ralph's eyes opened wide. 'We know it here. Folk know us. If we go someplace we're strangers, folk'll likely not take kindly to it.' He ran his fingers through his hair. 'Anyway, what work'd we do in Winchester?'

Emma stuck out her bottom lip. 'There's plenty in the cloth trade, Kit said.'

Ralph hooted loudly. 'And what d'you an' me know 'bout cloth? We're *farming* folk, Em…'

'We can *learn*. We're good workers, me an' you.'

'Good at farming. But for summat we don't know a jot about?'

Not knowing if he was right or wrong, Emma didn't answer. But Ralph seemed nettled by the conversation for, grabbing at his hood again, he threw open the cottage door and dived out onto the lane. Emma stared at the door. She knew where he'd be going. But, being Ralph, he wouldn't be there long. One pot and he'd be home again for supper.

She took a stool and sat outside the door, letting the early evening sunshine warm her face. Baby Bartholomew was sleeping and the girls were still out somewhere with their friends. And, as there was only bread and a small scrap of cheese for supper, she could afford a moment's rest.

And it gave her time to think.

It was about this time last year when the king issued a new statute, fixing wages to what they'd been before the Death. Ralph'd been so angry about it. The new statute was hardly any different from the first one, brought in two years before to stop labourers demanding more money when there were so many fewer of them. Ever since the first one, Sir Richard'd been paying below average wages, but, after the second statute, he planned to *cut* wages even further.

'He claims it's his duty to follow the letter o' the law,' Ralph'd said, pacing the floor and thumping a fist against the palm of his other hand. 'He says he must support the king's efforts to make the country strong again. Ha!'

She rarely saw Ralph so riled up. Her first husband, Bart, was given to daily outbursts in his rage against the world, but Ralph was mild-tempered and it took a lot to make him angry.

But, if Ralph was vexed by Sir Richard's plans, Emma was infuriated. Yet also fearful. She worried that Eleanor might want to cut *her* wages too, and was troubled because Eleanor had been good to her and Emma wouldn't want to let her down. She hated being beholden to people she liked. But, in the end, Eleanor didn't cut anyone's wages, and neither did most of the other employers in Meonbridge. Indeed, Emma plucked up her courage to ask for almost as much as Eleanor paid Will Cole, though it was annoying that even Mistress Titherige paid her, a woman, less than the man, no matter they were doing the same job.

But Sir Richard was still the biggest employer in Meonbridge and, after his decision to further cut the cottars' wages, Ralph took up again the position of dissent that he, and Emma's then husband, Bart, had held just after the Death. Then, it had been a dreadful, frightening, time. Lords and masters everywhere were trying to keep things as they were. But the tenants who'd survived the Death – villeins and cottars alike – were no longer willing to work for a pittance or give the manor unpaid labour, when it was clear working men were scarce and could say "nay" as well as "yea". Yet, despite Lady de Bohun – or so Eleanor had said – thinking they *did* deserve more, Sir Richard continued with his stubbornness, saying he couldn't afford higher wages, and anyway it was the law.

And, even now, he was *still* keeping cottar wages low.

And yet – and this was why Emma was churning this over now, it annoyed her so – Ralph remained resolutely *loyal* to Sir Richard. She let out a great sigh, even though no one was around to hear it. Sometimes she tried to encourage Ralph to work for other people, like some of the wealthier villeins – just as she did – but he always found some excuse. And now he was refusing even to consider making a better life for them all by leaving their tight-fisted lord and finding better-paid work in town.

It was all very vexing.

It was a pity, Emma often thought, that, since the Death, the little market that used to spring up every week on Meonbridge's green was now limited to once or twice a month. Though of course it did make sense, with so many fewer folk left to buy and sell.

Most stall holders were people she knew, selling surplus produce from their crofts – eggs, vegetables and, later on, a little fruit – and some of the villein goodwives brought cheeses they'd made from the rich milk of their goats or cows. But sometimes, especially in the summer, others came, from further afield, like the fishmonger who travelled from town to town, village to village, finding customers for his salted and dried fish. Merchants might come to sell cloth, or pots and pans, or soap and candles, or knives and spoons. But, more often, the market was just for village folk to buy the basics, merchants not bothering to make the trip if it wasn't likely worth their while.

Emma always enjoyed the noise and bustle of her neighbours gathering together on the green, pushing between the closely positioned stalls. Even these days, since the Death, the market could still seem busy on a bright spring day. She looked forward to exchanging greetings, and stopping to gossip a moment or two. She found pleasure too in browsing the goods for sale, even though she was often disappointed that her purse of coins was too light to let her make more than the most basic of purchases.

The morning of the market, before she went to work, Emma picked up the small, shabby basket she'd bought many years ago, and heaved open the heavy door.

'I won't be long, Bea. Mind you don't leave the baby by himself. You know the mischief he'll get into.'

Beatrix rolled her eyes. 'I *know*, Ma. You tell me *every* time.'

Emma chided herself. She must stop treating Beatrix like a child. After all, she was nearly nine.

She walked up towards the green. Bright mornings such as these always lifted her spirits, and it was good to feel the warmth of the April sun climbing up into the sky. But she had no time to relish the pleasures of the day, when she'd promised Eleanor two hours up at Riverdown before dinner. She hurried on, hoping to find the itinerant candlemaker there, for she was very short of tallow, and maybe one of the villein goodwives had brought some eggs, and perhaps the last of their leeks or kale.

As soon as she reached the green, the clamour of the little market made her smile. Many people were already here. She hoped there'd still be some eggs, and wove a swift path between her fellow purchasers, looking for the stall where Alice atte Wode usually sold her surplus produce. She soon spotted Alice, exchanging eggs and what looked like a cabbage for coins.

Emma ran over and bobbed a slight curtsey. 'Mistress atte Wode,' she said, giving her a sunny smile. 'I'm late.'

Alice placed the cabbage in her customer's basket, then gently laid the eggs on top, before turning to Emma, her eyes alight. 'Emma, dear, how nice to see you. How's that bonny babe of yours?'

Emma'd heard Alice was ailing, though from what she didn't know. She glanced at the older woman and took in the strangely sallow skin of her cheeks, and the stiff, stooping way in which she held herself.

'Naughty,' said Emma, 'but adorable withal.' She rested her basket on the edge of Alice's trestle table. 'And yourself, Alice?'

Alice wagged her head from side to side. 'Well enough.' Then, straightening up, she groaned. 'Feeling my age a little.'

Emma wondered how old Alice was. Ten years her senior perhaps? No more, surely, and yet she looked much older. Perhaps some ailment was weakening her, but it was not Emma's place to ask. Instead, she gave a chuckle. 'I feel the same myself after a morning up on Riverdown. Which is where I must go right soon, else Mistress Eleanor'll dock my wages.'

'Surely not. But best make your purchases and go?' Alice's eyes were twinkling.

Emma nodded. 'Four eggs, if you will, Alice, and d'you still have any leeks?'

Alice twisted around and bent stiffly down to delve into a sack. She groaned again as she stood up, and pressed one hand against her back as she held out two fat leeks in the other. 'Not many left,' she said. 'The leeks are rather old now, and you might want to remove the outer layers. Are these enough?'

Emma took one. 'Just this.' She'd keep as much of it as she could. She thought she saw a glimmer of understanding in Alice's eyes. 'And the eggs.'

Moments later, as Emma was looking for the candlemaker before she hurried home and then to work, she felt someone tweak the sleeve of her kirtle.

'Emma?'

Spinning round, she found Susanna beaming at her.

'I haven't seen you in a while.'

'Busy,' said Emma, shrugging.

'I know you are.' Susanna pursed her lips. 'Always working.'

'No choice.' Emma glanced at her friend's small basket, half-filled with cheese and sweetmeats. It seemed Susanna had money enough to buy whatever she wished, despite not having to labour beyond her house and croft.

Just then a boy came forward with a tray of pies. 'Ho, missis,' he said, 'hot pies for yer dinner? Fresh from the bakehouse.'

Emma sniffed: the tempting smell of meat and gravy wafted from the tray, cruelly filling her nostrils. But she shook her head.

'Aye, why not?' said Susanna, with a titter. 'One for Tom, and I'll take one down to Harry. He'll like that.'

Emma couldn't deny her envy. How she'd love to buy a treat for Ralph, or her girls. Her purse held coins enough, but the baker's pies were overpriced, and she refused to let her emotions get the better of her wisdom.

'Anyway,' she said, as Susanna placed the pies carefully atop her eggs, 'I must go. The lambs are waiting.'

Susanna nodded, and a sudden sadness crossed her face.

'What's the matter, Susy?' said Emma, placing her free hand on her friend's arm.

Susanna wagged her head. 'Oh, nothing. You'll think me foolish…'

Emma's eyebrows lifted. 'Tell me?'

'I envy you the lambs,' Susanna said, her voice a whisper. 'Somehow, those days with my Fran, when we *both* had to work…like you and Ralph… I miss that…'

Emma thought Susanna was being ridiculous: she'd married a man well off enough so she didn't have to do any extra work outside her home. Why complain of that? She'd not mind spending more time at home and with her girls. And not have to take the baby with her everywhere. She'd been carrying her babies to work since she was fifteen.

''Course you miss *Fran*,' said Emma, 'but surely not the work? Wi' your baby slung about your chest, your back screaming from being bent double all day long, your legs barely fit to walk you home. You're not telling me you miss all that?'

'No, of course not. I just wish Harry wanted me to work *with* him, like you and Ralph, and the Sawyers…' She drifted off, then said, 'You know, like what Master Hugo says is in the Bible, "a woman shall be a helpmeet to her husband".'

Emma frowned. 'But you *are* Henry's helpmeet, Susy. You look after the house and the croft and the children. That helps him.' Susanna gave the slightest of nods. 'You're *fortunate*, Susy. Why not just be glad you've got such a loving husband?'

'You must think me ungrateful.' She chewed her lip. 'Though I'm not sure he's protecting me from work because he *loves* me. He thinks all women should stay at home.'

'Ha! Well, that ain't possible for some of us. He must know that?'

'I'm not sure he does. Or else he's forgot it. Of course I know the truth. For you, as it were once for me, with Fran, and for Agnes Sawyer, trying to help her husband's business prosper.' She chewed at her lip again. 'Truly, Emma, Henry *needs* help. He's been working so hard these past few months. You know he's had three skilled men since he first took on the mill, but none of them have stayed?'

'Why don't he just take on another?'

'I don't understand it. He says he can't afford to but, surely, Em, that can't be right?' She stopped, and pressed her lips together. 'I shouldn't say it, but he just seems to be pig-headed.'

'Men can be very stubborn when they get an idea into their thick heads.' Emma grinned.

Susanna gave a small smile in return.

# 4

Eleanor was grateful for Sir Richard's insistence that she be compensated for the loss of her sheep. Nonetheless, she was beset by worry that the cottars might band together in support of Matthew and John, and refuse to work for her. She and Walter could not manage the flock alone, if Will, Emma and the other cottars who gave occasional help, abandoned her.

She lay awake at night fretting about what might happen. When at last she fell asleep, her dreams were full of crowds of cottars ascending the hill to Riverdown, brandishing pitchforks, billhooks and shearing scissors, their mouths agape in protest. But what were their complaints against her? She could not make out words above their muffled howls...

Waking, she had a sense of dread. The dream was fast dissipating, but she could still picture the impossibly huge crowd of cottars climbing up to Riverdown – there weren't that many folk of *every* degree in all of Meonbridge. She shook her head and the last vestige of the dream slipped away and, with its passing, her anxiety also eased.

She threw back the coverlet, rose and dressed, keen to reassure herself that the only crowds on Riverdown were white and woolly, their gaping mouths not reproaching her but merely bleating to their neighbours.

She loved this time of year, when the sun rose early and she could start her day well before the Prime bell rang. Of course, spring days weren't always sunny but, this morning, as she opened the shutter of the small solar window, she was delighted to see the sky was blue and free from clouds, and to feel the sun already giving out a little warmth.

She ran down the narrow staircase to the hall, where Hawisa was already tending to the fire.

'Mornin', missus,' said Hawisa. 'Gran' day.'

'Indeed. And I'm eager to be off to Riverdown.'

'You'll take a sup and bite to eat afore you go?' said the servant, although

Eleanor knew it was not a question. Few folk bothered much with breakfast, with dinner coming in only a few hours, but Hawisa always said her mistress must have "a little summat" before she began her working day. Eleanor decided long ago not to argue with Hawisa, who might only be her servant, but assuredly had her mistress's best interests at heart.

It was seven years past that Eleanor's mother had died in childbirth. Losing her mother's tender devotion was a particular misery to the fifteen-year-old girl, but she had thrown herself into looking after her little brothers and being a helpmeet to her father. Three years later, he took another wife, who was never much of a mother to Eleanor. She cared only for the son, Roger, she had brought with her, a spoilt child four years Eleanor's junior, who invaded her home like an irritating wasp. But only twelve months later her father lost his life to the Mortality, along with her three little brothers. Eleanor was bereft, alone with her stepmother and stepbrother. Yet it was not long before the Mortality took her stepmother too, and Eleanor and Roger were left to fend for themselves. When, a few months after the Mortality had passed, Eleanor asked Hawisa and her, rather older, husband Nathan to look after her house, she found in Hawisa a maternal kindness she had not enjoyed since she was a girl. And how much she had welcomed it.

So Eleanor sat down at her table and accepted the bread and ale Hawisa put before her. She ate quickly, wanting to get to Riverdown as soon as possible. But then she heard a knocking at the door, and Hawisa bustled across the hall to haul the great door open.

'Oh, it's you,' she said. Eleanor groaned inwardly: why was Hawisa always so sharp with people?

'Who is it, Hawisa?' she called.

Hawisa came back into the room. 'John Ward.' Her mouth twisted into a grimace.

Eleanor got up from the bench. Perhaps he had come to pay his dues? 'Do ask John to enter, Hawisa.' She stepped forward as John shuffled into the room, his head half bowed, his hands clutching at the hood he had clearly just pulled off, leaving his strawy hair sticking up in all directions.

'John, what can I do for you?'

He lifted his head a little, then raised his eyes. She saw that they were moist.

'Why, John, whatever is the matter?' said Eleanor, then bit her lip at the absurdity of her question. Young Arthur was still missing.

John raised his head a little further, and dragged the sleeve of his tunic across his face. 'I'm right sorry 'bout your sheep, Missus Titherige.' His voice was soft and a little shaky. 'My lad done wrong, but it weren't his idea, missus, you can be sure of it.'

Hawisa fleered. 'He done it, all the same.'

Eleanor held up her hand. 'Thank you, Hawisa. You may continue with your duties.'

Hawisa muttered to herself and bustled over to the table, where she made a noisy business of collecting Eleanor's breakfast leavings before taking a circuitous path out to the scullery.

Eleanor waited until Hawisa had left the room before moving closer to John, so that she could keep her own voice low. 'I am of course much distressed about my sheep, for their loss will hit me hard. But I do understand Arthur may well have been led astray by his cousin Luke. Though that doesn't mean what Arthur did should be excused.'

At this, John cried out, passing his hood back and forth from hand to hand.

Eleanor touched his arm. The last thing she wanted was for young Arthur to be punished for his part in the theft and slaughter of her sheep, and yet it *was* a crime. She remained fearful that, if the boys ever returned to Meonbridge, Sir Richard would take it upon himself to arraign them both, and the punishment might be the loss of a hand, or even hanging. She shuddered. It was unthinkable that such a fate should befall the gentle, if simple-minded, son of this good-natured, hard-working man.

'Perhaps the boys'll not return,' she said. 'Perhaps they're already making a new life for themselves elsewhere?'

John rocked a little, then raked his fingers through his hair. 'Mebbe, missus.' Then he took a great wet sniff. 'But I miss my little lad and want him home.' His voice had become the merest whisper.

What more could she say? If the boys came home they might be hauled before the sheriff and cruelly punished. If they stayed away, this poor man would live the rest of his life in abject grief.

After John had paid over the sum deemed by Sir Richard to be his share of the reparation for Eleanor's sheep, he left her house, saying he would encourage his brother to pay up too. Eleanor thanked him for his promptness, but he bit his lip and rubbed the back of his neck.

'I daresay Matt'll take some time to bring his share, missus. I 'ad a bit put by, but I reckon he'll have to sell summat to find the coin.'

Eleanor imagined Matthew had little or nothing to sell. 'It might be a while, then?'

John gave her a weak grin and, replacing his hood, walked away from

Eleanor's house towards the village and, she supposed, the manor fields. She fancied his step was a little lighter than when he came. Perhaps paying his dues at least relieved him of one aspect of his melancholy. Poor man!

Shortly afterwards, Eleanor left the house herself and sped down into the village. As usual, she then took the rough road through Meonvale, where the cottar hovels huddled close together on either side. The memory of her alarming dream made her quicken her pace still further. She kept turning her head to left and right instead of watching where she put her feet, and almost turned her ankle on the rutted surface. Halfway along the road, she was startled by a noise, albeit only a magpie's rasp, and broke into a run, despite the hazard of the ruts, and only halted when she reached the bridge over the river. A little out of breath, she stood a moment, chiding herself for being so ridiculous. For most of the cottars would surely be already in the fields.

Today Walter and Will would finish shearing the wethers, providing Eleanor with a barn full of fine fleeces ready to go to market, while she and Emma spent the day with the suckling ewes and lambs, checking all the babes were feeding well and their mothers healthy. All seemed well enough, the ewes nibbling at the fresh spring grass, and their happy lambs leaping and playing in the sunshine. It was always a sight that lifted Eleanor's spirits.

But Emma, some distance away, having made her inspections more quickly and efficiently than Eleanor, shouted out and waved her arm. 'There's one not right here.'

Eleanor hurried forward, weaving her way through the grazing flock. 'What is it?' she called, her heart beating a little faster.

'Just one.' Emma pointed to a ewe standing away from her sisters. 'See how that dam keeps kicking at her lamb, not wanting him to suckle. Help me catch her?'

While Emma caught the sheep by the hind legs, Eleanor moved swiftly to its head and held it fast. 'We need to turn her over,' said Emma.

The ewe's udder was red and sore. Eleanor wrinkled her nose. 'No wonder she doesn't want her babe pulling on her.'

Emma winced. 'I'd much the same meself wi' Bea.' Then she turned to her task. She lifted her skirt a little and straddled the sheep to stop her getting up. 'Can you go and fetch a cup?'

'Can you manage on your own?'

Emma nodded. 'Just be quick.'

Eleanor wondered what the cup was for, but did not stop to ask. When she returned, she held tight onto the sheep's head, to try to stop her struggling, while Emma massaged the ewe's udder gently. As she massaged, a little milk squirted from one teat.

'That's it,' said Emma, beaming. 'And now a little more.' As she massaged, she squirted some of the milk into the cup. She glanced at Eleanor. 'Can you hold her mouth open?' As Eleanor did so, Emma tipped the milk down the animal's throat.

'Why are you giving her her own milk?' said Eleanor.

'It's an old trick to help clear a blockage in a teat. Dunno why.'

Walter had come over and overheard her. 'You're right,' he said. 'Don't always work, but it often does. Good work, Emma.' Then he turned on his heel and went back to Will.

The two women shared a giggle. 'Goodness, Emma,' said Eleanor, 'praise from Walter!'

As the sun started to dip behind the distant forest, and a pink and yellow glow lit up the western sky, Eleanor bade good night to Will and Emma, and sat a moment on a fallen tree trunk gazing into the distance, while Walter busied himself with checking the new hurdle fences they had erected, to keep the flock from straying. The fences would not, Walter had said, stop foxes, or even determined boys, but at least at night they would contain the flock more closely to the summit of the down, where they had the barns and he his cottage. Eleanor agreed to the fences, as a compromise, for she still did not think she could afford to employ men to guard the sheep all night.

Last year, when the new statute of labourers was enacted, Eleanor had thought – much like Sir Richard and one or two of the richer villeins on the manor – it might be a justification for cutting the wages of her workers. For, then, she was still finding it hard to balance her expenses and her income. It was a time when she still felt troubled by her ignorance and inexperience, and would have liked to discuss her worries with John atte Wode. Yet, since their acrimonious parting three years ago, she could not bring herself to approach him. But his mother Alice was knowledgeable and wise, and Eleanor still felt able to ask her advice, as she had so often in the past.

Now, as she gazed across her pastures and the grazing flock, and reflected on how well everyone worked today – especially Emma – she recalled her conversation with Alice about the new law.

Alice was open-mouthed when Eleanor confided that she was thinking of lowering the wages of the cottars who worked for her.

'You can't do that,' said Alice, shaking her head with vigour. 'Think, Elly dear, of what might – no, would – happen. You'd lose them, those good workers, like Will and Emma. They'd go elsewhere, you can be sure of it.'

She demurred. 'But they won't find better wages anywhere else in Meonbridge.'

'So they'll leave.'

She gasped. 'They can't!'

'They *can*, Elly, and they will. Times have changed, you know that. Folk won't just accept what's offered here if they can get better somewhere else.'

At length Eleanor accepted Alice's advice. And, indeed, when Emma boldly asked for a little more, she paid it, understanding that Emma was a worker she truly did not want to lose. Although she was somewhat surprised to find her still disgruntled that she was paid less than Will.

But, now, how glad she was that she'd asked Alice's advice.

She got up and strolled over towards Walter, who was just walking back to his cottage. 'I'm going home now.'

He nodded. 'Been a good day.'

She smiled and touched him lightly on the arm. 'Good night, Walter.'

'Sleep well.' His eyes were bright, as he patted her hand and let it rest there a few moments.

Eleanor was in good spirits as she sauntered back down the hill and entered cottar Meonvale again. It was late and darkness was already falling, but it was still light enough to see clearly where to place her feet upon the rutted track.

But, just as she had that morning, she found her heart beating a little faster as she picked her way between the furrows of dried mud, careful not to slip and turn her ankle. For now there were plenty of folk about, mostly men, and, as she passed close to the ramshackle building that served as Meonvale's ale-house, she heard a clamour of raucous voices. A couple of the men standing around outside, clutching pots of ale, called out to her.

'Evenin', Missus Titherige. 'Ow's your sheep. Got them tucked up safe, eh?'

They guffawed, and slapped each other on the back.

They likely meant no harm, but she ignored them and hurried on. But, before she had taken many more steps, she heard a roar of fury and Matthew loomed before her. He punched her shoulder with his fist.

She could not help but cry out with the shock of it. Yet she made herself speak calmly. 'Please, Matthew, let me pass.' She turned, trying to step past him.

But he shook his head and laughed. Grabbing at her arm, he swung her round to face him. ''Ow'm I going to pay you, missus, when my lad's gone missing?'

Eleanor tried to pull away, but Matthew's grip was tight. 'You're hurting me. Please let go.'

But he shook his head again. 'What makes you think you can run a great huge flock o' beasts up there on *common* pasture?'

Two men standing nearby grunted. 'You're right there, Matt, 'twere common ground afore Edward Titherige stole it.'

Eleanor turned and glared at them. 'My father didn't *steal* it,' she said, her voice bold. 'He bought it honestly from Sir Richard.'

'Nah,' said Matthew. 'It were *common* land, where all could graze their ewes and lambs.'

'You don't have any sheep,' she said, incredulous that he, of all men, should be accusing her.

He squeezed harder on her arm. 'But I *might* have if it weren't for the likes o' you taking all the land.'

But then his brother John was there. 'Calm down, Matt. You've no call to be so offensive to Missus Titherige.'

Matthew sneered. 'Why not? If it weren't for her, my lad wouldn't be missing.'

'Don't be an idiot, Matt. It's not Missus Titherige's fault Luke an' Arthur've run away.' He grimaced. 'In fact, the fault is *yours*, for givin' the lad ideas.'

'What ideas?' Matthew snarled at his brother and flipped viciously at his shoulder with the back of his free hand.

'Claiming she weren't up to being a farmer. Calling her an "'aughty cow". Saying she'd no business raising sheep.' John raked his fingers through his hair. 'Luke'd not've thought of getting back at her if you'd not railed against her so.'

Then he stepped forward and grasped his brother's arm, trying to pull him off her. But Matthew held on fast, tightening his grip so much that Eleanor cried out.

At the same moment, another voice was shouting, and Nicholas Ashdown was at her side. Pushing forward, he raised his fist, aiming a blow at John, who was the nearer. Eleanor, seeing Nicholas's intention in an instant, cried out to stop him, and he held back. But Matthew let go of Eleanor's arm, thrusting her away so violently she staggered backwards. Then, swinging sideways, he lunged at Nicholas, so their faces were within inches of each other. Growling, he jabbed his fingers repeatedly into Nicholas's chest.

'Shove off,' he said, his voice low and menacing. 'This is naught to do wi' you, *incomer*.' He spat out the last word.

Eleanor was about to protest when Matthew drew back his arm. He pitched his fist at Nicholas with frightening force. Nicholas just managed to dodge aside, and the punch landed on his shoulder. Yet it still knocked him off balance.

And perhaps it was the shock of being suddenly unsteady on his feet, or perhaps it was Matthew's taunt, but Nicholas seemed to change in a moment from a wise man into an angry one.

For Matthew was momentarily off guard, boasting to his cronies of the power of his fist. Nicholas regained his poise and levelled a massive blow against the cottar's nose, causing him to howl and curse. Almost at once Matthew returned the punch and a fight ensued, both men falling to the ground, rolling and scuffling together like a couple of fox cubs.

A few of the cottars standing around were encouraging Matthew, but most silently shook their heads, including John, who, it seemed, thought better of trying to step between his brawling brother and his opponent.

But then more shouting heralded the arrival of the constable, two of his henchmen flanking him and brandishing fearsome-looking cudgels. Geoffrey signalled to his men, who weighed in with their weapons. Dragging Matthew and Nicholas apart, they hauled them to their feet.

As the two men were pulled upright, Eleanor saw with horror how bloodied both their faces were. The evidence of scores of drunken brawls and angry frays already disfigured Matthew's features. But Nicholas's once fair face now bore not only a broken and bloody nose, but deep cuts and scratches that would surely heal to scars and make him look as brutal as the cottar.

Nicholas was shaking, and she thought his nose must hurt him. His knuckles, too, were scuffed and bleeding, but he straightened his back and held his head high, as the constable called him and Matthew to come and stand before him.

'You're in luck,' said Geoffrey, addressing them both. 'I'm feeling gen'rous tonight. You two can make your peace and go your separate ways.'

Nicholas pressed his hand to his chest and bowed his head, but Matthew scowled.

The constable crossed his arms. 'If I find either of you making fools of yourselves again, I'll throw you in his lordship's dungeon. Understood?'

John agreed on his brother's behalf, then took hold of Matthew and pulled him away, back towards the ale-house. Matthew let himself be taken but went off cursing, seemingly neither contrite nor grateful for being let off what would be a harshly punishable offence.

Beneath the congealing blood, Nicholas's face was turning pale. Eleanor laid a hand on his arm. 'You should have your injuries treated soon.'

He nodded, then addressed Geoffrey. 'I apologise, master constable, for letting my anger get the better of me. It was foolish and dishonourable. Indeed, it's the first time I've ever let myself be drawn into a brawl.'

The constable uncrossed his arms and inclined his head. 'Perhaps, then, Master Ashdown, you'll resist the urge a second time?'

Nicholas tried to grin, but flinched and dabbed with his fingertips at the wounds on his face.

Geoffrey then bowed briefly to Eleanor. 'If you're wondering why I let Matt go, Mistress Titherige, when I understand it were you he assaulted afore Master Ashdown here came to your rescue...' He winked, and Eleanor nodded, then grinned at Nicholas. 'It wouldn't help none to throw Matt in gaol,' the constable continued, 'with him grieving for his froward son. I warrant too he's shamed by what the lad has done, so don't be too hard on him.'

Eleanor thought it unlikely that Matthew was ashamed of anything, but didn't say so. Neither did she say he didn't deserve to be given any mercy, being so lazy and unreliable, as well as violent.

'I'll escort you home,' said Nicholas, once the constable and his men had left, and the cottars had either squeezed back inside the decrepit ale-house or drifted off home.

'Don't be foolish, Nick, you need attention. I'll take *you* to Simon Hogge, so he can mend your wounds. Then I'll take myself home.'

He made a weak attempt at protest, but it was clear he needed the barber-surgeon's help and, at length, he let Eleanor take his arm.

When Eleanor at last reached home, it was almost dark, and Hawisa was pacing the floor of the hall. Even when Eleanor explained to her the complicated reasons for her lateness, she was by no means soothed.

'I can't imagine what your poor Ma'd think,' the servant said, flapping at her skirts, 'finding you've walked home in the dark *alone*.'

Eleanor pouted. 'You didn't know my mama, Hawisa. Anyway, I had no choice, as I have explained.' She slumped down in the one big chair, which used to be her father's, and leaned back against the cushions. Her eyelids drooped. 'I'm very tired.'

'I'm not surprised, wi' all those antics—'

Eleanor raised her hand. 'So I'm going to bed, Hawisa. Now.' She stood up again.

'Without your supper?' cried the older woman.

'Yes, Hawisa, entirely without my supper.' Eleanor grinned. 'I'm too tired to eat. And I think I can survive one evening without food.'

She would not have minded a small bite to eat, but the prospect of spending any further moments in Hawisa's company was exhausting. The horrible incident with Matthew had been upsetting, almost, but not quite, bringing her frightening dream to life. But insisting on taking Nicholas to Simon's to dress his wounds had calmed her, and now she was tired rather than distressed. However, she also wanted to be alone, to reflect upon Nicholas's brave intervention on her behalf.

In the summer months, it was always hot up in the solar, tucked up as it was beneath the rush-thatched roof. But this evening it seemed stifling, despite it being still only May. Eleanor undressed and put on her night chemise. She would have liked to sleep quite naked, allowing the smooth linen sheets to cool her skin, but it would surely be improper, with Nathan lying only just downstairs on the pallet he and Hawisa shared?

It would be cooler too not to have to draw the hangings around her bed, but again propriety persuaded her to close them, and she lay down in the muffled dark, drew up the sheet and coverlet, and folded her arms across her chest, like an effigy on a tomb.

She closed her eyes, and let her worries surface.

She itemised the elements of her situation in her head. First, she was a free woman and in most respects answered to no one but herself. Second, she had a fine house of her own, and servants. Third, despite a troubling few months immediately after the Mortality left Meonbridge, she had thus far made a fair success of her enterprise. Her father's flock was already in good heart before he died, and she had done well to build it up still further over the past three years. Indeed, she was now quite well-off – not wealthy, that would take years, but comfortable enough. So Eleanor Titherige was a free-woman, a farmer, and a businesswoman.

*But*, she was unmarried.

It was not a position in which she had expected to find herself at twenty-two. But, after her mother died, the fifteen-year-old Eleanor had taken on her role, caring for her little brothers and helping her father in his grief. If he had been planning marriage for her, it was forgotten. Three years passed before he himself remarried, relieving Eleanor of her motherly duties. She was already almost nineteen when her father found her a suitor but, two months later, the young man was dead from the Mortality, as were her father, her brothers and her stepmother.

Left alone, with her livelihood and her father's flock of sheep to manage, she had somehow failed to consider marriage – until now. Yet being unwed was not a position she could, or should, sustain. Even though, in truth, Eleanor resented the idea of *having* to marry just to prove her respectability, the fact was, in Meonbridge, indeed perhaps in the whole of England, being unwed at twenty-two, unless she was a widow or a nun, was simply not acceptable.

Yet it was not only social propriety that required her to get a husband. For, notwithstanding her success with her sheep these past few years, her business was still local and small-scale, and she was not making the best deals for her wool. It irked her to admit it, but she was sure a man would be able to make better inroads into the higher levels of wool merchant society where she needed to gain a foothold.

In particular, perhaps, a man like Nicholas. She let his face – the fair one, not the bloodied – float into her head.

Like her, Nicholas was the child of a prosperous Winchester wool merchant who also lost his life to the Mortality. Nicholas had been educated for the Church, but after the dread disease had gone, leaving devastation – yet opportunity – in its wake, he decided that neither Church nor trade were to his taste. Having a fancy to be a farmer (like her own father), he had left Winchester for the promise of Meonbridge land, offered by Sir Richard's son Philip in those dark days when the manor was overburdened with untenanted plots and pastures.

It seemed to Eleanor that she and Nicholas had much in common. She suspected he had been attracted to her ever since he first came to Meonbridge, though it was only recently he had been paying court to her. He was a handsome man or, rather, he had been until this evening's brawl had caused such damage to his face. And was not the very fact that he had intervened on her behalf, to rescue her – as the constable had hinted – from Matthew's violent intentions, an indication that he was the very sort of strong, decisive man she needed as a husband?

Yet might that not be said also of Walter? The man who had saved her from certain death at the hands of the vile Gilbert Fletcher, as he tried to strangle her to stop her revealing his part in the murder of Sir Philip. How very brave dear Walter had been that day, when he fell upon Gilbert and plunged his shearing scissors into his thigh.

So, Nicholas *or* Walter?

Her chest felt tight, and it suddenly seemed unnaturally hot beneath her bedcovers. She sat up in the dark, threw off the sheet and coverlet and drew back the bed hangings. Swinging her legs round, she got up from the bed and stepped across the wooden floor to the little shuttered window. It was so small that, even in daylight, it was scarcely possible to see much of the view across the meadows to the woodland that stretched for miles to the north. Nonetheless she pulled the shutter open and peered out into the darkness.

At that moment, clouds drifted away and let the moon's light shine directly onto the meadowland behind her house. It lit up the countryside as if a giant was holding aloft an enormous lantern. A family of foxes was in the middle of the meadow, a mother perhaps and her brood of three. The cubs were play fighting like little boys, the parent watchful, perhaps for danger, perhaps for prey. Then she trotted off towards the woods, the cubs not noticing she had left them until she called, an eerie howl that carried across the silence. The cubs stopped their tussling and held their heads erect. The moon was so bright Eleanor could even see their ears were pricked. Then the vixen called to them again and they gambolled after her, until all had disappeared into the darkness of the trees.

What a charming sight they were. Yet she thought at once that Walter would not think so. He considered foxes vermin, fit only to be caught in a snare and dispatched with a hard blow to the skull. Walter was not a cruel man, but of course he deemed the lives of their sheep of much greater value than that of any fox. And how could she not agree?

The air beyond the window was warm, and yet a sudden slight breeze wafting inside felt chilly, and she shivered. She closed the shutter and slipped back into her bed. She drew the bed curtains and lay down again beneath the coverings. She wanted to go to sleep but, more importantly, she felt she had to somehow *finish* her deliberations. She surely could not, should not, let matters drift…

Could she perhaps weigh up the *qualities* of Nicholas and Walter?

First – she folded over the tip of her little finger – although Nicholas had not wanted to be a merchant, he had expressed great interest in her enterprise and, with his education and his status, and the connections he must have in Winchester, he would surely be the ideal man for gaining the foothold in merchant society that she needed? Whereas Walter had neither status nor education – indeed he was by birth a cottar – and it was surely unlikely that he could convince a haughty Winchester merchant of the superiority of their wool. On the other hand – next finger – Walter knew everything there was to know about the husbandry of sheep, whereas Nicholas knew little about sheep at all and certainly nothing about managing a flock as large as she planned hers would be.

So that was two fingers counted. What else was there?

It was true that Nicholas made her laugh – middle finger – whereas Walter was mostly morose and serious. Nicholas spoke with wit and vigour – index – while Walter barely spoke at all, though she knew him to be thoughtful. Nicholas was tall and handsome, his skin still fair despite three years working his Meonbridge lands, whereas Walter stood scarce any higher than she, and his face was kind but its skin was darkened by a lifetime out of doors. She folded the top part of her thumb…

Walter's sun-browned face came before her. Her face flushed in the dark as she thought of the bond that had grown between them, after she had saved his life, then he hers. And how, because of the bond, she had, almost unwittingly, promised him a future with her and her magnificent flock. How pleased Walter had been. Yet she knew their partnership could not be merely one of fellow shepherds. She was mostly unwilling to admit it, even to herself, but she thought that Walter might love her. But what did she feel for him? She didn't know. Even though they had not only worked together for three whole years, but had been seen together often enough that most of Meonbridge might well consider them nigh on a couple.

She knew all this. Yet, when Nicholas paid court to her, she let him. Even encouraged him… Of course it was dishonourable of him, when he must know full well what all of Meonbridge knew. But it was surely dishonourable of her too…

Her cheeks grew hot again, and a few tears of frustration prickled at her eyes. She rolled onto her side and tried to imagine one of them lying by her side. Which one should it be? And on what grounds should she – could she – choose?

# 5

## SUMMER 1352

Agnes closed her eyes and put her fingers to her forehead, rubbing gently. The pain was getting worse. She had been in the workshop since first light, trying to better her turning skills. Yet she was still struggling to master them, after months of what seemed like fruitless effort. It was vexing that she found it so difficult. Was it truly because she was a woman, as Jack had said?

'A woman cannot unite in harmony the actions of her hand, foot and eye,' he'd said, his face solemn. She'd arched her eyebrows, thinking he must've heard it from some other man, for the words sat uneasy on Jack's humble lips. But his comment had irked her, and resulted only in making her all the more determined to succeed.

Yet now, though she still didn't see why it should be true, she wondered if perhaps it *was*, seeing how long it was taking her to learn. Of course it might be that just she, Agnes, was "inharmonious", rather than women in general. But it was certainly true that the results of all her efforts were pitiful, her bowls always askew, her newel posts invariably crooked.

She blew out her lips in a long sigh, then leaned down to rub at her left leg. It too was sore, and still trembly from pumping the lathe's pedal all day long, and her fingers were stiff from the strain of pressing the chisel against the turning wood. She could've done without her head adding to her discomfort. Even though it was easy enough to hide her quivering leg beneath the wide skirt of her kirtle, and she'd become quite adept at disguising the pain in her hands, a megrim always made her face pinched and grey, a clear sign to Jack she was suffering. Yet she must betray no inkling that her work might be causing her a problem, else he'd use it as an excuse to put an end to it.

As if he wasn't keen enough already to oust her from his workshop.

Agnes tried to distract herself from her multiple malaises by listening to her brother. John would sometimes visit Agnes in the evening, supposedly to play with his little nephews. If he was feeling melancholy, as he often was, they could usually lift his spirits but, this evening, she felt more than usually *un*sympathetic to his grumbling. She'd come home to start preparing supper, leaving Jack to finish in the workshop, and the girl she hired to care for the boys had not yet brought them home. So the house was quiet, and Agnes would've liked just to get on with her tasks. Yet she could hardly refuse to let her brother talk.

John was in ill humour, a choler that recurred whenever something reminded him of how he'd failed to win the hand of Eleanor Titherige. It was three years since their relationship had ended yet, in all that time, he hadn't stopped wanting her, or agonising over where it was he had gone wrong.

Agnes found her brother's continued self-loathing pitiable. She always said the same to him: it was his own fault for trying to push Eleanor around, a woman like her just wouldn't stand for it, and he needed to forget her and find someone else. And, every time she said it, he agreed, and promised to do something about it. But he never moved beyond the promise.

She gave John a pot of ale, and he slumped down on a stool, cradling the pot in his big, soil-darkened hands. As he talked, Agnes bustled about, clearing up, preparing supper. She cast occasional sideways glances at her brother, three years older than she yet, as ever, making *her* feel the elder of the two. For this *man* was behaving – still! – like a lovelorn boy. Yet, not only was he one of the best-favoured men in the village, tall, broad-shouldered, fair-haired and handsome, he was the respected reeve of Meonbridge manor, able, surely, to ask for the hand of any girl in the village?

How could he *still* be pining for a woman who'd so obviously left him firmly in her past?

'It was bad enough when she took up with Walter,' John said, 'no matter he were just a cottar—'

'She didn't "take up" with him, John,' said Agnes, pinching the top of her nose and briefly shutting her eyes. She opened them again and glared at him. 'Walter *works* for her.'

He shook his head. 'There's always been more to it than that.' He grunted. 'Anyway, that's all about to change, I warrant, for Nick's courting her more keenly now.'

'I'd heard.'

Nicholas Ashdown was another of the few truly eligible men in Meonbridge. Such men were hardly numerous since the Death. But what was it about Eleanor that had these strong men falling at her feet? Eleanor was certainly no beauty, with her dull red hair and freckled face. Perhaps it was her sheep? Agnes sniggered to herself. Yes, it was probably the sheep.

'He's had his eye on her ever since he came to Meonbridge,' John continued.

'But he's bided his time. P'raps her and Walter's fallen out, and Nick knows it?'

'And how would he know?'

'Dunno. But I saw them yestereve, him and Eleanor. There was a fight outside the hovel that passes for an ale-house among the cottars. Matt Ward, you'll not be surprised to hear.'

'But also Eleanor, and Nicholas?'

'It seemed Matt attacked Eleanor, over the stolen sheep, I warrant, and Sir Richard's insistence he and his brother pay her compensation—'

'Quite right too.'

'I agree, but Matt clearly doesn't. Probably hasn't got the money.' He took a deep draught of his ale. 'Anyway, Nick appeared like a knight errant to rescue her.'

'How thrilling.' Agnes grinned. Not only falling at her feet, but riding to her rescue too.

'Mind you, he got a bloody nose for his trouble.' John clearly couldn't help but smirk a little. 'A *broken* nose, from what I hear.'

'Well, that'll spoil his handsome face.' She paused, her eyebrows raised. 'Or stand as a mark of courage?'

Agnes was relieved when John drained his pot and said he had to go, as Ma'd have his supper waiting. She was weary of being asked to concern herself with her brother's love life, when she was more troubled by her own. For Jack's attitude had changed towards her, and towards her working in his workshop, and her fondness for him had begun to fade. Was *her* change of heart related to *his*? Likely so.

She crouched down onto the three-legged stool she kept close to the fire, so she could rest while cooking. She picked up her long-handled spoon and gently stirred the pot. The savoury smell wafted up from the simmering broth. It likely smelled better than it'd taste. For most of the meals she'd cooked lately were unappetising and watery. Her shoulders slumped. Surely she hadn't always been so wanting?

Staring into the bubbling liquid, she recalled how Jack had often praised her cooking when they first married. How she had adored Jack then. She was grateful, too, that he'd taken her on, that he'd truly loved her, despite her recent birthing of another man's – Philip de Bohun's – bastard child. When they came to Meonbridge a few months later, the plan had been just to visit, to see her parents, then move on somewhere else to establish a new life together. But somehow they'd been urged to stay, when the de Bohuns discovered her little Dickon was their grandson, and Sir Richard offered Jack the tenancy of the carpenter's shop.

And, at first, they were very happy.

It was actually *Jack* who'd suggested she learn a few basic carpentry skills, so she could help him in the workshop, and avoid him having to take on anyone else, for a while at least.

'Few skilled men are left,' he'd said, then pursed his lips. 'Fewer men of any kind, skilled or otherwise. Surely, Agnes, women'll *have* to take on men's work, in the workshops as well as in the fields?'

Agnes had given him a hug. She felt proud to be married to such a man, sounding so bold and modern.

And it had seemed a good solution. She learned fast, soon producing small rough-hewn objects, like whittled spoons and trenchers, then moving on to benches and boxes, anything that had straight edges and could be nailed together.

It was only when she tried her hand at turning, a few months ago, to make cups and bowls and chair legs, that her skill had proven wanting and Jack seemed to change his mind. Though it wasn't only her work that was a matter for dispute between them.

But, just as Agnes's unhappy musings leapt forward to the disputatious present, the clamour of crying children sounded from beyond the door – a noise that might shortly provoke another argument, if Jack was already walking home.

Only a moment or two later, Marye thrust open the heavy door, which flew back with a bang as it hit the wooden bench that stood beneath the cloak pegs. The girl almost fell into the room, unbalanced as she was, with baby Geoffrey clutched precariously under one arm, and dragging little Stephen with the other. Both boys were wailing.

Agnes pressed two fingers to her forehead, then looked at Marye, her lips pressed together. 'Where's Dickon?'

Marye jerked her head towards the door. 'Jus' outside.' She rolled her eyes. 'Says he won't come in.'

'Don't be ridiculous, Marye.' She strode over and took hold of the bawling, red-faced Geoffrey. 'Go and fetch him in.'

Marye muttered something unintelligible and shambled back outside, yelling Dickon's name. Agnes followed her out into the garden, jiggling the baby on her hip in a vain attempt to soothe him. She couldn't help smiling at the sight of Marye waddling after Dickon, as he ran off into the potager, weaving in and out of the planting beds. Marye was not a dainty girl, and couldn't match his speed, despite him being only three. Moments later, Dickon darted through the open door, crowing and roaring, then threw himself down onto the straw-filled pallet where he and his brothers slept during the day, and beat at it with his fists. Shortly afterwards, Marye reeled into the room, out of breath and as red-faced as the still-howling Geoffrey.

Agnes closed the door then grasped Marye by the shoulder. 'Why's Dickon in such ill-temper?'

Marye blushed. 'I jus' wanted to visit my friend,' she said in a whisper, 'jus' for a gossip.' She raised her eyes. 'She's expecting.'

'For mercy's sake, Marye,' cried Agnes, feeling her own choler rising. 'You *know* Dickon won't sit quiet while you chat. Anyway, I don't pay you to gossip with your friends, with child or without. I pay you to look after my boys.'

Marye shrugged and Agnes would've liked to hit her: she truly was the most vexatious girl. Why did she keep her on, when she so often brought the boys home peevish, leaving her to cajole them into eating and sleeping when she was already exhausted from her day?

'Go home, girl,' she said, and gave her a little push.

Marye pouted and opened the door again, just as Jack appeared outside it. Marye jostled past him, knocking him off balance, the door frame being not quite wide enough for both. Jack rebuked her as she trudged away. But she didn't answer or turn around.

Jack came inside and slammed the door. Dropping his tool bag with a clatter on the floor, he surveyed the scene before him. Stephen was sitting on the bench just at his side, his shoulders hunched, his feet kicking against the stretcher. Dickon was still thumping at his pallet, and Geoffrey was refusing to be pacified. Knowing how it must all appear to Jack, Agnes felt a throbbing in her head, as a hard smile of irritation distorted his mouth.

'That girl—' she started.

But Jack raised his hand. 'You can't blame Marye, Agnes. She's just a child herself.'

'Thirteen—'

'A *child*.' He bent down to lift up Stephen from the bench and held the boy against his chest, stroking his hair. Stephen nestled his fair head into his father's neck and crooned. As Agnes saw, not for the first time, how easily Jack could soothe the child, her megrim seemed to worsen. She closed her eyes and rubbed her forehead with her fingers.

Jack noticed and went over to her. He came close and bowed his head until his forehead was just touching hers. 'Don't fret so, Agnes. It doesn't help.'

She nodded, then moved her head back a little, hoping he might kiss her. But he didn't.

'Give me Geoffrey too,' he said. 'I'll rock him for a while.' He sat down in one of the fine chairs he'd made and she put the baby against his other arm. Jack jiggled his leg a little, gently bouncing Geoffrey, and quickly changing the child's misery into laughter.

58

For a moment, Agnes couldn't move, staring at her husband, wondering what magic spells he knew that so readily cast such calm upon his sons. She lifted up her apron and wiped the edge of it across her cheeks.

But shortly Jack looked up. 'You'll have to deal with Dickon...'

She gave him a small smile and crept over to her eldest son. He'd stopped pummelling his pallet, but was now sitting on it, picking at the straw poking through a hole in the linen cover. She squatted by his side, lifting her skirt and folding it over her knees. Dickon seemed unwilling to look her in the face, so she gently took his chin in her hand. How like his father he was, with his dark hair and bright blue eyes. 'What's wrong, poppet?'

The boy's shoulders slumped, then he jerked his chin out of her hand. 'Nuffin.'

'Something must've made you cross with Marye.'

He resumed his picking at the straw then, giving his mother a furious scowl, yelled at her. 'She's a stupid fat pig!'

Agnes couldn't stop her hand from flying out and slapping him hard across the face. At which, he shrieked, flopped back onto the pallet and wept.

It was quite dark by the time the boys were all asleep and Agnes and Jack could sit across the table from one another, spooning up some of the thin, tasteless soup she'd made what seemed as long ago as half a day. Jack drank a little, then tore off a chunk of coarse bread from the loaf and, dipping it into the broth, sucked noisily at the sops. He didn't seem to want to speak. Not because he was angry with her, she thought – even though he surely was. But rather that, after the uproar earlier, the peace that had now settled on the house was just too welcome to disturb.

Agnes pushed her bowl away, only half emptied. Even if she'd been hungry, the soup would still taste like pigswill. She took some bread and gnawed at it.

If Marye was proving hopeless, it hadn't always been so with other girls she'd hired. Soon after they decided to stay in Meonbridge, Agnes, in an effort to prove herself a full partner in their workshop, hired a girl to care for Dickon while she worked. She assumed Jack would approve, as he'd been the one to suggest she learn the craft. But in fact he was doubtful, feeling she was neglecting her son. They argued about it, though he didn't make her dismiss the girl.

A year later, when Stephen was born, Agnes hired a wet-nurse. She winced at the memory of Jack's anger.

'A *wet-nurse*,' he cried, running his fingers through his hair. 'Wet-nurses are for the gentry, Agnes, not the likes of us. You might have *some* sort of kinship with the de Bohuns, Agnes, but you're *not* them.'

She became upset, feeling he was deliberately misunderstanding her decision. 'It's not because of that, Jack, you know it isn't.' She had fought back tears. 'It was *you* thought I should work, to help the business grow. But I can't work and care for the children all at once.'

At length he did concede. But, when Geoffrey came along, Agnes just let the girl who then looked after Dickon and Stephen bring the baby to the workshop for his feeds. Jack considered that suitable enough, and, at least, that girl made a good job of caring for the boys. But she'd left earlier this year to marry, and Marye seemed to be the only possible nursemaid left in the village.

When Jack had finished eating, she cleared the table, while he went outside to check the animals. She hoped he'd not be long, for she craved her bed, and sleep. Her forehead was still throbbing, and only sleep would free her from the pain. Leaning against the table, she felt a tightening in her chest.

How was it she was only twenty, yet already felt older than her Ma?

# 6

Susanna was lifting the rows of onions she'd planted in the spring, and laying them out to dry across the hard and dusty earth. What joy her garden brought her, especially on a day like today, when, despite the coming autumn, the sun was still warm, the sky almost cloudless. She stood up and, pressing her hand against her back, gazed around at the extent of her croft, with its barns and sheds, the beds of vegetables and herbs, the orchard at the far end, running down towards the river: the river that was the reason for the relative ease of her life as Henry's wife. She did love it here. And how much better a place it was to bring up children than the dark, damp cottar cottage where she'd raised her first family.

She glanced back towards the house. Maud was playing dutifully with her little cousin Francis, on the tiny patch of grass Henry had agreed would serve well as a play place for their growing family. But then she realised Tom had vanished, despite being left in charge. He hated baby minding, considering it one of those "girls' chores" he thought he shouldn't have to do. Her brow creased a moment, but she soon let it melt away. She understood.

But, when wailing burst from the baby's cradle, she saw Maud was paying it no heed. Susanna tutted and, throwing down her weeding tool, jumped up and ran over to the children, wiping her hands against her skirt. As she came closer, she saw Maud had brought out her growing collection of wooden animals, which was kind of her as Francis was a clumsy boy, often unwilling to share toys, even when they weren't his own. But now the two of them seemed quite absorbed, in a game of Noah's Ark, she thought it was, for Maud had fashioned a little ship from a curl of tree bark. She stared at Maud a moment: how very pretty the child was, with her wheat-coloured curls bobbing lightly as she solemnly directed Francis in how to match up the pairs of creatures and march them into the Ark.

Susanna bent over the wooden cradle that had served all Maud's brothers and sisters – all lost in the Death, apart from little Peter's accident in the mill.

Baby Joan was more whimpering than crying. Cooing, Susanna leaned in and lifted the baby up into her arms and, in an instant, the child ceased her whining and, cooing in return, put out a hand to touch her mother's face.

Delighting, as she always did, in her baby's milky smell and soft squirmy warmth, Susanna eased herself down onto the grassy patch, first to her knees then, wriggling round, she sat with Joan cradled in her lap.

She'd been stung by Emma's remark the other day, that she should be grateful for her lot. She'd not meant to sound ungrateful – she'd just wanted to express her worry about Henry. But it'd come out all wrong. It had seemed hard-hearted, what Emma said, yet she was certain she'd meant no unkindness by it. And, indeed, wasn't Emma right? Susanna surveyed again what was her domain, the house, the croft, the children. How could she not be thankful?

She understood well enough why Emma might think badly of her. Henry's income was sufficient that she'd no need to work outside the house and croft, or so he told her.

But it wasn't so for Emma.

A while back, Emma had been bold enough to complain to her of what she considered Sir Richard's tightfistedness.

'He won't raise wages, saying the king's brought in some law or other to keep us workers in our place.' Emma had tossed her head in her frustration. 'Yet some of the other employers here, like Nicholas Cook and Alan Fuller, they don't let themselves be told what to do by some law made a hundred miles away.'

Susanna had nodded, though she'd not known how to answer. 'It don't seem right—'

But Emma was in full flight, and forgot all sense of tact. 'But Ralph's so faithful to Sir Richard, he lets himself be paid a pittance, despite his skills. I tell him he should go and work for Alan Fuller, but he won't.' She rolled her eyes. 'I work for as much money, and for as many different people, as I can. Why does he think he's in debt only to the de Bohuns?'

Susanna gave a little nod. 'Harry's loyal to the manor too—'

Emma had screwed up her face. 'Well, he *would* be, wouldn't he, seeing he's got the only mill in Meonbridge.'

Susanna had felt the warmth prickling on her neck, then rise quickly to her cheeks. Some folk did resent Henry's family and forebears having always held the manor's mill. She'd no reason to feel guilty about it – it was just the way things were.

Nonetheless, she'd been embarrassed then and was so again the other day with Emma.

She knew well enough what life was like for Ralph and Emma. It had been like that for her when she was herself a cottar wife. She and Fran both had to work, finding employment as best they could. They'd no choice if their family was to survive.

She lifted baby Joan into her arms and rocked her gently. How different life had been for her first family. They never had a patch of grass to play on. As babies, they spent their days strapped to her back or breast, as she laboured in the fields, and, as two- and three-year-olds, they'd not played at Noah's Ark, but endured endless days just sitting by her as she worked, and sometimes even had to work themselves... Susanna freed a hand and wiped away the moistness that had gathered in her eyes.

Why on earth would she want that life back again?

Yet a small part of her did wish it. Not *that* life, of course, not Emma's life. Just one where Henry considered her his helpmeet, let her share in his decisions, instead of ignoring her advice, indeed not even seeking her opinion. Perhaps it had always been like this, only at first she hadn't noticed because he was so loving too? But now he no longer seemed to love her, she felt much more keenly the distance he seemed to have put between them.

She nuzzled the baby's neck, then held her up and bounced her gently. Joan giggled, and Susanna pulled her close again and covered her with kisses.

Perhaps she had to be content with the children Henry had given her?

Henry had been at the manor today, called by the constable to be a juryman at a special court hastily arranged to try the case of a villein woman accused of assaulting her husband with a skillet.

'The case should've been taken to the Hundred court,' he'd said, 'or even held over till the sheriff's tourn. But it was agreed we wanted to keep the shameful affair within the manor – dealt with in our own way.'

Susanna had already heard about Elizabeth Wragge's supposed misdeeds. She was sister-in-law to the bailiff, Adam, who, by all accounts, was much discomfited that a relative of his, a hitherto respectable woman, indeed one of the village goodwives, should be brought before the court.

In a huddle of the village gossips, Ann Webb had teetered between indignation and amusement. 'Who'd've thought it of Lizzie Wragge?' Her eyes were alight. 'Attacking her ol' man wi' a skillet. They say Simon Hogge had to bind his wounds up real tight else he'd've bled to death.'

'An' him such a gentle young man,' said another. 'It don't seem right.'

'Mebbe there's more to it than meets the eye?' said Ann, with a knowing wink.

'What're you thinking of?' Susanna said. She knew neither Mistress Wragge nor her husband, except to pass the time of day, and thought both

63

seemed respectable and worthy people, though the wife was many years older than the husband, almost old enough to be his mother, which she'd always thought surprising.

But Ann just tapped her nose.

When Henry returned home from the court, he seemed almost eager to tell Susanna all about it.

'Elizabeth Wragge claimed poor Edmund was always finding fault with her. I warrant *she's* the harridan, not him. Edmund's one of the most courteous men I know.'

'But surely she wouldn't hit him just for finding fault?' The Church said it was a husband's duty to chastise his wife, so Susanna supposed if Edmund truly found Elizabeth wanting in some respect, it was his right to say so.

'You'd think not.' Henry grunted. 'But some women don't respect their husband's right to rule in his own household.'

Susanna gasped, and he raised his eyebrows. 'You disagree?'

She blushed a little, unsure how to answer. 'Of course not, Harry,' she said at length. 'The man's the head of the household. Isn't that what the Bible says?'

'And you acknowledge it?'

She nodded, yet inside she felt a little queasy. 'A husband always has the final word,' she ventured, 'but I don't think that gives a man the right to criticise his wife unfairly—'

Henry snorted. 'I hardly think Edmund were doing that. Rather the opposite, poor bastard. And her assaulting him's the final straw.'

'What did she say in her defence?'

'I reckon Lady de Bohun had a hand in Sir Richard's judgement, for at first his lordship were almost sympathetic to Elizabeth's claims.' He snorted again. 'She said she didn't see why she should stand for it any longer, when she'd brought such a dowry to their marriage—'

'Was her dowry especially large?'

'*All* his land was once hers. He'd none before he wed her. Don't you remember when they married, three years past?'

Susanna knit her brow, trying to remember, and gradually it came back to her. Edmund was the bailiff's younger brother by several years, an educated man once destined for the Church, left landless by their father, who'd given all his property to Adam, the eldest son. But, after the Death, Edmund decided after all he didn't want to be a priest, but preferred to stay in Meonbridge, where vast tracts of land had become available, many untenanted, some now held by women. One such woman was Elizabeth, a wealthy villein's widow, who was much older than Edmund but held three virgates of some of the best land in

Meonbridge. Despite the wide gap in their ages, Edmund married her.

Susanna remembered how the gossip had then seethed around the pump: how Edmund had wooed Elizabeth, and she was flattered because he was so young and handsome. She chuckled as she recalled what the sharp-tongued Alys Ward had said.

'I hear Elizabeth's much *enjoying* her new young husband.' Her eyes had held a wicked glint. 'An' Master Wragge's as happy as a pig in muck.'

'Though I've heard,' chipped in her friend Ann, 'he's only just realised he'll get no babes from her, no matter how spirited his ploughing.'

'Elizabeth's too old for it now,' said Alys, 'but then she's *never* had a babe. Yet young Edmund didn't seem t' think on that, his greedy eyes seeing the land an' not much else, I warrant.'

'I wonder,' Susanna now said to Henry, 'if it were when he realised she couldn't give him children he started to find fault with her?'

'That, and when she started hitting him.'

'Harry!' cried Susanna. 'Are you saying she's hit him more than once?'

He shrugged. 'As I hear it, she's been lashing out at the poor bastard for months. With her tongue, then with whatever she happened to have to hand – distaff, spoon or skillet.'

'I can scarce believe it. Surely Mistress Wragge's a gentle soul?'

'Not so. And, this last time, she drew blood and poor Edmund had to call in Simon to bind his gaping wounds.'

'Who raised the hue and cry?'

'Edmund himself.' Henry shook his head. 'Shameful business.'

Susanna bit her lip. 'What did the court decide?' What *was* the penalty if Elizabeth was found guilty? The stocks, perhaps? Imprisonment?

Relieved to see Henry smiling, Susanna thought the jury must, after all, have found in favour of Mistress Wragge. But, moments later, she felt a fool. Why did she imagine that Henry, of all men, would want her acquitted?

'We all agreed,' he said, 'we couldn't let her off, else all the wives in Meonbridge'd think they could hit their husbands.' He let the smile bloom into a broad grin. 'Everyone laughed at that, thinking it a great joke, but we could hardly let her get away with it.'

Susanna gasped at Henry's seeming cheerfulness. And at once it dawned on her that he was among the most vehement supporters of finding Elizabeth guilty.

'What'll happen to her?' she said, her voice a whisper.

'Ordeal by water,' said Henry, matter-of-factly.

Susanna cried out. 'Surely ordeals are not allowed. Didn't Lady de Bohun—?'

Henry let out a guffaw. 'Of course her ladyship tried to persuade Sir Richard that he should follow the law. But we all thought the woman – all women – had to be shown we'll not tolerate such behaviour here. We had to prove her guilty. And his lordship agreed with us.'

Susanna's heart beat a little faster. It was hard to believe this was her Harry talking. 'She might die,' she said.

But Henry made no answer.

The ordeal was carried out next morning, soon after daybreak, in the confines of Saint Peter's, with the priest and all the jurors gathered round. Sir Richard was not there. Susanna went along, joining the few villagers, men and women, who were curious to see it. She overheard some muttering that surely ordeals had been banned years ago, so how come Sir Richard was allowing it? She suspected he had little taste for harsher penalties than the usual fines or stocks, or else was urged by her ladyship to ignore demands from jurors for retribution. Yet it seemed that *this* jury – perhaps with Henry at its forefront? – wanted an example made of Elizabeth, and had persuaded his lordship that, despite its illegality, an ordeal would prove her guilt. So why was his lordship absent?

Perhaps he already regretted his decision? And Susanna thought maybe she did too. It was going to be a shameful spectacle, and she couldn't bear to watch the poor woman drown or, worse, see her float and then be dragged off to be – what? Hanged? She shuddered. Surely she should leave now, go home and take the children for a walk? Yet, she was curious too, and still hadn't moved when Master Hugo and the jurymen approached the church, with Elizabeth Wragge, her hair uncovered, her face red and shiny, lurching behind them. The constable, she noticed, was there too but seemed to be hanging back, his expression gloomy.

Almost at once, Susanna wished she'd gone home after all. For there, among the jurymen, she – of course! – saw Henry, who'd surely not be pleased to find her there. Yet if she tried now to leave, he'd be bound to notice, so she stood her ground, stepping a little sideways to hide behind Ann Webb and her friend Alys Ward. Alys was a bitter-tongued old shrew, who seemed almost gleeful at the prospect of Mistress Wragge's humiliation, but Ann, though sometimes she did speak out of turn, was mostly kind at heart.

After the Death, Ann and Susanna were both newly widowed and forced by Sir Richard's court to give up their only worthwhile possessions in order to pay the heriot for their husbands' deaths. Ann had nothing to give except her cooking pot, and had pleaded with his lordship to show mercy, for without her pot she'd not be able to feed her little boy. To the surprise of many,

Sir Richard had shown sympathy and agreed to accept the smallest of money fines instead of the pot, and Ann threw herself, weeping, at his feet.

How different were their situations now. For Ann still worked some days from first light till dark, at any one of the many jobs she was obliged to take to make any sort of living. Even then she'd barely enough to feed herself and her child, now a large and lusty boy of ten. Whereas Susanna... Well, she'd clearly found much better fortune.

Nonetheless, Susanna reached for the comfort of Ann's hand as one of the jurymen pushed Elizabeth forward to stand before the great barrel of water set up in the lee of the church wall. The woman was trembling, with fear rather than cold, Susanna assumed, until the juryman whisked away the cloak wrapped around her shoulders to reveal that she was wearing naught but her chemise.

A shared gasp came from the watching women, though Susanna heard a man standing close behind her snigger. She might have turned around to reproach him but decided not to draw attention to herself. Instead she squeezed Ann's hand, and Ann returned the gesture doubly.

Susanna scarcely knew Elizabeth but thought her likely a proud, haughty woman, for whom this ordeal would be the deepest humiliation. And Susanna's own unease at witnessing the woman's shame was made worse by knowing Henry had demanded it. Yet again it seemed to her impossible that her "Harry" would think it right for a respectable woman to be so dishonoured.

She could hardly bear to watch what was about to happen, but something stopped her from keeping her eyes entirely averted.

Master Hugo, looking grave, mounted the platform placed before the barrel and uttered some words of blessing over the water. Then one of the jurymen tied a rope around Elizabeth's waist, and he and another man hefted her off her feet. She thrashed her arms about, bawling like a baby and begging for mercy, but the men took no notice of her pleas and, struggling onto the platform and lifting her up high, slid her down into the barrel. Elizabeth was not a large woman, but she caused a mighty splash as she dropped, shrieking, into the water. She flailed for a few moments, her head and hands bobbing twice above the barrel's top. But then she disappeared.

Susanna couldn't stop herself crying out, and others cried out too, though some watchers were cheering. Confused, she turned to Ann. But Ann was grinning.

'Look at them men's faces,' she said, pointing at the jurymen and the priest. All were dark with anger. 'Their plot's failed. Now they'll 'ave to find her innocent.'

Susanna nodded then, relieved. 'Because the holy water accepted her?' She let out a great breath. 'So she'll live?'

But Ann's grin changed into a grimace. 'Not if they don't 'aul 'er out right quick.' And she yelled at one of the jurymen to pull Elizabeth from the barrel or have bloody murder on his hands.

At that, four men – one of them the constable – scrambled to the barrel's edge and thrust their arms down into the water, almost tipping in themselves, until they found Elizabeth and hauled her out, no longer thrashing but a dead weight.

Everyone pressed forward to look at her, as she was laid upon the ground. As Susanna looked, her hand flew to her mouth. Elizabeth's eyes were closed and, despite the holy water finding her innocent, she looked quite dead. And, almost worse, the way her soaking wet chemise clung tightly to her body further deepened her humiliation. Susanna saw a few men leering over the sight of her breasts and thighs, their shape clearly revealed now by the flimsy fabric.

Also noticing the leering men, the constable ran forward with the cloak and threw it over Elizabeth's body. But then he knelt down at her side and, rolling her over onto her chest, struck her several times hard upon the back. Susanna gasped, as did many of the other onlookers, but, moments later, Elizabeth coughed and a gush of water spilled out from her mouth. Geoffrey took her shoulders and lifted her up gently, until she was sitting with her head between her knees.

Ann nudged Susanna's elbow. 'Warrant she feels right poorly, after swallowing all that 'oly water. But 'least she's still alive.'

Susanna nodded. '*And* proven innocent.'

Ann pouted. 'But she ain't, is she?'

'Whatever do you mean?'

'Everyone knows how cruelly she treats poor Edmund. They say of an evenin' you can hear his cries for help clear across the river.'

Susanna wasn't at all surprised to find Henry most exasperated that Mistress Wragge had sunk inside the barrel of holy water, and had to be set free. He clearly agreed with Ann that Elizabeth wasn't innocent at all. 'But surely,' said Susanna, 'the ordeal proved she *was*? If she were guilty, she'd have floated.' Susanna was confused about it all, but decided not to press the point with Henry, who was trying to find a useful outcome, despite justice not being served in quite the way he and his fellow jurors had hoped.

'Mebbe, at least,' he said, 'the shame of her ordeal, and her *nearly* drowning, will make other Meonbridge wives think twice afore attacking their husbands.'

Susanna would've giggled, though she held it in. She'd not think even *once* about attacking Henry.

*

Next morning, when she went to the pump to fetch some fresh well water, Susanna found the other women there asserting it was indeed a shameful thing, not only to suffer the ordeal, but to hit your husband in the first place.

'No decent woman'd do that,' said Alys, and everyone muttered their agreement.

'But everyone knows,' said Ann, repeating her claim of yesterday, 'Lizzie Wragge *do* beat her poor Edmund...'

'Maybe she's got good reason?' said Agnes, who, Susanna noticed, recently came more often to the pump herself, instead of sending Marye.

Everyone turned to Agnes for an explanation. She flushed slightly, then bit her lip. 'I've heard Edmund never gives her any word of kindness, complains at everything she does, and spurns any advice she offers.'

Some of the other women mumbled their recognition of Agnes's claim.

'My man's just the same.'

'Huh! Mine thinks nothin' I say's worth hearin'.'

'An' my Rob treats me no better 'n the shit he scrapes off his boots.'

Agnes nodded. 'Don't most men think their wives weak-minded? Else they'd respect them like they deserve. Maybe it's surprising more wives *don't* act like Mistress Wragge?'

Susanna suppressed a gasp. Surely Agnes couldn't be saying Jack Sawyer, of all men, thought his wife weak-minded? And did Henry think that of her? He certainly refused to listen to her advice. But was that because he thought her opinions worthless, or just that he was pig-headed?

She giggled. 'Oh, Agnes, surely not?' She tilted her head. 'Yet, I warrant I do sometimes feel I'd like to slap my Henry, if I thought it'd knock some sense into him.'

Ann and Agnes chuckled, and a couple of the others agreed they'd like to thump their husbands too. But Alys fleered. 'You oughta watch your tongue, Susanna Miller, else you might find *yerself* dunked in a barrel of 'oly water.'

Ann cuffed Alys on the shoulder. 'Curb your wicked tongue, you ol' besom! Susy meant nothing by it.'

# 7

## AUTUMN 1352

Eleanor hadn't seen Nicholas Ashdown for weeks. She'd decided to test herself – to see if, or by how much, she missed his company. She would have liked to do the same with Walter but that was scarcely possible, when they worked together every day. She'd been trying to arrange it so, most days, it was Will who worked with Walter, while she spent her time with Emma, working with this year's lambs. But once the lambs were grown and separated from their dams, the males sent for slaughter, and most of the ewe lambs put out to pasture on their own, they needed little attention.

And now it was nearing Michaelmas, when they prepared the older ewes for mating, a task that needed all four of them to work together. It was a task she much enjoyed, moving through the ewes ripe for mating, pressing her hands against each one's back to check she was neither too fat nor too thin, and in the best condition for conceiving lambs and rearing them. Of course Walter was the best judge amongst them, and Eleanor relied on him to say if an animal needed richer pasture or a period of fasting.

This was hardly a suitable time for silence. Yet, here she was, attempting to distance herself from him, and she was sorry for his puzzled frown and downcast eyes. So, after a day or two more of struggling with her ridiculous constraint, Eleanor gave it up, in the interests of her business and her reason. It would be a relief to return to their usual easy association. But, when she saw Walter's face become less troubled, another wave of guilt washed over her, for the hurt she knew she must have caused him by treating him so coolly.

'Walter,' she said, smiling, 'please advise me.' His forehead wrinkled. 'Now we have examined all the ewes, should we turn our attention to the rams?' She scarcely had to ask, but hoped to demonstrate her need of his advice.

He gave a curt nod. 'We must, mistress—'

Eleanor winced. She hated it when Walter called her that. But she was of course entirely to blame if he assumed her coolness meant she had reneged on any intimacy between them.

'They're in fine fettle,' he said. 'I'm sure of it, but Will and me'll check them over in the morning.'

'You don't need my help?'

Walter shook his head. 'Will and me can do it. Rams are ill-tempered brutes when vexed, once we start prodding them and peering in their mouths.' He allowed a grin to lighten his face.

'Very well. But, next week, should we run the ewes and rams together?'

Walter knit his brow this time and stared at her, unspeaking.

Eleanor felt a flush bloom on her neck and rise up to her face. She had no need to ask about the rams, and Walter knew it. What must he think then of her unnecessary questions? That she was humouring him, perhaps, mollifying him as if were a querulous child? How much he would hate that.

Then tears were threatening to moisten her burning cheeks. Furious with herself, she blinked them away. But Walter had not noticed and was already trudging back towards his cottage. She followed, as far as the start of the track that led back down to Meonbridge, where she stopped and called out, 'Good night, Walter.'

He turned to face her. 'We'll run them together Monday,' he said, his voice peevish-sounding.

Eleanor nodded, then turned onto the downhill track. She wanted to run, but the tears were threatening again, and for a few moments she did not move. And the moments were long enough for Walter's voice to regain its usual gentleness, as he called out to her, 'Good night to you, Eleanor – sleep well.'

Looking back, she saw him raise his hand, and waved hers too. Then, ignoring her blurry eyes, she ran down the hill to home.

After three long days of lowering clouds and heavy rain, Monday's dawn was bright, but Eleanor's initial hopes of a dry and not too windy day on Riverdown were quickly dashed, as the pale sun soon slid back behind the scudding clouds, and did not reappear.

She had not been up to Riverdown for several days – since her foolish exchange with Walter about the rams. Indeed, she'd not been out of the house at all, deciding to spend this time when Walter didn't need her trying to fathom her accounts. But today she had to venture forth again and it was not a cheering prospect. The narrow village roads would, she knew, by now be muddy, the deep ruts likely full of rainwater, and the hill track up to the pasture could be slippery. She pressed her lips together. Was it already time for her heavy boots? Or even the wooden pattens, to keep her feet dry above the mud? The chill and damp of approaching winter had arrived, the warm, sunny days up with her flock – and with Walter – now just a lovely memory.

Nonetheless, as Walter promised, he and Will would surely have checked the rams, and today was the day he planned to run them with the ewes. And she was going to be there, muddy roads or no.

Sitting on the bench set by the outer door, she lined up her usual boots, her thicker winter boots and her pattens on the floor before her.

'Which do you think, Hawisa?' she said, as the servant bustled about the hall, clearing Eleanor's breakfast things and tending to the fire. 'How are the roads this morning?'

Hawisa clicked her tongue. 'Quaggy, mistress,' she said and, coming over, lifted the skirt of her kirtle to show the thick brown crusting on the hem. 'And that's just this morning.'

'So, winter boots or pattens, do you think?'

'Well, if I had them pattens, mistress, they're what I'd wear. Even the village roads're inches deep.'

So Eleanor pulled on her thinner boots and tied the pattens over them. Then she selected her thick winter cloak from the hooks behind the bench, and an extra hood and, well wrapped up, she heaved open the door and peered outside. It was not raining, although, as she stepped out onto the track outside her house and gazed up at the sky, she thought the clouds looked set to burst again before too long.

The track here was not too muddy, for the land drained well this side of the village, and the track was not much used, leading as it did only to her house and two others. But, as she entered the village, Eleanor found the roads were indeed quite thickly muddied, if not "inches deep". She picked her way, finding the heavy pattens uncomfortable and awkward, as she always did when she first put them on after long months of disuse.

She was unsurprised to find the narrow road that ran through Meonvale even harder to negotiate. She soon began to wish she had not worn the pattens after all, for they made it easier to slip off the ridge tops and plunge a foot into the muddy, rain-filled ruts. Which, just as she was passing Will Cole's cottage, is exactly what she did. The furrow was uncommonly deep and, as her foot sank into the muddy softness, cold brown water breached her boot top and trickled down inside, soaking her woollen stocking.

Unbalanced, she began to sway but, at that very moment, Will burst forth from his cottage and ran to her side, catching her before she toppled over.

'God's bones, missus,' he cried, 'that were close. You was nigh on flat on your face.'

'Oh, Will, thank the Lord you were here. What a sight I would have been, besmirched from head to toe in mud.' She managed a laugh, and Will joined in.

'If I'd been a moment sooner, missus, I could've stopped you slipping.'

'No matter, Will. I'm glad at least you stopped me falling over.' She peered down at her sunken foot. 'Would you help pull my boot out of the mud?'

Will grinned and, supporting her with one arm, leaned down and, grasping the top of the boot, heaved upon it. For a moment or two, the boot refused to yield. But then he gripped its back, and rocked it till the heel lifted from the mud, and Eleanor's booted foot came suddenly free with a squelch and a spray of muddy water that splattered both their clothes.

But, as Eleanor put her foot down, she almost toppled over once again. 'My patten!' she cried. 'It's been left behind.'

'Shall I dig down and find it, missus?' said Will, with a twisted grin.

'Thank you, Will, but no. It was wearing the wretched things that got me into trouble.'

Will helped her to a drier patch of road beside his cottage, where she bent down and untied the other patten. For a moment, she considered going home again to put on her winter boots, but decided not to, as Walter would undoubtedly be pacing forth and back, speculating on why she and Will had not yet come. Her thin boots would be ruined, but somehow that seemed to matter less than ensuring her shepherd was not too aggrieved.

She left the patten just inside Will's cottage. 'I'll send Nathan to retrieve it, and the drowned one, but not until the ruts dry out a little,' she said. 'But now you and I must make haste, else Walter will think he's been abandoned.'

They walked as quickly as they could, stepping carefully between the rain-filled ruts and often diverging from the track to take a drier path through some cottar's croft. One of them was the untidy plot surrounding Matthew's dishevelled hovel.

Will jerked his head towards the cottage as they hurried past. 'There ain't a stick o' furniture in there now. His pallet and his cooking pot – not that he uses it – are all Matt's got left.'

Eleanor gasped. 'But why?'

'He had to sell it, didn't he, to raise your money, missus.'

Eleanor gazed back at the ramshackle building. A lump came to her throat. 'I knew he'd struggle to find the money and, in truth, I would have let him off. But Sir Richard insisted I should have my reparation.'

'Quite right, missus,' said Will. 'It wouldn't've been right to let him get away wi' it.'

'But I do feel sorry for the man, despite my vexation about my sheep.'

As they crossed the river by the little wooden bridge, she stopped a moment and stared down into the rushing water. The Meon was much swollen by the days of rain, the muddy waters flowing fast beneath her feet, not all that far below the underside of the bridge.

'Anyway, missus, don't fret for Matt. He's brought everything upon hisself.'

'But poor John is not to blame for anything, and he must so miss his little Arthur.'

The track up the hill was not as difficult as she had feared but, where the chalk was bare of grass it had turned slippery from the rain and her thin boots kept sliding, making the walk more tiring than usual.

'Daresay Matt misses his lad too,' said Will. 'Without him, he's no money, only what his brother gives him.' He grunted. 'He were dour enough when he lost 'is Sarah and the girls in the Death, but now he's more an angry bear 'n ever.'

Eleanor nodded, remembering how fierce Matthew had been when he attacked her, and how, when he came to give her her money, he had almost thrown it at her at the door before storming off, his retreating shoulders stiff.

'Where do you think the boys can be, after all this time?'

'Dunno, missus.' He scratched at the hair beneath his hood. 'Though I reckon they're still in Me'nbridge.'

'Truly? But the constable's men searched—'

'But how *well* did they search? *All* the barns and outhouses?' He shook his head.

'So you think the boys are hiding somewhere *here*?' said Eleanor. 'But why do you—'

''Cause things keep goin' missing.'

'What sort of things?'

'Loaf o' bread, couple of eggs, a fresh-made cheese. Things folk weren't sure at first they'd lost, but then—'

'So has no one raised the hue and cry about the thefts?'

He shook his head. 'Cottar folk, we stick together. We soon suspected what were goin' on. An' if it were Luke and Arthur stealing, it'd be summat else for his lordship to charge 'em with.' He stopped walking. 'None of us wants that, missus.'

'Nor I, Will. I told Sir Richard I didn't want them brought before the courts, but I suppose he might think such misdemeanours should not go unpunished.'

'Which is why no cottar'll raise the hue and cry for the loss of a bit o' bread or piece o' cheese.'

When at last Eleanor and Will arrived at the top of Riverdown, Walter was pacing the patch of rough ground that fronted his cottage. As they approached, he stopped and stared at them, saying nothing. His face was dark, his shoulders stiff.

Eleanor ran towards him. 'I'm sorry we are so late, Walter. I had a mishap on the road – my boot stuck in the mud.' She laughed lightly, but he did not reciprocate, and she felt her heart squeeze with dismay. Nonetheless, she tried to keep her mood light-hearted. 'The roads are dreadfully muddy in the village—'

'When are they not?' said Walter. 'It *has* been raining.'

Eleanor's heart squeezed again and she felt the inevitable flush already blooming on her pale neck. 'Well, yes, of course,' she said, the words coming with unbidden pauses.

If he noticed her discomfiture, Walter did not show it. Instead, he strode away, whistling his dogs, towards the area of pasture they had fenced off especially for today's gathering of the mating ewes and rams.

'Shall we get on?' he called back, his voice low and impatient, and Eleanor felt tears pricking in her eyes, blurring her vision. Why *did* she seem to want to cry so much these days? She scrubbed vigorously at the beads of moisture with the edge of her cloak. The coarse texture of the heavy cloth at once made her eyes feel sore, but she had to ignore them and follow her shepherd. She beckoned to Will to follow too and, as he came forward, he touched her arm.

Dear Will. Somehow, *he* understood. This was supposed to be a happy day, but she had spoiled it already by vexing Walter. Though it seemed to her vexation came to him all too readily these days.

She blinked her eyes a few times to clear them, then she and Will fell in after Walter as he marched at speed towards the paddock where the ewes were waiting ready for mating.

# 8

Emma usually expected Ralph home from work the same time as herself, but it was almost dark by the time he heaved open the cottage door, swollen already by the rain, even though autumn had scarce begun. Emma was irritated he was late, for she'd made some pottage for her family, to warm them up after another damp and chilly day. And she was fed up hefting the pot off and on the tripod, trying not to let the liquid boil away, yet wanting to keep it hot for Ralph's return.

When she heard him scrabbling outside the door, trying to force it from its frame, she hurried over and stood before it, her hands planted on her hips, waiting for him to fall into the room. And, when he did, letting in a skirl of wind and a shower of driving rain, she opened her mouth to scold him for his lateness – and at once closed it again.

For, despite him being so bedraggled, with his boots thick with mud, his cloak and hood soaked through, and his long hair stuck in dribbling tails across his face, Ralph took one look at her and *laughed*.

Emma pulled a face. 'What's there to laugh at, husband?'

'You, Em, you. Standing there, hands on hips, your scold's mouth on your face, you're the spit of the old besom I've just left.'

'What "old besom"?'

Ralph laughed again. 'Ma, o' course,' he said, casting off his cloak and hood and throwing them to the floor. 'God's eyes, Em, please, please don't be turning into her.'

For a moment Emma thought the wet weather must've puddled her husband's brain. But then he stepped forward, his clothes dripping into the rushes, and, gently removing her hands from her hips and wrapping his arms around her waist, he kissed her full on the mouth, his drenched face soaking hers.

Then he stood back again and held her hands akimbo from her body. He grinned. 'No, you're not her. For your lips are soft and sweet, not rough and bitter.'

Then Emma understood poor Ralph must've just had one of his many altercations with her witch of a mother-in-law. Grinning back and wriggling her hands free from his, she began to remove his clothes, dropping each item on the floor. She groaned. 'Yet another lot to dry off.'

'Mmm, miserable, this endless rain.'

Emma went over to the small chest where they kept their few belongings, and took out a thin cloth. Coming back, she rubbed at Ralph's naked body. He grinned at the effect her touch was having, and grabbed the towel from her, jerking his head towards the girls, who were staring across the room.

Emma giggled. 'I'll fetch your dry – well, drier – clothes. They've been standing by the fire since yestereve, so at least they'll be warm.'

The same had been true of her spare kirtle, which had been hanging on the rack the best part of a day, but still felt damp when she put it on a while ago – but a little drier than the sodden one she'd taken off. How much she hoped this constant rain would stop. It had been only days, but she'd become accustomed to how easy the long hot summer made keeping clothes both clean and dry. Still, at least the children didn't have to leave the house. Emma took a chance on leaving baby Bart, as well as Amice, all day in Beatrix's care, which was a lot to ask of the girl, but a small price to pay for keeping them all warm and dry.

The pottage was a comfort but, as always on these wet and chilly nights, Emma longed for bed, when the family all nestled close together on the big pallet in the corner of the room, underneath a pile of blankets and, albeit still damp, cloaks.

Settling the two girls in the middle of the pallet, Emma crept back to the fire with Bart in her arms. Joining Ralph upon the bench, she rocked the baby back and forth, willing him to fall asleep. Then she nudged Ralph with her elbow.

'Tell me about Alys,' she said, her voice a whisper. 'Was she being difficult?'

Ralph laughed softly. 'Ain't she always?'

'But was it summat particular?'

'Summat specially nasty, 'bout Susanna Miller...'

'What's the old witch been saying?'

Ralph related what his mother had told him of the gossip at the pump, and what Susy had said about slapping Henry.

Emma's eyes widened, but he went on. 'Then Ma said, once Susanna were gone, she told the others, Henry Miller better watch out, or his wife'll do for him, and get all his property. And she said they all agreed with her.'

Emma's nostrils flared. 'Your mother should be ducked in the river for her wicked tongue.'

Ralph sniggered. 'I agree wi' you, Em.' There was no love lost between him and his mother.

'Susy's the last person in the world to hurt anyone,' said Emma, 'let alone her own husband. Surely she were jesting when she said it?'

'Dunno, love, but I'd've thought so. Anyway, it's time we bedded down.' He gestured towards the baby, sleeping soundly now in Emma's arms. 'I'll cover the fire.'

Emma shuffled over to the pallet, tucked the baby between the sleeping girls and, without bothering to take her clothes off, eased herself down alongside Beatrix, her arm resting lightly across her children. A few moments later, Ralph spread out all the coverings as best he could before lying down with his back towards little Amice. He was soon asleep, snoring softly.

But Emma couldn't sleep, tired as she was. She thought of Susanna, and her silly jest – for it surely *was* a jest? Yet, to the wrong ears – like those of her sour-tongued mother-in-law – it could be taken as a threat, and Emma knew only too well how folks' words could be misunderstood.

After one more day of rain, Emma's prayers were answered. It was still only October, with at least the possibility of fine weather before the winter settled in. And thus it was already proving to be, with the sun making a daily, if feeble, appearance. It was a relief to feel warm and dry again, if only for a week or two.

But if daily life was, for now at least, no longer damp and chilly, it had become peculiarly perplexing.

Emma always knew exactly what she had available to feed her family: bread, of course, a few eggs, dried beans, a couple of onions, sometimes a scrap of bacon or a small piece of cheese when she or Ralph had earned a little extra. It was never much, and never in such quantity she'd not notice something going missing.

So when, on her return from work, she looked over her small supplies to ensure she had sufficient for a meal, she was confused – indeed, shocked – to find the loaf of bread rather smaller than she remembered it had been this morning, and the precious cheese she'd bought only yesterday from Alice at the market, well... Emma stared at the cheese, doubting her own eyes. How much of it had they eaten at supper yestereve? Half of a half perhaps? No more, surely? Though it was so delicious everyone *wanted* more. But she didn't permit it... Surely? Yet the cheese was now a half moon, so how could that have happened?

Emma rubbed at her eyes, trying to think if, after all, she *did* allow her family another helping… But she knew she simply *wouldn't*.

So where was the missing cheese, and the piece of bread she was sure was missing too?

She looked across at her girls, playing quietly together with the two cloth dolls she'd made them years ago, threadbare now and each with a missing limb. It was unthinkable that either girl would take food without asking. They knew, young as they were, how careful they had to be with what they had. So had someone come inside and stolen it?

She went over to the girls and squatted down, folding her skirt over her knees.

'Beatrix?' she said, and the girl rolled her eyes.

Emma bit her lip. How silly she was to use Bea's full name – it always put her on her guard. She took her daughter's chin gently in her hand. 'Bea, I want to ask you something.'

The girl pulled away, freeing her chin and glaring at her mother. 'What?'

'I was just wondering if you saw anyone loitering here this morning.'

Bea squinted. 'Why?'

Amice scrunched her eyes together in imitation of her sister. 'Why?' she said, copying Bea's tone of voice.

Emma tried to keep her voice light. 'It's just I think some of Mistress atte Wode's lovely cheese is missing…' She trailed off, seeing what she thought was a glint of fear in her daughter's eyes.

Bea shook her head. 'How can that be, Ma?'

'I dunno. How can it?'

'No one's been here 'cept us, Ma. Mebbe you just forgot how much were left?'

'Mebbe.' Emma couldn't stop her brow from creasing. 'But I don't forget, Bea, do I?'

Bea shrugged, but Amice giggled. 'Poor Ma. P'raps you're getting old…'

'Amice, how dare you!'

It came out more fiercely than she'd intended and the child's face crumpled and she burst into tears. Emma leaned forward and clasped her to her breast. 'Oh, my sweet, I'm sorry. I didn't mean to sound so vexed.' She rocked back and forth, shushing the girl's weeping, and glanced at Bea, who just shrugged again.

Emma wished now she'd kept it to herself. She somehow thought Beatrix *did* know what'd happened, but she didn't want to press her. Despite her grumpiness, the girl had a kind heart. Perhaps she'd given the food to someone even worse off than themselves? But who could that be? And would Bea truly give food away when it meant she and her sister might go hungry? It seemed unlikely.

# 9

Jack paced up and down, anxious to be on their way. It took only an hour or so to travel the six miles to Wickham, but he wanted to be there well before the market started, to be sure of being in place and ready for when potential buyers came.

Agnes was eager to get going too. To make an early start, yestereve they'd loaded up the cart with a selection of her wares – boxes and small plain chests, flat trays and whittled spoons, as well as a few of her attempts at turning, cups and bowls. Though Jack was doubtful her turned items would sell, for – as she'd reluctantly admitted – they weren't of the highest standard. Jack himself had made a few items of furniture, stools with well-turned legs and small cupboards with quite finely decorated doors. It vexed Agnes how much more skilled Jack was, though of course he'd been practising his craft for years, from apprentice to journeyman to master. It was scarcely surprising his work was so much better than hers, when she was self-taught and working at it a bare two years.

Agnes was becoming agitated. Where *was* the girl? Even if it was an earlier start than usual, surely it wasn't too much to ask that, once in a while, Marye might shift herself to get here before first light? They couldn't leave until she got there, for they could hardly abandon the children without a nursemaid. Jack had gone out what seemed like hours ago to harness the hired pony to the cart shafts, and now he was annoyed that the beast was being kept standing in the yard.

Jack stopped his pacing and, throwing open the outside door, peered out into the gloom. Looking past him, Agnes saw a faint light in the distant sky. Jack saw it too, irritation on his face. 'If we don't leave soon, it'll not be worth the journey.'

'She'll surely be here shortly.'

Jack's lips were tight. But, moments later, Agnes heard the pounding of heavy steps along the track that led to their croft and a panting and – Agnes suspected, though couldn't yet see – red-faced Marye appeared at the open door.

Gasping for breath, Marye leant against the door jamb. 'Sorry, missus.'

Agnes grasped the girl's wrist and pulled her into the room. 'Is that all you've got to say for yourself? The boys are waiting.'

Jack cleared his throat. 'As, Marye, are we.' His voice was low but not harsh. 'You could've made a better effort.'

Marye's shoulders slumped, and Agnes now saw in the candlelight that her cheeks were scarlet, from running to be sure, but also, she hoped, from shame. 'Sorry, sir,' said Marye in a whisper. 'You get off now, an' I'll see to the boys.'

Jack gestured to Agnes to follow him outside. 'We must make haste. It's as well we decided to go to Wickham and not twice as far to Winchester.'

'Winchester only in the summer months, perhaps?'

Jack didn't answer, and Agnes knew he'd rather not waste a day going to the market, but apply all his energy to making crucks, rafters and beams, and doors, lintels and window frames, for constructing houses, barns and workshops, and renovating old ones.

Lately he'd been talking again of taking on an apprentice, and a journeyman or two, for there was much work to be had in Meonbridge and beyond and, with his reputation now well-established, Jack was well-placed to take on more. Agnes knew too that, if once he'd been pleased enough with the contribution her efforts made to the growth of his business, he no longer thought them worth her while.

Agnes let her head droop. She was very tired, and bouncing around on the rough seat of the cart didn't help her melancholy. She'd worked so hard the past few days, staying late each evening in the workshop to ensure they had a good batch of items to sell. But the turned items weren't much good, and Jack had been disinclined to take them.

They'd argued over it, and in the end he'd selected a couple of dozen bowls and cups. But he shook his head over the plates. 'You can't take these,' he said, picking one up and turning it over in his hand. 'See how uneven it is.' He placed it on the workbench, and it rocked. 'You can't expect folk to pay good money for a wobbly plate.'

She'd wanted to protest but just nodded her agreement to Jack's decision.

They spoke little on the journey, and Agnes noticed the stiffness in Jack's shoulders as he drove the pony forward along the rutted roads, guiding it as best he could between the furrows, sometimes diverging from the track where the verge seemed firmer than the road itself. It was hard work, and he'd rather not be doing it at all. Yet, when they reached Wickham and had set up their stall in a satisfactory location in the broad market square, he seemed to relax and, leaving her to deal with customers, sauntered around the little town in search of other tradesmen of his acquaintance.

If Jack cared little for coming to market to sell her wares, he did enjoy the chance of exchanging small talk with his fellow craftsmen. He'd joined a small group of diverse tradesmen in the village, but few carpenters worked within walking distance of Meonbridge, and he relished the company of men of his own ilk. In particular, she knew, he wanted to associate with the more powerful and experienced men he met here in Wickham, and even more so those in Winchester, for he aspired to being a master craftsman of the highest order. He thought mixing with men of standing might, somehow, cause their superiority to rub off on him. As a consequence, he listened eagerly to such men's opinions, even when they seemed contrary to what she was sure he'd once believed.

As the morning progressed towards dinner time, Agnes had sold all Jack's furniture and nearly all her chests and boxes, but very few of the bowls and cups. Folk might pick up a bowl and turn it over in their hands – just like Jack did with the plates – then peer at the roughness of the finish and put it down again. She had noticed another stall close by was also selling turned wood pieces, evidently more successfully than she. She pressed her lips together.

Just then, two men of the superior sort stopped at her table. Their opulent clothing, long, richly embroidered gowns and large floppy velvet hats, one blue, the other green, gave them the air of wealthy merchants rather than the usual market customers. Perhaps they were – she'd not seen either of them before.

To her mortification, when they picked up her bowls and examined them, they smirked with what she took to be derision. 'Just look at this,' said the blue hat, pointing out the uneven rim, where her chisel had snagged the wood. 'Very poor quality. Not the sort of thing we want our brothers offering for sale.'

The green hat murmured his agreement. Then he gave Agnes a thin smile. 'I recommend, mistress, you advise your husband to practise a little more before he comes to market.'

Agnes felt her cheeks suddenly afire, and while she should perhaps have agreed, or said nothing, in response, her affront at the supposition that the bowls could be only *man*-made loosened her tongue. 'They're not my husband's work, sirs, but my own,' she said, her voice a little shriller than it might have been.

The eyebrows of both men shot up beneath the brims of their floppy hats, and the green-hatted man smirked at her again. 'In that case, mistress, I recommend that *you* practise a *great deal* more before you bring your wares again to Wickham.'

Agnes's cheeks burned hotter but, realising silence was now the best response, she did no more than nod, before turning around and bending down, ostensibly to busy herself with the crate of unsold goods behind her.

But then she heard Jack's voice and stood up again to see him addressing the two men most cordially, as if he and they were well acquainted. And perhaps they were, for the men knew well enough Jack's name, though not, it soon emerged, that this was his stall and she his wife.

However, as the men began again to comment on the poor quality of Agnes's bowls, Jack, evidently recognising the awkwardness of the situation, drew the men away before responding, without acknowledging Agnes as anything to do with him. But Agnes wanted to hear what they were saying about her and, keeping herself mostly hidden by the canvas canopy of the neighbouring stall, she moved a little closer towards them.

'It's not a woman's place to become a craftsman,' the blue-hatted man said to Jack, who merely nodded. 'She may of course *assist* her husband in the administration of his business,' continued the man, 'and in the care of his apprentices. But attempt to mimic the skills of the master craftsman? No, no, no, that cannot be right.'

His companion agreed, but Jack demurred. 'That woman's only making small pieces,' he said, his voice a little hesitant. 'Perhaps it helps her husband's business in these difficult times?'

Agnes muffled a gasp. "*That woman*"? Jack was talking as if he didn't know her.

The blue-hatted man shook his head. 'An apprentice could be – should be – doing that, Master Sawyer.'

Jack scratched at his beard. 'You don't think that, perhaps, with so few craftsmen to be had since the Death, it's not a bad idea for women to play their part?'

Both men's faces took on grave expressions. 'I disagree,' said the green-hatted man. 'It's different when a woman is a craftsman's *widow* and continuing his business, but we masters must find and train *young men*, Master Sawyer. They're where our future lies, not with women, and especially not when they're incompetent.'

He winked and jerked his thumb back towards Agnes's rough-edged bowls, while she suppressed another gasp. But Jack inclined his head slightly to the two men. 'Clearly my opinion's not as well-reasoned as I'd thought. I bow to your greater experience of our trade.' The men appeared to grunt acceptance of his apology.

Then Jack bowed once more. 'But I must away. Good to have met you both again.' Then he walked away at speed, in the opposite direction from their stall.

Jack was as silent on the journey home as he'd been that morning. His body was hunched forward, his attention entirely on the pony. Agnes sensed he didn't want to discuss what had happened at the market. Instead, she churned it over and over inside her head, trying to decide whether or not it would mark an unwelcome, and enforced, change in her ambitions.

She was certain Jack *had* once been proud of how quickly she'd learned her carpentry skills. But when he became aware, first, of Sir Richard's scepticism about the suitability of her working instead of caring for his grandson; then the disapproval of other craftsmen in the village; and finally the almost hostile reaction of the master carpenters of Wickham and Winchester, Jack seemed to change his view. Though surely the change was only on the surface? She convinced herself he didn't *truly* agree that women should not be craftsmen.

Yet, later, when they reached home and had eaten some of the watery pottage Marye had made for them, Agnes asked Jack again if he planned to take on an apprentice, and his response was not what she hoped to hear.

'I suppose you heard what those men said? Those *masters* of the craft.' He arched his eyebrows. 'Apprentices are the future, Agnes. And I want to play my part in that future.'

'It weren't so long past you thought my learning the trade would be a boon to your business—'

'That *was* true, Agnes, but no longer. I need to build my business with those who can learn *all* the skills of carpentry, so we can build houses and repair barns. There's much to be done, and I can do it. But only with the right men to help me, and that means journeymen and, yes, apprentices.'

'Very well, but why can't some of the apprentices be girls?'

Jack guffawed. 'Because I'd be a laughing stock, Agnes – in Meonbridge and beyond. I suppose it might work in a big city enterprise with lots of apprentices, maybe taking on some small-scale work as well as building. But not here.'

'But women are the future as well as men—' she tried, but Jack held up his hand.

'Stop, Agnes, the answer's no. I don't want to be doing this small stuff any more, not even furniture. I'm a buildings manufacturer, and girls can't do that type of work.'

Agnes opened her mouth to protest, but Jack gave a slight shake of his head, and she closed it again. Then, shrugging, he stood up and strode over to the door. 'I'm going out,' he said, and took his cloak down from its hook. Then, pulling on his boots and throwing the cloak around his shoulders, he heaved open the door and dived out into the dark.

Agnes stared after him: Jack almost never went out in the evening. But perhaps a pot of ale and a chance to talk with other men would calm Jack's disquiet?

But what of *her* disquiet?

It had been a distressing day. Despite selling all her chests and boxes, she was vexed no one wanted the bowls and cups. It was obvious why they didn't, but to hear those men so damning of her efforts— And to watch Jack disowning her, not wanting to be tarred with the brush of her "incompetence", as that fellow in the green hat had said.

And now Jack was saying – for the first time – he no longer wanted to make the "small stuff", not even furniture. So there was no role for her in the business…

Perhaps there were other reasons for Jack's change of mind about her? He'd said he wanted another child. Maybe this apparent change of heart was more to do with Jack's idea of family life than what he wanted for his business? The man she'd married, only three years ago, who had adored her, despite her bastard boy, had then wanted nothing more than to make her happy. But now? He did still love her, she was sure of it, but he no longer seemed to think it mattered what *she* might want.

Her head began to throb, as it so often did when she felt upset. Perhaps it would be best if she gave it all up *now*, before Jack made her do so? She could just go back to being a wife and mother. Another child, a daughter perhaps, would surely be a joy?

Yet she so loved her time spent in the workshop, cutting wood and shaping it, creating objects other folk might find useful. Even learning how to use a lathe and chisel had been a pleasure, albeit not – so far – a great success. She didn't want to give it up. She wanted to do more – to be good at turning, to move on to making furniture, to be even better at it than her husband. These past two years had been more than just a means of helping to keep Jack's business afloat. They had opened her eyes to what was possible, for women as well as for men. For her. And she wasn't going to give it up without a fight.

# 10

It was chilly in Eleanor's hall. The rain of a few weeks ago had passed, leaving bright days but cool evenings and early mornings. Autumn was well advanced, the lovely warm summer days up on Riverdown already a distant memory. Eleanor was always saddened by the prospect of winter, the endless days of indoor gloom, the daily struggle to keep warm and dry, the longing for it all to end and for spring to come again.

As if to signal the start of this long dark time, Hawisa was in a more than usually irritable humour, threatening to abandon her battle with the fire, despite the urgent need to warm the house.

'I don't hold with these new-fangled chimneys,' she said, poking at the logs in an effort to encourage the feeble flames. 'A hearth in the middle o' the floor does a better job than this.' She gestured at the chimney with disdain. 'That great 'ole just keeps sending down a cold blast of air. It don't help none.'

Eleanor chuckled to herself. That chimney had been her father's pride and joy, a token of his success, of his ability to build a fine house with the latest innovations. She remembered how much her mother had welcomed being able to sit in her hall without the perpetual swirl and stench of smoke clouding the air about her head, as it always had done in their old house with its central hearth. As it still did in most of the homes in Meonbridge. Eleanor did not recall her parents' servants having trouble with the chimney fire. Yet Hawisa complained constantly about it, and Eleanor had to suffer both her grumbling and the lack of heat. Though, despite her grumbling, Hawisa always got the fire going in the end.

Eleanor wrapped two thick cloaks about her shoulders as she sat down to eat her unappetising breakfast – the breakfast Hawisa always insisted that she ate. In truth, a small bowl of Hawisa's flavourless but warming gruel would have been more welcome than the hard coarse bread, dry cheese and mug of cold ale set before her. But she had taken only one sip of the ale before there came a hammering on the door and the voice of, she thought, young Harry

Mannering, calling out her name. Hawisa tutted and, heaving herself to her feet, lumbered over to the door and hauled it open.

'What's all this noise?' she said and, lurching forward, dragged the boy inside by his tunic and slammed the door behind him.

'Hawisa!' cried Eleanor, rising from the bench. 'Don't handle the poor boy so roughly.' She went over to him. 'Has someone sent you for me, Harry?'

The boy removed his hood and held it in his hands. 'Aye'm, Master Cole. He said to fetch you, missus, as quick as we can be.'

'Do you know why?'

He bit his lip, and fiddled with his hood a moment.

'Speak up, boy,' cried Hawisa, but Eleanor raised her hand.

'Is something the matter, Harry?'

'It's your sheep, missus, they got out and are runnin' wild down by the river.'

'What do you mean?'

He bit his bottom lip. 'They run off is all I know. And Master Cole's trying to catch them.'

Within moments, Eleanor was by the door, sitting on the bench and pulling on her heavy boots. She closed the clasps on both her cloaks, and pulled the two hoods up over her head.

'You goin' without your breakfast?' cried Hawisa, and Eleanor half closed her eyes, then opened them again.

'Yes, Hawisa. I can shift well enough without it.'

She and young Harry hurried down towards the village as fast as the track, still rain-slicked despite the dry days, would let them. Eleanor envied the way the boy seemed able to skip lightly across the slippery surface, not minding if he slid, but she was, as ever, cautious, not wanting to lose her footing or fall over.

At the river bridge, she stopped to survey the scene before her, Will running hither and thither across the meadow trying uselessly to round up sheep. The beasts – most would be pregnant ewes – kept running away from him, further along the riverbank.

'Harry,' she said, 'please go and fetch Will. I want to speak to him.'

Harry jumped down from the end of the bridge onto the grass and sped off across the meadow towards Will. It took a while for the boy to catch up with the running man, but at length he seemed to have delivered Eleanor's message, for Will abandoned his chase.

When at last Will stood before her, he could not meet her eye but bent over, his hands on his knees, as he tried to calm his breathing.

'It's hopeless trying to round up sheep alone,' said Eleanor. 'You need a dog. I'm grateful to you for trying, Will, but maybe we should get some help?'

'Who from?'

'If we raised the hue and cry, maybe some villagers would come to help?'

He stood upright then. 'D'you think they'd come?'

'We won't know if we don't ask. I'll go up to Riverdown to see if Walter knows what happened...' She paused. 'You've not already done so?'

'I were on my way up when I saw these.' He pointed to the sheep, calmer now and cropping at the meagre grass. 'I thought I should try...' He grimaced. 'But you're right, missus, wi'out a dog, mebbe it weren't such a good idea.'

Eleanor couldn't help but grin. 'Maybe not. But, never mind, see if you can raise some help, and I'll go on up to Walter.'

When Eleanor reached the top of the hill, there was no sign of Walter. He was not in his cottage nor around the holding pens – not that she would expect him to be. She hurried on towards the pasture where, two months past, Walter and Will had fenced a large paddock for the pregnant ewes but, as she approached, it was clear that, while there were sheep in the paddock, many were missing. Going closer, she found a length of the new hurdle fencing smashed, how she could not tell, but it was almost certainly where the missing sheep had made their escape. Walking on, she saw Walter and his dogs, some distance away, rounding up some fugitives and herding them back towards the main flock. She stood and watched him, admiring the calm, efficient way he and his dogs gathered the scattered sheep together, his whistles and commands drifting clear across the still cold air. But, when he reached her, his face was black with anger. Without speaking to her, he guided the sheep back into the paddock and sat the dogs by the broken fence to guard against another escape.

Eleanor went to greet him. 'Do you know what happened here? Did the sheep break down the fence?'

He came forward, his eyebrows raised. 'I scarce think so.' He grunted. 'Nay, it were done deliberate. With an axe or summat.'

Eleanor's heart skipped a beat. 'Deliberate? You mean someone *meant* to let the sheep escape?'

Walter scoffed. 'What else? Broke the fence and chased them out.'

'Do you know about the ones that ran downhill to the river?'

'I assumed some must've, 'cause they're not all here.' He gestured at the flock. 'So whoever broke the fence down must've chased them, else they'd not've gone that way.'

'They're scattered all along the river bank,' said Eleanor. 'Will tried to round them up, but it was hopeless without the dogs. So he's gone to get help from the village—'

Walter scoffed again. 'That won't work. Not without the dogs.' He strode towards the flock. 'Help me get all these into the holding pens and barn. Once they're safe, we'll go down and round the others up.'

It took them a while to move the flock and distribute them between the pens and the only enclosed barn they had. By the time they went back down the hill, the "help" was under way, but clearly it was not going well. It would be, thought Eleanor, an almost comical scene, if the whole business were not so vexing. For women, children, and one or two old men, were chasing up and down, yelling and flapping at the sheep with arms and aprons, trying to make them turn and go back up the hill.

Walter's face grew even darker, and he snorted like an angry bull.

'They are only trying to help,' said Eleanor, seeing it had clearly been a bad idea.

'But they're not helping, are they?' He was almost shouting. 'Those ewes'll lose their lambs, the panic they're getting into.'

Yet several of the sheep had been brought together at the bottom of the hill. Eleanor ran across to thank the two women and their children who had helped to catch them. But Walter merely grunted at them, evidently unable to bring himself to show his gratitude. How churlish he could be sometimes!

Walter left one of the dogs, Meg, and Eleanor to guard the gathered sheep, and marched off with Dart to round up the remaining animals. When he returned with them, several of the sheep were wet, presumably the result of a dousing in the river.

'Two drowned,' he said. 'Must've fallen in and broke a leg.'

Eleanor gulped down a sigh. 'Oh, no, not more deaths.'

He shrugged then called to Will to come and help him retrieve the corpses. 'I'll skin them,' he said to Eleanor, 'then at least we'll have their wool and meat, even if the lambs are lost.'

While they had been busy bringing the sheep back up to Riverdown, Eleanor felt that she and Walter, and Will, were working well together, just as they always had. Once all the sheep were home again and put into the holding pens until the fences could be mended, Will went off with the dogs, saying he'd eat his dinner in the barn. Eleanor and Walter sat together inside the shepherd's cottage, sipping some warmed ale.

Walter sat down on a stool a little distance from Eleanor, and hunched over his pot, not speaking.

'The losses are not as great as they might have been,' said Eleanor at last, wanting to break the silence.

He scowled. 'Losses from foxes, the cold, scabies – you expect them sort o' losses. But when someone – and we know who, don't we? – attacks them out of envy or revenge or viciousness, I'd like to slit *his* throat.' His eyes were sparking.

'Walter! You shouldn't say such things—'

'Why not? An eye for an eye, the Bible says.'

She shook her head. 'Even if we *think* we know who did it, without any evidence, we can hardly accuse him of it.'

'I weren't thinking of *accusing*. More settling the matter.'

Eleanor stared at her shepherd. 'I don't believe what I'm hearing. This isn't you talking, Walter, so…so…vindictive—'

'It's him who's vindictive. He's got it in for you, Eleanor Titherige. And he won't let it go unless he's stopped.'

Eleanor got up and stepped away from Walter, though the cottage was so small there was nowhere to go unless she went outside. It was hard to hear such talk from Walter, a man she had always considered gentle, and generous. She understood how angry he was – so was she. But perhaps Walter felt *responsible* for not stopping Matthew – if that was who it was – and his anger arose from a sense of guilt?

She came back and sat down again. 'Was it a mistake to leave them outside overnight? You said it was impossible to keep them in cotes— Yet this is the result.'

Walter's eyebrows disappeared into his hair. 'What I said was it'd be hard to house them all as the flock grew bigger. You saw how crowded the sheep were in the pens and barn. Think how big the barns'd have to be to house them all.'

'So if they have to be outside, don't we need to guard them better?'

Walter ran his fingers through his hair. 'We've been through all this. You said you can't afford more men. So we agreed on fences.'

'You said they'd help, keeping the flock close… But they haven't.' She became aware that her voice had risen, and she sensed the inevitable threat of tears. She did so hate arguing with Walter.

'Naught's going to stop men like Matt Ward.'

'But perhaps *you* could have stopped him?' she said, not planning to say anything of the sort. 'When he chased the sheep down the hill, he, and they, must have run straight past this cottage. Surely they made a noise? Didn't you hear them?'

Walter almost choked on the sip of ale he had just taken.

And Eleanor wished the mud floor of the cottage would cave in and swallow her up whole. Hadn't she just accused Walter, of all men, of incompetence? What had made her say it? She truly did not know. And, in her misery and

91

confusion, she sprang to her feet and ran from the cottage, heading for the downhill track.

But Walter followed her and, easily catching up with her, grasped her arm and spun her round to face him.

'You accusing me of neglecting my duties?' he said, his voice shaking. 'And giving bad advice? Did I hear you aright, Mistress Titherige?'

She shook her head, but could not answer, not knowing if, in truth, Walter *had* advised her poorly, and *had* failed to stop the attacker scattering her sheep.

Walter let go of her arm. 'So be it, Mistress Titherige. As you no longer value my service, I resign.' He smirked. 'Perhaps your friend Master Ashdown can advise you better. I'll be gone by the morrow.'

He strode back to the cottage, from where sounds of banging shortly came.

Eleanor stood quite still, chewing at her lip. Had Walter truly said that he was leaving? He could surely not have meant it? Yet his voice was so full of hurt she thought perhaps he did. But he said he would go in the morning – time enough for him to change his mind…

She shivered. It was cold standing up here on the hill, where, even on a calm day like today, the wind seemed to cut straight through. She thought she would go and stand by the ewes awhile, where it was more sheltered, and the warmth of their woolly bodies might give her comfort.

She was surprised to find Will there, examining the sheep. He looked up as she approached.

'Missus. Just checking no harm's come to them. Apart from the dead 'uns.'

'Thank you, Will,' said Eleanor. She wanted to say more, but could not think what to say.

Will coughed. 'You an' Walter been arguing again?'

Eleanor felt herself flush despite the cold. She nodded.

'He's a good shepherd,' said Will, and she nodded again, but did not answer.

Shortly, Walter walked past the pens, carrying a bag of tools. He was heading for the paddock.

'Looks like he's going to mend the fence,' said Will. 'I'll go and help.'

'I'll go home for dinner and come back later.'

'Right, missus,' said Will and ran after Walter.

Eleanor watched Will go, feeling wobbly and light-headed. Surely, if Walter was mending fences, he did not mean to leave her?

But when Eleanor returned to Riverdown after dinner, she found that Walter had already put together his few possessions and gone, taking Dart, his favourite dog.

Will was waiting for her, pacing up and down in front of Walter's cottage.

'I tried to stop him, missus, but he refused to stay, saying you didn't want him here no more, and he'd go an' find an employer who valued his advice an' sense of duty.'

Eleanor winced. 'Was that truly what he said?'

'I remembered it specially so I could tell you.'

She flailed her arms around in grief and distress. What had she done? Again! For hadn't she driven away John atte Wode? What was *wrong* with her that she was so unkind to those she cared for?

Tears streaming, she took Will's arm. 'Please, Will, don't tell anyone Walter's gone. Not yet...'

Will's eyes smiled. 'You hopin' he might change his mind and come back?'

'Of course,' she said in a whisper. 'Though I daresay his pride will not permit it. But, just in case...'

Will pressed his lips together, and she knew what he was thinking.

That evening, Nicholas appeared on Eleanor's doorstep, the first time he had ever visited her house. When Hawisa opened the door to find him standing outside in the dark, she did not let him in until she had called her mistress to demand if she was taking visitors.

Eleanor was horrified, as she so often was, at Hawisa's ill treatment of a guest. And, hurrying to the door herself, she took Nicholas's arm and pulled him inside. 'I'm so sorry, Nick, do come in out of the cold.'

He was well wrapped up in a fine thick cloak that Eleanor suspected had been his merchant father's but, nonetheless, she drew him over to the fireplace and bade him take a stool.

She sat next to him and tilted her head. 'Have you come for a particular reason?'

He shrugged. 'I heard what happened with your sheep, and thought to come and see if you were harmed in the assault.'

'I wasn't involved in the attack on the sheep, only in gathering them up again.'

'D'you know who attacked them?'

'I have my suspicions. It's clear the sheep's escape was no unlucky accident, but done deliberately. Perhaps by Matthew, given what Will has said about how resentful he is against me.'

'It's likely to be Matthew,' said Nicholas. 'Will you bring an accusation against him?'

'I suppose I would quite like to but, no, for there's no evidence against him.'

'But the way he brags in the ale-house, it's possible he's already told his mates. I'll ask around. See if anyone's heard him say anything.'

'Thank you, Nick, that would be kind,' she said though, in truth, she was not at all sure she *wanted* to have the evidence to accuse Matthew. For, despite everything, she still felt sorry for the man.

They sat quietly for a few moments, until Nicholas asked, as if he had just thought of it, how Walter was.

She stared at him. Did he know Walter had gone? Surely Will was the only one who knew, and he had sworn he would not tell. But Meonbridge was a small place, and news always travelled fast.

'What do you know?' she said.

He bowed his head and laced his fingers together. 'I'd heard he'd left Meonbridge, but thought it couldn't be true.'

She bit her lip and did not answer for several moments. But at length she said, 'It is. He had a better offer, with more money and a far bigger flock, and decided to take it.' It was as well the room was gloomy from the lowering candles, for she knew her cheeks were burning from the shame of telling such a bald untruth.

But Nicholas pulled on his neat little beard. 'Are you sure? It's hard to imagine Walter leaving the flock after so long.'

Eleanor felt a sudden tightness in her throat. 'Are you saying that I am lying?'

He held up his hands. 'Of course not, Eleanor. I just wonder if Walter left for some other reason, one he decided not to tell you?'

He cocked his head and Eleanor felt sure she saw merriment dancing in his eyes.

And she wondered at that moment why Nicholas had really come to see her. Was it truly just to enquire about her health, or in fact to confirm if the rumour about Walter was the truth? For, of course, if Nicholas did consider himself a rival for her affections, he would be delighted to learn that Walter had gone from Meonbridge and left the field clear.

But Nicholas was seemingly not so crass as to press his suit right there and then. After a courteous further exchange of small talk, he rose to go. At the door, he took her hand and kissed it, something he had never done before.

Eleanor's heart turned over, but it was not because of the kiss. Rather she was realising how very foolish she had been. Now Nicholas knew the field was open, he was surely trying to worm his way into her heart? Yet somehow she already knew he'd not succeed.

For Nicholas could not advise her about her sheep – in truth, only Walter could do that.

But there was of course much more to it than just the sheep.

*

Eleanor came up to Riverdown at first light, as she had done every day since Walter left, to spend time alone in the shepherd's cottage. Soon, she thought, she would offer Will the shepherd's job, and the cottage, but she was not yet quite ready to accept that Walter was not coming back.

She folded back the hide shutter on the window to let in a little light, and sat down on a stool next to the long-dead ashes in the hearth. As she often did, she remembered sitting here with Walter, three years ago, when she had come to tell him that John atte Wode had asked her to marry him. Walter was so generous, so selfless, in his response, yet what relief she saw there in his eyes when she then told him she had not accepted John.

She did nothing to stop the tears spilling over and trickling down her cheeks.

How very far was her life now from the reverie she had nurtured then. She had pictured herself and Walter building up her father's flock, becoming known throughout the county for the quality of their wool. She had envisioned – yes, she had! – that she and Walter might, perhaps, become more than mere business partners.

Yet she never thought she *loved* him, not in the way she had felt about John atte Wode. Although she only realised how she felt about John after they had parted, on terms so acrimonious she had wondered if it was mere fancy she had ever held him in her heart. But she did recall, if only in retrospect, the tingle of excitement that accompanied John's nearness to her, or him asking if she would care for an evening stroll. At the time she scarcely recognised it, and how much she did regret it later, after she had so recklessly driven him away.

But she had never felt that way about Walter. She admired him, both for his skills and knowledge as a shepherd, and for his bravery in rescuing her from the savage intentions of Gilbert Fletcher. Of course she had also saved him from death some months before, and to some extent it was this shared debt of gratitude that had drawn them together.

Yet, as she sat here in this cottage, where he had sat every evening for so many years, stirring his small supper in the pot still hanging, cold and empty, on the tripod, she knew it was not just gratitude she felt for Walter Nash. She had known it three years ago, and she knew it still. And yet, just as she had John atte Wode, she had driven him away.

Yet could she bring herself to go after him and beg his forgiveness?

More tears wetted her cheeks, and were allowed to drip.

Even if she persuaded herself to do so, the task was quite impossible, for of course she had not the slightest idea of where Walter might have gone.

# 11

SPRING 1353

Henry had forgotten to take his dinner with him. The cloth and flask of ale had been waiting for him, as usual, on the bench by the door, so he wouldn't miss it. But miss it he did this morning. Perhaps because he was in such low spirits? Which was hardly unexpected, when last night was yet another he'd spent rolling and threshing beside her, unable to find sleep or respite from the cough that plagued him still – a cough that had persisted the whole of winter and was not abating even now the warmer weather had arrived.

Susanna was worried about Henry's health. He worked so long and hard, without sufficient help, that daily he came home exhausted. He'd worked in the mill for many years, since he was a lad. He'd become accustomed to the work, heavy as it was, and grown strong from the labour of it. But, at the start of winter, he began to cough. He said it were naught, and refused to seek a remedy. So she'd paid a secret visit to Simon, the barber-surgeon, to ask for his advice.

'I'm not a physician,' Simon had said, 'but coughs are thought to be caused by an excess of phlegm.'

She'd nodded. She knew little about how the humours affected health but trusted Simon's view. 'Can anything be done?'

He shrugged. 'I'd advise him to drink plenty, and to rest.'

Rest, he'd said! But when she told Henry that, he'd scoffed and told her not to fuss. She tried not to, for fussing only made him even more dispirited. But as the weeks passed, and the cough didn't let him alone, it was hard not to worry.

'I won't be long, Tom dear,' she said, picking up the bundle and the leather flask. 'I'll just take your pa his dinner, then we'll have ours. You can play outside a while if you like.' Tom pulled a face but didn't refuse. 'But mind you keep a close eye on little Joan.'

The boy lifted the baby out of her cradle as if she was a bundle of clothes and trudged over to the door that led outside. 'Come on, you two,' he said to Maud and Francis, his face long, and the little ones toddled behind him.

Susanna hadn't been to the mill for a long time, despite it being only steps away from the cottage. She could scarce remember how long ago it was. Had she once gone right up inside the mill house? Perhaps when she'd first married Henry? Aye, that was it. Then, he'd been pleased to show her where he worked, to explain how the rushing water of the Meon drove the great mill wheel, how the wheel drove the shaft that turned the millstones, and the stones then ground the grain to make the flour that he sold back to everyone in the village for the price of his share. She'd been almost frightened by the noise and confusion of the place, yet impressed that *her* husband was responsible for such a complicated engine, and held such an important position in Meonbridge's life.

Of course now she had no reason to go down to the mill, for Henry brought home any flour she might need. But, anyway, after that first time, Henry had made it clear he didn't want her there because, he said, it was such a dangerous place.

He'd hugged her when he said it. 'The mill's my domain, my sweet. Yours our home and croft.'

And, at the time, she'd been so happy that he wanted to keep her safe, thrilled that the domain he'd assigned her was such a lovely place to be. She couldn't then have imagined ever thinking it not Paradise.

As she approached the outside steps that led to the mill's upper floor, where she thought Henry would be, Susanna's heart was beating. She knew he'd be vexed with her for coming, but felt justified in bringing him his dinner. She wouldn't stay more than a moment – just put his bundle and flask down where he could see it, then leave.

At the bottom of the staircase, a door opened onto the ground floor, which housed the clanking wheels that turned the grinding stones upstairs, and from where, she recalled, the sacks of grain were hauled up through a trap door to the floor above, where the grain was then fed into the hopper to slither down between the stones.

Before she went up the steps, she peered in through the door, just to see if Henry was downstairs after all. He wasn't, but two others were: the two Collyere brothers, the idle young cottars he employed to do some of the heavy lifting and clean the mill machinery. They certainly weren't doing what he paid them for, but were sat together on a pile of grain sacks, gossiping, while Henry, she supposed, was working upstairs alone. For a moment, she considered chiding them for their idleness, but thought better of it – Henry'd not welcome her interference.

At the top of the stairs, she stopped and peered through the open door.

Henry was on the other side of the mill workings. How would he know she'd come, for the noise made by the water wheel outside and the machinery within was so loud that, even if she called out, he'd surely not be able to hear her?

She took a few steps forward, considering how to attract his attention. She waved, but Henry wasn't looking. She was nervous about going any further forward, but she'd have to if she was to show him she'd brought his dinner.

She stood a while, reminding herself of how the engine worked. It was certainly a wondrous sight, though she still hated the appalling din. But the other thing she noticed, which she'd not remembered from before, was the dustiness of the air. A shaft of sunlight, slanting through the one high window, was full of motes of grain, hanging like minute insects in the brightness of the beam. And, as she watched, fascinated by the way the specks seemed to float and dance by turns, she felt a tickle in her throat and began to cough. Then she could hear Henry coughing too, and thought the dust must be another reason why he coughed so much.

But what could she do to help him?

He could hardly stop working in the mill. Though perhaps he might work a little less, as Simon had suggested? If he had at least one proper, permanent employee who knew what he was doing, surely that'd make a difference?

He'd not welcome her advice, yet her concern for the welfare of her husband, the father of her children, made her bold. When, a few moments later, Henry did raise his head and see her standing by the door, his dinner bundle in her raised hand, she beamed. And, instead of scolding her, as she'd feared, he came across. And, when he took the flask and bundle from her, he gave her a fleeting smile.

'Thank you, wife. I'd thought I'd have to come and fetch it.'

'I know you don't like me coming here, Harry, but I thought I'd save you the trouble.'

'Thanks,' he said again, then turned back to his work. 'I'll eat it in a while.'

She knew he'd want her to go at once but, somehow, she couldn't stop herself saying what was on her mind. 'Harry?' She put out a hand to touch his arm.

He spun round again to face her, his expression already sullen. 'What, Susanna? I must get on.'

'Aye, I understand...' She hesitated. 'And yet...'

'Well?'

She hesitated another moment. 'It just seems to me, Harry dear, you need help here – proper, expert help. A journeyman...' Deep lines appeared on his forehead, but she pressed on nonetheless. 'And those two cottars downstairs— They're idle louts, you must know that.'

The moment her words were out, Susanna knew she should've held her tongue. For Henry's frown became a scowl and he put down his dinner on a nearby joist.

'I've said before, Susanna, I won't have you interfering.' His voice was stern.

She felt a little sick, and could scarcely answer. 'But I—'

He raised his arm. 'But nothing, wife. Go! Leave me to my work.'

But Susanna, the power of her concern overcoming her sense of caution, didn't move. 'Harry, please. You're ill. The air here's so dusty, is't any wonder you cough so bad? And surely you recall what Simon said, about you resting more? If you spent less time here—'

But Henry shook his head. 'So, what d'you suggest, woman? That I give it up and let the children starve?' He lurched back towards her. 'Leave,' he growled. 'Now.'

Yet still she didn't move, certain of the rightness of her concern, and of her remedy for it. Just then, another beam of sunlight shone through the high window, and she turned her head to see the dust dancing there again. But, a moment later, a sharp stinging on her cheek made her gasp and she was stumbling, falling against the joist where Henry'd put his dinner. Her elbow nudged the bundle as she slammed against the timber, and it toppled off the joist into the machinery below. She heard herself cry out, and put her arm up across her face to shield it from the blows still coming from Henry's hand.

'For God's sake, woman,' he yelled into her face, 'stop pressing me to accomplish what I can't.'

She was shaking. Her shoulder, still pressed against the timber, felt bruised, and her cheek was being pricked with pins. Yet, not understanding what he meant, she persisted.

'But what's stopping you, Harry?' she said, her voice unsteady. 'Surely you can afford to take on a skilled man instead of just those useless oafs? It must be worth the cost if it means you don't have to work so hard?'

Henry didn't answer but, lunging forward, grasped the arm protecting her face. He hauled her to her feet and raised his other hand as if to strike her again. But, this time, she found herself resisting, using all her strength to push him away, to stop him. Yet she was surprised when he let go of her arm and tottered backwards, bursting into a fit of coughing. He took two or three stumbling steps before his heel caught against a jutting beam and he fell back against the grain hopper. She heard the thud as his head slammed into the hopper's rim. Then his body seemed to crumple and he slid down to the floor.

Susanna rushed over, knelt down and put her arm around him. 'Oh,

Harry, I'm so sorry,' she cried. 'I'll go and get help...'

But, only moments later, Henry shook his head and, pushing her away, struggled upright. His fingers went to his head, where a trickle of blood oozed from a deep cut, and he glared down at her, still crouched on the dusty floor.

'I said, "go", wife,' he said, his voice low, 'and I meant it. Don't persist in disobeying me.'

Knowing she must now do what he bade her, she scrambled to her feet and reeled towards the door that would lead her away from a Henry she no longer recognised, and to fresh air.

She ran down the outer steps and back towards the cottage. As she hurried up the track, she thought she heard someone, a customer perhaps, coming the other way. Not wanting whoever it was to see her as she was, her wimple adrift, her cheek possibly reddened from Henry's blows, she left the path and, skirting her cottage, slipped down towards the river.

She sat down on the fallen trunk of an ancient tree where, in happier days, she and Henry often sat together, enjoying the peaceful burbling of the water. She reflected on her foolhardy behaviour. She'd known Henry would be annoyed with her for speaking out, yet she still didn't understand *why* he was so unmoving in his views, or why his stubbornness and melancholy had so suddenly turned to violence – the first time he'd ever raised his hand to her.

She felt confused. Had Henry *always* thought it right for a husband to strike his wife if she vexed him? She was certain he'd not done so when they first wed. Yet when there was all the fuss over Mistress Wragge, it seemed then that he *did* think the Bible was right when it said that a husband had the right to rule, a duty to chastise his wife...

Of course it was common enough for men to beat their wives. Her first husband, Fran, had never raised a hand to her, but she remembered how her own mother often had bruises on her face and arms. Her father never asked, only demanded. And if her mother argued, he hit her. She knew too of other women in Meonbridge who'd suffered at their husbands' hands, and not only cottars. She recalled how, four years ago, Matilda Fletcher was said to have been abused by her wealthy but cruel and, it turned out, murderous, husband Gilbert.

Her head was spinning, and she heard the sound more than once before she realised that, above the river's noisy babble, a child's cry was coming from the direction of her cottage. She sprang up from the trunk but, still light-headed, she tottered a little before steadying herself enough to hurry back through the orchard to her garden.

From the corner of her eye, she could see strands of hair escaping from her wimple. Tucking them back in the best she could, she winced as her fingers brushed against her cheek. Then, looking at her fingers, she saw there was a little blood. Tom would surely notice, so what could she tell him? Just that she had slipped and banged her face against a beam? Yes, that would do. And it would serve too as a warning of how dangerous the mill could be.

# 12

If Jack didn't seem to agree much these days with what Agnes said, they were at least united on the subject of Marye. The girl was useless: lazy and unreliable, always needing to be instructed on her duties. Agnes had employed her to make life easier for herself, to enable her to spend time in the workshop, but Marye's ineptness was just making Agnes's life all the harder.

Jack said it: it was a hopeless situation. But he went further. 'I see no point in keeping her on. You can care for the boys yourself, now James has come.' Which was, after all, what Jack wanted her to do.

Since the day they went to Wickham back in the autumn, Jack had made it clear he no longer supported her ambition to become a craftsman. Then he proved it when, just after Christmas, he took on a young man from Wickham as his journeyman, the nephew of one of Jack's rich cronies – one of those floppy-hatted men, she thought. She did still go into the workshop once or twice a week, determined not to let herself be beaten. But she made only the most basic pieces, for Jack no longer let her use the lathe, claiming that James, being a skilful turner, was obliged to use it daily.

It was all over, scarcely before it had begun, and she didn't, after all, have the energy to fight it.

Agnes sat down at her mother's table for a while, staring at her hands. She'd not gone to the workshop this morning, for her brother John had paid her an early visit.

'Ma's sick,' he'd said. 'I told her to stay abed and you'd go to see her later, take her her dinner...'

Agnes held her temper. 'Can't you leave her something to eat?'

He'd stared at her open-mouthed, as if she was half-witted. 'I have to go to work—'

Agnes clenched her teeth. 'As do I—' she started, but John held up his hand.

'But you don't *have* to, do you, sister?' He'd seemed to be looking through her, and she could've thrown a pot at him.

But she could hardly argue. It was a woman's job to feed her family and, if the woman was sick, the job fell to her daughter, not her son. She pressed her lips together. She didn't say so to John, but she'd not cook for him. He and their little brother could shift for themselves – at Mistress Rolfe's, no doubt.

As dinner time approached, Agnes had packed some of the food she'd prepared for her own family into a cloth and, leaving Marye in charge of serving Jack and the boys their dinner, had left the house to walk the short distance to her mother's.

The atte Wode croft was close by the mill, the path leading up to the village from the mill running between their croft and the Millers'. Agnes often went to the mill herself these days, for she'd found Marye incapable of getting her order right.

As she approached her mother's croft, Agnes had been surprised to see Susanna Miller hurrying up the path from the mill. She couldn't recall the last time she'd seen her there, and indeed why would she ever need to be? Agnes wondered idly at the reason for her visit now, as she'd such an air of agitation about her, her head darting from side to side, her hands clutching at her cloak, pulling it close about her like she was hiding something.

Agnes raised her hand, about to call out, when Susanna suddenly darted from the path and, rather than go to her cottage, ran down through the orchard towards the river. Agnes dropped her hand, supposing Susanna not in the mood for talking, and went into her mother's cottage.

Alice didn't rise from her bed, and ate nothing of the food Agnes had brought. It had been a waste of effort and of time. Nonetheless, now she was here, Agnes thought she'd stay a while. Her mother went back to sleep and, with her brothers evidently eating their dinners out, Agnes welcomed the opportunity to enjoy the peace and calm of her mother's tidy hall.

She liked being alone, for it gave her the chance to think, without the distraction of the boys. Yet, what was there to think about? Why was she still bothering with the workshop when Jack didn't want her there? She'd told herself to fight for it, for the chance of a better life, for herself and for other women. But perhaps it was simply the sin of pride? Yet surely it was not sinful to gain pleasure from your work?

She stretched her hands out on the table's top and examined them. They looked like the hands of an old woman, rather than one of twenty. Well, they weren't wrinkled or brown-spotted, but certainly disfigured by old scars and more recent cuts, where a chisel slipped, or a splinter of wood had shorn off and pierced her skin.

She let out a bitter laugh. She need no longer have these old woman's hands!

Agnes eased herself up from the stool – sometimes her body too felt more than twice its age – and went to see if her mother needed anything.

Alice was awake again, and Agnes helped her to sit up.

'How are you, Ma?'

'My belly pains me,' she said, her voice lacking its usual strength. 'Something I ate—'

'That's unlikely, Ma. You're ever careful with your food.'

'Even I can make a mistake.'

Agnes pursed her lips. 'So d'you want anything? A little hot broth?'

Alice seemed to consider it. 'No, thank you, Agnes, I'll let it be.'

'So, shall I sit with you, or would you rather sleep?'

'Sleep,' said Alice, already shuffling herself back down and pulling at the covers. 'You go home to Jack and the little ones.'


As Agnes was gathering together what she wanted to take home with her, she heard the noise of women shouting. Opening the door and running up the path towards the road, she saw Alys, followed by Ann and two other cottar women, hastening towards the village, yelling for folk to come out of their houses.

As Ann hurried past, Agnes ran forward and grabbed her by the arm. 'What's happening? Is something wrong?'

Ann, caught off balance, was wild-eyed. 'It's Master Miller,' she said, her voice full of alarm. 'He's dead. Alys just found him.'

Agnes stared at the other woman. 'Dead? How?'

'Dunno, Agnes. Alys didn't say. She's gone for the constable.'

Agnes stepped back into the cottage. As it was so close to the mill, she might be asked to help find out what had happened. She'd better not go home yet, but wait for the constable to come.

Had Henry had an accident? The mill was a dangerous place, as everyone in Meonbridge remembered from four years ago. Yet surely not for Henry, sure-footed in the place he'd worked for fifteen years? Perhaps he'd collapsed? He'd certainly looked quite sickly lately. But then she recalled Susanna, running from the mill.

Before long, the noisy women were coming back, with a few more village folk, mostly women and children, though Jack was with them, and the constable with his henchmen. As they reached the cottage, Agnes stepped outside again.

Geoffrey greeted her. 'You been at your mother's this past hour or two?'

'At least that long.'

'You heard aught untoward? Shouting, mebbe?'

'None till I heard Alys calling out the hue and cry.'

He bowed his head, then addressed Alys, who was shuffling from foot to foot. 'Let's go to the mill,' he said, 'and see what's afoot.' Alys's eyes seemed to light up, as Geoffrey beckoned everyone to follow him and strode off along the path leading down towards the mill.

As they passed the mill cottage, Geoffrey stopped. 'Mistress Miller must be told,' he said, and sent one of his men to find her. Everyone watched as the man knocked on the door, but received no answer. He opened the door to look inside, but soon came out again, shaking his head.

'No sign of her,' he called out, 'nor the little ones.'

'Susy walks a lot,' suggested Ann.

'We'll find her later,' said Geoffrey, nodding. 'First, we must attend to her husband.'

Agnes, who'd never joined a hue and cry before, was struck by the merriment of the gathering, all chattering excitedly, asking of each other how Henry might've died. But when they arrived at the mill, everyone was shocked suddenly into silence, for the dreadful clanking noise coming from inside the building sounded very wrong, even to Agnes's ears.

Geoffrey rubbed at his neck. 'Summat ain't right,' he said then, gesturing to everyone except his henchmen to stay below, took the outside staircase to the floor above two steps at a time. Moments later, one of the men flew back down the stairs again, and sped over towards the millrace and the great waterwheel. Agnes couldn't see what he was doing but, a short while later, the wheel stopped turning. The awful grind and clatter of the machinery above began to slow and at last ceased altogether, followed by a collective murmur of relief.

'Thank the Lord for that!' said Alys. 'Wha' a row.'

'Were it making that noise afore?' said Jack to Ann and Alys, who shook their heads. He nodded. 'Perhaps it'd begun to run on empty? No grain betwixt the stones?'

The others murmured agreement, just as the man returned from stopping the waterwheel and ran up the stairs again.

A while later, the constable and his men appeared at the upper door, bearing Henry's body, then staggered down the narrow staircase, trying to manoeuvre their unwieldy load. The men were sweating by the time they reached the ground and, laying Henry's body down, they stood up with a groan and flexed their shoulders.

Geoffrey blew out a long breath. 'Big man,' he said, and his men grimaced in agreement. Geoffrey laid his hand on the shoulder of the man who'd stopped the wheel. 'It were as well you knew to drop the sluice gate.'

The man shrugged and Geoffrey turned to Jack. 'Reckon he were just in time. The stones was grinding naught but dust, and there were a right strong whiff o' smoke.' His eyes opened wide, and he shook his head. 'The whole place might've gone up.'

Jack nodded. 'I thought as much. Not that I know aught about mills.'

The group of women shuffled forward and peered down at the corpse. Alys pushed herself to the front, claiming precedence as first finder of the body. Agnes scarcely wanted to see poor Henry dead, but found herself pressing forward too.

'See what I told you,' said Alys. 'He's been hit on the head by summat.' She pointed to the wound upon his forehead, gaping a little and bloody.

Geoffrey shook his head. 'Nay, Alys, you can say his head were hit, but not necessarily *by* aught.'

Alys pouted. 'What you saying, master constable?'

'We don't know what happened, Alys, and have to find the truth of it.'

The other women murmured agreement, just as Simon, carrying his surgeon's bag, came hurrying to join them.

'Ah, surgeon, good,' said Geoffrey. 'Mebbe you'd just inspect the body? See what you can tell us?'

Simon knelt at Henry's side and, unfastening the lacing on his shirt, laid his hands upon his naked chest. 'He's still quite warm,' he said, 'so he's not long dead.' Geoffrey acknowledged the surgeon's comment, then Simon examined the wound on Henry's head, and pressed lightly on the skin, gently prodding at the eyelids and the face.

'Well, master surgeon?'

Simon gestured at Henry's forehead. 'See here, constable, there's two wounds, close by each other.' He pointed. 'The blood is drier there, and wetter here.'

Geoffrey leaned down to look and nodded. 'Hit his head twice, you thinking?'

Simon shrugged, then stood up. 'Anyways, the stiffening of the body's not begun so, with the other signs, I reckon he's been dead less than two hours. Indeed, with the wetness of that blood, it could be much less— Not even an hour past, perhaps?'

Geoffrey pursed his lips. 'Thank you, surgeon, for your opinion.'

'So what'll you do now?' said Jack.

The constable pulled himself up tall and puffed out his chest a little. 'Ask questions, Master Sawyer. Find out what folk know of this unhappy incident.'

'I know what 'appened,' said Alys, pressing forward again and planting herself in front of the constable. 'Ask *me* yer questions.'

Geoffrey exchanged a grimace with Jack, over Alys's head. 'Very well, Alys, tell us what you know.'

And she told how, after dinner, she'd come with Ann to buy their flour from the mill. 'And it were eerie quiet here,' she said, her eyes bright. 'No one about. Not that Fulke and Warin who work here mornin's, nor—'

She was stopped mid-flow by Geoffrey, holding up his hand. 'Ah, yes, the Collyeres. Go and fetch them here,' he said to one of his men. 'Tell them they're needed urgent.' The man hurried off towards the village, while Geoffrey gestured to Alys to continue.

'Not the Collyeres nor Master Miller,' she said. 'Ann and me, we called out his name and got no answer. So, at length, I climbed the steps to see where he were.'

'And you found him?' said the constable.

'He were lying crumpled on the floor, up agin the workings, his head smashed open like he'd been hit wi' summat heavy, or shoved so hard by someone—'

Geoffrey held up his hand again. 'Nay, Alys, you're jumping to conclusions again. An' his head's hardly "smashed open", is it?' He exchanged a grin with Simon. 'Henry might've just collapsed and hit his head by accident.'

'Mebbe,' she said, seeming disappointed.

'At all events,' continued Geoffrey, 'whatever happened, it's not all that long past, from what Master Hogge's just told us.' He seemed to think a moment. 'Did anyone come to the mill earlier today? Afore dinner, say?'

A woman from the village held up her hand. 'I did, master constable. This morning, midway 'tween Terce and Sext, I'd say. Henry seemed well enough. Hardly in good spirits, but fit enough to carry two sacks of flour to my handcart.'

'Anyone else?' the constable said, scanning the gathering. But everyone stayed silent.

Until Agnes, wondering if what she knew was relevant, decided to tell the constable what she'd seen on her way to her mother's house.

Geoffrey pulled on his beard and creased his forehead. 'What're you saying, Agnes?'

'Only that I saw Susanna leaving, and she seemed upset.'

But she soon wished she'd not spoken out at all, for Alys, the old witch, clearly saw an opportunity for her own kind of mischief and repeated, with a knowing wink, what Susanna said that day at the village pump. A murmur of disquiet hummed around the company.

'You suggesting Mistress Miller might've wished to harm her husband?' said the constable.

107

'I'm just saying what I heard,' said Alys.

Ann scuttled forward and poked her in the shoulder. 'But she meant nothin' by it, you ol' besom. You know Susy wouldn't hurt a fly.'

At that moment, Fulke and Warin came hurrying towards them, urged on by the constable's henchman. All three were red in the face from running, but Agnes thought she saw fear too on the brothers' faces. They weren't Meonbridge folk but had come up to the manor as boys, looking for work and a place to live, after their hamlet, Upper Brooking, had been all but emptied by the Death.

'Ah, at last,' the constable said. 'Some questions, lads.'

But the cottars were bent over and struggling to catch their breath, and Fulke, the elder of the two, held up his hand. 'A moment, cons'able, if yer please.'

Geoffrey folded his arms across his chest and instructed his men to find the means to make a litter. He tapped his foot. 'Well?' he said to the cottars. 'Can you yet answer?'

Whether they were ready or not, the constable insisted the brothers told him what they knew. Seeming unwilling to say anything at all, at length they admitted to hearing their master arguing with his wife aloft, and several heavy thuds.

'Like he were hitting her?' said Fulke, his voice faltering. Geoffrey shrugged at that, but didn't speak.

A while later, the brothers agreed, they saw Mistress Miller run down the stairs and away from the mill.

'And when was all this?' asked the constable.

They blinked, then Fulke scratched at his neck a while, and Warin delved beneath his greasy cap.

'Afore dinner?' Fulke said at length. ''Cause we don't work after.'

'So, after hearing all that noise, you didn't go upstairs to see your master was all right?' said Jack.

The brothers exchanged glances. Then Fulke bristled. 'It were our dinner time,' he said, his voice rising, but Warin was shuffling his feet.

'So you just went home without bothering to check?'

Both blinked again, and shuffled, but said no more.

Geoffrey was pulling at his beard once more. 'We need Mistress Miller's version of events,' he said. 'Master Sawyer, would you lead a search party, to find her and bring her to the manor to be questioned?'

When Jack came home much later, he told Agnes that Susanna had been easily discovered, down by the river at the place where, four years past, she'd found baby Maud lying amongst the reeds.

'The three little ones were with her,' he said, 'but not Tom. She'd taken them for a walk after dinner, just as Ann had said.'

'How was she?'

'When I told her of Henry's death, she swooned,' said Jack, running his fingers through his hair. 'And when I said she'd been seen leaving the mill in some distress—'

Agnes swallowed. 'You didn't tell her it was me who saw her?'

'No, Agnes, I didn't.' He looked asquint at her. 'But, as I was about to say, she seemed truly shocked at any suggestion she might be to blame for Henry's death. She admitted she'd gone to the mill – to take Henry his dinner, she said – and she and Henry had argued. But when she left, she said, Henry was certainly alive. Indeed, she expected him home as usual, and had been about to return home to start preparing supper.'

'So, where is she now?'

Jack frowned. 'Despite what she said, and what Simon said about how long past Henry had died, Geoffrey saw fit to hold her, and Sir Richard didn't disagree.'

'So where's she being held?' said Agnes. 'Not in Sir Richard's dungeon, surely?'

Nausea rose in her throat, as she suddenly understood the possible outcome of her assertion about Susanna. Yet she could hardly gainsay it now. Anyway, what she'd said was true, though it didn't mean Susanna killed her husband, either by accident or with intent. She slumped down onto a stool and, resting her elbows on the table, grasped her head between her hands.

'No,' said Jack, 'Lady de Bohun was there and insisted she was given a room inside the manor, under guard, until the coroner comes.' He laid a hand on Agnes's shoulder. 'Sir Richard seemed relieved at her suggestion.'

'Are they truly thinking Susy could've killed her Henry?' said Agnes in a whisper. 'That surely can't be right?'

'Perhaps she didn't mean to?'

She lifted her eyes to Jack. 'What do you mean?'

'Fulke and Warin said they heard noises from upstairs, like someone being hit—'

'Henry hitting Susy, they said.'

'But they wouldn't know which, would they? Mistress Wragge's just been accused of beating Edmund—'

'She were found innocent—'

'But everyone knows she's not.'

*

109

After a long, upsetting day, Agnes was glad to go to bed. Jack suggested that, for once, the baby might sleep with his brothers in the truckle bed, and Agnes was so exhausted she readily agreed. Jack took it upon himself to put the boys to bed and sit with them until they settled down to sleep. She was grateful to be relieved of what was often the most difficult time of day. She covered the fire, and snuffed out most of the tallow candles, before shuffling across the room to the wooden bed and truckle Jack had made, in small imitation of the fine beds at the manor. The truckle was pulled out at her side of the bed, and Jack was sitting on its foot, crooning as the three boys drifted off. Grasping the hem of her kirtle with both hands, Agnes pulled it up and over her head, then laid it across the chest – another of Jack's creations – that stood at the end of the bed. Then, pulling off her chemise as well, she climbed, naked, onto the bed and drew the sheet and blanket over her.

Only moments later, Jack had stripped off his clothes and was lying next to her. She welcomed the warmth of his body. And when he faced her and, sliding one arm beneath her shoulders and the other around her waist, drew her to him, she let her body melt into his. She slipped her arm around him and pressed her hand against his back to bring him even closer, grateful that she was here, nestled against her husband. Yet her comfort was disquieted by the lump rising in her throat, as she thought of Susanna, all alone, perhaps awaiting accusation, while her husband lay dead and cold in the manor dungeon vaults.

When, a little later, he stroked her breasts then, kissing her mouth softly, rolled on top of her, Agnes didn't think to resist him, relieved that at least Jack still seemed to love her. Despite his change of mind about her working, despite his angry assertions that she was neglecting the children, despite all the arguments and resentments between them – he did still love her.

Even if she was no longer sure she was in love with him.


It was four days before the county coroner, Hubert Gastingthrop, arrived in Meonbridge. Jack, as one of Meonbridge's freemen, was summoned to the manor as a juryman at the coroner's inquest. The coroner spent two days in Meonbridge, but it was only after he'd gone that Jack told Agnes all that had happened at the manor.

She'd been up there herself, repeating to the coroner what she'd already told the constable. The coroner questioned all the folk who'd said their piece before – Fulke and Warin, Alys, Simon…

It seemed stifling hot inside the manor hall, despite the cloudy day outside. As she waited to be called to speak, Agnes felt a thickness in her throat, and kept fiddling with the ring on her left hand. And, when she rose from the bench to go to stand before the coroner, her left leg trembled and almost let her down. She bowed her head as she repeated her brief account of seeing Susanna coming from the mill.

But the coroner wanted to know more. 'What do you imagine Mistress Miller was doing inside the mill, before she ran away in so much distress?'

Agnes didn't know, so how could she answer? But the coroner repeated his question and, when she raised her face to him, she felt a little dizzy as his black eyes bored into her. Was he wanting her somehow to implicate Susanna in Henry's death? She repeated only what she'd said before, and while the coroner loured at her, perhaps unsatisfactory, reply, his clerk scribbled furiously on his parchment. How glad she was to leave the manor as soon as she'd said her piece. She didn't want to stay and listen to any more.

But poor Jack had to sit through it all.

'It were a grim business, viewing poor Harry's body,' he said.

Agnes's hands flew to her face. 'You mean—?'

'I won't describe it, Agnes.' His eyes became moist. 'We had to watch while the coroner poked and prodded Harry's decaying flesh.'

'In the manor hall!' Agnes said, aghast.

'No, no, outside on the bailey. He was laid out on a bier.' He wiped his hand across his face. 'Then, once the coroner were done, he were taken away to be prepared for burial. I don't think I'll forget the sight, and smell, of him.' He was silent then for several moments. 'Anyway, after that we all went inside for the inquest.'

'Inquest?'

'You know, all the questioning. Like when you came in. After he'd questioned you and Simon, and the others, he then had Susanna stand before him. And he was so hard on her, I thought she might swoon again.'

'What did she say?'

'She'd gone down to the mill because Henry had left his dinner at home. She said she'd seen how dusty the air was inside the mill, and the dust caught in her throat, making her cough. She claimed Simon had already advised Henry to rest, to help ease the cough he'd had all winter. So what with that and the dust, she begged him to get skilled help again, so he'd not have to work so much. But he dismissed her advice and told her to leave the mill. "He always hated me being there," she said. Then they began to tussle—'

'Tussle?'

'I don't know what she meant. Perhaps he pushed her towards the door, and she resisted?' He shrugged. 'Anyway, she said, during this tussle, both of them fell over. First, she banged her face against a timber pillar, then Henry tripped against a beam in the floor and hit his head against the mill machinery.'

'And she thought he was dead?'

'No, not at all. She said he got to his feet and insisted again she leave. Which she did. But she said she was upset by the argument and, when she heard someone coming down the mill path – that must've been you – she ran off the path and round into her croft through the orchard.'

'So she was just upset that they'd argued?'

'I suppose so. But the coroner seemed not to believe her, for he continued to press her about the so-called tussle. He asked how it was an experienced miller such as Henry could trip over in his own mill, and she said she couldn't remember how it happened. And she became so distressed she couldn't say no more, and the coroner seemed to take that as a sign of guilt.'

'Guilty of striking him?' Agnes bit her lip. 'So if I'd said nothing about seeing her—'

Jack put his arm around Agnes's shoulders. 'You only spoke the truth.'

But now she wished she hadn't. Especially when Jack then told her further witnesses were found – men who, he said, avowed that Henry complained often of Susanna's constant nagging.

'Then some old fellow got up,' continued Jack, 'and said she came from "bad stock", as he put it. "Like father, like daughter", he said, and tapped the side of his nose. And the coroner actually *smirked*.'

'Why did those men only come forward today, and not before?'

Agnes saw anxiety in the glaze in Jack's eyes and the tension in his neck, as he told her more of Hubert Gastingthrop.

'I fear that man has an especial hatred of women,' he said, his voice low. 'It's not a coroner's job to prosecute, though he can recommend Susanna's sent for trial before the king's judges. But I reckon he saw an opportunity to accuse a woman of petty treason.'

'Petty treason?'

'He seemed only too delighted to explain it to us. Last year, he said, the king issued a new treason law. Women who just *tried* to kill their husbands, he said, were no longer guilty of petty treason—' Jack grimaced. 'In fact, Agnes, the old bastard seemed quite disappointed by that. But, anyway, it still held that women who *did* kill their husbands must be arraigned—'

'And that means what?' said Agnes.

'Less than treason but still a capital offence.' Jack bit his lip. 'For which a woman's punishment is burning—'

Agnes let out a cry and, for several moments, couldn't speak. Could Susanna really be accused of murder – and *burned*? She stepped forward and

112

nestled her face against Jack's chest. 'That surely *can't* be right,' she said, her voice a whisper.

He folded his arms around her. 'It's only the penalty if she's convicted.'

Agnes nodded her face against his tunic. At length, she looked up at him. 'So what happened to her?'

'The coroner said he was recommending she be sent for trial and was entitled to arrest her. The sheriff had to confirm his recommendation, but he was confident of that. She'd be kept in the sheriff's gaol in Winchester till whenever the king's judges come to try her.'

'And didn't Sir Richard try to stop him?'

'He did protest, but the coroner cited the case of Elizabeth Wragge. "If that case had come to the sheriff's attention," he said, "she'd not have got away with it." His eyes were glinting and Sir Richard looked embarrassed. I suppose the coroner was chiding his lordship for trying her here instead of at a higher court. And was saying it was his fault Mistress Wragge had been found innocent. "Surely, Sir Richard," the coroner said, "you don't want Meonbridge women to think they can assault their husbands without scruple? Women are getting above themselves, my lord, and we need to put a stop to it!"' Then Jack almost grinned. 'Lady de Bohun was near speechless with indignation. But the coroner said he'd the sheriff's authority to arrest a felon, and Sir Richard seemed just to crumple.'

It seemed ridiculous to hear of Susanna, of all people, being called a felon. But the news of Susanna's arrest was all Agnes needed to tip her over from feeling a simple prick of guilt to plunging into the deepest of low spirits. Surely, she repeated to herself a hundred times a day, it'd be entirely her fault if Susanna *was* found guilty, for speaking out when she could've held her tongue?

It didn't help that the brief period of renewed affection between her and Jack had already waned. She hardly blamed him, knowing well enough how difficult she was being. She'd dismissed Marye, as they'd agreed, but letting herself be so distracted by her worries about Susanna meant she was neglecting the children. And Jack, of course, had noticed.

Yet, only days after losing Marye, he'd brought home their first apprentice – another boy, of course. Agnes thought it tactless of him. It seemed the final nail in the coffin of her failing attempt to become a craftswoman, and she knew she was already being unduly hard on Christopher, and knew too how angry Jack was with her for being so unkind.

And, when she stopped to watch and consider – which wasn't often – she saw that twelve-year-old Christopher was quite different from her little sons.

He was thoughtful and keen to please, and could be an asset to her household if only she would let him.

But she rarely did.

Instead, she found fault with everyone, and chided Jack daily for not seeing what she saw. But he didn't often argue back and, if she looked into his eyes, it was disappointment more than anger that she found there.

# 13

Eleanor still loved being up on Riverdown, with the just risen sun giving the promise of a warm day, albeit it was still only April. A light breeze riffled the loose tendrils of her hair, flicking them against her face. Stopping at the top of the track, she gazed around her, at the view back down the hill to the river meandering alongside the village, and to the thatched roofs of the cottages and the glinting windows of the manor house. Then she scanned the horizon where, in one direction, thick woodland strode across the distant hills and, in another – although she had still never seen nor could she imagine it – the sea stretched far away to distant lands. She turned again to take in the pastureland rolling across the downs, where her growing flock was grazing.

Yes, it was glorious up here. She could see it, but nonetheless it *felt* bereft.

Despite the great flock of sheep over in the pasture, Riverdown seemed empty, and so did she. And, when she came up here to work with Will and Emma, it was with resignation, rather than contentment.

It was simply not the same without him.

It was five long months since Walter left, and Eleanor wondered if she would ever recover that contentment that she felt before.

She heard the sound of voices and, pulling herself back into the present, she ran past the shepherd's cottage towards the pasture. Will and Emma were both there, waiting for her. Eleanor waved to them as she approached. The working day had to begin, thoughts of Walter swept away, for now at least.

Will was a happy man. Since Walter left, he had been working full time on Riverdown, carrying out all the shepherd's duties. He did them so well that Eleanor decided it was only fair to give him Walter's job and, to convince him of her trust in him, she bought him a new puppy to train alongside Meg.

It was annoying that Emma seemed aggrieved at Will's advancement.

'Yet again,' she had said, 'a woman don't get considered for the job.'

Eleanor was very fond of Emma, and she was excellent with the lambs, but she did find her complaints a little testing.

'But Will has experience of *all* a shepherd's tasks,' she said. 'Anyway, you have a family to care for, and a husband, whereas Will's a widower and alone, and more than happy to live up here in the shepherd's cottage.'

Emma shuffled her feet a little and gave a rueful nod.

Despite Emma's tacit acceptance of Will's new position, Eleanor sensed that she was still unsettled. She had talked in passing, more than once, of her and Ralph leaving Meonbridge to find new "prospects", as she put it, although what she thought they might be she did not say. But as she had also said, in a rather resentful tone of voice, that Ralph was not keen on leaving Meonbridge, Eleanor hoped that meant Emma would be staying too.

Eleanor contemplated Emma's desire for change. She thought it somehow odd, for were not most women content to be wives and mothers, and overseers of their households and crofts? Would she herself not have been quite content with that? It was of course what she had expected – she could never have imagined, four years ago, being responsible for a great flock of sheep. And, if her father and brothers had not died in the Mortality, she would surely now be the wife of a successful merchant, with a great house in Winchester to manage, and at least one child, or maybe even two.

Yet, perhaps she was doing "most women" an injustice in assuming them contented with their lot? For Emma was not alone in thinking that, since the Mortality had turned the world upside down, women might – or even should – grasp any opportunities it offered. Eleanor thought of Agnes, learning to be a carpenter, though she had heard lately that Jack had changed his mind about it all, and wanted Agnes back home as a wife and mother.

Eleanor smiled to herself. One advantage of *not* being married was that she did not have a man telling her what she could and could not do. Nonetheless, the good reasons for *being* married – respectability, the chance of children and, of course, having a knowledgeable partner in her business – had not changed, and she could not deny that she still wanted them.

Nicholas had continued to try his luck with her, since that evening when he first visited, soon after Walter's leave-taking. She had waited several weeks for Nicholas to tell her whether he had discovered that it was Matthew who had chased her sheep off Riverdown and down to the river. But he never brought that information to her, even though she heard from Emma that Matthew was most certainly the culprit, from what Ralph had overheard him saying in the ale-house in Meonvale.

So Eleanor deduced that Nick's visit then was, as she had suspected, intended not to offer her his help, but to check if Walter had really gone, leaving the field of courtship clear for him. Nonetheless, she let him escort her to the manor's Christmas feast, and allowed him entry to her house on a few occasions when he called on her, ostensibly to enquire again after her health.

But, at length, despite all Nicholas's admirable qualities, she could not bring herself to give him any further encouragement. A month ago, she had instructed Hawisa now to tell him always that her mistress was not at home, and she hoped that he would take the hint.

Eleanor knew which man she wanted to marry and, if he did not want to marry her, well, then she would remain a spinster, and let the establishment of the Titherige flock be the focus of her life. It was inappropriate, and not what she wanted. But, while she had still charge of her own life, she was determined to maintain it, and not simply surrender to propriety if she did not have to.

Eleanor saw little of her stepbrother, Roger, though she still invited him occasionally to share her dinner. Roger had grown a lot since he took on the blacksmith's shop – both into manhood and in his mastery of his trade. Four years of hammering iron and bending it to shape had wrought in him the stature of a well-built man, neither particularly tall nor handsome, but very much conforming to his family name. At first, orphaned by the Mortality, they both felt much like frightened children, unprepared for making their own livelihoods, but having little choice. For the first two years, Eleanor had cooked their dinner and helped him manage his little cottage, as well as her own house and – despite her own need to work long hours with her sheep – to support his efforts to become Meonbridge's blacksmith. It became easier when she took on Hawisa and Nathan, and even more so when, a year ago, Roger had become affluent enough that he too could employ a servant.

But she had been so wrapped up in her own concerns that, as she listened to her stepbrother telling her of Susanna's arrest and removal to Winchester, Eleanor's mouth fell open in an undignified gape.

She knew that Henry had been found dead in the mill a week ago. And that Susanna, and many others, had been questioned by the constable about what had happened. But the coroner's visit had passed her by. She chided herself now for being so selfish she had not even bothered to visit Susanna and offer her condolences for Henry's death. She assumed he had been taken ill, for he had undoubtedly been looking sickly of late. It had not occurred to her that Susanna, or indeed anyone, might be held *accountable* for his death. Yet this was what Roger was telling her.

But, surely, it was impossible to imagine that Susanna would kill anyone, let alone her husband, except perhaps by accident? Eleanor chewed at her bottom lip, scarcely believing her own lack of thought for her friend. And now it was too late, for Susanna was alone in Winchester, and possibly in great danger.

She put down her spoon and pushed away her bowl. She stood up so sharply that her stool wobbled, then fell over, as her kirtle skirt swept against it. Lurching towards the fireplace, she gripped the back of her father's cushioned chair, her head bent, her cheeks burning.

She heard Roger clear his throat and speak her name, asking if she needed help. She shook her head, but did not turn around. Her ears were pounding, and her head seemed full of bees. In truth, she wanted to weep, for the shame and sadness overcoming her.

Moments later, she heard Hawisa bustle into the room. 'All done?' the servant said, her tone brisk, then cried, 'What's this, mistress, not eating?' Then, coming over to the fire, she took Eleanor's elbow. 'What's up wi' you?' she said, her voice more kindly now than brisk.

Eleanor shook her head, unable to reply.

Roger answered for her. 'Elly's just found out Susanna Miller's been arrested.'

'Ah,' said Hawisa, 'so that's it.' She clicked her tongue, then shook Eleanor's arm. 'She should've been paying better heed to her friend's plight, instead of fussing all the time about herself.'

At that, Eleanor wrenched her arm from Hawisa's grip and stood upright, glaring at her servant, her eyes afire. 'How dare you speak of me as if I am not here,' she cried. 'Or speak of me as if I've been neglecting my friend—'

Hawisa stared back, never one to shy away from confrontation, even with her mistress. 'Well, ain't you? Ain't you been so wallowing in your own troubles, you clean forgot to ask your so-called friend 'bout hers?'

Eleanor was suddenly very hot, and her heart was pounding in her chest. How could Hawisa be so unfair? She slumped down onto the chair and leaned back against the cushions, twisting her fingers through her hair and making it a tangle. 'Susanna *is* my friend,' she said at last, her voice cracking.

'Then you'd best do summat to 'elp her.'

After she had rinsed her face and hands with cooling water, combed the tangles from her hair and changed her work kirtle for a cleaner one, Eleanor threw her best cloak around her shoulders and opened the door.

'I'm going to see Lady de Bohun,' she said to Hawisa. 'Please send word to Will and Emma that I'll not come to Riverdown this afternoon, and they are to carry on without me.'

Hawisa lay her hand lightly on Eleanor's arm. 'You need summat to take you out o' yerself.' Eleanor knew that she was right.

At the manor, Margaret de Bohun, as always, expressed delight at seeing Eleanor again. 'I see little of you these days, my dear. You are so very busy with your sheep.'

'Indeed,' said Eleanor, then flushed. 'So busy – or, rather, so concerned only with my own affairs – that I have been neglecting those of my friends.'

'Mistress Miller, perhaps?'

Eleanor pressed her lips together. 'Susanna cannot possibly have killed Henry. Surely you agree?'

Margaret lifted her shoulders a little. 'I cannot say, my dear Eleanor. Although I do admit it seems unlikely—'

'No, your ladyship,' cried Eleanor, 'it is *impossible*. Susy is such a gentle soul, she could not hurt the smallest creature, let alone her husband.'

'I have always thought that of her.'

'So please help me discover the truth of what happened at the mill. I beg you, Lady de Bohun, do say you will.'

Margaret stood up from her chair and took a turn about the solar. Then she came and took Eleanor's hand. 'I cannot go against Sir Richard's wishes.'

'But will he not also agree?'

Margaret wagged her head a little. 'I am not sure. The coroner – what a vile man he was! – persuaded Richard that he could not risk another guilty woman "getting away with it", as he so crassly put it.'

Eleanor gasped. 'Whatever do you mean?'

'The Elizabeth Wragge affair.' Margaret's nostrils flared. 'What a ridiculous blunder! Forcing her to undergo ordeal by water – an *illegal* ordeal. I do not know what Richard could have been thinking of.'

'I thought ordeals were no longer permitted.'

'They have not been permitted for *decades*, Eleanor. In those days, defendants might choose to submit themselves to ordeal in order to prove their innocence.'

'Believing they would sink?'

'Indeed. But, in this case, the *jurymen* suggested it, presumably believing to the contrary, that Mistress Wragge would float, and thus be proven guilty. Why they would think that, I truly cannot imagine. And, even more so, I cannot imagine why *Richard* let them do it.' She threw her hands into the air.

'Why could the jurymen not just find her guilty?' said Eleanor.

Margaret spread her hands. 'It is quite beyond my understanding. There was evidence enough that she *did* hit her husband.'

'But the ordeal failed the jurymen, did it not?'

'Quite.' Margaret looked triumphant. 'But how shameful for such a dreadful *barbaric* thing to happen here in Meonbridge. In truth, Eleanor, sometimes I think my husband must be becoming brainsick, to let himself be so persuaded.'

Eleanor could not resist a smile at that, for it seemed to her Sir Richard's mind was quite intact. But her ladyship did seem to relish criticising his judgement, perhaps not out of rancour but frustration.

'And now he is worried,' continued Margaret, 'that all the women in Meonbridge might consider Mistress Wragge's acquittal an excuse for them to beat their husbands. Ridiculous! As you say, he should simply have found her guilty, as all the jurymen believed she was, and given her some suitable punishment. Then that would have been an end to it.' Her nostrils flared again. 'Instead of which, the coroner used the whole business as an excuse to send Susanna to be tried before the king's justices, to ensure that she did not also, as he put it, slip through the net. Which is why Richard conceded to the wretched man taking the poor woman away.'

'But does a coroner have such authority?' said Eleanor.

'Apparently he does. He can recommend a trial, although the sheriff must approve it. But I am of the impression that what the one recommends, the other will not gainsay.'

Margaret was clearly furious with Sir Richard for letting the coroner outwit him, yet Eleanor suspected her ladyship did not vent her anger quite so vehemently in his presence as she was doing now. But could Margaret possibly be right about his lordship being brainsick? After all, he was not so very old. Yet Eleanor did recall how distracted he became during the riots that followed the Mortality. Then, he seemed unable to decide how best to deal with the situation, and was being pulled this way and that by his son Philip, and Robert, the bailiff who in the end proved to be so traitorous. Both men wanted to take a hard line with the rioting tenants, but Margaret advocated a more conciliatory approach. In the end, her view prevailed, and Meonbridge at length returned to something like a peaceful community. But, by then, both Philip and Robert were dead.

'But do you think that, despite everything, Sir Richard might yet be willing to investigate what happened at the mill, to find the truth of it?'

'He might. We will have to ask him.'

Margaret sent word to her husband, in the hope he was still somewhere close at hand and could come to talk to them. Then, while they waited for his lordship's answer, she told Eleanor all about the "vile man", Hubert Gastingthrop. She had been present throughout the coroner's inquest.

'Not officially, you understand,' she said, a rather mischievous curve upon her lips. 'But the inquest was held in the manor hall, and there was no reason why I should not sit down beneath a window with my sewing.'

Margaret was able to relate, with remarkable clarity, all the questions the coroner had asked, of whom, and what their answers were. By the time Sir Richard appeared in person in the solar, Eleanor felt she knew enough to be able to convince him of the urgent need to pursue Susanna's case.

She repeated to Sir Richard what she had said to his wife, and he pulled on his beard. 'I understand your concern, my dear, as Mistress Miller was – is – your friend. But I am inclined to let justice take its course.'

'But if we do that, your lordship,' said Eleanor, her heart thumping, 'Susanna might lose her life.'

Deep lines furrowed his brow. 'You think so? The evidence against her is—'

'*Unconvincing*,' said Eleanor, her eyes bright. Sir Richard looked startled at her spirited interruption, but she continued, repeating what Margaret had told her about the coroner and her suspicion of his dislike of women.

Sir Richard raised an eyebrow at his wife.

'That is what I believe, husband,' she said. 'That loathsome man is likely to press for a conviction, whether the evidence is clear or not.'

Sir Richard nodded slowly. 'So let us review the evidence, Mistress Titherige.' He gestured to Eleanor to sit down in one of the two tall, deep-cushioned chairs that stood either side of the fireplace, while Margaret took the other. Sir Richard planted himself before the fire, barely alight this warm spring afternoon.

Eleanor cleared her throat and tried to piece together what Margaret had told her of the coroner's inquest into a coherent story.

'At present, your lordship, as I see it, there is no clear evidence that Susanna killed her husband, deliberately or otherwise. She told the coroner what happened at the mill, and surely we have no reason to disbelieve her? Coupled with the evidence of the Collyere brothers and Agnes Sawyer, it appears there was an argument between her and Henry, and they tussled.' She paused. 'I'm not quite sure what Susy meant by "tussle" – that was, her ladyship said, the word Susy used.'

'From what Susanna said, it sounded as if there was a bit of pull and push,' said Margaret, 'although even that seems strange, for two such gentle-natured people.'

'It does, yet the Collyeres said it sounded more like they were fighting. Anyway, Susy said that during the tussle she hit her face, and then Henry tripped over backwards and banged his head. Perhaps the coroner assumed violence on Susy's part? That she pushed him hard enough to make him trip?'

'Is *pushing* an act of violence?' Margaret said, her forehead wrinkling.

Sir Richard shrugged. 'It would have needed some strength on his wife's part to push a big man like Henry to the floor.'

'It surely would,' said Eleanor. 'But I refuse to believe that, even if Susy did push Henry, she *intended* to hurt him. It must have been an accident that he fell? And she said he wasn't badly hurt. His head was bleeding, but he was soon on his feet, telling her again to leave.'

'Although Master Gastingthrop did not believe her,' said Margaret.

'But Simon reckoned Henry died no more than an hour before he was discovered by Alys, which was surely as much as *three* hours after Agnes saw Susy running away.'

Sir Richard rubbed at his beard. 'Unless he died later, having hit his head an hour or two before?'

'Would that still be murder,' said Margaret, 'if Susanna pushed him and he fell over and hit his head, but did not die till later?'

'I cannot say. If a man dies following a fight, it is not always judged as murder. It is dependent on the circumstances.'

'So Henry's death,' said Eleanor, '*could* be judged an unhappy accident?'

'Or at least not a deliberate killing.' Sir Richard rubbed his beard again. 'Yet we must not forget the evidence of what Mistress Miller had said, about wanting to strike her husband. Another reason, I think, for the coroner taking a hard line with her.'

'But that was surely not a statement of *intent*, Richard?' said Margaret. 'Mistress Ward may have made it sound so, but Susanna must have said it as a jest? Everyone else who heard her say it thinks so.'

'Alys Ward does tend to mischief-making,' said Sir Richard, 'and her evidence should perhaps not be taken as the unblemished truth. Yet it cannot be ignored – and Master Gastingthrop chose not to.' He winked. 'After all, we already had the case in Meonbridge of a woman who did beat her husband – almost to death, it seems – and got away with her misdemeanour.'

Eleanor exchanged raised eyebrows with Margaret.

'But, Sir Richard, it is hardly just to compare Susy with Elizabeth Wragge,' said Eleanor. 'Everyone in the village knows Mistress Wragge *was* violent towards poor Edmund—'

'And if you had not sanctioned that foolish trial by water,' said Margaret, her voice rising, 'you could have judged her guilty yourself and dispensed her some fit punishment.'

Sir Richard glowered at his wife, perhaps vexed by her censure. 'Yet it does appear that Mistress Wragge has ceased her intemperate behaviour,' he said, 'from what I am told.'

'But there is no sign,' continued Eleanor, 'that Susy was *ever* violent towards Henry—'

'Until that day,' said Sir Richard. 'Perhaps she had been working up to it? Several men came forward to say that Henry complained often of her nagging him.'

Lady de Bohun sprang suddenly to her feet. 'And at whose instigation did they say it, I should like to know? Master Gastingthrop's, I daresay. What is most likely is that there was a tussle between husband and wife and, by unlucky chance, Henry tripped and hit his head. He was well enough when Susanna left him, but died later from – what? Perhaps the wound was more grave than it appeared?'

'Yes, that makes sense, your ladyship,' said Eleanor. 'Although perhaps there is another explanation.' She glanced at Sir Richard, who gestured to her to continue. 'That Henry had another visitor after Susy left and it was *then* that he received the fatal blow?'

'Now that *is* conjecture, Mistress Titherige,' Sir Richard said.

Lady de Bohun touched his arm. 'It is, of course, but what is very clear, husband, is that there may be more than one explanation of what happened at the mill. It is our responsibility to ensure that the outcome of the case does not result from a single, one-sided explanation, given by a man who seeks to rid the world of women.'

Despite Sir Richard's resigned acceptance of Margaret's entreaty that he support Susanna's case, Eleanor did not expect him to ask her to accompany him to Winchester. But a week later, they were travelling to the city, Eleanor riding one of Sir Richard's rounceys, and Hawisa bouncing alongside on an appropriately bad-tempered mule. They rode in the middle of a small company of Sir Richard's servants, well-armed and alert to danger.

Eleanor did not enjoy the journey. Though she had ridden often enough as a girl, she had become quite unaccustomed to it in recent years. She hated the discomfort of the side-saddle, but could hardly demand to sit astride the horse, which would be most improper. And then there was her anxiety about the potential peril of the road, and Hawisa's constant stream of protest. Hawisa had not wanted to come at all, but Lady Margaret would not countenance Eleanor travelling without a female companion, so poor Hawisa had little choice.

When at last they arrived in Winchester, Sir Richard said they would immediately seek an audience with the sheriff. Despite the fine, dry weather, he rejected Eleanor's suggestion that they leave the horses with his servants at the stable and walk the short distance to the castle.

'My dear Mistress Titherige, you evidently have no idea of the filth and danger of a city's streets.'

She flushed a little. It was true that this was her first time in Winchester. As they had ridden in, she had marvelled at the fineness of the city's streets. She admired the bishop's castle and the magnificent cathedral, and the many fine churches and grand houses, the latter, Sir Richard told her with a knowing grin, being the fruits of Winchester's success as the centre of the wool trade.

'My father must have been born here,' she had said, unable to suppress a delighted giggle, 'and become one of those merchants.'

Sir Richard had pointed to a grand three-storey house. 'Perhaps that was it?' His eyes were twinkling.

Eleanor had giggled again. Was that her father's home, or one of the other sumptuous-looking houses? Whichever it was, he lived there until he moved to Meonbridge.

'No, young lady,' continued Sir Richard now, 'we will ride right up to the castle door, so that we arrive with our boots unsullied and our throats uncut.' He winked at her, and she managed to return a rather feeble smile, shocked that her life could possibly still be in danger here amidst such wealth and splendour.

The sheriff doubted that Eleanor and Sir Richard would discover anything of value from talking to Susanna, reckoning the coroner had carried out a thorough enough enquiry. 'Master Gastingthrop's report was scrupulous and there is sufficient evidence for the woman to be presented to the king's justices. I will keep her here until whenever it is they come to Winchester. Which may be soon, or may be not...' He smirked.

Sir Richard cleared his throat. 'So you have already decided?' he said. 'Are we not able to present further evidence to support Mistress Miller's case?'

The sheriff rubbed at his nose. 'Not now, Sir Richard, but there is no reason why you cannot support the woman at her trial.'

Eleanor felt nauseous with horror for Susanna's plight. 'But we can still see her?'

'Of course, mistress,' he said. 'We welcome visitors to our prison *guests*.' Eleanor was sure she saw him wink.

'We have brought her food,' she said, 'as well as blankets and clean clothes.'

'Good, good,' the sheriff said, raising one hand in a dismissive wave, as he returned to his desk and wrote out the permit they required to gain entry to the gaol. He handed it to Sir Richard, a smirk on his lips again. 'Visit as often as you wish. It may well be many months before the king's judges return to Hampshire.'

When Eleanor and Sir Richard first entered Susanna's cell, she was lying on the bed, her face to the wall. Eleanor glanced around the little room, taking in the coldness and the feel of damp, the narrowness of the only window, too high up to see outside, the meagreness of any source of comfort. The rushes on the hard stone floor were sparse; the straw mattress filthy and leaking stalks; what passed for a blanket threadbare and fetid. She exchanged a look of revulsion with Sir Richard, who frowned and nodded.

Susanna did not move until Eleanor spoke her name. Then, rolling over, her eyes grew wide and glassy as she saw Sir Richard standing before her. Her fingers scrabbled at the mattress to help herself sit up, then she perched on the mattress edge, her shoulders stiff and her breathing shallow.

Eleanor crouched down and took Susanna's hands. 'Don't be afraid, Susy. Sir Richard has come with me because he's as determined as I am to find out the truth of how Henry died.'

'The truth?' she whispered.

'Indeed, Mistress Miller,' said Sir Richard. 'Mistress Titherige does not believe you are responsible for your husband's death, no more do I. The truth of what occurred that day must be discovered.' He touched Eleanor lightly on the shoulder, and moved towards the door. 'I will leave you two alone to talk.'

But Eleanor demurred. 'No, Sir Richard, please stay. I'd rather you were party to our conversation.' She hesitated. 'Please, Susy, don't take this amiss, but I think it best if his lordship is witness to what you say, in case I mishear or misconstrue your meaning.'

Susanna, for all her evident distress, agreed, and Sir Richard opened the cell door and called the gaoler. When the man came, grumbling, his lordship pressed a coin into his grimy hand. 'Three stools, if you please. At once.'

The man shuffled off, still muttering, and returned moments later holding two grubby, rough-hewn tripods. 'These're all I got, m'lord,' he said, sniffing, and put them down.

Sir Richard harrumphed. 'Very well. You can go.'

Susanna stayed sitting on her bed, while Eleanor and Sir Richard took the stools. Eleanor took Susanna's hand. 'Please, Susy, will you tell us what happened the day Henry died.' Susanna's face crumpled, but Eleanor squeezed her fingers. 'We want to understand,' she said. 'That is all.'

Susanna chewed at her bottom lip. 'I told that coroner everything.'

'But *we* want to hear it, Susy.'

So she told them about the argument with Henry, and the "bit of a tussle", as she put it, there had been between them. 'Then Henry tripped.' She knit her brows. 'I don't know how it happened, maybe when I were pushing him away? But his boot caught on a floor beam and he fell back against the grain hopper. He banged his head and it were bleeding. But moments later, he got up and ordered me again to go.' She bit her lip. 'I obeyed him then and Henry *were* alive when I left the mill.'

'Perhaps his head wound was more serious than it seemed?' said Eleanor.

'I've thought that myself. Or maybe he somehow fell again and hurt himself more badly? Though that don't seem likely with him working at the mill so long... Oh, Elly, I've thought and thought about how Henry might've come to die. But I truly don't know the answer. All I know 's he were alive when I last saw him.' She turned from Eleanor to Sir Richard and back again, her eyes imploring them to believe her.

Eleanor felt certain Susanna had not expected Henry to fall and hit his head. Did she push him away because he was hurting her? She was about to ask, when she saw that Susanna had bowed her head again, and her shoulders were hunched. She laid a hand on her friend's arm. 'You look tired, Susy. Shall we leave you now?' In truth, she did not want to go yet, but there would be another day for questions.

But Susanna shook her head. 'Not till you've told me about my little ones.'

Eleanor was glad she had paid a visit to Isabel Foreman before she came to Winchester. 'They're well, Susy. Missing you, of course, and confused about what's happened to their father. But Isabel is taking good care of them.'

Susanna whimpered. 'They must be so upset. But mebbe Tom's helping them to understand?'

Eleanor's hands flew to her face. 'Tom? But he's not with Isabel.'

Susanna cried out. 'Why ever not? When the constable took me to the manor, Tom were out with his friends. The little ones were taken away, to Isabel, you say, and I thought someone'd go and look for Tom and take him to join his brother and sisters.'

'Oh, Susy, I think that no one did—' She was aghast at the appalling realisation that everyone seemed to have *forgotten* about Tom. How was that possible?

'Tom's missing, then?' said Susanna, rocking back and forth now on the bed and plucking at her skirt.

But Eleanor leaned forward and stilled Susanna's hands. 'He might not be missing, Susy. Perhaps he's simply caring for himself at home? I daresay no one's been to check.'

Susanna's eyes seemed to brighten. 'Mebbe that's it. It'd be just like him.'

Sir Richard cleared his throat and pulled on his beard. 'We will enquire into it, Mistress Miller, as soon as we return to Meonbridge.'

Eleanor squeezed Susanna's hands. 'We *will* find him, Susy, and send word that he is safe.'

But Susanna was chewing at her lip again.

# 14

Emma linked her arm with Ralph's and briefly leaned her head against his shoulder, as together they strode up through the village towards Saint Peter's church. Beatrix and Amice trotted along behind, though Beatrix was struggling to keep a grip on her squirmy baby brother, Bart. Perhaps the boy was too big now for Bea to carry? Emma lifted her face up to Ralph's and they exchanged a grin. The sun was already warm on their backs this bright Sunday morning and, for a few moments at least, Emma felt a small surge of happiness. The return of spring and dry, warm weather often had this effect on her, though of course the feeling never lasted.

Emma sometimes wondered why they bothered coming to church at all, except Ralph said they must. 'If we don't go,' he'd said, 'the priest might think we're not mindful of our souls.' She'd pulled a face at that, but agreed it were best not to risk a chiding. And, indeed, on some days, church could even be a joy.

Four Sundays back was Easter Day, the one day in the year when most folk almost enjoyed going to church. They all confessed their sins and were permitted to kneel before the altar and accept the communion bread and wine. It was also the only day that Master Hugo seemed at all happy in his calling, when the entire congregation raised their hands and voices in celebration.

But, most other Sundays in the year, like today, folk just shuffled in and stood, unmoving and unmoved, listening to Master Hugo mumbling out the Mass in some language no one but he could understand – Latin, Ralph said it was, but what that was Emma didn't know – and only taking the bread and wine himself. Then folk just shuffled out again and went about their Sunday business. Ralph said it were enough just *being* there while Master Hugo spoke the Mass, and it was no matter if they didn't understand the words. She weren't sure she agreed, but didn't argue.

Though Emma preferred those boring sorts of Sundays to the few occasions when Master Hugo Garret thought his parishioners needed his advice and teaching. For that meant a sermon, and a sermon invariably sent her home with a quaking heart.

So when, after he'd recited the Mass and taken his communion, the priest climbed the steps up to the platform he'd had installed two years past to raise him high above his flock, Emma let out such a mournful groan that many of her neighbours chuckled. But Ralph poked her hard with his sharp elbow and whispered a reproof and, when she pouted, he knit his brow and gestured to her to listen.

If she'd known it was to be a sermon day, Emma would've stayed at the back of the church, so she could slip out unnoticed. For she'd never much cared for Master Hugo's lessons, especially since Bart's funeral, when, with her beloved's body lying cold upon the bier, the priest had accused him of stirring up God's wrath with his sinful defiance of Sir Richard, risking the Death's return to Meonbridge. Emma thought Master Hugo then a cruel, unfeeling man, who took no heed of how his words might wound. It was true he spoke, from time to time, of love and of forgiveness, of God's longing for his people to obey Him. But, it seemed to Emma that this priest took every opportunity to chide his flock, every chance to make them fear their likely fate beyond the grave.

Master Hugo took his place up on his platform and glared down at his flock, his lips pressed tight together, evidently waiting for the murmuring to cease. When it didn't, he coughed, and those who'd mebbe only just noticed he was there cleared their throats, and silence fell.

The priest then raised his hands and let his lips broaden into a thin, unwelcoming smirk.

'My friends…' he began, letting his hands fall again. 'In the great wisdom of his calling, King Solomon tells us that a quarrelsome wife is like the endlessly dropping rain.'

He grimaced. 'We know all about rain, do we not, my friends? The tedium of it, the discomfort of it, the constant drip-drip-drip of it. And that is exactly what, said the shrewd and perceptive king, it is like to have a nagging wife, a wife who does not obey her husband, a wife who will *not* still her tongue.' He thumped one fist against the other.

Emma found it hard to suppress a gasp, but many of the men around her chuckled and mumbled agreement with the priest.

'Let me relate to you,' continued Master Hugo, 'two tales, *exempla* they are called, anecdotes that serve to illustrate a greater truth.' He cast his gaze across his flock, the smirk still fixed upon his mouth that Emma thought looked sly.

'First,' he said, 'the story of a widow, given a second chance at happiness by a young man, whose only wish was to love and cherish her. Just as the Bible tells us that a husband must. But the Bible also says that a husband's love includes a duty to chastise his wife if she is at fault, just as a father gently chides his son to teach him manners, and as our Father in Heaven admonishes us, his children, for our misdemeanours, because he so wants us to be worthy of his great Love.'

He raised his hands again, somehow inviting the silent company to listen closely.

'And this young man *did* love his wife,' he went on. 'He gave her all that she desired. He was sensitive in his reproaches to her, despite her failing to provide him with an heir, nor performing her domestic duties with much skill or satisfaction. Because he *loved* her. Yet this thankless wife spurned her husband's love, did not respect his gentle efforts to teach her her duties, refused to obey his solicitous commands. Instead—' he hesitated, leaning forward a little, 'instead, she answered his love with *violence*.' He brought his fist and hand together again. 'She struck him, this ungrateful wife, and often, first with her hand, then her distaff, and finally with a skillet, until, at last, she almost killed him.'

A cry came from the congregation and Master Hugo paused, his head bowed and shaking slowly from side to side. Then he lifted his head up again, his brow creasing with deep furrows, his eyes in a penetrating stare. He raised one arm and pointed towards the nave's high vault. 'How wicked, how *unnatural*, is such a woman in God's eyes!' he cried and, bringing his arm down, he let his quivering finger sweep across the now wide-eyed congregation, and hover fleetingly over two or three of the women standing there, drawing from them moans and cries.

As Emma watched the priest's menacing finger, her heart was thumping. For everyone, surely, knew what he'd just said weren't a *tale* at all, but his own judgement of Mistress Wragge. And others thought it too, as a murmur of angry-sounding voices erupted but was quickly stilled, as Master Hugo glared and coughed again.

'And now,' he said, his sly simper wiped from his face, 'for my second tale, that of another widow, also given a second chance at the joy of matrimony. Her husband, a man of principle, a godly man, strove only to provide for his wife and their growing family. But what reward did this honest man receive for his endeavours? The daily scolding of a nagging wife! Always demanding more of him. Despite all that he had given her, she was never satisfied. And so intemperate is womankind that, in the end, her dissatisfaction with her lot also turned to violence. But, in this case, such violence that her poor husband *died*. Killed by his wife's own hand. *That* was her thanks to him for working so hard to provide the best for her and her spawn.' He glared around the nave. 'What, think you, is God's opinion of *her*?'

Later, as everyone shuffled out of the gloomy church and emerged blinking into the sunlight, the women were mostly silent. But from the mumbled conversations of their husbands, it seemed to Emma that many of them accepted the "truth" of Master Hugo's so-called tales.

Ralph was not among them. Once they were home, he drew Emma to him and held her close. 'It were obvious what the priest were getting at. I were as shocked by it as you.' She nodded her head against his chest, tears pricking.

'It were wicked,' she said, pulling away and wiping her fingers across her eyes. 'I'm going outside a while, for a bit of air.'

Ralph opened his arms to let her go and she went out into their tiny croft. She knelt down by her meagre herbary with her weeding hook and fork. She'd learned from Alice long ago how to grow a few herbs, thyme and sage and marjoram, parsley, mint and clary, to add flavour to their simple food. She'd have liked to grow vegetables as well, onions and cabbages, but the plot just wasn't big enough. She often thought with envy of Susanna's croft, with not only space enough for vegetables of many kinds, and trees of apple, pear and cherry, as well as herbs, but also for a flock of fussy hens, and even a sty with two fat pigs. She'd landed on her feet, Emma had often thought, but now, with Susanna facing trial for murder, Emma knew who was the better off, no matter if she'd no money and no land.

After a while, Ralph came out to find her, and crouched down by her side as she pulled weeds fiercely from around her precious herbs. 'Don't fret, Em,' he said. 'That priest don't know what he's talking about.'

'But he's God's servant.'

'Don't mean it were God's word he were preaching.' He sat back on his heels. 'He were right about a man loving his wife, even chiding her if she's at fault—'

'But not wives their husbands?'

Ralph put out his hand and lightly tweaked her nose, making Emma giggle.

'But,' he went on, 'even if his first story – 'bout Mistress Wragge – were true enough, he weren't right with the second—'

'I'm not sure he were even right about Elizabeth. It weren't fair to accuse her of not giving Edmund an heir, when she's *never* had a child. Everyone *knows* she's barren.' She frowned. 'If Edmund wanted children, he should've married another. He were just greedy for her *land.*'

'Though mebbe she weren't much of a wife? And Master Hugo *were* right when he said Edmund only chided her with words.'

'He said a nagging wife were like the constant drip of rain, but a husband can

131

nag too.' She tilted her head. 'Mebbe Elizabeth couldn't bear *him* drip-dripping no more?'

Emma gathered her tools together and stood up. Picking up the bucket of weeds, Ralph went and threw them onto the midden heap then, returning to his wife, put his hand against her waist as they walked back to the cottage.

After a dinner that rather matched her mood, Emma asked Beatrix to clear away and Ralph to go with her for a walk. 'As it's such a lovely afternoon,' she said lightly.

Beatrix pulled a face and muttered something Emma couldn't hear, but which almost certainly included the word "unfair". Ralph crouched down next to the girl and whispered something in her ear. Beatrix shook her head. As Emma watched them apparently coming to some sort of agreement, she thought yet again what a good, kind man she'd married. She'd never imagined loving another after losing her darling Bart, but it was hard not to love Ralph too, when he was so considerate and thoughtful, to her and to her daughters.

Emma wanted to carry on the conversation about Master Hugo's sermon, but didn't want Bea and Ami listening in. It was hard enough to understand the priest's intentions, without having to answer questions from the girls.

As they often did, they took the track down to the river, then crossed the bridge and climbed the hill to Riverdown. Once up on the down, they could walk for miles, but had promised Bea they'd not be gone too long, so she could go out to play with her friends a while. Skirting Eleanor's main flock, they went only as far as a stretch of empty downland where they could sit undisturbed by sheep.

Emma always enjoyed being up here, even when she was working. It was peaceful, apart from the bleating of the sheep, and its long view of distant places made her wonder what else there might be in the world for her and Ralph – and for the girls and little Bart – away from Meonbridge, away from everything they knew. It was a frightening thought, yet somehow thrilling. She'd tried to urge Ralph to think how they could profit from the changes brought by the Death but, favouring what he knew over what he didn't, he was unwilling to leave Meonbridge. Which was a pity, as Emma felt sure life'd be better for them all in Winchester.

Though it wasn't better there for Susanna, locked up in the sheriff's gaol, waiting for the king's judges to come, whenever that might be.

'Poor Susy,' she said, as they sat down on the grass.

Ralph lay back with his head resting on his folded arms, his eyes closed against the brightness of the sun. 'Mmm. She shouldn't be in gaol, *or* facing trial.'

'You was right about Master Hugo's second tale,' said Emma, 'It weren't fair on her—'

'Or on Harry.'

The very idea of the Millers fighting was daft. Emma recalled their lovely wedding day, with all the music and the dancing. It had been such a joyful day after the horror of the Death and, then, the loss of little Peter and his poor mother, Joan.

'Harry were so happy to have her as his wife,' said Ralph. 'D'you remember how much he cared for her?'

'An' they was both such gentle people... So when did it all go wrong?'

He shrugged. 'Harry's become so full of melancholy, and he's been grumbling for months about her nagging.'

'In the ale-house?'

'Mistress Rolfe's. I go there sometimes – the ale's better than the cat's piss sold in Meonvale.' He winked, but Emma frowned. 'The old Harry hardly ever went to an ale-house,' continued Ralph, 'but lately he'd been there most every evening.'

'I'm not surprised he'd been finding her a nag,' said Emma. 'But she were so worried about him, getting so tired and ill. I daresay nagging don't help, but she'd been working herself up into a lather about it.'

'Harry said she kept pressing him to get proper help again. Even his brother Thomas told him she were right.'

'Thomas?'

'He comes out quite often now. He's getting better, slowly. "The mill ain't a one-man job, Harry," he said. Mind you, Em, I've heard no one *wanted* to work for Henry no more.'

Emma blinked. Ralph'd never said that before.

'Think on it, Emma,' continued Ralph. 'He had three journeymen. The first one were a poor worker, according to Harry, so he sacked him. Then the second Harry said demanded too much money, and the third left for a job in a bigger mill, again, so Harry said. But losing three in so short a time?' He scratched at his head.

'So you thinking they left 'cause he were a bad master?'

He shrugged. 'I know he'd been looking for a replacement, but mebbe nobody applied? You'd've thought *somebody'd* want the job. But mebbe word got round he were too miserable a master?'

'An' it's been months since that last one left,' said Emma. She frowned. 'Susy thought he'd not been looking.'

'But he *had* been. I reckon he'd not told her it were why he were making do with the Collyeres, 'cause no one else'd risk it.'

'But it's odd, isn't it, Ralph, when Harry used to be so full of jollity and good humour?'

'But he'd changed, Em, an' in more ways than just his temper.'

'What d'you mean?'

Ralph's nose wrinkled. 'Harry's face lit up when Ivo the mason said once, in conversation, like, women were getting above 'emselves. "What 'bout that Agnes?" said Ivo, and thumped his pot down on the table. "I told Jack he oughta put a stop t'it. Where'll it all lead, if women start thinking they can run the place?"' Ralph pulled a face. 'Most seemed to agree with him, Harry included—'

'But not you?' said Emma.

''Course not, Em. I'm happy for you suggesting how we do things.'

'Not that you ever take much notice.' She tilted her head.

Ralph sat up, laughing. 'Anyways, I thought they was all talking hogwash, but I kept quiet. Though now I wish I hadn't, 'cause Harry were lapping it all up.'

'You might not've changed his mind.'

'But he were saying things he'd never said before, Em, things I'd not think he'd ever say.'

'Like what?'

'Like what the priest were saying, about a husband's duty to chastise his wife. I always thought Harry must be joking when he said it.'

'Why?' Emma gave a mischievous grin. 'It's what the Bible says, ain't it? An' don't *most* men slap their wives if they talk too much, or don't do what they're bid?'

Ralph let his mouth fall open, though Emma knew he was pretending to be shocked. '*Some* do,' he said, 'but, no, not most. And *not* Harry. I don't understand what changed him. It's hard to believe the man I used to know would hit his wife, no matter how heavy-hearted he'd become, or what he might've said after a few pots of ale.'

'An' I can't believe Susy'd hit *him*,' said Emma, 'no matter what the Collyeres thought they heard.'

'But there's another thing,' Ralph said, ''bout Harry. You know he were a juryman when Mistress Wragge were brought to court? Well, I heard he were set on her being found guilty. Like they had to make her an example. An' *that* don't seem at all like the Harry I used to know.'

Next day, half way through the morning, Emma was glad when Eleanor suggested they all stop work for a moment's rest, for the sun was burning fiercely, and the breeze was so light there was scarcely any cooling relief, even up on

Riverdown. Will said he'd take Meg and the puppy for a stroll. Emma smiled at the sight of the little creature bouncing around Will's feet. It had been good of Eleanor to buy it for him.

'He needs two dogs,' Eleanor had said, her eyes brimming with tears. Emma knew she was thinking about Dart, the other dog, gone with Walter. The loss of Dart much saddened Eleanor, though she said she didn't really begrudge Walter at least one of the dogs he'd trained up from a puppy.

She pressed her lips together. 'I'm grateful he thought to leave us Meg.'

Will whistled the dogs to come then, together, the man striding, the dogs racing ahead of him, they disappeared from view across the down. Emma walked with Eleanor back to the shepherd's cottage and they sat down on the rough-hewn log bench Walter had made for taking in the view on summer evenings.

'I've seen Susy,' said Eleanor, after a few moments. 'At the gaol.'

Emma gasped. 'You was brave to go alone.'

'Sir Richard came with me. I think he feels a little guilty for letting the coroner take her away.'

Emma clicked her tongue. 'An' so he should. She *can't* be guilty.'

'I agree, yet it's hard to know how to prove it.'

'It's hopeless, then?'

'I don't think so. Although Susy just repeated to us what she'd told the coroner, I'm not at all sure it was the truth. I feel she's hiding something.'

'Why would she? Anyway, what sort of thing?'

'Oh, I don't know,' said Eleanor. 'I just wonder if Henry *struck* her – perhaps with force and deliberation – and, if she then hit back, it was to defend herself?'

'Then why didn't she say so?' said Emma, frowning.

'Perhaps she has somehow cast it from her mind?'

''Cause she can't bear the thought Harry might've hit her on purpose?'

'Something like that. What do you think?'

'Me and Ralph don't believe she'd've hit him with no reason. Yet it's hard too to imagine Harry striking her... He did love her so.'

Eleanor took Emma's hand in hers and squeezed it. 'We *must* find the truth, somehow.'

Emma agreed but couldn't imagine how.

'Anyway,' continued Eleanor, 'I wanted to ask you something else.'

She told her what she'd learned from Susanna about young Tom.

Emma could scarcely believe it. 'I thought he were with Issy Foreman,' she said, 'but what with the Foremans living the other side of the village, I've not seen the little ones since Susy went to Winchester.'

'Well, he's not with Isobel. I told Susy he must be at the cottage, looking after himself, but he's not there either.'

Emma bit her lip. 'So where is he?'

'That's what I want to ask you, Emma. To help me find him. He must be somewhere in the village. Though why he's hiding, if that's what he's doing, I don't understand.'

'Why didn't he go to Issy with the others?'

Eleanor plucked at her skirt. 'He wasn't with them when Susy was taken to the manor, and the little ones to Isobel. In all the upset of her being arrested, poor Tom was just forgotten.' She wrung her hands together. 'Oh, Emma, I feel so ashamed. I can't believe no one in the village wondered where he was. How could he just have been forgotten?'

'I s'pose he were with his friends, or on his own. As he were most of the time, as Henry wouldn't let him work.'

'But you'd have thought, when he went home, he might have wondered where his family was and gone to ask someone. Or perhaps he never did go home? He may not even know his father's dead, or his stepmother's been arrested for his murder.'

'Or mebbe he *does* know, and is hiding 'cause he's afraid?'

'But why would he be afraid?'

'Mebbe *he* went to the mill too, after Susy left?'

Eleanor nodded. 'Could he have found Henry dead before Alys did—?'

'And ran away, afeared he might be accused?'

'But why would anyone think *Tom* responsible for his father's death?'

'Folk know how much he and Harry argued—' Even as she said it, Emma couldn't believe that Tom, of all boys, might be thought guilty. She shook her head. 'But he's such a gentle, good-natured lad, not the sort—'

'No, not the sort at all.' Eleanor smiled and patted Emma's hand. 'So, if he is hiding, it's simply because he's frightened.'

'So we must try and find him.'

The following evening, before the dark had settled in, Emma went out with Eleanor to look for Tom. They'd decided to keep their search to themselves, in case Tom *was* somehow in trouble, though Eleanor agreed Ralph could be told, as he might know where a lad might hide.

Ralph reckoned the boy would likely hide out in one of the deserted cottages or an unused building on a neglected croft. There were plenty for Tom to choose from, most of them in cottar Meonvale.

Emma suggested she and Eleanor start their search in the area of Meonvale closest to the river, where the crofts were the first to be abandoned after the Death passed on. The ground was prone to winter flooding, the cottages much given to damp, and the folk who'd lived in them moved to better crofts, left empty by those who'd perished. Some did fear taking on those houses, thinking the sickness might still linger in cracks in the walls or the spent rushes on the floor. But when none more were afflicted, and the months passed by, fear was at last shrugged off for the sake of a better house.

Whispering without knowing why, Emma led Eleanor from croft to croft, skirting collapsing midden heaps, climbing over piles of junk, leaning hard against the swollen doors of cottages and barns to grope around their dark interiors. They found nothing but discarded belongings, decayed food and the odd item of broken furniture, the only occupants fat spiders lurking in great dusty webs, mice scurrying along the beams, and sometimes birds nesting in the rotting roof thatch.

But no Tom.

Then in a cottage a few plots distant from the river, there were signs of recent occupation, despite the crumbling daub in the walls and holes in the reedy thatch.

Emma went in first, then called out to Eleanor to come. 'Look,' she said, pointing to the hearth. She bent down and held her hand over the ashes, then touched the iron pot hanging on the tripod. 'They're warm. Someone's been cooking here.'

A filthy pallet lay close by, its straw stuffing escaping from a rip in the cover, a torn and smelly blanket heaped on top.

'Could it be Tom?' said Eleanor.

'Would he try to cook?'

'He might. It's been two weeks, so he'd be hungry.'

'But where'd he find the food?'

'Susy's garden? Although there'd hardly be much to take at this time of year.'

'So where's he now?'

'Out foraging? Unless he saw us coming and ran off. But if it is him, he'll be back. So somehow we must keep watch.'

# 15

Eleanor stood at the spicerer's stall, breathing in the curious nose-tingling perfumes rising from the colourful sacks of seeds, barks and berries, and on the edge of a sneeze as pungent dust drifted from the peppercorns the merchant was scooping from a sack.

She had always loved coming to the fair. Because it was held only once a year and lasted three days, it encouraged a few merchants to travel from much further afield. The fair would attract a good crowd of purchasers too, and many of the wealthier sort, who could afford the more expensive goods on offer.

For these foreign merchants sold mostly manufactured goods, which were often of much better quality, or more exotic, than anything the local merchants could offer – the finest woollen cloth, well-made pewter ware, and jewellery – and, sometimes, spices. A spicerer did not come every year to Meonbridge but, in the summer months, an employee of the spice merchant in Winchester would travel between a few Hampshire fairs, bringing cloves and cinnamon, and ginger and mace, as well as pepper. How delighted Eleanor was to find that the spicerer had this year chosen to come here.

She had already treated herself to a length of fine cloth for a new kirtle, and wanted to please Hawisa by buying a little spice and sugar for her to add to a pie or pudding. It could not be much, for she was not one of the wealthier sort, but Hawisa could make a little go a long way.

Eleanor put her purchases into her basket and, after handing over the coins to the spicerer, wheeled around to move on to the next stall. Then, a short distance away, she spotted a black and white dog – a dog she knew very well.

Her heart began to race and she took a couple of steps forward, hoping to see the owner of the dog. And there he was, hidden slightly by some cottar women browsing at a nearby stall. Dart was sitting quietly by his master, his head turning this way and that, taking in the market smells perhaps, but not fussing to go and sniff them out. Walter was talking, amiably it seemed, to two or three other men, cottars he would have known from boyhood.

Her heart still thumping, Eleanor waited for him to stop his conversation. In truth, she was fearful of approaching him, yet how could she bear not to? Had he after all come back to her? Perhaps he was asking those men if they had seen her?

Moments later, Walter was walking in her direction, Dart trotting at his side, and she tucked herself a little behind the awning of the spicerer's stall, waiting for them to come closer. They took quite a while to cover the short distance, as Walter, she supposed, was talking to the folk he met. But then she knew he must be near, for Dart appeared at her feet, his tail wagging, whining and pawing at her skirt.

Eleanor emerged from her hiding place and found herself face to face with Walter. The inevitable flush soon warmed her neck, and she was sure it must be already rising to her cheeks.

She tried a smile. 'Master Nash.'

But, to her dismay, he frowned. 'Mistress Titherige.' His nod was curt. Then, looking down at the dog, he spoke sharply. 'Sit.'

Dart sat at once, but placed himself between them, twisting his lovely head back and forth, looking up at each in turn. Eleanor could not help but bend down and stroke his neck, then fondle his soft, silky ears.

Then she stood up again. 'Are you well, Walter?' she said, trying to sound relaxed.

'Well enough. Yourself?'

She gave the slightest of nods in answer, hesitating to ask what she most wanted to know. She let her hand drift to Dart's ears again, before being bold enough to look Walter in the eye. 'Have you returned to Meonbridge?'

'A visit only. I received word my aunt was ill.'

Eleanor's heart turned over with disappointment. 'I had heard Mistress Nash was ailing. How is she?'

He shrugged. 'I've not yet seen her.'

Eleanor felt a flush rise to her face: she should not have to *ask* Walter about his aunt! She herself should have – could have – visited Cecily, for the old lady's cottage was only a short distance from her own house, just along the track that led to Upper Brooking. If she cared for Walter, she ought to have shown proper concern for his aging aunt. She surely had been *meaning* to...

Of course Lady de Bohun was attentive to the elderly of Meonbridge, and she had a close relationship with Cecily. For, after the Mortality, she had placed herself under the old lady's tutelage – somewhat against Sir Richard's wishes – so she too could understand the healing power of herbs. Though she only ever used her knowledge for medicinal purposes, never prescribing love potions to infatuated maidens, as Eleanor was certain Cecily used to do.

But Margaret's loyalty to her mentor did not absolve Eleanor from her own neighbourly responsibilities. She cast her eyes down again to Dart and, raking her fingers through her hair, teased some strands of it forward a little to hide her cheeks.

'Will you be staying many days?' she said, not looking up.

'Long as necessary.'

Eleanor felt almost faint. 'Then you will leave again?'

'I've my job to return to.'

She looked up then and met his eyes. 'Is it a good job?'

'Head shepherd with a flock twice the size of yours.'

'Where?' she said, her breathing shallow.

'Sussex way.'

She could not think what else to say, and Walter half-turned, about to walk away.

'I must go,' he said. 'My aunt's waiting.'

'She knows you're coming?'

He knit his brow. 'Of course. I sent word.' He fixed Eleanor's eyes with his. 'Though I knew *she'd* want me here.'

Eleanor looked away again, and fiddled with her hair. She felt tears pricking and did not want him to see her cry. She wanted him to leave now, yet she could not bear for him to go, afraid she might never see him again.

Walter did not move at once. Dart nudged his nose against her hand, and she leaned down to stroke his muzzle.

Then Walter repeated that he had to go.

'You must,' she said, her voice a whisper. But she did not let go of Dart, entwining her fingers into the thick fur on his neck. The tears brimmed and, pretending to have a speck of something in her eye, she wiped her sleeve across it.

'Are you all right?' said Walter.

She nodded. 'Perhaps a bit of fur? It's nothing.'

'I'll go then.' He tied a rope around Dart's neck and pulled on it gently. 'Come.' Then, he brushed past Eleanor and, without turning round, raised his hand in a gesture of farewell. 'Good day to you, Mistress Titherige.'

Dart trotted on beside him, but looked back at her three times, before she retreated to her hiding place, tears streaming down her cheeks.

# 16

The first shaft of early morning sunlight was just poking through the high, narrow opening that was the only window in Susanna's cell. She sensed the brightness through her closed eyelids. She wished the new day hadn't come. For there'd be no chance now of the sleep denied her all night long, until her cell was dark again. And even then…

How many nights had passed since she'd slept through? Would she ever sleep again?

Shifting her body awkwardly on the unforgiving straw-filled mattress, she rolled to face the wall and pulled the woollen blanket up over her head, trying to block out the morning. But it was hopeless. Despite the narrowness of the window slit, the sun was filling the cell with light. It wouldn't last, of course. Her cell was always at its brightest now, for the window faced the rising sun. But as the sun travelled across the sky, the light would fade and the room become gloomy once again. Knowing that, she told herself, as she did every morning, to get up from her bed and take advantage of the light. Yet what was there for her to do?

She opened her eyes and stared at the wall, inches from her nose. Putting out her hand, she let her fingers trace the edges of the stones, shivering at their chilly hardness. She was grateful to Sir Richard for enabling her at least to have a room to herself, a bed and a blanket, and the ministrations of Edith Wyteby, the landlady of some nearby ale-house, who'd agreed to bring her food and drink each day, and rushlights and clean bedding from time to time. Others here were much less fortunate – crowded together several to a room, forced to rely on alms from charitable citizens, or to go out each day to beg for food on the streets. She was at least spared that humiliation.

Susanna rolled away from the wall and, swinging her feet down to the hard earth floor, she sat up and flexed her aching back. Pressing her hands down against the edge of the low rough-hewn wooden bed frame, she eased her shoulders, then closed her eyes again and bowed her head. She scarcely even wanted to stand up, or to accept the time had come for her to face the day.

Perhaps Edith would come early? The few moments of Edith's company were what Susanna welcomed as much as the food – though her morning visit often brought fresh-baked bread, its warm yeasty smell enticing Susanna to eat, despite her failing appetite.

Susanna opened her eyes again, confused. The room seemed less bright than she'd thought – the shaft of sunlight no longer beaming through the window slit. And she was lying down again, so had she slept a little after all?

A jangling sound was coming from beyond the door, the noise that must have woken her. The gaoler was outside, riffling through his ring of keys. Perhaps Edith had come? But, moments later, the door flew open and, when the gaoler stepped inside, he was alone.

Susanna heaved herself up from the bed and stood to face the man, now planted foursquare before her, his short, bandy legs astride, his broad shoulders set. But the corners of his mouth were downturned, his doleful eyes made gloomier by the unkempt locks of greasy hair hanging limp before them. She was used to the gaoler's melancholy mien. He seemed unhappy in his job but she thought him by nature kindly. For, whenever he came to see her, which was never with good news, she felt his disappointment was always heart-felt and personal.

She assumed it was not good news he brought today.

He bobbed his head briefly in greeting. 'Missus Miller.' He shuffled his feet a little and fingered the fastenings on his grubby tunic. Then he raised his eyes to hers, and his shoulders heaved. 'Sheriff sent me wi' a message.'

Susanna's heart thumped in her chest. If the news was good, the gaoler surely would be smiling?

'He's approved the coroner's advice,' the man continued. 'You're to go for trial afore King Edward's judges.'

Despite her gloomy reckoning, Susanna's body folded and she slumped heavily upon the bed.

'You're to stay here till they come to Winchester,' said the gaoler.

'And does the sheriff know when that might be?'

He scratched at his neck. 'We never know, missus. Could be weeks, or could be years—'

'*Years?*' Susanna cried out.

'God willing, not, missus,' he said, then tugged at his matted beard. ''Tis been a while since they was here, so they must be due a visit.' He let his mouth curve a little. 'Let's hope 'tis soon, eh, missus?'

She couldn't answer, but raised her eyes. The gaoler shuffled backwards out of her cell, leaving her perched upon the edge of the bed frame, her shoulders hunched, willing herself not to cry. The news was hardly a surprise, yet it had numbed her.

She sat, unmoving, for a long while – how long she didn't know – until she realised Edith hadn't yet come, and her mouth and throat were dry. Her tongue felt large against her teeth and she found it hard to swallow. She glanced across at the wall opposite, and her eyes fell upon the leather flask Edith had brought yesterday, lying on the low shelf that served as her only table. Getting up, she took the two steps needed, and picked up the flask. Bringing it up to her ear, she shook it. She could hear a drop of ale still swilling around inside and, with anxious fingers, she pulled at the stopper and lifted the flask up to her mouth. A trickle of the weak ale wetted her lips and dribbled into her mouth, but there was scarcely enough to reach her throat. Tip it as she might, the flask was empty. She licked the film of ale from her lips, but the cooling wetness quickly dried, and her thirst remained unsated.

She lay down again, trying to forget the dryness of her mouth, wishing Edith would come. She'd never been one to cry, even as a child. Her mother had said only babies cried and, once walking, were babes no longer. Susanna grew up in the belief that crying got you nowhere. Yet, now, when neither her mother nor anyone else was here to see it, she let a few tears flow.

It could be years, the gaoler said, before the king's court came. She thought she mightn't live that long, if this was to be her world for all that time. She conjured up a vision of her lovely croft – her garden full of newly sprouting vegetables and herbs just coming into flower, the white apple blossom in the orchard, the hens warbling as they pecked for worms, the pigs snorting and snuffling in the mud. Was anyone caring for the animals, tending to the young plants? A sob came to her throat unbidden, as she realised she'd not asked anyone to care for either – there'd been no time or opportunity.

She must remember to ask Eleanor next time she came...

When Susanna next heard the gaoler's jangling keys, she almost sprang up from the bed, so relieved that Edith had come at last. She smoothed the skirt of her kirtle, and managed to apply a smile to her face as the door swung open and Edith Wyteby bustled into the little room.

Edith plumped her basket down on to the bed, and grinned at Susanna. 'Mornin', Mistress Miller.'

But Susanna's smiling mouth had already crumpled to a pout. 'Oh, Edith,

I thought you'd never come,' she said, unable to keep a note of resentment from her voice. Yet the moment she'd said it, she wished she hadn't.

Edith's lips pressed tight together. 'I'm no later than usual, mistress—'

Susanna's hand flew to her mouth. 'I'm sorry, I didn't mean—' And, stepping back, she slumped onto the bed. 'I've scarce had any sleep...' Her shoulders shook.

Edith moved the basket and sat next to her and, putting a motherly arm around her, drew her close. 'Now, now,' she said. 'You're worn out, dearie. From worry as much as lack of sleep, I warrant.'

Susanna nodded against Edith's shoulder. 'The gaoler just told me the sheriff's sending me for trial,' she whispered.

'He told me too,' said Edith. She rocked back and forth a little, as if comforting a child. But then she removed her arm and held Susanna away from her. Cupping her chin in her hand, she lifted her face. 'But your lord said he's certain you're not guilty.'

Susanna tried to smile, but couldn't. 'Did he? Elly thinks so too.'

'That Missus Titherige?'

Susanna agreed, but then a sob escaped from her throat. 'But how can I not be found guilty, when the coroner's so certain of it?'

Edith didn't answer at once. 'Perhaps your Missus Titherige'll find a way?'

Edith had put on the shelf a fresh-baked loaf, a round of soft cheese, and a new flask of small ale, promising to return later, as always, with Susanna's supper. But Susanna clung to her, and Edith was forced to prise her hands away.

'I must go, dearie,' she said. 'I got my ale-house to run.'

Susanna kept hold of Edith's hand, not bearing to let her go, but at length she let her withdraw her hand and leave.

As soon as Edith had gone, Susanna remembered how thirsty she'd been before she came. She went over to the shelf and picked up the new flask. Unstoppering it, she put it to her lips. The liquid ran down her throat, so cool and reviving she had to stop herself emptying the flask – she had to make it last till Edith returned with more. Feeling a little better, she put down the flask and picked up the loaf, putting it to her nose and breathing in its sweet, yeasty aroma. It smelled delicious. At Sir Richard's bidding, Edith always brought her the best bread, a small luxury to lighten her daily gloom. She broke off a small chunk and bit into the crust, then scraped the soft pale dough into her mouth with her teeth. She closed her eyes – her only pleasure now a hunk of bread...

She sat down again on the bed – the only place she had to rest – and thought of what Edith had said. Had she been right – could Eleanor possibly find a way to free her? Susanna couldn't imagine how. For what she'd told the coroner surely led him to believe that, whatever happened in the mill, she was responsible for Henry's death? What could change that?

She didn't believe she'd killed her husband, yet she couldn't remember clearly now what had happened in the mill – so how could she be sure? Every time she tried to bring the events of that day to mind, a veil seemed to fall.

The coroner didn't believe her when she said it was an accident that Henry fell. But was he right to disbelieve her? Henry did fall backwards, but why did she push him? It was that she couldn't quite remember.

As she tried to bring the scene to mind, while one moment it was there, somehow it always faded, just as dreams grow dim as soon as you awake. The one image that did keep coming to her mind was of Henry lying on the mill floor, his head bleeding, and her crouching down beside him, saying she was sorry…

But was Henry still alive then, as she had thought, or was he dead? Now, she truly didn't know.

# 17

It was three weeks since Emma and Eleanor first found the derelict cottage with signs of someone living there. They'd agreed to keep an occasional watch on the place, so each time Emma walked past on her way up to Riverdown, or back down again, she cast her eyes towards it, just in case she saw signs of movement. But she never did, and neither did Elly.

Many times, Emma had walked down to the cottage after supper, pretending – if anyone asked – to be enjoying the lighter, warm spring evenings. She hid for a while behind a crumbling barn a short distance from the cottage, waiting to see if Tom came or went, but she never saw him. Yet when she went and looked inside the cottage, she found, just as she had before, a ragged blanket on the pallet, the ashes and cooking pot still warm and, the last time she went, a few scraps of bread. But no boy.

It was disappointing. But she'd keep on trying.

At supper yestereve, Bea'd gulped down her food and flounced off through the door, without a backward glance, saying she was going to see her friends. Emma bit her lip. Bea was acting very strange these days. She'd gone off like this each evening for a few days now. She stared at the closed door a moment. Perhaps the girl did just want a bit of fun after a day tending to her peevish baby brother?

Emma took her cloak from the hook by the door. 'Can you look after Ami and Bart a while?' she said to Ralph. 'I'm going down the road—'

Ralph's forehead puckered. 'You shouldn't go no more, Em. Taking an evening stroll in Meonvale just ain't something folk do, 'less they're heading for the ale-house, or up to mischief of some sort.' His frown changed to a grin.

'I know,' she said. 'But one last time...'

He shrugged, and she threw her cloak over her shoulders and stepped out onto the dusty road.

Quite apart from the suspicion her "stroll" might arouse if her neighbours saw her, Emma now knew her efforts were probably a waste of time. Likely Tom was watching out for *her*, and keeping well out of her way. Maybe this *should* be the last time, though she didn't want to give up on finding him…

As always, she hid a while behind the barn before clambering over the junk in the yard to reach the cottage door. She approached quietly, then waited by the door jamb, listening for sounds coming from inside. When she heard none, she heaved open the swollen door and stood still for a few moments, letting her eyes accustom to the dark. But, once she could see, a lump came to her throat. For the ragged blanket was no longer on the pallet and, when she went over to the hearth and leaned down to touch the pot, it was cold, as were the ashes underneath. Days' long cold. Tom had gone.

One evening, after Ralph had returned from working in the fields, he took a stool outside the cottage door, as he often did. This time, Emma joined him.

'I've got summat to ask you,' she said, pushing her hand through the gap between his body and his arm, and leaning her head upon his shoulder.

'So what d'you want now, wife?'

'You know you said I shouldn't go looking for Tom Miller no more? But Elly and me still think we ought to find him. He's only eleven, Ralph – we can't just leave him out there on his own.'

'I'll not gainsay it. But what d'you want me to do?'

'Look for him? Say you've been asked to check on all Meonvale's derelict buildings? It's not unlikely bailiff'd ask you to, seeing you're chief cottar.'

Ralph hooted. 'I'm not *chief* cottar, Em. Whatever gave you that idea? And why'd you imagine Master Wragge'd want a check on *cottar* hovels?'

'Ain't there been talk of repairing some of them?' she said, tilting her head.

'But I *haven't* been asked to report on them.'

Emma pouted. Ralph was ever a stickler for the truth.

But, in the end, he agreed. When he returned the second evening, he'd a broad grin on his face. He sat down with a pot of her good ale, saying he'd got news. He took several gulps of ale and nibbled on a crust of bread, while she sat across from him drumming her fingers on the table. She knew very well he was teasing her.

'Well?' she said, grabbing the crust from his hands.

He pursed his lips. 'Good news, I think, and not-so-good…'

'For Jesu' sake, Ralph, *tell* me.'

'I found signs of *three* people living in the most isolated, most decrepit, barn in Meonvale. Down near the river, at the far end of one the longest of the abandoned crofts.'

'*Three?*' Emma threw up her hands. 'Luke and Arthur too?'

'Mebbe. Or could be a group of vagrants…' He rubbed at his close-trimmed beard. 'Anyway, three pallets were laid close together, but there were no blankets so I s'pose, whoever they were, they'd moved on again. But it looked like they'd been getting food.'

'*Food?*'

'Well, I found a few crumbs of bread an' a scrap of cheese, fallen into the rotten rushes.'

'I've heard a few folk saying lately they were missing food again. Like last autumn.' She patted Ralph's leg. 'You remember how I thought then someone'd stolen some of our cheese and bread?'

Ralph nodded. 'Others said the same. But then the thefts just stopped.'

'I'd forgot all about it.'

'And now it's started up again?'

'But not from us,' said Emma.

Ralph scratched his ear. 'Anyway, if it's the boys, they can't be stealing it themselves, 'cause no one ever sees them.'

'So mebbe someone's taking it *to* them—' And, as she said it, Emma's hands flew to her face, as she remembered the expression on Bea's face all those months ago when she'd asked her about the missing cheese. And then the strange way she'd been behaving lately.

Ralph stared at her, and gently took her hands away from her face. 'Em?'

Emma bowed her head. 'Oh, Ralph,' she said in a whisper, 'I think it might be Bea.'

After supper, Emma refused to let Bea go out. At first, Bea tried to push past her, out through the door to the road, but Emma caught her arm and pulled her back into the room.

'Pa and me've got summat to talk to you about, Bea.'

The girl rolled her eyes, but her face paled too and, wrenching herself from Emma's grip, she folded her arms across her chest. Ralph went over and put his arm around her, but she jerked away from him too, and Ralph arched his eyebrows at his wife.

'Bea, look at me,' she said, taking the girl's chin gently in her hand. Bea didn't resist and lifted her eyes towards her mother. 'Pa and me just want to ask what you know about Tom Miller.'

'What's to know? He's run away, ain't he?'

'Why "run away"?' said Ralph.

She shrugged. 'He's not round here no more.'

'But what makes you think he's not just lost, or hurt – or even dead?'

Bea stayed silent, turning her face away.

Emma gritted her teeth, then glanced at Ralph, who nodded. 'Bea, look at me,' she said again, but the girl didn't look around. 'Pa's found someone's been living in one of the old barns.' Bea didn't move. 'We think it might be Tom...' Bea twitched a little, and Emma glanced at Ralph again. 'Don't you think he must be frightened being all alone?'

At that, Bea turned and her eyes were gleaming. 'He's *not* alone,' she cried, 'he's with Lu—' But then she burst into tears, and shook her head. 'No, no, I didn't mean— You mustn't— They'll get hanged for—' She trailed off, wet sobs overwhelming her.

Ralph put his arm around her and, this time, she didn't resist as he pulled her close and stroked her hair. 'Hush, Bea, love,' he said. 'We're not looking for Luke.' She sniffed. 'We just want to find Tom, make sure he's all right.'

'So they're still in the village?' asked Emma but, when Bea didn't answer, she glared at Ralph in frustration.

'Please tell us, Bea,' he said.

'Can't,' she whispered between the sobs. 'I promised.'

'But you've seen them, Bea? You've been to where they're hiding?'

She gave the barest of nods.

'And why did you go there?'

'Took food,' she said at last.

'Food you stole from folk in Meonbridge?'

Bea gave a single nod. She looked away again but at length turned back to her parents. Her eyes were wide. 'I'll not break my promise, but I'll tell you *why* Tom's hiding.'

Next morning Emma ran almost all the way up to Riverdown and, by the time she reached Eleanor and Will, she was panting. She wiped her shawl across her glowing cheeks.

Eleanor's brow wrinkled. 'Is something wrong?'

Emma shook her head, and waggled her hand. 'Shouldn't've run so fast.'

'Why did you?'

'Got news.' She then stared hard at Will.

'Can see I'm not wanted,' he said, grinning, and, whistling to Meg and the puppy, strode away towards the pasture, the two dogs scampering beside him.

'What is it?' asked Eleanor.

Emma grinned. 'Tom.'

Eleanor's eyes lit up. 'You've found him?'

'Not exactly. But Ralph found summat in a falling down old barn. Then, later, Bea said she knew Tom were hiding.' Emma turned her face away from Eleanor, ashamed at the half-truth.

'How did she know?'

'Oh, you know how children like playing in old buildings… Anyway, one day she found Tom.' Emma was certain she was blushing, though Eleanor didn't seem to notice.

'Did he tell her why he'd run away?'

'That's what I wanted to tell you. It's what we thought. He did go to see his Pa that day, and must've seen him *after* Susy left.'

'And did he talk to Henry?'

'Didn't get a chance. Soon as Henry saw him, he roared at him to leave. Then, Tom said, he flew at him and struck him round the head, hurting his ear and making him all dizzy—'

Eleanor's hand flew to her mouth. '*Henry* struck his son?'

'That's what Tom told Bea. She said his ear were all red and swollen, so I s'pose it must be true.'

'Poor boy. Henry had never hit him before, had he?'

Emma shook her head. 'He's always been so gentle. Anyway, Tom said he were so scared he ran off. Later he overheard folk in the village saying his Pa were dead, and Tom were *then* so terrified he might've somehow killed him, he hid.'

'Did Bea tell him Susy's in prison?'

'She mightn't have thought of it.'

Eleanor went quiet for a while, then took Emma's hands. 'If Henry did hit little Tom, our idea makes sense that he was also violent towards Susy. I've always thought it unlikely Susy could push Henry over – and why would she? – *unless* he somehow attacked her. I can't imagine her having the *strength* – Henry was a big man – unless she was so agitated or afraid she couldn't stop herself.'

'What you thinking?'

'That Henry *did* strike out at her, and she was trying to stop him doing it again. Don't you think you'd somehow get the strength you needed to defend yourself in such a situation?'

Emma shook her head. She'd never had to fight off a man. Her own Pa had been strict but never beat his children, and her beloved Bart had been a wastrel and a fool at times, but the gentlest of husbands. As was Ralph.

'Because I remember,' continued Eleanor, 'when Gilbert Fletcher tried to kill me. I found strength I didn't know I had to fight him off, although of course in the end Walter rescued me, thank Jesu.' Emma noticed a hint of sadness in her eyes.

'Mebbe you're right,' said Emma. 'It'd make sense too, from what Ralph's said.' Eleanor cocked her head. 'He said Henry'd changed. Become gloomy and downhearted, grumbling all the time 'bout Susy nagging. And when he said in the ale-house how it were right for a man to *punish* his wife for nagging, all the men who heard him said they often gave their wives a slap if they talked too much.'

'But Henry wouldn't do that—'

'Not the Henry we *used* to know. Not my Ralph, neither.'

'So does Ralph know what changed him?'

Emma shook her head. 'It's hard to understand.'

'Do you know, Emma, what folk say about the humours? About our bodies needing to be in balance?'

Emma shrugged. 'I'd heard Simon thought Henry had too much phlegm, whatever that is, an' it were what were making him cough so bad. But then Ralph's said he's heard melancholy comes from too much black bile.' She found it all rather confusing. 'Is that what you mean?'

'I think so, though, of course, I don't really know. Perhaps the excess of phlegm was one aspect of his imbalance, but it was the black bile that changed the normally good-natured, *sanguine* Harry into the melancholic Henry?'

'Either that, or the Devil was whispering in his ear.'

Eleanor raised her eyebrows, but continued. 'And perhaps his melancholy made him so downhearted that everything annoyed him, even when Susy was trying to help? Does that make sense?'

'I s'pose so. An' it might mean what happened in the mill really weren't Susy's fault, but his.'

# 18

It was extraordinary how well the manor gardens had recovered since the Mortality. No one, not even Margaret, had any interest in gardening when most folk thought the world was coming to an end, and afterwards, Sir Richard had refused to let any of the surviving tenants spend time gardening when there was so much fieldwork to do. And although Margaret understood his reasoning, it upset her to see her splendid gardens fall into such decline. The beds of herbs were overrun with weeds and, although the sages, thymes and lavenders were a blaze of blue and purple, the plants were so tangled and unkempt that she had feared she could never bring them back to health. The roses were same: the once-neat bushes, though full of flower and heady scents, had grown into wild thorny thickets. The shape of the little hedges that divided the beds had been sore in need of clipping, and the narrow paths criss-crossing the gardens were knee deep in coarse grass.

But, eventually, the crisis eased and Margaret had been able to employ the services of a few men to help bring her precious gardens back to life.

Eleanor had been hurrying across the bailey when Sir Richard appeared at the main door of the house, running down the steps. He raised his hand in greeting.

'Ah, Mistress Titherige,' he called. 'Good that you've come promptly.' One of his squires came forward with his horse. 'As you see, I am expected elsewhere.'

'Why did you want to see me, Sir Richard?'

'Thought you would want to know that I have learned the king's court comes to Winchester in August.' He raised an eyebrow. 'Mistress Miller is fortunate it is so soon. It might have been *years* before they came down here again…'

Eleanor felt suddenly light-headed. So it had come at last. 'That *is* good news, Sir Richard, yet I cannot but feel nervous of the outcome.'

'I agree.' He took the reins from the squire and lifted his left foot into the stirrup. 'We must make a plan, Mistress Titherige.'

'A plan?'

'To ensure Mistress Miller's freedom.'

Eleanor gave a nervous laugh. 'Yes, of course.' She was surprised at his lordship's seeming eagerness to free Susanna. 'Indeed, I do have news that may help her case.'

He swung up into the saddle, and peered down upon her. 'What news?'

'Young Tom—'

'Is found?'

'Not yet, your lordship, but maybe soon. But it seems that *he* may have been the last person to see his father alive. If we can find the boy, he could at least confirm that Henry was still living after Susanna left him.'

Sir Richard knit his brow. '"We"?'

'Ralph and Emma are helping me,' she said, and Sir Richard stroked his beard.

'But might not the boy himself then be in trouble?' he said.

Eleanor gasped. In truth, she had not thought of that. 'But he's only a child – surely no one would think he could hurt, let alone kill, a man like Henry?'

'I agree it seems unlikely.'

The horse began to step and prance, anxious perhaps to be on its way. Sir Richard leaned forward and patted its neck. 'I must go. But we must talk further, Mistress Titherige. Come back this evening, if you will. I am sure Margaret can stretch our small supper to feed three.' He winked, and Eleanor laughed at the silliness of his jest.

After a day up on Riverdown, Eleanor was always hungry. Even if she returned home at Sext for dinner, as she often did, her appetite was again raging by the end of the afternoon. So, she was disappointed to discover that Sir Richard had not been jesting. Supper at Meonbridge manor was far more meagre than she had expected. Yet, what little was offered was of the highest quality: soft white wheaten bread, a little fresh butter and a delicious sheep's cheese, both made in the manor dairy, and a bowl of cherries picked from the orchard – and a large flagon of rich Gascony wine.

Sir Richard must have told his wife that Eleanor had news of Tom, for Margaret was eager to hear what she had to say. Yet, the model of good manners, her ladyship waited patiently for her guest to sate her hunger, nibbling idly on a piece of the richly piquant cheese and sipping delicately at her wine. Eleanor, on the other hand, was almost matching Sir Richard in her enthusiasm for the food, helping herself to bread and cheese until the platter was nearly empty, and accepting every offer to refill her goblet.

But, at length, Eleanor felt satisfied and gave Margaret a rueful grin. 'I am so sorry for keeping you waiting, your ladyship.'

'It is hungry work, perhaps, nurturing sheep?'

'It is. Though I do enjoy it withal.'

Margaret tilted her head. 'Despite the loss of your shepherd?'

Eleanor blushed a little. 'I have another. Will is very diligent and attentive.'

'I am sure he is, although not quite as experienced or expert as Walter?' Margaret's eyebrows lifted, and a sly simper played upon her lips.

Eleanor was certain that her ladyship was teasing her, and lifted her napkin to her face to hide the mounting pinkness on her cheeks.

At that moment, Sir Richard also finished eating and, draining his goblet in a single gulp, then refilled it. His eyes twinkled as he leaned forward. 'Well now, Mistress Titherige, I think we should keep her ladyship in suspense no longer.'

Margaret tutted at her husband's comment, while Eleanor lowered her napkin and gave her an apologetic smile. 'Yes,' she said, 'I must tell you what I have learned.'

She related what Beatrix had told her mother, that Henry had hit Tom, damaging his ear, and frightening him so much that the boy ran away. 'We know Tom has been hiding in a derelict barn in Meonvale—'

'So why don't you go and get him?' said Sir Richard, waving his goblet in the air.

'Because he is no longer there. Perhaps he discovered we were looking for him, and was so frightened to be found that he ran off somewhere else.'

'Does the boy know his father is dead?' said Margaret.

'It seems so. Little Beatrix said he was so scared he might have killed him that he decided to stay hidden—'

Sir Richard frowned. 'Why would he think he had killed his father?'

'Bea didn't say. But I suppose he might simply be confused about what happened?'

'He is still only a child,' said Margaret. 'If he heard the news of his father's death soon after he last saw him, he might well suffer a sudden aberration of understanding. Do you not think so, Richard?'

He shrugged. 'You may be right, my dear. We need to ask him.' He poured himself more wine. 'We need to find him, Mistress Titherige. I will send out a search party.'

Eleanor agreed that Tom must be found and brought home, but was uneasy at the prospect of Sir Richard's henchmen blundering about the manor trying to track him down. She thought it likely that Tom would take fright again and disappear completely.

'Please, your lordship, before you do that, why not let Ralph, Emma and myself try to find the boy? Emma thinks her daughter will, in due course, lead us to him and we don't want to frighten him unduly.'

'I agree,' said Margaret. 'Poor child – he must be terrified out there on his own.'

'But how long might it take?' said Sir Richard. 'We only have two months before we must make our case.'

Margaret took in a sudden breath. 'You are proposing to *make a case?*' she said. 'Am I to understand, husband, that you plan to *speak* for Mistress Miller before the court?'

Sir Richard harrumphed. 'The evidence the coroner has against her is flimsy, Margaret. Despite his conclusions, and his insistence on comparing Mistress Miller's case to that of Mistress Wragge, I see no similarity. Mistress Wragge was clearly guilty of what she was accused, despite the verdict of the court.' At this, Margaret rolled her eyes at Eleanor, who could not help but grin. 'Whereas,' continued his lordship blithely, 'it is as likely as not that Mistress Miller did *not* kill her husband.' He gulped some wine. 'And I intend to prove it.'

'Thank you, Sir Richard,' said Eleanor. 'And something else might help.' She told him what Emma had said about the changes in Henry's humour and, to her surprise, Sir Richard agreed.

'Master Miller had indeed become most melancholy of late,' he said, 'in great contrast to the merry fellow we used to know.'

'In truth, I hardly saw him, as Hawisa always went to the mill, but she said he was always gloomy and downhearted. Yet, you are right, Sir Richard, it is not long past that he always made folk laugh.'

'But what relevance has this, Mistress Titherige?'

'Just that the coroner deduced that Susanna attacked Henry, whereas it seems to me more likely that *he* attacked *her*. I can't believe Susanna would have struck Henry or pushed him over without provocation.'

'Yet Mistress Miller did say that she pushed him,' said Margaret, 'as if there *were* no provocation.'

'But I have thought that perhaps she somehow cast it from her mind, because she could not – could not bear to – *believe* that he had struck her? Is that possible, do you think?'

'I have never heard of such a notion, but I suppose it might be so.' Margaret seemed to seek agreement from her husband, but he simply shrugged.

'And there is another thing, Sir Richard. I've always wondered if the coroner *encouraged* Henry's drinking companions to say Susanna was a constant nag, to help *his* case that Susanna – like Mistress Wragge – was likely to be violent towards her husband.'

'Are you suggesting that those men's evidence was falsely given?'

'Not exactly. But Ralph and Emma believe that Henry had somehow become an *advocate* of wife chastisement – which he'd certainly not been before.'

Sir Richard got up and paced the floor a little.

'I wonder, your lordship,' continued Eleanor, 'if you should perhaps question some of those men again? Not just those who bragged of slapping their wives, but also Henry's more peaceable friends, like Nick Cook and Jack?'

'A splendid idea,' said Margaret, and Sir Richard wagged his head.

Eleanor bowed her gratitude to Margaret. 'For my suspicion is that Henry, though he had never struck his wife before, just boiled over during the tussle and lashed out at her. You remember she had a wound on her face?' Both de Bohuns nodded. 'She said she unbalanced, and fell against a beam. But perhaps it was actually a blow from Henry that made her fall? Then, when she pushed him away, to defend herself, by chance he tripped.'

'The mill certainly has many hazards underfoot,' said Sir Richard.

'And if Henry had changed from the gentle man he used to be to a more ill-tempered one – as, according to Ralph Ward, he seemed to have done – then his striking out at, first, his wife and, then, his little boy would not be a surprise.'

'Perhaps, dear Eleanor,' said Margaret, 'you should try to get Susanna to recall the tussle once again, but in more detail, to see if she can remember more clearly what truly happened.'

'That is what I want to do. Will you come with me again, your lordship?'

Eleanor accepted Sir Richard's hand to help her alight from her horse, and she stepped down on to the dusty road, just outside the great oak door that gave onto the sheriff's gaol. They had left Meonbridge at first light, hoping to arrive in Winchester well before the dry heat of these June days had risen to make travelling unbearable.

Nonetheless, the journey had been mostly disagreeable. With the scarcity of rain since March, the roads' winter slough had become hard-baked – and no less treacherous than slippery mud to horses' hooves. Guiding the horses between the stone-hard fissures demanded all the riders' skill and patience, and the twelve miles seemed twice or thrice the distance. And Winchester's roads were scarcely any better than those out in the country. Here any fissures were shallow ones, for the quaggy winter mud must have been scraped smooth, the hills and valleys evened out. But the more level surface was still stone hard and, now she was standing upon it, Eleanor saw how vigorously the dust rose into the air, swirling giddily about and casting smuts upon her gown and grit into her eyes. The roads and paths of Meonbridge of course were dusty too. But, here in the city, perhaps it was the greater passage of carts and animals and people that threw up a cloud so thick, at times it almost obscured the sun?

Eleanor pulled her hood up over her head and drew the sides together to protect her eyes and nose, while clamping her lips tight shut. Sir Richard grimaced at the unpleasantness of the air and, taking Eleanor's elbow, hurried her to the gaol door and hammered on it. It was soon opened and the two visitors stepped inside, relieved to be out of the choking dust, yet Eleanor already sensed how much the chill behind these walls contrasted with the warmth of the streets outside.

In Susanna's cell, it felt not only cold but dank, and Eleanor wished she had brought another blanket or a thicker cloak, but with so many weeks of warm dry weather, she had not thought of it. She regretted her lack of foresight the moment she saw Susanna. She and Sir Richard exchanged glances of dismay, so much changed was she since their last visit.

If she had not thought of blankets or warm cloaks, Eleanor had at least gone to the mill cottage to fetch a change of clothes. Yet, when she saw how very thin Susanna had become, she realised that the kirtle she had brought would hang on Susanna's body like a shroud.

Sir Richard cleared his throat. 'Mistress Miller, may I ask, is Edith Wyteby serving you well enough?'

When Susanna looked up at him, her eyes were dry and distant, but she gave him a thin smile. 'Thank you, sir. Edith attends me well.'

'Yet the rations she provides are insufficient?'

But Susanna shook her head. 'No, no, sir,' she said, her voice almost a whisper, 'don't blame her for my condition. Dear Edith tries her best to tempt me with good bread and tasty cheese, and even a little roasted meat. But my appetite is poor…'

Her voice drifted into silence, and she slumped back down onto the bed, her breathing shallow. Then she pointed to the shelf on the other wall, and Sir Richard went over to inspect what lay there: most of a good white loaf, a whole small cheese, and a leather flask. He picked up the flask and shook it – there came no sound from it. But the food, as he indicated to Eleanor, was largely untouched.

Eleanor felt a tightness in her chest. 'But, Susy, you *must* eat. You must keep up your strength, both for the trial, and for your children.' She sat down next to her and, taking her hand, squeezed it, noticing how light and frail it was, almost like a child's.

Susanna bobbed her head but did not raise her eyes. 'I've no strength, Elly dear,' she said, in scarcely more than a murmur. 'An' I doubt I'll ever see my little ones again.'

Eleanor's eyes were damp as she sought Sir Richard's face. How had Susanna declined so fast? When she last saw her, she was of course distressed but in seemingly fair health. Yet that was, Eleanor realised with horror, five weeks past. Had she truly neglected her friend for so very long?

Sir Richard nodded, in what Eleanor took to be understanding of her thoughts. He coughed again. 'Do not even think that, Mistress Miller. You *will* see them again, and soon.' Susanna lifted her face to his, but her eyes were dull. 'Have you received news of the king's court?'

Susanna shook her head.

'They have not told you when the trial will be?' said Eleanor.

Susanna's face seemed to crumple, so perhaps, Eleanor thought, she *had* been told but had put it from her mind. She gave Sir Richard the slightest of nods, and he acknowledged her unspoken request.

'We have heard,' he said, 'that the king's judges will come to Winchester in August.' Susanna gasped at that, making Eleanor deduce that the information was indeed quite new to her.

She squeezed her hand again but lightly. 'So we must prepare ourselves. Sir Richard is proposing to plead your case.'

'But I've no case, Elly. That coroner were quite certain of my guilt...'

Eleanor let go of Susanna's hand and grasped her bony shoulders, pulling her gently round to face her. 'But Sir Richard and I are quite certain of your *innocence*, Susy, and we intend to prove it to the court.'

Susanna blinked. 'How?'

'I want you to try and remember *exactly* what happened in the mill.'

Her face crumpled again. 'But I've already—'

Eleanor gave her a little shake. 'I know, Susy, but I want you to try again. I think what happened may have been a little different from what you told the coroner, and what you told us when we were last here.'

'I can't remember...' Susanna lifted her eyes and stared at Eleanor. 'I keep thinking Harry must've been dead when I left the mill. It were only in my *imagining* he were alive.'

'You mustn't think that, Susy. Harry *wasn't* dead, I know he wasn't. I want you to picture in your head exactly what happened, very slowly, step by step. I will help you.'

Susanna's shoulders slumped, but Eleanor thought she also saw a faint gleam in her eyes.

'Start right from the beginning, when you first arrived at the mill.'

Susanna stood up and wiped her fingers across her eyes. Then, her words slow and hesitating, she described how she approached the outer staircase and peered in through the downstairs door to see the Collyere brothers idling. She'd thought of going in to upbraid them but, knowing Harry wouldn't want her to, just went on up the steps. Harry was at the far side of the loft, but she didn't know how to attract his attention. Looking about her, she noticed – for the first time, she thought – the dreadful dustiness of the air, and realised it must be making Henry's cough worse. And Simon had already advised him to rest. So, even though she knew he'd not welcome her advice, somehow she was set on giving it.

'How did Henry greet you when you first arrived?' said Eleanor.

'He smiled at me and thanked me for his dinner.' She bit her lip. 'I should've left at once – I'd intended to. But I were somehow driven to speak my mind, and I said yet again how fearful I was for his health, and how he had to find another journeyman, so he could work a little less. But he were vexed with me for saying it and ordered me to go.'

'But you didn't go?' Susanna slowly shook her head. 'So what did you do?'

Her brow knit but she said nothing. Eleanor thought maybe she was trying to bring the events to mind.

'Susy?'

At that moment, a shaft of sunlight pierced the narrow window. Eleanor looked up and saw the dustiness of the air hanging in the beam. Susanna tilted her head up too, and then cried out.

'Harry *hit* me!' She shook her head, this time, it seemed, as if she was trying to dislodge the memory. Her eyes were staring. 'He *struck* me, Elly, across my face, so hard it sent me reeling.'

Eleanor took in a sudden breath, and exchanged a brief smile of satisfaction with Sir Richard. 'You've not said that before, Susy.'

'I must've forgot it—' She put her fingers to her brow. 'Harry'd never, never, struck me before.'

'And did you fall over?'

'Aye, I landed heavily against a joist. It hurt my arm.' She gave the slightest of grins. 'Harry's dinner was on the joist, and my elbow knocked it down into the machinery.'

Eleanor caught Sir Richard's eye. 'It might still be there.'

He nodded. 'We'll investigate when we get back.'

But Susanna was already continuing her story. 'Then Harry hauled me to my feet and raised his arm, like he were going to hit me again—but—but I pushed him—aye, I pushed at him with all my strength to stop him.' Her eyes were darting wildly about the room, and she spun around, her hands up to her face, then slumped down onto the bed. She stared at Eleanor. 'I do remember now,' she said, her voice a whisper.

Then she spelt out the rest, quite clearly, as if a veil had been taken from her eyes. And she concluded that Henry was most certainly alive when she left the mill. 'He'd quite a deep cut on his head where he'd banged it, and it were bleeding, but he was on his feet, demanding that I leave.' She let out a small sob. 'But the Harry I left there were not the man I'd known.'

Moments after Susanna finished retelling her story, a rap on the cell door announced Edith's arrival, come with Susanna's breakfast and dinner. After an exchange of greetings, Sir Richard asked to see what Edith had brought. If the landlady felt aggrieved she was being accused of something, she hid it well enough, uncovering her basket and taking out what it contained. Susanna had been right – Edith was attending well to her needs, and it was not her fault if her charge refused to eat what she had provided. She left the new provisions and put the old into her basket.

Then, bidding Susanna farewell, with a promise to return in the evening, she turned to leave.

'I will walk with you to the street, Mistress Wyteby,' said Sir Richard, and the woman bobbed a curtsey and allowed him to let her pass first out of the cell.

Eleanor sat down again by Susanna's side and took both her hands. 'I'm so glad you remembered what truly happened, Susy. I knew you could not possibly have killed Henry. And I've heard from others how changed a man he had become.' Susanna raised her eyes. 'The man who struck you was not the man you married. Poor Henry was ill, and it was surely, at least in part, what changed him from the cheerful man into the gloomy.'

'D'you truly believe that, Elly?'

Eleanor squeezed her hands. 'I do.'

They sat quietly for several moments, then Eleanor stood up and, fetching a piece of bread and a little cheese, urged Susanna to eat. Susanna pressed her lips together a moment, but then took the food and nibbled at it. Eleanor insisted she keep nibbling until it was all gone, and at length Susanna allowed a small smile.

'Thank you, Elly,' she said then, standing up and shuffling the two steps to the shelf, she picked up the flask and sipped some of Edith's good ale. Then she returned to the bed. 'I've been thinking, Elly, about Tom. How is he?'

Eleanor made a sudden business of bending down and searching for something in her bag, chiding herself for not thinking how she would answer Susanna's inevitable question.

When she sat up again, she had decided to tell her only half the truth. 'He would not stay with Isabel, but wanted to look after himself.'

Susanna gave a little nod. 'That's just like him.'

'He's a brave lad,' said Eleanor. She felt ashamed, lying to Susanna, but told herself she did it for the best of reasons. She would atone for it on Sunday.

But if she would not tell Susanna that Tom was missing, she could at least tell her he was probably the last person to see Henry alive, and not her. Although it might upset her even more to learn that Henry had struck his beloved son. Eleanor argued silently with herself for several moments, but then Sir Richard returned and she was distracted. In the end, she said nothing and, later, when they were travelling back to Meonbridge, she found herself relieved that she had kept quiet, just in case Tom was never found.

The next morning, the constable knocked early on Eleanor's door. Hawisa, in her customary ill humour, muttered curses as she lumbered to the door and threw it open.

'Constable,' she shouted across the hall to Eleanor, who was picking at her unappetising breakfast and wondering whether she should investigate alone Susanna's claim about Henry's dinner falling into the machinery. Tutting yet again at Hawisa's lack of courtesy, Eleanor hurried to the door.

She glared at her servant. 'Invite the constable inside, Hawisa,' she said, her tone scolding. But Hawisa neither seemed to notice her mistress's displeasure nor obeyed her bidding, but waddled back into the hall and pretended to clear the table.

'Do come in, master constable, and tell me of your business,' said Eleanor, and he stepped inside, a bemused grin on his lips.

'His lordship bade me come,' said Geoffrey. 'He wants you and me to go with him to the mill.'

'Ah, yes, I was only just now thinking of it. We need to check something Susanna told us yesterday.'

'He said he'd meet us there.'

Eleanor threw her light summer cloak around her shoulders and followed the constable along the track back towards the village.

Sir Richard was waiting for them on the path leading down to the mill. He was pacing back and forth, although he greeted Eleanor with a beaming smile.

'I'm sorry to have kept you waiting,' she said.

'You have not, my dear. But I would be glad withal to do this quickly.'

'Does the miller know we are coming?'

Sir Richard had managed to find a journeyman to take on the mill, but he was, it seemed, merely on loan from a large mill in Winchester, and would stay only a few months in Meonbridge, until a permanent replacement for Henry could be found.

Sir Richard's eyes twinkled. 'I thought a *surprise* visit might serve a secondary purpose. As well as enabling us to confirm Susanna's story, I can see how well young Master Langelee is doing his job.' He chuckled as they continued down the path and reached the bottom of the stairs to the loft.

As they approached, Eleanor heard the sound of raucous laughter coming from the ground floor room, and touching Sir Richard's arm, she drew his attention to the noise. Frowning, he crept forward and peered in through the open door. Eleanor stepped forward too, just as Sir Richard roared the names of the Collyere brothers, and the unhappy youths emerged blinking into the sunlight.

'Well?' said Sir Richard, his face twitching. 'What have you to say?'

The young men hung their heads.

'You're just as idle now as when Henry Miller was your master,' growled Sir Richard. 'They weren't working, master constable, but simply taking their leisure at my expense.'

'Always been lazy louts, these Collyeres,' said Geoffrey. 'In my opinion, my lord, their idleness contributed to poor Henry's demise.'

At that, Fulke shook his fist at Geoffrey. 'Oi, that ain't right. We never killed him.'

Geoffrey's eyebrows lifted a little. 'I never said you did. But if you'd done your share o' the work instead of taking your leisure, as his lordship puts it, Henry might've better kept his head above water.'

Eleanor bit her lip. Fulke and Warin were undoubtedly lazy, and perhaps not as grateful as they should be to Sir Richard for letting them stay in Meonbridge. But it was hardly fair to blame them for the drastic change in Henry's humour, or for his stubborn refusal to seek out another journeyman, though perhaps it was true enough that, if they had made a proper effort to do what they were paid to do, Henry might have managed better.

Sir Richard was stroking his beard. 'I am inclined to agree with the constable—' The two young men's faces crumpled. 'I should throw you out of here and put you back to midden clearing.'

Their faces now were going red, and Fulke was rubbing the back of his grimy neck, while his brother, Warin, bounced from foot to foot. It was clear his lordship was well aware of their agitation and revelled in his ability to taunt them. But surely he would not force them out, for the young miller could never manage entirely on his own?

Sir Richard stroked his beard some more, and looked them up and down, shaking his head. They were quaking now more bodily, but at length he let a smirk play upon his lips.

'Ha!' he cried. 'Fortune smiles upon you, Fulke Collyere, and your unworthy brother. For I cannot let down young Master Langelee, and so must keep you on, despite my reservations. Indeed, I *command* that you stay, that you work a *full* day every day, and I will be demanding a report from your master on your betterment – or otherwise.'

His lordship's eyes were twinkling again. Some might have thought his treatment of the Collyeres overweening, but Eleanor was certain it was mischief more than malice. For, since the Mortality and the dissent that followed it, Sir Richard had – with Margaret's guidance, Eleanor thought – come to regard his tenants almost with respect, perhaps recognising that, without their cooperation, his manor could not function. Some might have thought the Collyere brothers, being outsiders, as well as rather sluggish workers, did not deserve respect, but perhaps his lordship thought it worth his while to make harder-working tenants of them if he could.

Fulke and Warin slunk back to their work and the sound of vigorous activity came forth shortly from the ground floor room. Sir Richard raised his eyebrows at Eleanor and Geoffrey, then pointed to the steps.

Eleanor had never been upstairs in the mill house before – customers were always served downstairs. In the loft, she was struck by the noise of the water rushing beyond the walls, coupled with the constant clatter and grind of the great toothed wheels, and the grating of the millstones, one against the other. She saw too what Susanna had noticed: the air was full of flying debris, motes of grain floating in the beams of sunlight slanting through the loft's high window, and great clouds of dust rising from the turning stones.

Not venturing much beyond the entrance, Sir Richard hailed Master Langelee, who was working, shirtless and glistening with sweat, just beyond the machinery. He had to call several times before the miller heard him, but then he made his way carefully across the floor, stepping over joists and skirting jutting objects. He bowed his head briefly to Sir Richard, then again to Eleanor and Geoffrey, who were standing a few paces behind his lordship.

Sir Richard – Eleanor presumed but could not hear – told the miller why they had come, and the young man nodded. But Sir Richard then came back to her.

'He suggests you do not come any closer, my dear. Because of the danger of your skirts becoming caught in the machinery.'

He and the constable went forward, towards where Susanna had said the dinner bundle had fallen off the joist. Geoffrey knelt down and pushing his arm down behind the joist, he was able to reach the cloth and pull it up. He held it up to show Eleanor, and she nodded back.

Sir Richard was meanwhile inspecting the timbers above the place where the bundle must have begun its fall. A few moments later, he pointed, and Geoffrey bent down, and the two men nodded to each other. Eleanor was eager to know what they had discovered, but they then moved closer to where the miller was working, and seemed to be searching the machinery for something.

When at last they returned to her, Sir Richard was grinning. 'In the first instance we found a daub of blood upon the timber, which might accord with what Mistress Miller said about her falling and hitting her face. Then, on the machinery, another, much larger, smear that might be where Henry received the wound upon his head.'

'So Susanna's story does seem right.'

'Or does at least make sense.'

When they left the mill, the constable was still carrying the bundle.

'Are you keeping that?' said Eleanor.

Geoffrey nodded. 'His lordship thinks it'll help prove the truth of Mistress Miller's story.'

Eleanor noticed a ragged hole in one corner of the linen. She pointed. 'But is there anything left inside it?'

Geoffrey frowned and, opening the bag, peered inside. Then he delved in and pulled out a small hunk of stone-hard bread, well gnawed, and a few scraps of dried out cheese. 'Looks as if a mouse or summat has had a go,' he said.

'It's surprising,' said Eleanor, grinning, 'it didn't eat it all.'

Sir Richard harrumphed. 'It will do. But keep it safe, Geoffrey, well out of reach of any other vermin intent on destroying our valuable evidence.'

# 19

Agnes went out soon after sunrise, leaving the children in Jack's care, with a promise to be quick. But it was Midsummer's Eve and she wanted to join the other village women collecting fleshy sprigs of purple orpine, delicate birch branches and the bright yellow blooms of Saint John's wort. She cut quickly, and didn't try to fill her basket, knowing Jack would be pacing, anxious to start his working day.

Back home, with the boys gnawing at their breakfast bread, she tied the gathered stems together in mixed wreaths and bunches, then hung some from the house eaves and nailed others to the door. In times past, when their much-loved priest, Master Aelwyn, had tolerated – though not encouraged – the tradition, the women would've decked Saint Peter's church as well as their houses. But Hugo Garret was chary of such adornment, saying it stank of witchcraft or magic, declaring Midsummer's Eve a celebration of Saint John's birth, not some unholy pagan ritual, as he put it.

Agnes thought the priest a killjoy.

She told Jack how, as a girl, she'd believed some plants became magical on Midsummer's Eve. 'I used to put flowers of yellow wort beneath my pillow,' she said, smiling fondly at the memory, 'in hope my future husband'd walk into my dreams.'

Jack rolled his eyes. 'Maids do have such foolish notions. My only desire on Midsummer night was to down sufficient ale so I could take a girl into the fields.'

Agnes of course pretended to be shocked, though she knew full well what young lads did. And Jack, perhaps wistful for the Midsummer pleasures of his youth, had apparently decided his young journeyman would not be denied them.

'I've let James stop work early,' he continued, 'so he can join the revelry.'

Agnes pursed her lips. 'Is that wise? He'll be awake all night, drinking and making merry, and goodness knows what else.'

'He's not a child, Agnes. With a holiday on the morrow, he can sleep off any excesses. You'll take care of Christopher? He's too young to join the merrymaking, though he mightn't think it.'

His presumption was annoying but, really, she didn't mind at all. For she'd at last learned to accept the young apprentice into their family, if only because he was so clever at amusing her unruly boys. Everyone seemed to be better at it than her... She sometimes wondered if she wasn't meant to be a mother, when she was still so inept. But surely *all* women were meant for motherhood, weren't they?

In the past few weeks, Agnes had spent hours in the garden, working on the potager, or in the herbary, and sometimes resting in the shade of the small rose-covered arbour Jack built two years ago. She'd found how pleasant it could be to have the children play outdoors. On a hot and airless summer's day, the boys would still of course have tantrums, but their screeches somehow seemed more bearable for being out of the stifling confines of the house, scattered into the open air.

Agnes perched upon the arbour's turf bench, the grassy seat brown now from the relentless lack of rain, the crisp blades pricking through her skirt. Jack had decided to close the workshop after dinner, so Christopher, free for the afternoon, sat beside her, while Dickon and his two brothers sprawled upon the blanket she'd spread over the hard, dry ground.

If Jack hadn't found her tale of wort's magic power amusing, perhaps the boys were still innocent enough to find wonder in anything fantastical.

'Do you know any Midsummer tales?' she said to Christopher.

He nodded eagerly. 'My Ma said Midsummer were when evil spirits were abroad.' He twisted his mouth. 'She said, if we weren't careful, we might get carried off by faeries.'

Dickon's eyes grew wide. 'Faeries?'

'Or elves.'

'Wha's elves?' said Stephen, mimicking his brother's bright gaze.

Christopher grinned. 'Same as faeries. Little people with magi—' He bit his lip. 'Is't all right to speak of magic?' he whispered.

She laughed. 'Your Ma told *you* about them, and so did mine tell me. Surely there's no harm in it?'

'Ma'd all sorts of tales about keeping safe from wee folk, as she called them.' He giggled. 'She said you should carry an iron nail in your braies—'

'Ah,' said Agnes, 'my Ma said yellow wort'd do it, or a sprig of rue.'

'What's rue?' said Christopher, and Agnes got up and, crossing to her herbary, returned with a short stem with thick blueish leaves and small yellow flowers. She held it out to Christopher, who thrust his nose into the blooms. He at once recoiled. 'Aargh, it's horrible,' he cried, rubbing vigorously at his nose, and Agnes laughed, and her little boys joined in.

'The smell alone would surely stop the faeries,' she said, and held the sprig down to Dickon, who bawled his dislike of the acrid smell and, jumping up, ran around the garden screaming.

Agnes exchanged a grin with Christopher. 'Any excuse to dash about and squeal like a piglet.'

'I've seen how much he likes to make a noise.' Then his cheeks went pink and he bit his lip.

Agnes leant forward to touch his arm. 'He *does*. And I don't mind you saying so. But *I've* noticed you seem well able to calm him.'

'I got two little brothers, and a sister, an' I've always been good with them.' He stood up. 'Shall I get him?'

'If you would.' She was sorry she'd been so difficult with Christopher when he first came to them. But he seemed not to have noticed her earlier curtness, or simply chose to ignore it. Thank Jesu for the boy's good humour!

Christopher chased Dickon around the garden, making it a game, until at last he caught him. He whispered something in his ear, and Dickon grinned. Agnes watched as he dragged his tunic up over his head then, turning it inside out, pulled it back on again, and resumed his frantic dash in and out of the potager beds. At length, he ran shrieking back to the arbour and threw himself onto the blanket, tumbling into his little brothers as if they were a couple of cloth poppets. Both of them fell to wailing, while Dickon crowed that he'd escaped the faeries.

Christopher came back too and threw a grimace at Agnes when he saw both Stephen and Geoffrey crying. 'Sorry I got Dickon so excited,' he said, reddening again, but Agnes shrugged, picked up Geoffrey and bounced him on her knee.

'He *is* very easily excited. What was it you said to him?'

'If he turned his tunic inside out, he'd confuse the faeries and make sure they couldn't catch him.' He grinned. 'So that's what he did.'

At that moment, Jack emerged from the house, drawn outside, Agnes supposed, by the noise. She pulled a face at Christopher, who chewed at his bottom lip.

Jack strode down the path and over to the arbour. 'Why're the babies wailing, Agnes?' He bent down and picked up Stephen. Jiggling him up and down a moment, he frowned at her. 'Why *do* the children always end up crying?'

Agnes shook her head. 'Dickon got over-excited and knocked them over.

They're not hurt, Jack, just taken by surprise—'

He stared at her a moment, then looked away. Stephen was already calmer for being in his father's arms. Jack whispered in his ear, then lowered him gently to the ground. The boy toddled off towards Christopher, who took his hand and led him over to the potager, where they crouched down side by side to inspect the onions.

'So what's Dickon so roused about?' said Jack.

But when Agnes told him, he rolled his eyes. 'Why'd you want to put such ideas into the children's heads?'

'Oh, Jack, it's only what folk say—'

'What *some* folk say, Agnes. Folk who should spend less time worrying about being led astray by malicious sprites, and more time praying to be kept on the path of righteousness.'

Was this truly *Jack* talking? He'd never before been a champion of prayer. Indeed never, until recently, very keen to go to church. Yet, these days...

He started back to the house, then spun round again. 'We'll go to church this evening?' he said, making it sound like a question, though she somehow knew it wasn't.

She sighed. She'd been hoping to join in some of the Midsummer revelry, perhaps to dance a little, thinking it might lift her melancholy. Or at least help her feel more like the young woman she still was, rather than an ageing matron. But if Jack wanted to go to church, she could scarcely refuse to go. It was after all the celebration of Saint John as well as Midsummer, and some folk *would* spend all night long in prayer. But she thought most would prefer to consider it a "pagan ritual", as Master Hugo had it, and spend their evening feasting and drinking, and in song and dance, till the sun rose again tomorrow. She knew which she'd rather do too but, with Jack's strange new obsession, she had little choice.

'All night?' she said.

'The little ones could hardly manage that. But we can join the candlelit procession, then pray a while before we bring them home to bed.'

'Oh?' said Agnes, 'I'd rather hoped to watch the setting of the fires.'

He tutted. 'Folk shouldn't be setting fires at all, with everywhere so dry.'

'But they will, Jack. It's what folk do at Midsummer.'

Apart from the plague year, when she'd been far away from Meonbridge, she thought she'd probably never missed the setting of the fires. She remembered how people always wore garlands of yellow wort, lit lanterns from the flames, and stumbled from fire to fire in a festive procession around the village. But, in her fond reminiscence, it was true her family *never* joined in the merrymaking, for her father Stephen always insisted they went to church as soon as they'd watched the first bonfire being set.

So the revelry she longed to join was denied her even then, in preference for prayer and supplication.

And now it seemed Jack too wanted to deny his family any Midsummer fun. Yet he'd not denied her the past two years. They'd left the children with her mother – content enough these days to miss the celebrations – and even joined in a little of the merrymaking. So had Jack now truly lost his sense of fun?

Perhaps he saw the disappointment on her face, for he shrugged. 'We'll go and watch the fires, just for a while, before we go up to the church.'

Jack was turning into her father!

Most folk were God-fearing, went to church every Sunday and paid their dues to the priest. But her father was more than usually pious, as was her older brother Geoffrey, who'd been training to become a priest. Agnes and her brother John were less inclined to fall in with what their parents asked of them, though they rarely openly denied their father's wishes.

But it took little wit to realise why *Jack* was becoming seemingly more devout than he'd ever been before. The change had begun last year, when he laid his plan to become a master craftsman of renown. For piety and sobriety were essential attributes of the stanchion of village society he wanted to become.

The sun had just made its final descent behind the distant woodland that divided Meonbridge from the next manor to the west, its bright glow hanging briefly above the trees. The sky was darkening rapidly, pinpricks of light already scattering the mantle overhead. It was the finest of evenings, the air both warm and still, perfect for the setting of Midsummer fires. The setters would soon be at their posts across the village, ready to ignite the fires, for the flames to ward off evil spirits and purify the air, and of course give light to the gathering revellers.

Jack kept his promise. He picked up Stephen, and Agnes cradled Geoffrey in her arms, while Christopher kept tight hold of Dickon's hand, and they walked together the few yards down into the village where the first bonfire would be lit. Agnes had made herself a garland of Saint John's wort, and Jack's eyes lit up as he lightly touched the yellow flowers.

'They're as bright as your lovely hair,' he said and, lifting his hand, let his fingers delve beneath the edge of her wimple and tease out a lock of hair. 'It's a pity you have to hide it.'

Agnes pushed the lock back underneath the fabric. 'Really, I'd rather not.

Especially when the air's so warm. It's wonderful to let your hair fly free. But I'm a respectable married woman.'

'So only *I'm* allowed to admire your golden curls?'

She gave him a sunny smile and tucked her free arm through his.

The first bonfire was set on the edge of the grassy area in the centre of the village, a good distance from the broad bole of the ancient oak. In most years, on Midsummer Day, a great circle of blackened grass remained after the fire had burned away but, this year, there was scarcely any grass left to scorch, most of it already shrivelled up from the lack of rain.

As they approached, the setter was just poking the ignited char cloth into the tinder at the bottom of a great pile of wood and bones. The dry tinder caught at once, and flames surged up through the pyre.

Dickon's eyes grew wide as he watched the fire climb, then he shrieked when the pile – two or three times taller than him – shifted and subsided a little, and sparks erupted on all sides. His shrieking set off his brothers, and Jack blew out a long breath, which Agnes assumed meant he thought coming here a bad idea. But she just smiled at him and, jiggling Geoffrey up and down, walked around the fire pointing out the colours of the flames and the pretty sparks flying up into the air.

A small crowd had now gathered, some carrying lanterns, a few clutching pots of ale they'd bought in Mistress Rolfe's ale-house, only yards away. It was still early, yet several of the young men were already raucous and unsteady. Jack's brow wrinkled at the sight of them, and Agnes suppressed a grin at the thought that he'd so suddenly become quite old. Yet, only this morning, he'd been recalling his own youthful Midsummer excesses, to justify young James joining in the revelries.

She sidled over to her husband and nudged his elbow. 'You *were* like them once.'

He looked asquint at her. 'Was I?'

'So you said.'

He let out a brief guffaw. 'So I did. I suppose misbehaviour always looks unseemly when you're not a part of it.'

She nodded, then pointed to a couple of youths who'd put down their ale pots and were taking off their boots and tunics, and tucking their shirts into the tops of their long braies. 'I think they're going to leap the fire.' She gave him a sidelong glance. 'Did you ever do that, Jack?'

'Not that I recall.'

'But then you're not a country lad,' she said. 'Maybe folk didn't think so much about the harvest up in Chipping Norton?'

'Harvest?'

'The height of this year's crop.'

The half-stripped youths were talking to the man in charge of the fire, telling him, perhaps, not to feed the flames till they'd made their leap. Then they took themselves off a few yards from the fire and prepared to run at it.

'Usually lots of lads take part,' continued Agnes. 'The one who jumps the highest, that'll be the height of August's harvest.'

'Looks to me as if they'll get singed feet,' said Jack, a wry grin on his face.

The fire was burning more fiercely than Agnes thought it should be. But, at that moment, the first lad ran, and jumped, and at once let out a blood-curdling yell. His dangling feet must've touched the dancing flames. He collapsed on the other side of the burning heap, wailing and clutching at his feet. One of his friends picked up his pot of ale and, stumbling over, threw its contents but missed the scorched toes by inches. The second leaper, his face pale in the firelight, apparently thought better of making his jump, for he returned to his discarded clothing and was already struggling to pull his tunic back over his head.

His friend still writhed and wailed upon the ground, then someone ran up with a bucket of water and tipped it over the bottom of his legs. Shortly afterwards, Simon, the barber-surgeon, pushed his way through the gaggle of onlookers – some anxious for the injured lad, others full of reproof for his foolhardiness – and knelt down in the puddle.

Jack gestured with his head. 'Simon'll help him. Shall we step across to the church now?'

'It's surely much too early yet for church,' said Agnes. 'Let's walk up to Riverdown – there'll be a fine fire on the hill.'

Jack agreed, if reluctantly, and they skirted the group to take the road down through Meonvale, then up towards the pasture where Eleanor Titherige ran her sheep. But they'd walked only a few yards when the priest loomed across their path, come perhaps from the church on the other side of the green. Agitation showed in his sour, reddened face and in the stiff set of his shoulders.

Jack hailed him, and he spun around. 'Ah, Master Sawyer.' He didn't acknowledge Agnes standing at her husband's side, but cocked his head towards the fire. 'It's not the fires *per se* I object to,' he said, his voice strangely hoarse, 'but the mischief that accompanies them.'

'There's just been an incident,' said Jack. 'Young lad singed his feet.' Master Hugo twisted around to stare at the group of villagers standing beside the fire.

'They'd do better on their knees in church than getting drunk and leaping fires. Give their wicked souls some chance…' Then he shook his head again, and Agnes thought a gleam lit up his eyes. 'Not that *those* wretches' souls have much chance of salvation.'

As he stared, the priest's face changed from ruddy to dark and, paying no further heed to Jack, he spun around and hastened towards the group.

Jack shook his head and turned again towards Meonvale, but Agnes put out her hand and touched his arm. 'Let's hear what Master Hugo has to say.'

Jack pouted. 'Why?' But she just followed the priest back towards the fire.

As Master Hugo advanced upon the group, he was waving his arms and shouting 'Make way, make way.'

Several people grumbled but a few stepped back to let him pass. He stood before the lad with the burned feet, sitting up now but still groaning. Towering above him, the priest glared down at the unhappy youth, his expression not one of compassion but contempt. 'This is the result of intemperance and wickedness,' he roared, pointing a quivering finger at the lad, who peered up at him and seemed to quake.

Simon stood up and faced the priest. 'It were only a prank, Master Hugo. A prank lads've played as long as I can remember.' He grinned. 'And sometimes the fire catches them by the toes.'

The priest glared at him. 'Fire is the Devil's artifice, master surgeon, not something to be trifled with.'

Simon shrugged, but the onlookers were mumbling, with what sounded to Agnes more like hostility than agreement. She touched Jack's arm again. 'They don't want Hugo's opinion.'

'Yet maybe they should listen to him?'

Agnes glanced across to where Hugo looked to be squaring up to Simon. 'You'd have thought he might have more compassion for the injured lad.'

But Jack shrugged. He seemed unwilling to criticise Master Hugo.

The priest then spun around to confront the bystanders. 'I urge you all, leave this devilish place and come to church. Don't join in this pagan depravity but come, celebrate the birth of the blessed Saint John.' He took a few paces in the direction of Saint Peter's. 'Come!' he cried again, holding out his hands. 'Spend your evening in prayer not prodigality.'

But no one made a move to follow him, except perhaps for Jack, who Agnes sensed had shifted slightly away from her. She put out her hand again, and this time grasped his elbow. 'No, Jack, please, don't be seen to gainsay our neighbours.' He pulled his arm away so sharply she feared he might defy her, but he stood his ground, though she heard him breathing heavily.

The priest spun around once more to face the villagers, his face darkening again. A trembling seemed to come upon him. 'All sinners, then?' he said, almost spitting out the words. 'Drunkenness, gluttony, nay, even lechery, will surely set your souls onto the slippery path to Hell!' A few villagers moaned, but it seemed none were ready to give up their pots of ale or their planned procession from fire to fire.

Master Hugo turned away again, muttering to himself. But, after only a few steps, he swung around yet again, the skirts of his cassock flapping against his legs. Then he thrust his right arm out, his quivering finger directed at the fire, burning fiercely anew after a replenishment of dry wood and bone.

'Fire is the Devil's artifice,' he said again, his voice low and thick, 'and a *fit* punishment for the wicked, both in Satan's fiery kingdom and here on earth...'

Moving closer, Agnes then saw the flames dancing in his eyes, and the heat of choler on his cheeks. She was afraid of what she saw. And her fear sharpened as the priest's quivering finger swept across the gape-mouthed villagers, resting briefly on each of the women standing there, some of whom let out a cry and swooned against their neighbours.

'...to answer for their heinous crimes,' he went on, both arms now raised to heaven. 'Crimes defying God's natural order, the love of God for us his children, the love of a husband for his wife, the duty of both God and man to chastise and not suffer retribution.'

Agnes leaned her head against Jack's arm. 'What's he talking about?' she whispered.

'A husband's duty, and a wife's obedience,' he said in her ear.

'Ah, yes, that again,' said Agnes, and saw in their faces that her neighbours too had gleaned the meaning of Master Hugo's words.

'And when,' he went on, 'a disobedient wife seeks *unnatural* revenge against her husband, her wickedness renders her the Devil's slave and only fire can purge her of her sin!'

If Agnes's neighbours had, moments ago, been frightened into silence, they now howled their outrage at the priest's insinuation. It was obvious to all exactly *which* wife he meant. Several rushed at him, roaring curses, some even raising their hands against him, until he fled back towards the church. One or two men chased after him, and Agnes heard him bellowing his own, unfamiliar, fear.

Agnes's heart was racing, and her head felt a little dizzy. The priest's vile words were frightening, but so too was the sudden ferocity of her neighbours' wrath against him. She leaned again upon Jack's shoulder.

'How can a man of *God*,' she said, her voice muffled against the cloth of his tunic, 'accuse Susy so viciously?'

Jack didn't answer at once. 'I think he may be mad,' he said at last. 'And yet—'

Agnes lifted her head. 'Yet what?' She bit her lip. 'Surely you don't believe Susy's the Devil's slave?'

'Of course not. It grieves me to think it, but I believe it's the priest who is.'

'I'm going to tell Sir Richard about him,' she said to Jack a little later, as they were walking back from watching the fire up on the hill. They weren't going to church after all. Agnes couldn't bear to, and even Jack, despite his earlier enthusiasm, seemed less keen now to spend any more of his evening listening to their priest.

Nonetheless, he frowned. 'Why?'

'Because I daresay his lordship doesn't know of Master Hugo's vicious tongue.'

Jack said nothing. He'd been quiet ever since the priest's outburst around the village bonfire. Perhaps he'd been chastened by the violence of his words. Despite their recent fallings-out, Agnes was proud of her husband – he was a good man, an honest, forward-thinking man – and his recent turn towards the church surely signalled his wish to stand alongside Meonbridge's most respected men. He must be shocked to find one of them was a vile-tongued, indeed barbaric, denouncer of women.

Of course, she'd been vexed by Jack's change of mind about her working. But, even if he no longer considered her necessary for his business, he'd not become a man who thought women feeble-minded, dangerous sinners, for whom burning was the only fitting punishment. And she was certain he never would.

Next morning, Agnes marshalled the children into some sort of obedience.

'You must be good,' she said, to Dickon in particular.

He pouted. 'It's boring.'

'Perhaps Libby'll be there. You like her, don't you?'

Dickon pouted again. 'She likes *dolls*.' He spat out the last word.

'But I don't suppose she *only* likes dolls. I'm sure she enjoys running about in the garden too.'

Dickon had met Libby Fletcher once or twice, but had spent little time with her. She was the daughter of Matilda and her long-dead husband Gilbert, one of the murderers of the de Bohuns' son, and Dickon's father, Philip. Agnes felt sorry for the little girl, having such a father, and indeed such a grandfather – for Matilda's father Robert was guilty too of Philip's murder. She'd heard what happened to the former bailiff, though she'd not witnessed his fatal tumble from the church tower – a tumble that saved him from the gallows.

Agnes felt sorry for Matilda too, who bore the taint of her husband and father, and, because of their crimes, had inherited nothing of their substantial property, and had been left homeless, destitute and a mother. Agnes didn't quite understand why her ladyship had been so generous to Matilda, taking her in as her companion. But it seemed that, whatever the horrors of her past, Matilda had brought up her little girl to be gentle, polite, and well-behaved, and, as she was only a few months younger than Dickon, Agnes had wondered if she might be a suitable, calming, playmate for her boisterous boy.

Not long after dawn, Jack had allowed Agnes to send Christopher to the manor with a message, asking if Sir Richard would meet her on a matter of importance, and Christopher had run all the way back to say she should go now, as his lordship had business off the manor today.

Jack helped to dress the children, and Agnes was soon ready to leave. She hesitated, then tilted her head to one side.

'Might Christopher come with me? It's so difficult to have a proper conversation with the children around my feet.'

But she was not surprised when Jack shook his head. 'He's a carpenter's apprentice, Agnes, not a children's nurse.'

She pouted. 'A pity. He's so good with Dickon— Anyway, we must hurry, else Sir Richard might ride away without seeing me.'

Lady de Bohun seemed to be waiting for Agnes in the hall. For, as Agnes stepped through the door from the bailey, ushering Dickon and Stephen before her, her ladyship came forward to greet them, a broad beam on her face.

'It has been so many weeks since you brought the children to the manor,' she said.

Agnes blinked. She was certain it was *months*, rather than weeks. 'We're so busy, my lady.'

Dickon and Stephen were pressing close to Agnes's skirts, while Geoffrey wriggled in her arms. She hoped her ladyship might suggest finding a maid to take the children, as she'd done in the past. It'd make her conversation with Sir Richard the easier.

'I am afraid that Richard is not here after all, my dear,' said Lady de Bohun. 'He bade me apologise, but he had to leave here sooner than expected.' She tilted her head. 'Can you tell *me* what you wanted to discuss with him?'

Agnes hesitated but only a moment. She could hardly refuse to talk to her ladyship, when she'd always been so kind to her. 'Of course.' But then she bit her lip. 'Jack couldn't mind the children…'

At that moment, Geoffrey – bless him! – let out a piercing shriek, and struggled so vigorously to be put down he almost fell from Agnes's arms. She bent down and set him on his feet. He lifted his face to hers, then toddled away as quickly as his stumpy legs would let him. His brothers dashed after him and all three were soon tumbling together among the herb-strewn rushes spread across the floor. Lady de Bohun smiled and summoned a young page, perhaps twelve or so. The boy ran over, his face scarlet, his teeth catching at his lips.

'Yes'm?' he squeezed out.

She patted his shoulder. 'You need not look so worried, child. You are not in any trouble.'

The boy's mouth relaxed.

'I would like you to spend a while playing with those little boys,' her ladyship continued, pointing to the still tumbling Sawyers.

'*Play*, m'lady?'

'Indeed. Their mama,' she indicated Agnes, 'and I wish to talk a while. You can help us by keeping the children out of mischief. Can you do that?'

'Yes'm. Now?'

She suggested he thought of games that kept the children inside the hall. He seemed happy with the arrangement, and hurried over to kneel down with Agnes's boys.

'Shall we now slip away to somewhere quieter?' said her ladyship, gesturing towards the narrow stairway that led up to the solar.

Agnes hadn't seen this room for years. Nowadays, on the few occasions when she did bring the children to the manor, they stayed downstairs in the hall. But, when she was a girl, she had often come up to the family's private rooms. Her mother, Alice, had made clothes and furnishings for her ladyship. But Lady de Bohun had – or so Alice had said – welcomed her as more than just a craftswoman, indeed almost as a friend.

'I think poor Margaret must be lonely,' Alice had said, 'with Sir Richard away so often.'

When both women gave birth to a baby girl in the same month, their already uncommon friendship deepened, and her ladyship asked Alice to bring little Agnes often to the manor, to be a companion for her own Johanna.

Now, as Lady de Bohun ushered her into the room, Agnes's heart grew heavy, as the memory of the last time she had been here came back to her.

Despite the difference in their stations, she and Johanna had, like their mothers, developed a deep affection for one another, a close bond that – just months before the Death came to Meonbridge – was torn asunder by the reckless behaviour of Johanna's brother, Philip. Agnes had run away, to give birth to her first son alone and far from home. But, after a year's absence, she'd returned to Meonbridge with Jack and baby Dickon, and was relieved the de Bohuns were pleased enough to find they had a grandson, albeit he was illegitimate. It was when she'd asked if she might see Johanna that her ladyship had invited her and Alice to come up here to the privacy of the solar chamber, where her daughter might perhaps agree to meet them.

Agnes had been shocked to see how desperately unhappy Johanna was. She was of course grieving for the death of her brother Philip, murdered only two months before. But she was also still nurturing a terrible remorse for her part in the events that had led to Agnes's flight more than a year before. Agnes thought Johanna's wish to atone for that guilt must be behind her decision to become a nun, though she didn't understand *why* Johanna should feel so responsible for what had happened. But Johanna had fallen into a dismal melancholy, keeping mostly to her own company, her former joyfulness seemingly lost forever. It was the saddest of reunions, and Agnes had not seen her childhood friend again.

Nonetheless, Lady de Bohun had made it clear to Agnes that she'd welcome the occasional visit from her new grandson. Afterwards, she and Alice, too, met often, their friendship restored after the rift caused by Agnes's disappearance. Yet, now, it seemed that Alice's sewing days might be over, for she rarely stitched, though she and her ladyship did still sometimes share a cup of wine and sweetmeats, or stroll together in the manor gardens, and Agnes was glad of it.

As for herself, she always found Lady de Bohun warm-hearted towards her, the mother of her only grandchild, though Jack insisted that Agnes should never presume upon her ladyship's good will.

The lady bade Agnes sit. 'Would you like something to drink, my dear?'

'It was rather a rush this morning…' said Agnes, and bit her lip.

But her ladyship tutted. 'And all for nothing. I am so sorry if Richard made you hurry.'

Agnes shook her head. She could hardly complain of her lord's lack of consideration.

Lady de Bohun sent her maid Agatha for some refreshments. 'And how is my grandson?' she said. 'He seems full of energy.'

Agnes rolled her eyes. 'I think he's his father's son,' she said, then blushed.

But the lady smiled. 'He certainly looks like him. Behaves like him as well, then?'

'I think so, my lady, from what you've told me.'

Agatha returned with a tray bearing a jug of cordial, and a dish of sweetmeats, and placed it on the table close to her mistress's chair, then withdrew.

'So, my dear,' said her ladyship, 'what was it you wished to talk about?'

Agnes felt her flush blooming once more on her cheeks, at the awkwardness of what she was about to say. She bit her lip, then met the lady's eyes.

Lady de Bohun placed her hand upon Agnes's arm. 'My dear? Is it distressing for you to speak of?'

'A little.' Agnes took a sip of cordial and bit into a greenish ball-shaped sweetmeat, made from what she'd no idea. Then she straightened her back. 'But I must say it.' And she related what she knew of Master Hugo, what he'd said in church a few weeks past, and what he said last evening at the bonfire.

Her ladyship's eyes grew wider. Her mouth inelegantly agape, she brought her hands up to her face. 'I can scarce believe what I am hearing, Agnes,' she said, then, flinging one hand from her face, she patted Agnes's arm. 'Not that I am denying the truth of what you say. I would hardly think you would invent such a dreadful account.'

Agnes shook her head. 'It's no invention, my lady. You might ask many others, and hear the same account of his vicious tongue. It just don't seem right a man of God should speak so. Master Aelwyn was surely never so unfeeling?'

Lady de Bohun grasped both Agnes's hands in hers. 'You are right, my dear. Our beloved Aelwyn never flinched from trying to teach God's laws, but he did it with a kind heart and compassion, not the seeming malevolence you have described.' Her forehead puckered. 'I have never heard Hugo give a sermon. I thought he rarely did so—'

'Not often, but lately he seems only to want to frighten folk and threaten.'

Her ladyship clicked her tongue. 'I suppose he never would say such things before Sir Richard and myself.'

'That's what I thought.'

'I will speak to Richard later,' continued the lady, 'and insist he approach the bishop for a more Christian-minded replacement to Master Hugo Garret. The man is clearly excessively eager to find poor Susanna guilty.' She narrowed her eyes. 'It is partly Richard's fault of course—'

'Sir Richard's?'

'Indeed. When he allowed that preposterous ordeal to go ahead. It was Hugo who suggested it, you know.'

Agnes blinked. 'Really?' She nodded. 'Jack thought Master Garret might be mad.'

'I agree with him,' said Lady de Bohun. 'Even *suggesting* the ordeal was surely the act of a madman? Ordeals are illegal, and it is much more than a hundred years past that the Church *forbade* priests to take part in them. But, Agnes, there are other zealots in the village – men who fear women are taking unfair advantage of the Mortality's dreadful outcome.' She frowned. 'Men who wanted to be seen to support the pastor's view. They urged Richard to agree. Which he did, despite, in truth, *not* agreeing. He regrets not following the customary procedure and simply giving Mistress Wragge an appropriate penalty for her misdemeanour.'

'What penalty?'

'The stocks perhaps? Something that would shame her but not threaten her life.'

Agnes inclined her head.

'But Richard also regrets,' continued her ladyship, 'allowing that unpleasant Master Gastingthrop to take Susanna to Winchester, when I am certain that he was not at all persuaded that she was to blame for Henry's death.'

'Truly?'

'Indeed. He said often enough that Mistress Miller could not be guilty of murder, yet he was swayed by the coroner's assertion that all women are sinners and must be punished.'

'Poor Sir Richard,' said Agnes, 'not making the right decisions.'

But Lady de Bohun threw her head back. 'Ha!' she cried. 'Not only not the *right* decisions, Agnes, but, in truth, the most *absurdly* wrong ones.'

# 20

Emma handed over a coin to Fulke in exchange for a fresh-baked loaf of the rougher sort baked by Master Langelee. Henry had long ago lost interest in baking bread. Or perhaps he'd just let the ovens go cold, overwhelmed by the sheer effort of milling flour on his own. The mill's bakehouse became shrouded in cobwebs and dust, while a rival obtained approval from Sir Richard and set up in the centre of the village. But young Master Langelee held the view that milling and baking were two aspects of the same craft, and had restarted the ovens, determined to bring the people of Meonbridge back to the mill for their flour *and* their bread. Making Fulke responsible for serving customers seemed to Emma a risky way of ensuring a profit but, today at least, Fulke was merrier than she'd ever seen him; the hands passing over the bread looked clean, and the coins seemed to be clinking into the appropriate bowl.

As Emma reached the road at the top of the mill track, she glanced left towards the village and spotted Bea hurrying in her direction along the road, dusty from the lack of rain. She was carrying one of Emma's baskets and, despite the persistent summer heat, she'd pulled her hood up over her head, mostly concealing her face. But Emma knew it was her daughter. She was walking quickly, her head bent forward, not looking left or right.

Emma stepped back onto the path, concealing herself behind some bushes growing on the boundary of Mistress atte Wode's croft. She wanted to see where Bea was going.

Directly across from the mill track and the corner of the atte Wode croft, sideways to the main village road, was the narrower path that led to Eleanor's grand house, and those of two others of Meonbridge's wealthier folk, then on to the hamlet of Upper Brooking. Emma was somehow not surprised when Bea turned left onto the path.

She decided to follow her, but held back a while, waiting until Bea had put a little distance between them. She felt bad to be spying on her own daughter, but Bea was being so secretive still, refusing to say where Tom was hiding, and disappearing for hours on end.

Beyond the third big house, the track became even narrower, barely recognisable as a path, the lack of footsteps having allowed grass and weeds to overwhelm it. Ahead was a broad patch of woodland, and just before it, Emma knew, stood the rundown cottage of Cecily, Walter's elderly aunt, the last house in Meonbridge before the hamlet of Upper Brooking. Cecily was the oldest woman in the village: her back was very bent, and her cloudy eyes saw nothing now, but, according to Eleanor, her mind was as bright and alert as it'd ever been. Emma knew Cecily was harmless and sweet-natured. She'd sat through the night with her beloved Bart, after he fell – or was pushed – off the haystack, and tried to save his life with her herbal physic. Yet, the village children always thought her cottage a frightening place – even when Emma was a girl, they shunned it. And, now, Bea skittered off the track, and carved a wide arc through the scrubby heathland, before returning to the path once she'd passed the "witch's lair", as Emma's young friends had once liked to call it.

Once in the woodland, Emma could follow a little more closely, keeping herself hidden within the trees. But, as the trees thinned, the track emerged into another short stretch of open scrubby land, with few places to hide, and she worried Bea might turn and see her. She didn't want her daughter to feel she was betraying her. Yet, with the fixed set of her head and shoulders, the girl seemed intent on her journey and didn't turn round once.

Emma wondered if she was scared, being alone on this deserted path. But then she felt proud of her little girl, being so brave to help her friends. Yet Emma was herself afraid Bea was getting into trouble, helping escaped felons – if Luke and Arthur were there – and maybe even stealing food.

Upper Brooking had just four cottages clustered tight together that, until the Death, had been the homes of four related families, all Collyeres, all charcoal burners. Everyone who lived there had perished in the Death, except Fulke and Warin, who weren't brave or bright enough to stay in the isolated hamlet all alone and had moved to Meonvale. The three nearest cottages were in ruins, their walls crumbled away, the roof thatch rotten and fallen in. But the last one, the one into which Bea disappeared, had standing walls, and its roof looked more or less intact.

So what now? Emma had no intention of confronting the boys, especially if Luke was there. He mightn't be a big lad, but he was as ill-tempered as his father, as ready with his huge fists to thump someone rather than trouble himself to talk. Anyway, if this was where Tom was hiding, she'd fulfilled her mission. She'd report back to Ralph and Eleanor, then they could all decide what next to do.

She crept towards the cottage. It had only one window opening, high up so no one inside could see out. Taking very careful, quiet steps, she sidled over to one corner of the building, the window opening on the front wall just a couple of feet away. Much of the daub had fallen away, exposing the laths, and now she noticed wide gaps through which the boys could maybe see outside. So she stayed by the corner, and listened, the voices travelling clearly through the gaps. And she was soon assured that all *three* boys were there.

Bea must've brought them food and drink, because Emma heard them tearing apart a loaf of bread and gulping down some liquid.

'Where d'you get it this time, Bea?' someone asked – Emma thought it was Tom's voice.

Bea didn't answer at once. But then Luke's deeper, rougher voice spoke. 'D'you steal it from your Ma?'

'No,' said Bea, firmly, and Emma had to stifle a sob of relief with her fingers.

'Where then?'

Again Bea didn't answer.

'It's easy stealing food,' continued Luke, ''specially this time o' year, when everyone's in the fields. You can just walk in an' take it. I been doing it for months, ain't I, Arthur?'

Arthur didn't confirm it out loud.

'I *knew* it were you,' said Bea, her tone sour. 'Last year. After you ran off. Ma noticed some bread and cheese were missing. She thought I'd taken it, but it were you all along.'

Emma's heart turned over. It was true she'd blamed Bea then, though only in her head.

'Yeah,' said Luke, bragging again.

They all went silent, more interested perhaps in eating.

'What was it like, then, being with them outlaws?' That must be Tom, thought Emma, but kept her fingers pressed to her mouth.

Luke crowed again as he said what a good time they'd had, living in the forest.

Arthur spoke up then, though his voice was quavery. 'It *weren't* good, Lu. Those men were 'orrible, an' there were this woman…' He trailed off, perhaps not wanting to admit to what the woman did.

How much Emma wanted to go and hug poor little Arthur.

'So why d'you come back?' said Bea.

Arthur found his voice again. 'Lu got into trouble wi' the man, and 'e threw us out—'

Luke scoffed. 'Nah, I told 'em we didn't wanna stay there no more. Anyway, half-wit here wanted to come home to his *pappy*—' The last word was said with a sneer, and the sound of cuffing, then Arthur – Emma was certain it was Arthur – let out a yelp.

Then he began to cry. 'I'm hungry,' he whimpered, and apparently received another thump for his complaint.

'Shuddup, *baby*,' said Luke.

But Arthur just cried some more. 'I wanna go home,' he stuttered between his muffled sobs.

Emma's heart felt heavy now. Arthur may be eleven, the same age as Tom, but they couldn't be more different. Tom was brave and strong-willed, ready to stand up for what he thought. But Arthur was a child. He followed Luke around because he protected him from the taunts of other lads. But it seemed Arthur had grown tired of being on the run – it'd been more than a year – and, even if Luke enjoyed it, Arthur had had enough.

Then it was Tom speaking. Emma thought his voice sounded shaky too, despite his usual mettle. 'How long can we keep this up, Lu?'

Luke snorted. 'Long as we have to,' he said, which was no answer at all.

Emma put away the meagre food she'd bought and went out into the herb garden. There was nothing much for her to do, but she was happier outside in the sunshine and fresh air. And somehow she found it easier to think outdoors.

She heard Bea return a while later, but let her be. She didn't want to talk about what was going on, in case Bea went to tell the boys.

Later, when the children were in bed, she drew Ralph outside, and they walked down past the low fence marking the end of their small croft. They sat down on the fallen trunk of a long-dead apple tree that Emma remembered giving fruit when she lived here as a child. She gazed out across the common fields of barley and rye towards the woodland in the distance for a moment before telling Ralph what she'd done and everything she'd overheard.

He squinted at her. 'You been spying on your daughter?' He clicked his tongue, then grinned. 'Good thing you spotted her.'

Emma nodded. 'She's been so quiet and secretive lately. We suspected, but now we know the truth of it.'

'But it's not like Bea to *steal*,' said Ralph. 'I'm surprised she can keep doing it, without getting caught.' He scratched his beard. 'How long is it now?'

'Not so very long. Only since Tom went into hiding. The thefts a year ago were Luke. I heard him say so.'

'Taking a little bit of food for Tom is one thing, but stealing enough for three—'

'She can't be getting much. Which is why little Arthur complained of being hungry.' Emma pulled a face. 'Have you heard folk say food's going missing again?'

'Not this time. But mebbe not every wife's as mindful of her stores as you.' He smiled then knit his brow. 'But how does Bea do it, Em? When we're out, she's supposed to be looking after Ami and the baby.'

'I don't know, but we've got to stop it now, Ralph. Bea's in trouble already, but if she stops now—' She bit her bottom lip. 'I know she's scared, Ralph. I could tell.'

'You think Luke's threatening her?'

'Daresay. He must keep hidden, mustn't he? He's in much more danger than the others.'

Ralph agreed. 'He's almost a man, and everyone in Meonbridge knows what he's like, with his fists an' all. And everyone knows Arthur would've just gone along with what Luke said, not grasping the risk of it. If Luke's caught, he'll probably be hanged for stealing the sheep, whereas Arthur might even be let off—'

'And Tom ain't done anything wrong, except keep company with a thief.' Emma leaned her head against Ralph's shoulder, and rested her hand in his. 'I think Luke might be keeping Arthur 'gainst his will, just to keep *himself* safe. And maybe Tom's staying just to keep Arthur company?'

'I wonder why Luke came back at all?' said Ralph.

'To get rid of Arthur? Mebbe he's planning to leave him here and run off again?'

'So why ain't he gone already?'

'Dunno. But I do think Tom, an' 'specially Arthur, would be happy to be found. Mebbe then Luke'll leave and go and join some outlaws?'

'Then you and Eleanor should go and fetch 'em home.'

Emma lifted her head. 'And mebbe the tithing-men should go and get Luke, now we know where he is?'

'We haven't agreed.'

'Mebbe you should. Sir Richard weren't pleased you didn't go after him when he first ran off. What'd he think if he knew you didn't raise the hue and cry over the stolen food?'

Ralph shrugged. 'He don't know about that.'

'He could still fine you for neglecting your frankpledge duty. Luke's not worth the risk, Ralph—'

'But he's my cousin's son!'

'An' *he's* not worth it either. Luke stole Eleanor's sheep, then let them die. He's stolen food. He's been with outlaws. And he's been keeping Arthur 'gainst his will. Mebbe Tom too.'

Ralph's brow knit into deep furrows but didn't answer.

'We won't try an' bring Luke back,' Emma continued. 'I don't want to risk one of his great fists in my face.' Ralph grimaced. 'It's only Tom we want and, if Arthur wants to come, we'll bring him too. But, if Luke runs, we'll let him.'

'I reckon that's best,' Ralph said.


Next morning, soon after sunrise, Emma went to Eleanor's house, then together they took the track to Upper Brooking. As they passed Cecily Nash's house, Eleanor told Emma what happened when Walter came back to see her.

'I'd heard,' said Emma, then she bit her lip. 'He went up to Riverdown one evening when you and I weren't there. Will said.' Turning to Eleanor, she saw her eyes looked a little damp.

'Will didn't tell me,' said Eleanor.

'I think Walter must've told him not to.' Emma tucked her hand through Eleanor's arm. 'But surely he'll come back again. After all, he's bound to come back to visit her.'

'Only as long as Cecily's still alive,' said Eleanor, her voice quiet.

When they reached the derelict cottage the boys were hiding in, they crept towards it just as Emma did before. Standing by the corner, they listened to a little of the hushed, rather drowsy-sounding conversation, then Eleanor gestured to Emma and, moving swiftly to the doorway, Emma pushed open the door.

The boys were barely awake, still curled up on rotten-looking pallets. Luke was the first to leap up, his fair hair sticking up like cut stalks of wheat. He cursed Bea for ratting on them, then made a move towards the door but both women were standing in the doorway and he hesitated from pushing past.

The younger boys sat up slowly, each rubbing their eyes and scratching at their rumpled hair. Arthur seemed a little dazed but, when he saw Emma, he struggled to his feet.

''Ave you come to get me?' he said in a whisper, his eyes large.

'D'you want to go home, Arthur?' she said, and he shuffled across the room and put his arms around her waist. She folded her arms around him, and her heart turned over as she felt the bones of his back protruding and the trembling of his skinny body.

She glanced across at Tom, now standing too, his face crumpled. 'Can I come too?' he said.

Eleanor went to him and put her arm around his shoulder. 'Have you had enough of adventures?'

'I think so.' He bit his lip. 'Will we be in trouble, Arthur an' me?'

Eleanor shot a glance at Emma, who gave a slight shake of her head. 'I can't say, Tom,' said Eleanor. 'Let's not worry about that now. You both need to go home, to some proper food and rest.'

But Arthur began to cry. 'What's goin' to happen to me?' he stammered out.

'Let's just get you home to your Da,' said Emma.

Luke was hopping from foot to foot. '"Let's go home to Da",' he repeated, mimicking Emma's gentle tone. 'Yeah, get the milksop back to his pappy. So what 'bout me? You reckonin' on taking me home too?'

'You're not a child, Luke. You can please yourself.'

'Well, I know what'll happen,' he said, 'so I'm not staying to find out.'

With that he rushed forward and barged past Emma and Arthur, out through the door. Eleanor ran out too but soon returned. 'He fled across the scrub towards the woodland,' she said. 'I knew I'd never catch him.'

Emma sniffed. 'I told Ralph he should've called out the tithing-men.'

Tom and Arthur seemed cheerful as they followed Emma and Eleanor back to Meonbridge. Neither boy spoke much, save to answer Emma's questions about their health. But their eyes grew brighter and both grinned often, now they no longer had to worry about feeling hungry or being scared.

Emma'd agreed with Eleanor to take the boys straight up to the manor. His lordship was already planning, Eleanor said, to put Tom forward at Susanna's trial as a witness in her defence, and would be eager to hear his story.

Yet Emma was anxious about what Sir Richard might do with Arthur. She refrained from asking Eleanor, in case the boy overheard. But, when they reached the manor and climbed the bailey steps to enter the great hall, Emma felt afraid, wondering – far too late – if bringing Arthur here had been a terrible mistake.

However, it was Lady de Bohun who came to greet them. A beam lit up the lady's face as she approached them and saw Tom. She leaned forward and touched the boy on his head. 'You have been such a worry to us, Tom.'

Tom's cheeks flamed red, and he stared down at his boots. 'Sorry, m'm,' he said, his voice scarce above a mumble.

Emma felt someone clutching at her skirts and, looking behind her, found Arthur. Emma grasped his wrist and pulled him forward. 'And this is Arthur Ward, your ladyship,' she said, and thrust him forward a little further. He, too, stared at the floor.

'Ah, yes, *John* Ward's son, I believe?'

'Aye, m'lady. He's a good lad, truly.' Emma felt her face flush. She was eager to prove Arthur innocent, yet it wasn't Lady de Bohun she needed to convince.

'This is the child involved in the loss of Eleanor's sheep?'

'Aye, m'lady, but he—'

Eleanor touched Emma's arm. 'It's our belief, your ladyship, that Arthur was cozened into the theft by his much older cousin. We think he likely did not understand the consequences of what they did.' Her ladyship inclined her head, and Eleanor continued. 'And we suspect the poor boy has been kept from his father against his will.'

Lady de Bohun's eyebrows arched. 'Are you saying the child's cousin kept him prisoner?'

'Not exactly a prisoner, but I think Arthur has been a most unwilling outlaw.'

'And where is the cousin? Luke, is it?'

'I am afraid he ran away again. Our main concern, Emma's and mine, was to bring Tom home. And we thought to rescue Arthur if we could. In truth, your ladyship, we did not try to persuade Luke to come with us.'

'He'd not've come willingly, m'lady, and might've tried to harm us,' said Emma. 'He's a lot to lose if he's caught.'

'You are right of course. I understand that you could hardly *arrest* him yourselves. But I do know Sir Richard is somewhat vexed that he has remained at large for so very long.' She knit her brow.

Emma flushed again. She'd *told* Ralph he should've called out the tithing-men. They'd be in real trouble for failing to bring Luke to justice.

But Lady de Bohun continued. 'No matter. We must be relieved to have young Tom back with us. For it is not long now until Mistress Miller is brought before the king's justices, and Sir Richard is impatient to have all his witnesses and oath-helpers in place.' She leaned down towards Tom and took his chin in her hand. 'And you, Tom, are a very important witness.'

The boy flushed and shuffled his feet.

Eleanor gave little cough. 'Your ladyship, we have not yet talked to Tom about the trial. So he does not understand the importance of his story.'

Tom's gaze shifted from Lady de Bohun to Eleanor, and then to Emma, bafflement on his face.

'Indeed,' said her ladyship, nodding. 'You have not yet had the opportunity. Of course, Sir Richard will wish to talk to him—' Tom looked alarmed, but she patted his head. 'You have nothing to fear, child. His lordship will be delighted to find you returned to us, for he is eager to hear your story.'

Tom didn't answer, and chewed his lip. Eleanor put her arm around his shoulder. 'Are you hungry, Tom?' She raised her eyes to her ladyship, who lifted a hand to summon a servant.

'Take these two to the kitchens for some food,' she said to him. The servant bowed his head, though Emma was sure she saw a scowl twist his lips.

Tom and Arthur both stared at the women, their faces pale, but Emma gave Arthur a gentle push.

'Go on, Arthur,' she said. 'You *must* be hungry.' The boy shrugged, and Emma rolled her eyes at Eleanor. John might be poor but his lad was always properly fed. Yet now he looked like what Emma's Ma'd said folk were in the famine, all sharp corners and baggy tunics.

Nonetheless, Arthur held back, his lips pushed out and quivering. But then the servant cuffed his arm. 'Get on wi' you,' he said roughly, and gestured to both boys to follow. Shoulders hunched, they went, following the man across the hall.

'Sir Richard will be back for dinner,' Lady de Bohun said to Eleanor. 'You may leave the boys here, if you wish, and return this afternoon.' Then she turned to Emma. 'You too, my dear.'

Emma exchanged a nod with Eleanor. It was generous of her ladyship to look after the boys, so she and Eleanor could get on with some work. But she suspected that, as soon as John heard his boy'd been found, he'd be anxious to have him home. Though, as she thought it, a tightness gripped her throat, for perhaps Sir Richard wouldn't let him go. For a child Arthur may be, but he was also a felon.

After spending the rest of the morning up on Riverdown with Will, then sharing a quick dinner, Emma and Eleanor hurried back to the manor, hoping to find his lordship ready to discuss the future of the boys. But, when they arrived and entered the great hall from the bailey door, they were startled to find Ralph and some of the other men of the Meonvale tithing stood before the high table. A disgruntled-looking Sir Richard was slouching in his great cushioned chair, with everyone in noisy and peevish-sounding discussion around him.

Dinner at the manor was over, for most of the tables had been dismantled and the benches pushed back against the walls. A servant was examining the strewings on the floor for dropped food, a scruffy dog at her side gobbling up what scraps she found. The sight of it made Emma smile. Lady de Bohun was clearly stricter than most about not allowing filth and droppings to gather in the rushes.

As Emma approached with Eleanor, the cottar men turned their heads, and Emma bit her lip at the sight of Ralph's red face. Perhaps the tithing-men *were* now in trouble with Sir Richard? Lady de Bohun had already said his lordship was annoyed with them for failing to arrest Luke, and indeed Arthur, for the theft of Eleanor's sheep. Though, in fairness, it was the constable who'd given up the search. But the Meonvale tithing – which included Matthew and his wilful son – still had a duty to bring to justice any of their number who broke the law.

It were her Ralph who'd agreed *not* to raise the hue and cry over the stolen sheep, at the fearful pleading of his cousin Matthew, then didn't raise it again over the missing food, even though Sir Richard knew nothing of that. And, because Ralph were Meonvale's chief tithing-man, he was most at fault. Emma felt a tightness in her chest. Was Sir Richard now reproaching Ralph for neglecting his duty? Would he demand from him a huge fine, or worse?

But, after a few more heated words from both his lordship and the cottars, Sir Richard banged his fist down on the table and stood up from his chair.

'Enough! I have had my say, and you have had yours. You are good men, all of you— Well, most of you.' He arched his eyebrows. 'I have no wish to punish you now, when you have, at last, if tardily, brought the felon home.'

Emma gasped. Maybe, after her conversation with Ralph, he'd raised the tithing-men after all, and followed her and Eleanor out to Upper Brooking? When Luke ran from the cottage, were they waiting, ready to chase after him? She exchanged a wry grin with Eleanor, who looked as surprised as she was.

Eleanor stepped forward. 'Sir Richard? Has Luke Ward been found?'

'Indeed, my dear. The young knave's tithing finally looked to their duty and rounded him up. He is locked up below, and I will present him to the king's justices next month on a charge of sheep stealing, sheep killing, and theft.'

'Does he *have* to go before the judges? I—'

Sir Richard held up his hand. 'My dear Eleanor, I know you did not want to bring charges against him, but he has gone too far. Stealing your sheep was enough to make Luke a felon. Letting them die, then the food thefts—' Emma's hand flew to her face and Sir Richard noticed. 'Yes, Mistress Ward, I have finally learned of the thefts in Meonvale—' He glared at Ralph and the tithing-men.

Emma knew she'd gone bright red. Did he know, too, about Bea's part in the thefts?

But his lordship just carried on. 'And then it seems he ran off with his young cousin and took him to live with outlaws, beyond the protection a boy like Arthur needs. I am afraid Luke Ward has grown into the unenviable image of his father. But he is not a child and must take the consequences for his actions.'

Emma felt her flush cooling a little. Perhaps Sir Richard still knew nothing about Bea, as he'd not mentioned her. Ralph surely wouldn't have told him. But what of Arthur? His lordship spoke as if he thought the boy didn't share Luke's guilt.

'Will you present young Arthur too, your lordship?' she said in a whisper.

Sir Richard stroked his beard. 'I have not yet decided upon it, Mistress Ward. I am minded to present him to our own court, and find some suitable punishment, one that teaches him a lesson, and indeed any other Meonbridge lads with a taste for theft, but does him no lasting harm. The boy may be eleven,' he continued, lowering his voice, 'but he is nonetheless a child. Others may care to, but I have no stomach for maiming children.'

# 21

Susanna stumbled as the gaoler ushered her across the bailey towards the castle door. He was grasping her so tightly by the elbow she thought he'd bruise her arm, yet she was scarce in any state to run away. Perhaps he felt obliged to stop her toppling over? She certainly felt light-headed, like she might fall into a faint. Her stomach twitched, protesting. She'd eaten little for weeks, her once-hearty appetite overcome by tedium and fear. This morning, Edith came especially early to bring her a few sweetmeats – a honeyed treat, she'd said, to give her heart. But nausea and terror stopped her taking more than the bite or two she'd forced herself to swallow, so as not to seem ungrateful.

Now, as they approached the door of the castle's great hall, Susanna stumbled again, and was grateful for the gaoler's grasp.

'Whoa, there, missus,' he cried, throwing out his other arm to steady her. 'Be strong, now. His lordship's speaking for you today.'

He was nodding, his mostly toothless gums bared in a grin.

Eleanor had told her Sir Richard was to speak for her, along with other folk who'd swear her innocence. But, after so long in her lonely cell, Susanna had convinced herself the judges would still believe no one but the coroner, and would sentence her to burn.

She tried to swallow her foreboding, but it stuck there, lodging in her throat. 'I'll try, master gaoler.'

He grinned again and, putting his arm around her shoulder, helped her step through the great arched door. But, when she saw the vastness of the hall, the dizzying height of the rafters, the huge length of the walls, and the throng of chattering people, she stumbled yet again. Nausea rose and, heaving, she fell against the gaoler's broad chest. 'I can't,' she whispered.

'But you 'ave to, missus.' He grasped her shoulder with one strong hand and eased her upright. 'You got no choice.' His eyes were sad, as they so often were.

How could she do this? The outcome was surely not in doubt, for all Eleanor's kind words and his lordship's speaking for her. But the sooner it began, the sooner over, the anguish of not knowing ended…

At length she stood up tall. 'Where do I go?'

'Over 'ere,' he said, pointing, and helped her skirt the noisy gathering, down towards the far end of the hall, where a great table was raised up on a platform, with three high, cushioned chairs placed behind it. To one side of the platform stood two long benches, set at an angle, and in front of it, on the rush-strewn floor, were a few smaller benches, and the gaoler gently pushed her down onto one of these, then stood beside her, his big hand resting on her shoulder.

She closed her eyes and tried to breathe deeply, hoping it might calm her.

'Susy?'

Another, smaller, hand touched her arm.

'Susy? It's Eleanor.'

She opened her eyes, to see Eleanor's sweet face smiling down at her. Sir Richard stood behind her. 'How glad I am you're here,' she whispered.

'Have you seen how everyone has come to support you?' said Eleanor.

Susanna shook her head.

'Turn around and look.' Eleanor gestured at the crowd behind them. And, when she looked, Susanna saw many familiar faces. 'See,' continued Eleanor, 'how many Meonbridge folk have come?'

Susanna had come here once before, years ago. It was a bit of an outing when the king's justices came to the county. She couldn't recall the cases they'd come to hear. But what had brought the Meonbridge folk here today? To see her accused? To hear her sentenced to be burned?

Eleanor's eyes were bright. 'Many have come as oath-helpers, to swear your *innocence*, Susy.'

Susanna gave a brief nod at that, but inside herself she was still shrugging. She couldn't think they'd make a difference.

A small man, clad from head to foot in black, stepped forward and stood quite close to her. Suddenly aware of him, Susanna looked up, as he pulled himself up tall and pushed out his chest. Then he startled her with his booming voice.

'Oyez! Let all who have business and owe service to our king draw near. The court of the king's justices is in session, in the county of Hampshire, this Friday after the Assumption of the Blessed Virgin Mary, in the twenty-seventh year of our sovereign King Edward the Third.'

Susanna raised her eyes as three men, all grey-haired, all dressed in thickly embroidered black robes, took their places in the chairs behind the table. Two of them had long faces, with furrowed brows; one's mouth was tight-lipped, the other downturned and sneering. Her nausea rose again. *They'd* surely not have any sympathy for a woman such as her. But, when she glanced up at the man sitting between the two stern faces, for a moment her heart felt a little lighter. For, instead of his mouth twisting into a scowl, his face seemed mellow, his eyes somehow kind.

But her moment of ease soon passed, as the jurymen shuffled in and sat on the two side benches. She stared at them from beneath her lowered lids: twelve men, none of whom she knew. Grand-looking men, she thought, not a peasant or artisan amongst them, and no one from Meonbridge. What could *they* know of her case? Along with the nausea, the thickness in her throat returned. Surely, those sorts of men'd just take the coroner's word? She shook her head from side to side, struggling to catch her breath. Then Eleanor was at her side, her arm around her shoulder. 'Breathe slowly, Susy dear,' she said, and squeezed her shoulder gently.

The loud-voiced man announced the start of the proceedings. 'Lord Justice Sir Anthony Appylton is presiding. Be silent for His Lordship.'

Moments later, Susanna heard her name. Raising her eyes, she found Justice Appylton peering down at her.

'Mistress Miller,' he said again, 'please stand.'

She tried to obey but, shaking, found her legs too weak to lift her up. Eleanor cupped her elbow and gave her a little push. Tilting her face towards the judge, Susanna saw the faintest of smiles curve his lips. He inclined his head to her, then scanned the crowd, now hushed to silence.

'Master Hubert Gastingthrop, the coroner,' he said, 'has presented very detailed evidence of this case. Witness statements, the defendant's testimony—' He again peered down at her.

He shuffled the parchments spread before him and selected a few. She heard him read the coroner's summary of what had happened at the mill – an account that seemed to her not quite as she recalled it. Then he read out Simon's report on the condition of Henry's body, and the words of various witnesses.

Eleanor muttered over the claims of several Meonbridge men that Mistress Miller was known to be a scold. 'Who told them to say that about you, Susy?' she whispered, and squeezed her hand. 'Our priest perhaps?'

But finally, it seemed, the judge had read enough. 'Well, Mistress Miller, how do you plead?'

Not understanding what he asked, and confused by what she'd just heard read out, Susanna couldn't find the words to answer. She turned to Eleanor, but Sir Richard was then on his feet.

'Mistress Miller,' he said, 'is clearly much distressed by her ordeal of arrest and imprisonment, my lord justice. I will speak for her.'

'And you are?'

'Sir Richard de Bohun, lord of the manor of Meonbridge…'

Susanna heard him then reel off a list of other manors, but she didn't catch the names. Her mind was foggy, unable to believe she was here, facing death on the nod of all those nameless men.

'So how *does* Mistress Miller plead?' she heard the judge say once again.

'*Not* guilty, your lordship,' said Sir Richard.

'You have evidence to prove her innocence?'

'I do, my lord. I will provide a more detailed and accurate narrative of events at the mill the day of Henry Miller's death, and also the testimony of a dozen oath-helpers who will attest to Mistress Miller's innocence of her husband's murder.'

'Very well, proceed,' said Justice Appylton. 'Sit, Mistress.'

She slumped back onto the bench, and Eleanor took her hand once more. 'Try to listen, Susy.'

Susanna would've preferred to let her thoughts wander from this place, to that happy time when she and Henry were first married. But, nodding, she straightened her back and tried to fix her eyes upon Sir Richard.

He cleared his throat. 'The coroner's brief account, my lords, gives three erroneous impressions of Mistress Miller. First, that she both nagged her husband and refused to obey his wishes. Second, that she deliberately caused him to fall and hit his head that day at the mill. Third, that she then ran off, knowingly leaving him for dead. None of these impressions bears scrutiny. Moreover, your lordships, Master Gastingthrop's account does not reflect what truly happened. I can offer a more plausible version of events and will call, first, upon Mistress Miller, and then on others, to tell the court the truth of what occurred.'

He came across to her and put out his hand. Then, taking her arm, he drew her to her feet and led her forward to stand before the judges. Feeling the nausea rise yet again, and a dizziness in her head, she feared she might collapse, and grasped Sir Richard's arm.

He leaned his face towards her ear. 'Be strong, my dear,' he whispered.

'I'll try, sir,' she whispered back. Her heart was thumping but she forced herself to stand up tall and, clasping her hands together at her waist, faced the judges.

Sir Richard cleared his throat again. 'Mistress Miller, I want you to recall the events of that day once more. First, tell us why you went to the mill.'

Gulping down the nausea, she closed her eyes a moment and thought back to when Elly had questioned her. Opening her eyes again, she spoke. 'Henry'd forgotten his dinner—'

Several of the jurymen leaned forward, and one cupped his hand behind his ear. She cleared her throat and raised her voice a little. 'Sometimes,' she continued, 'he'd come home for it, but I thought I'd take it down, to save him the trouble. It'd only take me moments.'

'And what did you see when you first reached the mill?' said Sir Richard.

'I saw Fulke and Warin in the lower room, but I thought Henry'd likely be upstairs, so I climbed the stairs.' She closed her eyes again to picture what she saw. 'Up in the mill room, I saw dust flying about, so thick you could scarce see 'cross the room. It caught in my throat and made me cough. An' I knew then it must be what were making Harry worse.'

'And did Henry see that you had come?'

'Aye, he were pleased at first I'd brought him his dinner. I put the bundle down, and it were then I said about the dust and about what Simon the surgeon said about him needing rest. I were so worried 'bout his cough, m'lord, I just wanted to say again about him getting proper help.'

'And what did he answer?'

'He didn't like me saying it. He thought me meddling and told me to leave.'

'And did you?'

'Not at once.' She bit her lip. 'I were so worried 'bout him...'

'Of course you were. So what did Henry do then?'

She hesitated a moment, a great lump in her throat. 'He struck me hard across the face,' she said at last, her voice returned to a whisper. 'And I fell to the floor. I hit my elbow 'gainst a beam, and knocked his dinner down into the machinery.'

'My lords,' said Sir Richard, turning to the judges. 'The constable accompanied me to the mill to look for the dinner bundle and we found it, now somewhat devoured by vermin, but precisely where Mistress Miller said it would be.' Justice Appylton bowed his head.

'So what happened then?' said Sir Richard to Susanna.

'Henry grabbed my arm and dragged me to my feet,' she said, lifting her voice a little. 'Then he raised his hand again to hit me. To stop him, I leaned forward and pushed him away with all my strength. An' it were then he caught his foot upon a beam, and fell back 'gainst the machinery.'

'And did you run away?'

'No!' she cried. 'Of course not, sir. My Harry'd hit his head, so I went to him, thinking he might be hurt. But he weren't *much* hurt, for he soon got up, and told me again to leave.'

'And did you?'

'I thought it best to do his bidding.'

'The Collyere brothers, your lordships, can confirm that they saw Mistress Miller leave. They reported that they then heard their master moving about upstairs before they went home for dinner, not to return that afternoon. What is clear, my lords, is that Henry Miller was *alive* when his wife left the mill. I will now call several witnesses to confirm the truth of that.'

First, Agnes came forward, to say she'd seen Susanna leave the mill around Sext. 'She appeared upset,' she said, 'as if, maybe, she'd been arguing with her husband.' She gave a mischievous grin. 'I know that feeling well enough.' And a few of the women in the court chuckled at that, but the grumpy judge on the left glared at them, and Justice Appylton, his eyebrows raised a little, called for silence.

Alys then bustled forward to say she'd found Henry's body well after dinner time. 'We 'eard the bell for Nones, when we was raising the 'ue an' cry.' The constable confirmed her story, then it was Simon's turn to speak.

'Simon Hogge, my surgeon, your lordships,' said Sir Richard, gesturing him forward, 'who has, for many years, accompanied me on the king's campaigns.'

Simon stood tall and straight-backed before the judges, looking directly at them. 'I examined Henry's body soon after its discovery and, in my opinion, he'd died no more than one hour before.'

Justice Appylton peered down his nose at Simon. 'So, well after the time that Mistress Miller left the mill?'

'Indeed, sir. The wetness of the blood coming from the wound on Henry's head suggested a much more recent fall.'

Susanna was sure she'd not heard Simon say that before. A small bubble of relief rose in her chest.

'Thank you, Master Hogge,' said the judge. 'More, Sir Richard?'

Sir Richard signalled to someone at the back of the crowd and, to a fizz of gasps, a small boy jostled his way through the throng towards him. As the boy came close, Susanna sprang to her feet and ran forward to clasp him to her. Tom wrapped his arms around her waist and held fast for long moments until Eleanor stepped forward and gently prised them apart.

Sir Richard coughed. 'Young Tom here, your lordships, was, I believe, the last person to see his father, Henry, alive.'

There was more clamour from the crowd, and Susanna leapt up, crying, 'No!'

But Sir Richard held up his hand. 'Though that is *by no means* to suggest the boy is responsible for his father's death.' He waved his hand at her to sit, and she sank back onto the bench, her heart hammering with confusion.

'Let me explain, my lords. Young Tom has given me a full account.'

Then she heard Sir Richard tell how Tom saw his father long after she'd left the mill, and how Henry shouted at him and hit him, so hard as to damage his ear. Susanna wanted to cry out again, but stopped her mouth with her fingers. Had Henry truly hit her beloved boy? A few tears sprang to her eyes, and she bent her face down to wipe them away.

He went on to tell how Tom had run away and, later, when he overheard someone in the village saying his father had been found dead, he was so afraid, he hid. A friend – a child, Sir Richard said – found him by chance and agreed to bring him food. Then he fell in with two other boys, runaways, and they decided to stay together, moving out of the village to a deserted hamlet, where they were eventually discovered.

'So that is the background, your lordships,' said Sir Richard. 'But now I want young Tom to tell you in his own words what happened at the mill.'

Tom's narrow little shoulders shook as he stood before the judges, and when he began to answer Sir Richard's questions, his voice was quiet and quavery, and Susanna felt sure he must be crying.

'Pa always got angry when I kep' saying 'bout wanting to work with him in the mill.' He sniffed. 'I were afeared of him, him being so angry all the time—' He rubbed his hand across his face, and Susanna wanted to go to him and hold him tight.

'He weren't like my Pa no more,' said Tom, his shoulders heaving. 'Anyway, I just wanted to tell him I weren't going to complain no more.' He lifted his face to the judge. 'I thought Pa might stop being angry with me if I did.' This last he said so quietly, Susanna wondered if anyone but the judges and herself could hear it.

She brought her hands up to her face, breathing deeply. The poor, poor boy, to be so frightened of the man he once so adored.

But then Tom straightened his back. 'Pa were downstairs,' he said, 'hooking grain bags on the pulley and sending them aloft. When he saw me, he roared at me to leave. He were lumbering round, like those 'uge black bears at the fair. He looked funny, like he'd drunk too much ale or summat, and he'd got a bloody wound, here...' He pointed to his own forehead, high up beneath his floppy hair. 'But I didn't get a chance to say aught, 'cause Pa flew at me, and hit me 'round the head, making me all dizzy.'

Then he pulled at his left ear. 'He hurt my ear – I can't hear in it no more. Anyway, I were so scared I ran away. I hid 'til evening, then crept back to the village and overheard folk in the ale-house saying Pa were dead. Now I were proper terrified, thinking I might've somehow killed him, though I couldn't think of how. So I hid in an old empty cottage, like his lordship said.'

'Thank you, Tom,' said Sir Richard. 'Sit down now. So you see, my lord, Henry Miller was alive well after his wife left him at the mill.'

One of the nasty judges glowered. 'The boy could be making it all up.'

But Sir Richard returned the judge's glare. 'I doubt the boy would have invented that it was *downstairs* he encountered his father. Moreover, we discovered evidence of blood on the grain sacks down below, presumably from Henry's head wound. So Henry did go *downstairs* and then up again before he died, blood oozing from his head wound all the while.'

The judge's eyebrows knit together but then he shrugged.

Justice Appylton addressed Sir Richard. 'Your witnesses have provided us with a very detailed picture of the events that day. However, I have some questions – for clarification.'

Sir Richard inclined his head.

'First,' said the judge, 'Master Gastingthrop gave evidence that the tussle was violent. But when the coroner asked Mistress Miller to explain exactly what had happened, exactly how her husband received his injuries, she *refused* to say, suggesting guilt.'

Sir Richard shook his head. 'It is clear, my lord, that the so-called tussle was indeed violent. The Collyere brothers, working below, heard both shouting and scuffles overhead. What you have heard Mistress Miller say, however, is that her husband *attacked* her and she was forced to defend herself. It was when she did so that her husband tripped and fell.'

'Why did she not say that to the coroner?'

'Because she was so shocked, both at the incident itself, then at being arrested when Henry was discovered dead. The painful memory of her beloved husband *striking* her – something he had *never* done before, my lords – cast itself from her mind. She did not *refuse* to explain, my lords, but was simply *unable* to do so.' He straightened his shoulders. 'However, later, after gentle enquiry by her close friend, Mistress Titherige here, Mistress Miller at length regained her memory of that day and, as you have heard, has since been able to furnish us with a clearer account of events.'

Justice Appylton bowed his head. 'A second question, then, Sir Richard. Is it likely that Master Miller would "trip" in his own mill?'

Sir Richard held up his hand and called out, 'Thomas Miller!' And, to Susanna's surprise, Henry's brother raised his arm.

'Here, m'lord,' he called, and Sir Richard beckoned him to come forward.

Thomas pushed his way through the crowd of onlookers and stood before his lordship, fumbling and passing the edge of his cap between his fingers.

'Thomas, tell their lordships what happened when *you* tripped in the mill – how easy it can be, even for an experienced and long-serving miller.'

And, haltingly, Thomas related the sad story of the day when his last son, Peter, brought *his* dinner to the mill and, in his anxiety to protect the boy from danger, he had moved too fast, and caught his toe against a beam and, falling forward, knocked his own child down through the hatch, through which the bags of flour were hauled up from the floor below.

Tears sprang to Susanna's eyes yet again at the retelling of *that* terrible day. Yet her heart lifted at the clarity of her brother-in-law's account, when she'd thought him lost to the world of rational men.

'Thank you, Master Miller,' said the judge, gesturing at him to go. Thomas turned the wrong way to rejoin the crowd and, seeing Susanna sitting on her bench, grinned at her. She wondered at it, the first time she'd seen him smile for more than four years.

'Thirdly,' continued Justice Appylton, 'may I ask, what of Master Gastingthrop's evidence of Mistress Miller's apparent *intention* to strike her husband?'

Sir Richard shook his head. 'I am afraid, my lord, that Mistress Miller has been much misrepresented. I can bring before you witnesses whose evidence to the coroner was, shall we say, somewhat unproven.'

One of the other judges grunted. 'Are you saying you have persuaded these witnesses to *change* their evidence? With a little sweetener perhaps?' He rubbed his thumb and forefinger together and glared.

Sir Richard's eyebrows shot up. 'I most certainly am not. In the light of Mistress Miller's recovered memory and the evidence from young Tom, I gathered together those who had made statements to the coroner, to present the new evidence to them and ask if they still held the same view of her guilt. I did not, your lordships, ask them myself. The constable interviewed them.' He glared at the judge, his eyes as piercing as a hawk's. 'There was no "persuasion" of any kind, my lords.'

Justice Appylton, his lips slightly curved, waved his hand at Sir Richard to continue. Then, one after the other, Meonbridge folk came forward to say their piece.

Alys admitted that what she'd claimed Susanna said at the pump was her own interpretation. Ann piped up from the crowd to say Susanna was a gentle, upright soul, who couldn't kill a fly let alone her husband. Three men, red-faced, came forward to say they were encouraged by the priest to say Susanna was a scold, and the crowd erupted into a hiss of gasps.

Justice Appylton stared at one of the men. 'The *priest* persuaded you? Explain.'

The man, scarlet now, shuffled from foot to foot, his eyes darting wildly at his companions, but seemed unable to answer.

'Well?' barked one of the other judges.

'Shall I assist, my lords?' said Sir Richard, and Justice Appylton gestured to him to proceed.

Sir Richard turned to the quaking man. 'Did not Master Hugo – the priest in Meonbridge, your lordships, until recently – denounce Mistress Miller as the Devil's slave, a wicked wife who sought revenge against her husband? A denunciation made,' he raised an eyebrow, 'without the slightest speck of evidence to support his outrageous claim?'

The man lowered his eyes. ''Tis true, m'lord.'

Sir Richard addressed the judges. 'I am afraid, my lords, that our priest had become a madman, spreading lies and calumny about the good wives of Meonbridge without any justification.'

'He is still your priest?' Justice Appylton said, staring down his nose.

'No, your lordship. I have asked the bishop to find us a replacement. Master Garret has gone.'

The judge turned to the man. 'So,' he said, 'are you saying that Mistress Miller was *not* a scold?'

The man mumbled his reply. 'Master Miller were a changed man, your honour. He were once a cheerful fellow, who never had a bad word to say of his wife. But he got that ill-tempered, he started saying she were a nag. But everyone in Meonbridge knows she ain't...' He trailed off.

The judge turned to Sir Richard. '*Everyone* knows?'

Ralph stepped forward. 'Master Ward here,' said Sir Richard, 'was not asked to speak to the coroner. But, as a good friend of Henry Miller, he was a close witness to the change in his character.'

'Henry were once the happiest of men,' said Ralph. 'Gentle-natured. He *never* struck his wife, treated her always with love and respect. But he got gloomy and downhearted, and vexed too at his wife's urging him to do what he thought he couldn't. Yet I warrant he never told her *why* it were he couldn't get another journeyman. The truth was, m'lords, no one'd work for him 'cause he'd become so doleful a master.'

'But doleful is not violent, Master Ward.'

'Indeed, sir. But, in his downheartedness, he let slip to his drinking cronies he found Susanna's urging irksome, and *they*, m'lord, said she were a nagging wife. And, at length, Henry believed it too, and began to talk of chastising her, which he'd never done before, not even in words, let alone wi' his hand.'

Some men in the crowd and a few of the jurors laughed, but one juror, not laughing, stood up and faced the judge. 'But it says in the Bible, or so we're told, m'lord, a man has a *right* to chastise his nagging wife.'

Then a man in the crowd called out that he'd heard Henry say oftentimes how mad his wife were making him with her nagging, and how he thought one day he'd snap.

Justice Appylton held up his hand. He nodded to Ralph and, waving him away, turned to Sir Richard. 'Enough evidence, I think?'

Sir Richard bowed his head. 'But if I may just give a summary of my thoughts, my lord,' he said, and did not wait for the judge to agree. 'When his wife brought him his dinner, Henry Miller was in a deep melancholy, and overreacted to her natural concern for his welfare. He fell by chance and hit his head during an altercation with his wife, in which he struck her and she defended herself. His later aggression towards his son, which he had never shown before, was simply another sign of his melancholic humour. It has to be assumed that the injury to his head was more severe than Henry might have thought, and that he collapsed and died some time later, perhaps from the sheer exertion of his labours.'

'Thank you, Sir Richard,' said the judge then, pressing down on the table edge, pushed himself to his feet. 'We have heard a deal of evidence. As it is already well past Sext, I suggest we break now for a small dinner. Return to this place in one hour.' Then he and his fellow judges swept out of the hall.

Susanna sat with Eleanor, hands clasped together. Sir Richard gave Ralph some money to go and buy hot meat pies from a street trader, and when he returned with the pies steaming in their wrappers, the two men and Emma tucked into theirs with relish. Susanna claimed not to be hungry, which wasn't true, but she knew that any lumps of meat would stick fast in her throat and make her choke. For, despite all the evidence and folk speaking in her favour, she was still sure the case would go against her. She noticed Eleanor eyeing her own pie, cooling on the bench.

'Try to eat a little, Susy,' said Eleanor.

But Susanna shook her head. 'You eat, Elly. I can't, but don't let yours go cold.'

When the judges returned, Justice Appylton made short work of saying the evidence against Susanna was so thin, and the many oath-helpers so certain of both her innocence and the dramatic change in Henry's temper, together with the surgeon's view of his likely time of death, he was obliged to conclude that Henry's demise was most probably an accident. He was still alive well after his wife left the mill, and indeed after his encounter with his son. The bang on his head was likely graver than it seemed, and the cause of his later death.

When he asked the jury to consider their opinion, Susanna assumed they'd all leave the room. But the twelve men just shuffled along the benches and, leaning their heads together in a huddle, whispered to each other for a few moments before one of them stood up.

'We agree with your conclusion, your lordship,' he said, and bowed his head.

'Are all twelve agreed?'

'We are.'

Justice Appylton smiled down at her. 'So, Mistress Miller, you are free to return to your home and family…Mistress Miller?'

Eleanor then touched her hand. 'Susy, his lordship says you are innocent.'

The corners of the judge's eyes were crinkling. 'Go home to your family, Mistress Miller.'

Susanna wobbled as she got up from the bench. 'Thank you, your lordship.' Tears filled her eyes. 'Thank you, sir.' She dropped a small curtsey, then Eleanor took her arm and led her across to sit with Emma and Ralph.

Justice Appylton lifted an eyebrow at Sir Richard, who put his hand upon Tom's shoulder and gave him a little push.

'Come forward, young Tom Miller,' said the judge, 'and tell me more about those other runaways.' He pulled on his beard. 'Why did they run away?'

The colour drained from Tom's face. 'I d-d-don't know…' he stammered, then burst into sobs. He glanced at Eleanor, sheer terror on his face.

She exchanged a nod with Sir Richard, who stepped forward. 'I will bring the runaways before you shortly, my lord, and I am afraid they are – or rather one of them is – guilty of serious misdemeanours. But young Tom here knows nothing of those crimes.'

'Yet he lived with them for, what, several weeks?'

'That is true, my lord. But—'

Justice Appylton smiled and raised his hand. 'Come a little closer, Tom. Do not be afraid.' Tom shuffled forward to the table and the judge leaned forward. 'I want to tell you, child, that hiding out with felons was a dangerous thing to do. It tarred you with their brush, when you were innocent of any misdemeanour. I must warn you not to let yourself become involved again with such individuals. When you are home once more, be a good son to your stepmother, a good brother to your siblings and a hard worker for Sir Richard.'

Tom whispered something Susanna couldn't hear. Then he wiped his face on his sleeve, as Sir Richard put his arm around him and brought him to sit beside her. Tom leaned his head against her arm, and the sleeve of her kirtle dampened with his tears. Shifting her arm and putting it around his shoulder, his little body slumped against her, and she pulled him closer. Her eyes also filled with tears, and wiping them away didn't stem the flow. But it was no matter. She and Tom were safe.

She glanced up just as Justice Appylton grinned at Sir Richard. But then he let the broad smile slide away, and replaced it with a furrowed brow.

'So what of these two runaways?'

# 22

Eleanor sat on Walter's rough-hewn bench outside the shepherd's cottage. She was gazing at the sun lowering in the western sky, dipping behind the distant trees in a vivid pink-red glow. But the sunset's beauty blurred, as she recalled the events in Winchester earlier in the afternoon. Her gaze fell upon the cottage, and she wished Walter might come out through the door and stroll across to sit down next to her. And yet she knew, even if he were here, he would have no sympathy with her distress.

Will understood. Indeed, he shared her horror of what had happened in the court, even though the outcome was scarcely a surprise. Moments ago, Meg and the puppy at his heels, he had strolled off down the hill to Meonvale for a pot of ale or two.

'You'll be all right, missus?' he had said, his mouth taut.

She had nodded. 'Go, Will. I'll be fine.' She raised a tear-stained face to his. 'Am I foolish to be so upset?'

'Dunno, missus. It were a harsh punishment. But no more 'n we expected.'

'I just feel it's all my fault.'

'Now that *is* foolish. It were young Luke's fault, missus, not yours. He's no child. He knew what he were doing.'

She nodded again.

Will placed a hand lightly on her shoulder. 'You'll be off home afore I'm back?'

She laughed lightly. 'I must go soon, else Hawisa will be sending poor old Nathan out to look for me. Just a few moments longer, then I'll follow you down the hill.'

Hawisa and Nathan had chosen not to join the village outing to witness Susanna's trial, but to spend the day – it could be a holiday, Eleanor had said – visiting Hawisa's niece in West Meon, a few miles from Meonbridge, and a good walk upstream along the banks of the river. They were still out when Eleanor arrived home from Winchester, and she decided to go up to Riverdown before dusk fell to see Will and the sheep.

After they had discussed the flock, Will's mouth had drooped. 'I've heard about Luke,' he said, his voice croaking.

He had also not travelled to Winchester, agreeing to stay and mind the flock. She wondered who had told him about Luke but did not ask. 'The judge was so kindly towards Susanna,' she said, 'I hoped he might be merciful with Luke.'

'Mebbe he *were* merciful? He could've sent him to the rope.'

Eleanor felt a lump come to her throat. She knew Will was right. Luke's penalty was harsh enough, but at least the judge had spared him death – an act of mercy, Sir Richard had said, in recognition of Luke's responsibilities to his father. Although Matthew, tough as he was, collapsed onto the floor when he heard the judge announce Luke's sentence, and had to be revived with a bucket of cold water.

'So what happened?' said Will.

Eleanor pointed to Walter's bench and they sat down facing the lowering sun. 'You know that, after Emma and I found all the boys in Upper Brooking, and the tithing-men captured Luke, he and Arthur were put into the village lockup.' Will nodded. 'Poor Arthur was so miserable, but the constable thought it best if they were treated the same, until the court could decide on their guilt or innocence.'

''ard on little Arthur,' said Will.

'I agree. And there was a great commotion when the boys were brought into the court, with their hands bound, some declaring it was a shame Arthur was being so harshly treated, others that it was about time Luke faced the consequences of his actions.'

Will sniffed. 'Them'd be the ones he stole from.'

Eleanor nodded. 'Anyway,' she continued, 'I heard somebody weeping, and learned later it was John. Poor man! He didn't deserve such anguish.'

'John's a good man.'

'But then there came a great shout, and Matthew was hurtling forward, pushing through the crowd until he reached the front, where Luke and Arthur were standing.'

'Did he cause an uproar?'

She nodded. 'He ranted and raved against Sir Richard, and the judges, *and* the jurymen. I doubt it did Luke's case any good at all. Even Justice Appylton, who had been so kind towards Susanna, was dark with anger, and ordered Matthew to sit down.'

'Trust Matt to make a bad situation all the worse.'

'Indeed. Anyway, the two boys were made to stand before the judges. Poor little Arthur was quaking, weeping as if his heart might break, his face all shiny with the leakings from his eyes and nose.' She bit her lip.

'I warrant Luke weren't weeping.'

'No. He stood with his legs astride, a wide smirk on his face, gazing around him as if he hadn't a worry in the world.'

'Idiot boy!' Will scoffed. 'So what happened then?'

'Sir Richard related everything the boys had done. First, stealing my sheep and letting them die, then stealing food while they were hiding out in Meonvale. Then running away—'

'Didn't the judge ask why they hadn't been found in the hue and cry?'

'Sir Richard brought the constable forward, and he admitted that, although his search party looked hard for the boys after my sheep were stolen, they had to give it up. He was pretty red-faced, poor Geoffrey. But then Sir Richard told the judge that it was *his* decision not to chase around the countryside, as he put it, because he couldn't afford the manpower for a lengthy search. And the judge agreed it was difficult these days with so few men available for all that needed to be done.'

'Sounds a fair-minded fellow.'

'In truth, I think he was. Anyway, Sir Richard went on to tell how the boys joined a band of outlaws—'

'Outlaws?' Will guffawed. 'They fell in wi' renegades?'

Eleanor was not as much impressed as Will with what he seemed to consider adventurousness. 'Sir Richard said that Arthur hated it and wanted to come home, but Luke refused to leave, knowing, I suppose, what would happen if he came back to Meonbridge. As Sir Richard put it, Luke was holding Arthur against his will.'

'Poor little lad. He should never've kept company wi' his cousin. Luke's always been a bad lot, like his Pa.'

'The boys travelled with the outlaws for a long time – months – but in the end they threw them out or, rather, threw Luke out, because he fought with the leader. When they came back to Meonbridge, they found Tom, then Luke bullied his cousin Bea into stealing food—'

Will's mouth dropped open. 'Bea Ward *stole…?*'

'Poor Emma was distraught. Bea came forward and confessed that she had already taken a little food to Tom. But she said, when Luke and Arthur came, Luke threatened to kill Tom and eat *him* if she didn't keep bringing food, and she believed him. Poor child! She was so scared she kept on trying to take them food, even though it was almost impossible to find enough for three.'

'I warrant Luke got nasty?'

'I think he did. Poor Bea. Justice Appylton peered down his nose at her, and his fellow judges frowned. She looked so frightened. But the judges and the jurymen agreed that, when she stole food for Tom, she did so out of misguided charity, and when she continued stealing for Luke and Arthur, it was out of fear. So they declared she would not be punished, on the understanding Ralph and Emma controlled her behaviour in future. Emma almost fainted with relief.'

'So what did the judges say 'bout the Ward boys?'

'When Justice Appylton asked them each in turn both to give their plea, Arthur just stood there open-mouthed, not understanding what he meant. So Sir Richard spoke up for him, saying he was too young and simple-minded to be truly guilty of any of the crimes.'

'"Simple-minded" were a bit below the belt.'

'Perhaps, but his lordship wanted to make sure the boy wasn't harshly punished.'

'And did he speak for Luke?'

She shook her head. 'He thought Luke old enough to speak for himself.'

'And did he?'

She bit her lip. 'He refused. I don't know what he was thinking, but he just shrugged at the judge's question and acted as if he was— Well, I don't know what, Will.'

'So he got what he deserved.' He rolled his eyes.

'No, Will. Angry as I am about my sheep, I would never have wished Luke to suffer such a punishment. How can he work with just one hand?'

A few Meonbridge folk had gone to watch Luke having his left hand hacked off, but she could not bear to. It was enough to hear his screams, carrying on the still summer air across the castle bailey to the great hall where she waited. The sound of it would live with her forever.

Sir Richard had tried to have Luke's punishment commuted to one less damaging, but the judge took the advice of the sheriff that mutilation was the only choice. He had slumped down on the bench next to Eleanor and Geoffrey, his face grey. His shoulders hunched forward and he bowed his head. 'I failed,' he said. 'Mutilation it is.'

Eleanor had cried out and Geoffrey cursed. 'It's not often these days, lord,' he said, 'a thief suffers mutilation. A heavy fine's more common by far, to help replenish the king's meagre coffers.' Sir Richard grunted his agreement. 'But, as the Wards have no money,' continued the constable, 'nor any goods left them to sell, mebbe we shouldn't be surprised the sheriff advised a corporal punishment of some kind.'

'And hanging,' said Sir Richard, with a grimace, 'would serve only to deprive the manor of yet another worker. Not that Luke has ever been much of an asset in the fields. He will be even less effective with one hand missing.'

As the sun made its last descent, Eleanor knew that she should go. Yet still she did not move. Until, at last, imagining her servant's shrill reproof for staying out after dark, she eased herself to her feet and set off home.

Hawisa appeared to be waiting for her when Eleanor pushed open the heavy door and stepped inside her hall. But the older woman kept her counsel.

'You look all in, mistress,' she said kindly. 'Sit down and rest yourself.'

Eleanor sighed. 'I *am* exhausted, Hawisa. Will you bring me something to drink?'

'Ale, or mebbe a little wine?'

'Wine, I think.' It might revive her spirits.

When Hawisa returned with a goblet and a jug brimming with red Gascony, she put them on the table at Eleanor's elbow, then poured a goblet full.

'Thank you, Hawisa,' said Eleanor, expecting her to go back to the kitchen. But the woman did not move. Eleanor tilted her head. 'Did you want to say something?'

'Just to ask what happened at the court.'

Hawisa scurried back to the kitchen to fetch Nathan and then Eleanor repeated to her servants everything she had said to Will.

'It's no more 'n he deserves,' she said, echoing Will's words. Few in Meonbridge, it seemed, had much sympathy for Luke. 'Though how him and that good-for-nothing Pa of his'll cope only the Good Lord knows.'

Nathan would not dare argue with his wife, but he said, 'Matt's had it tough since the Death took 'is wife, and the two little maids—'

'Pah!' cried Hawisa. 'Lots o' folk lost loved ones – they don't meet ev'ry problem wi' their fists, or worse.'

Next morning, John presented his son to the constable for Arthur's punishment to be carried out. If Eleanor could not have borne to witness Luke's, she told herself that, in attending Arthur's, she would at least be showing support for John. Not that she planned to stay.

'You have stocks in Meonbridge, Sir Richard?' Judge Appylton had demanded. 'Then Arthur, son of John Ward, is to be confined in those stocks for one whole day a week for three weeks. During his confinement he must be given water, but no food. Between times, and thereafter, the boy must be given into the care of his father and bound over to keep the peace.'

John, brought forward to stand next to his son, had cried out as he heard the judge's words and, sobbing, slumped down onto a bench. Eleanor let out her breath and exchanged an expression of relief with Emma, who went across to John and put her arm through his.

Now, as the constable led him forward, the boy was shivering, despite the comforting warmth of the rising sun. But how gently Geoffrey was treating him, speaking quietly and touching him only enough to help! Arthur did not struggle, and Eleanor's heart clenched to see how brave the lad was being, despite his fear.

She recalled the last time she had seen the stocks on Meonbridge's green in use. Four years ago, Emma's first husband, Bart, was ordered to be confined by Sir Richard's son, Sir Philip, his penalty for refusing to carry out his tenant's duties. The bailiff's henchmen had manhandled Bart into the stocks. Two men dragged him here, straight from the manor court, hauling him by his arms so his boots scraped along the cobbles. Then they threw him down next to the stocks and roughly pushed his arms and legs through the holes, before slamming down the top board and chaining it shut.

It was raining, she recalled, the grass around the stocks slippery with mud. But this morning, with the sunshine, the warmth and Geoffrey's gentleness, it did not seem quite so terrible as it had done then.

Nonetheless, Arthur was still a child – in his mind, if not his body – and would surely find it hard to be imprisoned in that contraption all day long. She went across to John and touched his arm. 'Arthur's being very brave.'

'I told him not to be afeared. It's only for a day. An' I'll sit with him.' He rubbed his hand across his face. 'But he won't understand if folk come an' stare at him, or throw—'

'They *won't*, John,' said Eleanor. She squeezed his arm. 'Do you remember when Bart Coupar was in the stocks? Folk let him alone, not wanting the bailiff to think they approved the punishment. It will be the same with Arthur. If they come at all, it will be out of sympathy.'

'You think so, missus?' A sob escaped John's lips. 'My poor lad! I should've kept him away from my brother's worthless bastard of a son.'

Eleanor patted his arm. In the matter of Matthew and his wayward son, she did not know what to say to bring John any comfort. The horror of finding her stolen sheep dead or near to death paled beside that of Luke's mutilation. Of course, Will was right, Luke *had* brought it upon himself. Yet sometimes she wished she and Emma had not found him in the cottage in Upper Brooking, but he had been able to run far from Meonbridge, to a life of which she would have no knowledge, and need feel no guilt.

As summer drifted into autumn, the woodland that fringed the edge of Riverdown gradually changed from green to gold, bringing sunshine to the dense stand of oaks and beeches even when the day was cloudy. This year, the leaves seemed to be remaining gold rather than deepening to rusty red.

'Been too dry this summer,' said Will, shaking his head. 'Rain's needed early on to bring out the colour.'

It seemed surprising that a man like Will even noticed the changing colours of the leaves. Yet why shouldn't he? Walter did. She thought of those few happy late afternoons – two autumns ago perhaps – when, at the end of the working day, she and Walter would sit together in the shelter of the woodland, the flock grazing placidly in the pasture that sloped away below them and, far in the distance, the glorious gold and russet glow lit up the broad forest that lay beyond the bounds of Meonbridge.

'It fair lifts the spirit,' Walter had said. 'The beauty of it.'

That was all he said, but she did not need more words to feel the power of his... What? She had thought then – hoped perhaps – it was his affection, for her as well as for the world. But she had never asked him to say so, nor would she.

Were the trees as beautiful wherever he was living now? And was there perhaps some other young woman with whom he sat upon a hill, gazing across to the horizon? She turned away, not wanting Will to see her tears.

Despite it being Michaelmas, the summer heat still lingered through the day and, up on Riverdown – "closer to the sun than down in Meonbridge", Emma often said – their clothes were soon damp with sweat.

The three of them had been preparing the ewes for mating, checking they were in the best condition for producing lambs next spring. It was a job Eleanor found satisfying but, without Walter's expertise, she felt less confident this year than last that their judgements would be sound. It had been around this time last year that the rift between her and Walter had begun to widen, and it was hard now to remember what in truth had led to him, a few weeks later, leaving her and Meonbridge – yet impossible to forget her foolish part in it.

Now, she tried to remember exactly how Walter had carried out the checks. Of course, Will and Emma did know how to do them too, and between them they worked through the flock, pressing their hands firm upon the animals' backs to decide if they needed feeding up or fasting before being put with the rams next month.

They had checked only a few when Emma blew out her lips and threw off the woollen shawl she had put over her kirtle against the early morning chill. She wiped a corner of the shawl across her glistening face. 'It'll not be much longer afore we're complaining of the cold,' she said, grinning, 'so I s'pose we oughta enjoy it while we can.' Then she flung the shawl over a nearby hurdle fence and they continued with the ewes.

As she often did, Eleanor took a final walk around the pastures with Will – a stroll she used to take with Walter – checking that the sheep were secure enough, the gates shut, the fences sound.

'Hey, missus, look,' said Will, and strode over to a length of fence, coming back with Emma's shawl. ''Em forgot it.'

'I suppose she was rushing off home to her children,' said Eleanor. 'But she might need it tomorrow, so I'll drop it off on my way home.'

Eleanor was always nervous walking past the cottage occupied by Matthew and Luke, or the ale-house a few paces further along the road. She could never quite forget the day when Matthew threatened her, indeed assaulted her, before getting into a fight with Nicholas. Yet there was no avoiding Meonvale on her way home from Riverdown – there simply was no other road to take.

She had seen John and young Arthur several times since the poor boy's punishment in the stocks, and she was surprised daily that she had still not set eyes on either Luke or Matthew. But Emma had told her they were keeping to themselves while Luke's injury was healing.

'It's mending well enough, but Luke's nowhere near ready to start work again.' She bit her lip. 'An' it's hard to see how he'll ever be of much use with just one hand.'

'One of my father's servants lost his right hand fighting for the king,' Eleanor had recalled. 'I was fascinated by it as a child, yet it didn't seem much to bother him. And do you remember Sir Giles Fitzpeyne, who came to marry Lady Johanna?'

'And got sent away again when Sir Philip were found murdered...'

Eleanor grimaced. 'He'd lost a whole arm, or so I heard.'

'But it'd be different for a man like him,' said Emma, sniffing. 'Ralph said he wore a false metal arm, wi' a hand that moved. I'll warrant your Pa's servant didn't have one o' them, and neither will Luke.'

'Yet I remember that our serving man carried out many tasks with his one hand, using the stump of his other arm to help. I used to think how clever he was, although I suppose it was just practice. Maybe Luke too will learn in time?'

'But mebbe your man were proud to have lost his hand fighting for the king, and were willing to learn to live without it. Whereas Luke'll just be aggrieved, and 'e'll make no effort to help himself. Just like his Pa.' She paused, and bit her lip. 'An' if Matt were ill-tempered afore, Elly, you won't believe how bitter he's become, almost like he's lost his wits.'

Since that talk with Emma a few days past, Eleanor had become alarmed that Matthew might still vent his fury on her. Every time she passed the cottage, she held her breath, glancing sideways. Yet she tried not to hurry, not to look as if she was afraid.

When she saw no sign of Matthew or Luke, Eleanor released her breath and, side-stepping a small puddle caused by last night's rain, reached Emma's door. She raised her hand to knock. But her knuckle had not even touched the wood before she heard a shout, and her name called out, and she turned her head to see Matthew leaping the low wall of his croft and galloping across the muddy road towards her, his gait lop-sided.

'Oi, Eleanor Titherige!' he yelled. 'You 'appy now?'

She rapped hard upon the door, but Matthew reached her and grabbed her by the elbow. His face was dark, his eyes flicking from side to side. 'Eh, missus?' he said, his voice hoarse. 'I'm talking to you.'

She shook her arm free and faced him. 'Master Ward. If you are suggesting that I am *happy* that Luke has lost his hand, you are quite wrong. I am most *un*happy.' She struggled to keep her tears at bay, refusing to be cowed. 'Unhappy that he stole my sheep. Unhappy that he let them die. Unhappy that he held his gentle cousin against his will.' She paused. 'Unhappy too that you have so ill-treated him that—'

But she could not finish, as Matthew's hand flew across her mouth in a sharply stinging slap. She gasped, and twisted her head towards Emma's door, willing it to open.

But Matthew's grimy fingers were prodding her in the shoulder. 'Don't you say that 'bout my son. You know naught about us. 'Cept now he's a cripple 'cause of you. You know *that*, don't you?' He spat the words wetly into her face, then drew back his hand and hit her once again, the violence of the blow throwing her to the ground.

Eleanor let out a cry, at the shock of being hit, and the sudden pain that shot through her leg, twisted awkwardly beneath her in the mud. She winced too at the sting of blood as it spurted from her cut lip. But, behind her, at last, the door was opening and Emma was shouting curses at Matthew. She thought she could hear Ralph there too and, beyond her dizzy head, the scuffle of feet hurrying along the hard dirt road, until a small group was gathered around her, shouting.

Eleanor's head was spinning, her ears pounding. The shock of what had just happened, and the pain in her leg, kept her prostrate on the ground. But she could still hear Emma yelling at Matthew, and him cursing her in return.

But then Emma stopped shouting and was kneeling at her side, her arm around her shoulder, gently helping her to stand. And, as Eleanor struggled upright, wincing as she put weight upon her leg, Ralph and another man, William Mannering, grabbed Matthew by the arms and held him fast.

Then John came running, Luke and Arthur with him. Eleanor was aghast as she saw, for the first time, how loosely Luke's shirt seemed to hang on him and how his face was drained of colour. Blood still stained the filthy wrappings on his stump.

John stepped forward and touched Ralph's arm with his hand. 'Cousin, please set my brother free.' John's eyes were wet. 'I'll take him home.' He sniffed. 'You know how distracted he still is by all that's happened.'

Ralph's shoulders slumped, and he, and then William, loosed their grip on Matthew. Matthew shook himself free, hooting and flailing his arms above his head. But, a moment later, he let fly a punch at Ralph. 'You always take the gentry's part,' he yelled.

Ralph was quick enough to dodge the flying fist, so it only clipped the side of his head. Nonetheless, a trickle of blood oozed from his ear.

'Eleanor's hardly gentry!' cried Emma, taking Ralph's head in her hands and dabbing at his ear with a corner of her apron.

'But she ain't one of us,' said Matthew, his voice cracking.

One or two onlookers appeared to mumble their agreement but Ralph, freeing his head from Emma's hands, shook it slowly.

'It weren't Mistress Titherige's fault Luke were brought afore the court,' he said. 'She'd every right to accuse him for stealing her sheep, yet she didn't. She were more 'n generous, not wanting to make things worse for him.'

Matthew looked as if he would let fly at Ralph again, but John grabbed his brother's arm and bid William do the same.

'But, after stealing the sheep,' continued Ralph, 'and letting them die, he stole food from his neighbours – from us! – then kidnapped his little cousin, and fell in with them outlaws.' Ralph's face then twisted into a sneer. 'An' forced *our* girl to steal for him.' He stopped, his fury at that final insult written on his face.

Emma lurched forward and thumped Matthew with her fist. '*Our* girl,' she cried. 'How *dare* you!' This last was a scream.

Ralph gently took hold of his wife's arm and pulled her away. He glared at everyone. 'You all know the rules. Luke and Matthew are members of our tithing – it's our duty to bring any wrongdoing to justice. We was generous enough at first, following Missus Titherige's lead, not wanting to make things worse for them.' There was a general murmuring of agreement. 'But 'nough's enough. An' it weren't *our* decision Luke were brought afore the king's judges, but his lordship's, as y' all well know. An' it weren't our decision Luke lost his hand.' He touched his still-bleeding ear and winced. 'For all his crimes, he might've lost his head.'

More men and women had emerged from the ale-house and were coming across, some with pots of ale in their hands. Most onlookers seemed be accepting the truth of what Ralph said, though one or two of the new arrivals – unsteady on their feet already, despite the early hour – wanted to take Matthew's part, and urged him to stand up for what was only fair, as one of them put it in a slurred string of abuse.

Emma shook her head at that. 'What's *fair*?' she cried. 'What's fair is a lad who stole sheep and let 'em die were punished. A lad who duped his little cousin, who stole from us all here in Meonvale, were punished. It'd be no more fair Luke getting away with all o' that than anyone else.'

Eleanor felt very dizzy. As well as her leg, her head was hurting now, inside and out. She thought she might fall down again and leaned against the wall of Emma's house. But, as she did so, Matthew broke free from his captors once more and lunged at Emma. He was wild, flailing, weeping. He raised his hand as if intent on striking her, but Ralph stepped between them and Matthew lowered his hand.

'No more fighting, Matt,' said Ralph.

Matthew shook his head, tears flooding down his face.

'What'll happen to us?' he wailed, then, seemingly defeated, spun away in the direction of his house.

Eleanor blew out a deep breath, and closed her eyes. Was it all over? Her head seemed to be full of bees, and everyone around her appeared blurry, like in a dream. But then Emma was taking her arm in one hand, her other around her waist, and pulling her gently towards the open door. Opening her eyes again, she nodded her gratitude.

But then Matthew was swinging around again. With three strides, he reached Ralph and punched him squarely in the face. Ralph reeled but stayed on his feet, then lunged forward, his arm raised. But, as the two men closed, Matthew thrust his fist into Ralph's belly. Ralph wheezed then, collapsing to his knees, cried out. He was clutching at his belly, and blood was spurting from between his fingers. As he toppled forward, Emma – Eleanor already abandoned – half-caught him and they fell together down onto the mud.

Emma cried out too, for someone to fetch Simon. And a man ran off, though Eleanor did not see who.

Emma was wailing, Ralph groaning, as she ripped her apron from her waist and, bunching it, pressed it against the wound.

The onlookers surged forward, arguing between themselves, but it was clear to all that Matthew had used a knife against his cousin.

Eleanor, her own discomfort and distress forgotten, shouted at William Mannering, hovering beside his fallen friend. 'William, arrest Matthew Ward!'

But William was at once bewildered. 'He's gone,' he roared.

'Then call out the hue and cry,' she cried. Then, as William and a few others ran off after Matthew, yelling to all who could hear to join the chase, she sank to her knees, slumped against the house wall, nausea threatening to overcome her.

It seemed a long while before Simon came, although in truth it may have been no more than minutes. He found Ralph still groaning but seemingly not on the point of death. And, after he had examined the wound, he let out a long whistle.

'Not so bad as you might've feared,' he said to Emma. 'Not that deep. And Ralph's strong. He should recover.'

Emma uttered a cry of relief and stumbled across to Eleanor. The two women put their arms around each other.

Dusk was advancing now and clouds had built up thick enough to obscure the pale moon. Simon called for a lantern, then rolled Ralph onto his back. Emma's neighbour brought the light and held it steady as the barber-surgeon spread a little honey around the puncture in Ralph's belly, then stitched it and dressed it tightly.

Ralph had been helped up to his feet by the time the constable arrived. Only moments later, the tithing-men returned, all out of breath and heaving.

William shook his head at the constable. 'No sign of 'im.'

Geoffrey frowned and pointed at the darkening sky. 'No sense widening the search now,' he said. 'We'll wait till first light.' Then he tilted his head towards Ralph. 'Mind you, Ralph, if you're not too badly injured, perhaps – yet again – we should be generous to Matt and not hunt him down?'

Emma cried out 'No!', but Ralph agreed, despite his evident pain. 'Let's consider my injury the outcome of a fair fight.' Emma continued to protest, but he put out his hand to stay her. 'Tell that to Sir Richard, Geoffrey.'

The constable nodded, but Eleanor thought doubt showed in his tightened lips. Was he thinking, as Emma probably was, and she certainly was herself, that Matthew had received generosity enough?

# 23

## AUTUMN 1353

Agnes gazed at Susanna, bustling about her cottage, chatting to her children, bringing them drinks, fetching them toys, simply relishing being a mother once again. How remarkable she was, recovering her old cheerful spirit so soon! Only weeks since her trial and release from prison, she'd already regained most of the weight she'd lost. Her face too showed how well she was putting behind her the horror of those terrible months, in her rosy cheeks and bright eyes, and the invariable smile on her lips.

Agnes sighed. This was – what? – the fourth week of their new arrangement, her coming here for an afternoon to let Stephen and Geoffrey play with Susanna's little ones, while Dickon was up at the manor with his grandmother and Libby. She should surely be uplifted by Susanna's new-sprung cheerfulness?

Yet Agnes felt anything but merry.

At least the nausea of the last three months had passed. But she still had six months of increasing discomfort and exhaustion, though maybe at the end of it there'd be a daughter, which was certainly something to look forward to.

She stared at pretty little Maud. She was of an age with Dickon but as different from him as it was possible to be, with her sweet cherubic face, wheat-coloured curls, and her disposition by turns earnest and funny.

Then there was baby Joan, Susanna's last child, not as pretty as her older cousin but charming in her way, and certainly none so boisterous as her own Geoffrey, born the very same month.

Still, girls or boys, pretty or no, all the Miller children had given Susanna good reason to embrace the world again, to try to forget the terror of her arrest, imprisonment and trial. And so too had the mill. Agnes knew it'd been at Margaret's bidding that Sir Richard agreed to let Susanna be in charge of the mill, though she could never be the miller, which was no job for a woman.

Master Langelee, it seemed, was more interested in the baking side of the business and had asked Sir Richard if he might give up the milling but stay on as master baker. His lordship was happy to accept his proposition, provided he could find another miller. So he'd asked Thomas, who, after his surprising lucidity at Susanna's trial, seemed much more his former self.

And Thomas was glad to agree.

Now, said Susanna, he was so delighted to be working again, he was almost the man he used to be, jesting and wagging with his customers. Warin still laboured on the mill's ground floor but, despite his happy return from the darkest depths of melancholy, Thomas couldn't – didn't try to – manage the milling operation by himself, so another young journeyman was brought in from Wickham, again through Jack's connections, as it happened.

'And,' she said to Agnes, her eyes alight, 'Thomas asked me if he should give young Tom his wish.'

'To take him on as an apprentice?'

'You can imagine how thrilled Tom were.'

Agnes felt a brief surge of happiness for them both. 'But how are you coping, Susy? With so much to do?'

Susanna waggled her head, but her face still beamed. 'It's so good to be busy again, Agnes—'

'But you were never idle.'

'That's true. I always loved the house and garden and, of course, the children.'

'Yet now you've got the mill as well.'

'Well, only the accounting. And making sure Thomas has all he needs.'

Agnes laughed. 'You make it sound like nothing. Yet – the accounting? How d'you know what to do?'

Susanna shared her laughter. 'I'm learning—' Then she bit her lip. 'It were the one thing Harry let me help with. At first, anyway...' She went quiet. But she brushed her hand across her face and it lit up again. 'Mustn't let memories overwhelm me.' She stood up, and smoothed her skirt. 'It's not too chilly out, so shall we take the children to the river?'

Agnes gave a quick shrug and Susanna smiled and went to fetch her children's boots.

Agnes felt unsettled by what seemed like Susanna's rise and her own decline. She'd not been to the workshop since before Midsummer. Jack insisted now that all his efforts be directed towards the building business. Her "fiddling about", as he unkindly put it, was no longer needed.

She was scarcely any less busy than Susanna now, and wondered how she'd ever found time for the workshop. But the fact was she missed it.

She'd been surprised by how much she enjoyed making things, and was still loath to give it up. She'd been pondering upon it for a while, and thought yet again that, if she admitted defeat in the matter of the turning – thus removing the need for a lathe – Jack might let her carry on her work at home. Making small boxes and chests, trays and whittled spoons, toys perhaps? Perhaps he'd let her use one of the outhouses? Though she could imagine the expression on his face when she mentioned her idea.

She'd have to talk to him very, very sweetly…

Despite agreeing to Susanna's suggestion, Agnes thought it barely warm enough to let the children play outside. The sun had surrendered to the clouds some days ago, and the wind was easterly and brisk. She'd been surprised when Susanna suggested going to the river, given the unhappy memories it must hold, both for her and for Maud, though she supposed the child probably couldn't remember what'd happened to her mother all those years ago. But she'd agreed because Susanna wanted to show her boys what she called the "secret place" where, two years ago, Henry – still then a happy father – had dug out a tiny tributary to make a shallow pool, secluded behind a stand of overhanging willows.

Susanna led the way. 'He made it as a surprise for Tom and Maud – their special place, he said…' Her eyes glazed a little. 'Dear Harry, he were so happy then, with Tom and Maud, Francie a baby, and Joanie on the way. He were never so content as when he were doing things with the little ones.'

'He was a good father, Susy,' said Agnes. 'Remember him that way… The man who died last April wasn't the real Harry.'

Susanna touched her arm. 'I know. I think of *that* man as "Henry", not my lovely "Harry".' Her eyes glistened, and Agnes decided to change the topic of their conversation.

If Agnes thought it too cold for outdoors play, and even more so for paddling in an icy pond, her boys seemed not to notice, no more did Maud and Francis, nor even little Joan, as they all flopped down onto the chilly grass to pull off their boots. Then, barefoot, they waded into the shallow water and devised a game of sea battles, making a flotilla of little boats from fallen leaves.

Susanna was laughing at their antics, whilst Agnes's heart felt heavy at her own seeming inability to enjoy the simple sight of her children playing. She felt exhausted by everything, and knew well enough it was naught to do with lack of sleep.

'You *are* carrying, Agnes,' said Susanna, sympathetically. 'It's always tiring.'

She grimaced. 'It's not just that. I find so little joy in anything.' As she was saying it, she knew she shouldn't be. It was a betrayal of Jack. Yet she seemed unable to stop herself.

'Not even in your little boys?' said Susanna, joy clearly on her face as she gazed across at Stephen and Geoffrey, playing so amiably with Maud and Francis.

Agnes shook her head sadly. 'I don't think I was meant to be a mother.'

But Susanna rolled her eyes. 'Every woman's meant to be a mother, Agnes.'

'It doesn't feel so to me,' said Agnes, an empty feeling in her belly. 'I love my boys, of course I do, but when I see how much joy you seem to find in your children, I wonder why I—' She stopped, and let out a long breath. She really *shouldn't* be laying out her heart like this to anyone.

As Agnes reached the house on her way back from the river, Jack was already home. She found him trying to poke the fire into life, and he raised his head as she struggled through the door, with Geoffrey wriggling on her hip, kicking his muddy boots against her skirts, and Stephen pulling on her hand. Both boys were grizzling and wet. She tried to smile when Jack lifted his face to her, his eyebrows raised, but her smile died as he leapt up to his feet.

In two strides, he stood before her, his hands lifting Geoffrey from her arms.

'What the Devil happened, Agnes?' he said, his voice low and hard. 'Why does something always *happen*?' He barked the last word, as if it meant some sort of calamity, then carried Geoffrey over to the fire and began to remove his dripping clothes.

'Francis got over-excited,' she said, following Jack over with the grizzling Stephen in tow. Sitting on a stool, she stripped off the child's tunic. 'They were playing sea battles in the pool, with little leaf boats...' She tried smiling, but Jack's eyebrows lifted again. She bit her lip. 'It *was* an accident.'

Jack grunted. 'Isn't it always?'

She tugged at Stephen's shirt, cold and clinging to his little body. He wasn't helping, jiggling from foot to foot and complaining of the cold.

'The quicker we get these wet clothes off you,' she said, 'the sooner you'll be warm.' But he wailed as she dragged the shirt up over his head, the wet fabric catching on his ears. Geoffrey then joined in his brother's protests with a shriek, as Jack removed his braies and hose, leaving him naked and shivering before the still feebly flickering fire.

She'd wanted to tell Jack what a lovely time the boys'd been having with Susanna's children. How the excitement of having a pool to play in, and the fun of looking for suitable leaves to act as war boats, had brought them such merriment. And, eventually, even she found joy in the sight of her boys, so oftentimes peevish and ill tempered, playing so affably with the others. They were better behaved without Dickon, she'd thought, for he always seemed to bring out the worst in them.

But, in the end, it wasn't either of her boys who'd brought about the mishap, when the three older children had collapsed into a scrabbling heap of arms and legs, fighting over whose ships were whose.

'Oh, the babies!' Susanna had cried, as Geoffrey and little Joan were being jostled by the others, and about to topple over.

She ran towards them. She plucked Joan from the pool, her little kirtle already wet but not yet soaked through, but Geoffrey was not quite within her reach. Then, as Francis tussled with Stephen and his cousin Maud for possession of the boats, his flailing arm struck Geoffrey's shoulder. The younger boy fell forward, face down into the water.

But Agnes didn't tell Jack anything. He'd say it was ridiculous to let such small children play in a fast-flowing river. He might think Susanna irresponsible for suggesting it. He'd certainly think Agnes irresponsible for agreeing. It was best to hold her tongue about it all.

'I should go and collect Dickon,' she said instead. 'Can you finish dressing these two?'

Jack nodded curtly. 'Don't be long.'

She ran up the slight incline that led to the manor. It was already dropping dark, and Margaret might well be wondering why she'd not yet collected Dickon. Though Agnes knew that having her grandson play in her house for a few hours was as much for Margaret's own benefit as it was for Dickon's.

Three months ago, when Agnes had gone to report on Hugo Garret's alarming behaviour, Margaret had given the boys into the care of a young page. The two women had later found Dickon sitting with Matilda's daughter, Libby, their heads close together, deep in earnest conversation, while the page was playing a game of tag with Stephen and Geoffrey.

Margaret exchanged a smile with Agnes. 'Well,' she said, 'it seems that we have found a companion for Dickon.' And she then suggested continuing the arrangement every week. 'It will give me a chance to see my grandson,' she said, 'even if he does not know he is a de Bohun.'

'You don't want to tell him yet?'

'Richard believes him still too young. Best leave it until he is old enough to understand the implications.'

Agnes wasn't sure herself of the "implications". Sir Richard hadn't yet made it clear whether he intended to make Dickon heir to Meonbridge and his other estates. She rather assumed he would, yet the thought of it disturbed as well as delighted her. For what might it mean for her? Nonetheless, she'd agreed with Margaret, and indeed with Jack, not to speak of it to Dickon for another two years or more.

Agnes was out of breath as she climbed the steps up from the bailey to the heavy oak door that gave onto the manor's hall. She lifted the latch and, heaving the door open, stepped into the smoky warmth. Her ladyship was waiting for her, sitting at one end of the long table already being laid for supper, with Dickon at her side. Her face was a little gloomy, but it brightened when she saw Agnes come through the door.

Agnes ran across the hall. 'I'm so sorry I'm late, your ladyship. Stephen and Geoffrey had a little accident—'

'Nothing serious, I trust?'

'No, they just fell into some water and got a little wet. I had to take them home to dry out.' She noticed Margaret's eyebrows lifting, and wondered at it. 'I left Jack dealing with them.' Then she glanced at Dickon, who was oddly quiet.

Margaret seemed to notice her quizzical expression. 'Dickon too has had a somewhat *wet* afternoon.' She pinched her lips. 'Libby is upstairs now with her mother.'

Agnes's heart turned over. What *had* they done? She cast her eyes around the hall and spotted the young page, red-faced, on his haunches with his shoulders slumped, tending to the fire.

When Dickon had first come here, his afternoons with Libby were spent quietly, chatting and playing with Libby's toys. The page was again entrusted to mind them, but he was rarely called upon to do any more than simply watch.

But, after a few weeks, the children had apparently become bored with indoor play and begged their minder to let them go outside, so they could run around. He agreed, but as each week passed, they wandered further and further afield within the manor grounds.

Last week, Margaret had told her that the page was distraught when at last he brought them back. 'He thought I would accuse him of letting them get out of his control. But I told him they were a pair of rascals, and he was not to blame himself.'

'But surely he shouldn't let them run wild, your ladyship?'

Margaret had agreed to lay down some rules. 'Though, in truth,' she'd said, 'Dickon is *exactly* like his father at his age.' She seemed about to smile, then waggled her head. 'It was most difficult to stop Philip doing whatever he wished. And I fear our little Dickon is proving to be much the same.'

'Were you ever able to stop Philip?'

'In a way. Richard was abroad a lot in those days, and I employed Matilda's father, Robert, who was then the manor clerk, to be Philip's tutor and mentor. Philip was five, and Robert remained his tutor until Richard insisted the boy went away to start his knightly training two years later.'

Agnes wondered if she had heard aright. 'Robert Tyler?' she said, her voice a whisper. 'The man who later murdered—'

'Indeed. Robert was not always wicked. He was a great help to me when Philip was a child.' She bowed her head, then dabbed at her cheeks with her handkerchief. 'In truth, Agnes, I do not know when he began to change into what he eventually became.'

It was then Agnes began to change her mind about Libby.

When she first saw the girl with Dickon, she'd hoped she'd be a calming influence, a companion who might *stop* Dickon running wild. But now she wondered if, with such a grandfather – and she knew Matilda herself had had a reputation as a girl for being headstrong – Libby might in fact be every bit as unruly as Dickon. Perhaps Dickon should no longer come here to play? Yet she could scarcely tell Lady de Bohun she couldn't see her grandson, and it *was* a relief to have Dickon out of her own hair for a whole afternoon. She considered discussing it with Jack, but in the end decided to keep her counsel.

But now, it appeared, the children had been more disobedient than ever.

Margaret rose from the bench and, telling Dickon to stay where he was, drew Agnes away. 'They went far beyond the boundaries of the manor grounds,' she said. 'They were found down by the river – right down in Meonvale by the bridge that crosses over to go on up to Riverdown.'

Agnes suppressed a gulp.

'They were playing in the river with some cottar children. By the time the boy found them, they were wet and muddy. He brought them home at once, and we too, Agnes, had to dry them out. I have told them both that, if I find them doing it again, they will be punished.'

Agnes chewed her lip. Margaret didn't say what form such punishment might take, but Jack would be aggrieved if anyone raised a hand or stick to one of his children – even Dickon, not his own but, for now at least, his responsibility. If anyone smacked the children, it was Agnes. Jack never did, believing a stern reprimand more effective than a beating. She disagreed, and they argued often over it. Yet, now, she was surely proven right? Just *talking* to Dickon was not the answer to controlling his behaviour...

But, right now, she decided to let Margaret deal with her grandson's misdemeanours. She herself had other matters to discuss with Jack. And if he thought she couldn't control the children, he certainly wouldn't agree to her continuing her work at home.

# 24

Emma started awake. Amice was shaking her shoulder.

'Ma,' the girl said, her voice an urgent whisper. 'Wake *up*, Ma. There's summat wrong with Pa.'

Emma opened her eyes wider. With no light seeping through the shutters, it was still dense black in the room. Amice shook her again. 'Ma, *geddup*!'

Emma struggled to be fully awake. She reached out across the bed, across Bea's gently snoring head, and across the snuffling baby Bart. But beyond Bart the bed was empty.

She sat up and, taking Amice's arm, drew her close. She whispered in her ear. 'Why aren't you asleep, poppet?'

'*Pa* woke me up.' Amice pulled her arm from Emma's grip, and grabbed at her mother's chemise. 'Get *up*, Ma! There's summat wrong with him,' she said again, her voice a little louder.

'Where is he?' said Emma, swinging her legs to the floor, then scrabbling around in the dark for her shawl and throwing it around her shoulders.

'Outside.'

'But it's freezing—' started Emma, then panic rose in her chest. 'Oh, Blessed Virgin, why's he outside?' Then she was on her feet and she could see the door on the other side of the room. It was ajar and a faint light from outside was seeping through the gap. She hurried over, with Amice close behind her.

'Where is he, Ami?' Emma said again.

Amice grasped her hand and pulled on it. 'Out here.'

Outside, Emma could see her breath floating on the chill night air. Dark clouds scudded across the sky, and the moon hung like a ghost behind them, its faint glow casting a meagre light down onto the croft, enough for her to make out vague shapes ahead. But they'd gone only a few paces before Amice pointed at a dark mound on the ground. 'There!'

Emma ran over and knelt down by Ralph's prostrate body, naked apart from the long shirt he'd had on when he came to bed. 'Oh, my love,' she whimpered, 'why're you out here in the cold, an' with so little on?' His face was turned to the side, and she lowered her ear to his mouth. He was breathing, but the puffs were short, uneven.

'Ami, go and fetch Bea, now.'

Moments later, a bleary-eyed Beatrix was at her mother's side. 'What's wrong wi' Pa?'

'I dunno. He's ill. Quickly, Bea, go and ask John Ward to come.' It was only a few steps down the road, and she'd rather ask Ralph's cousin for help than her neighbours.

Emma stood up and paced a little. She couldn't move Ralph by herself. She had to wait for John.

When Bea returned, Emma told her now to run to Simon's and bring him here. Then she touched John's arm. 'D'you think we can try and carry Ralph indoors?'

Arthur had come too, and the three of them lifted Ralph up from the ground, John and Arthur at his shoulders, and Emma at his feet. Ralph cried out as they struggled with their awkward burden back into the house. They reached the pallet, where baby Bart was still sound asleep. Amice darted forward and, picking the child up, took him to his cradle, so Ralph could be laid down upon his back.

'Thank you, John, Arthur,' said Emma and, with shaking hands, lit a tallow candle. She carried it over so she could see Ralph more clearly and, as she did so, let out a cry. 'Oh, John, come and look.'

Ralph's long shirt was dark with a thick mass of blood. Emma tried to lift the hem of the shirt, wanting to see beneath, but the blood was sticking the linen to his belly, and he cried out as the fabric pulled at the wound. Whimpering, Emma leaned over him, intending to stroke his face, but instantly reeled back, nausea rising in her throat at the stench coming from his belly. 'Oh, Simon, please come soon,' she whispered.

Emma got up and put the candle on the table, leaving Ralph in deep shadow. But she noticed his body twitching violently, then he rolled over to his side.

'Em,' he whispered, his voice cracked and feeble, 'Simon can't do aught for me. I'm done for.' Then he clutched at his belly, and cried out again.

Amice began to weep, and Emma put her arm around her. The girl's face was strangely pale in the candlelight, and Emma could tell she was trying to be brave. Arthur was slumped on a stool next to Amice, and his face too was ashen, and twisted with what she thought was fear.

John came over to his son and whispered in his ear, at which the boy pouted a little but opened the door and went outside. 'Gone to wait for

Simon,' said John. Emma saw fear also in his eyes.

He began to pace, clenching and unclenching his fists, then stopped. 'It'll go bad for Matt if Ralph—'

Emma rounded on him. 'Don't say it, John! Simon'll be here soon.' Yet it seemed forever before she heard the sound of footsteps on the road outside, and Bea burst into the cottage with Simon close behind her.

'What's up wi' Ralph?' he said and Emma, holding back her tears for the children's sake, pointed to the bed.

'His wound's gone bad,' said John.

Simon knelt on the edge of the pallet and gently pulled at Ralph to roll him onto his back. He laid his hand upon Ralph's forehead. 'Can you bring some light?'

John lit a rushlight from the candle and left it on the table, taking the brighter burning candle over to the bed.

'Hold it...there,' said Simon, moving John's hand to ensure the light fell exactly over Ralph's belly. Simon groaned. 'God's bones, Ralph! It shouldn't've come to this.'

He rummaged in the bag he always carried with him, and drew out a flask of wine. 'Warm water, Emma?'

She'd already begun to prod the fire into life, and now jabbed at it more furiously. A little water was left in the tub and she ladled some into a clean pot, then hung it on the tripod over the fire. 'It'll be a while.'

'Soon as you can,' said Simon. Then he leaned forward. 'Ralph? I must uncover the wound.'

Emma came over to hold Ralph's hand. He opened his eyes and stared up at her. His face was ash-pale in the candlelight, and he was shaking – from cold or pain or fear, she didn't know. She bent down and kissed his lips. 'Be brave, my love,' she whispered, and he gave her a single nod and closed his eyes.

Simon held the flask to Ralph's mouth. 'Take some,' he said, and Ralph parted his lips and let some wine dribble in. Simon urged him to take more, then called to John to check the water.

'How much d'you want?' said John. 'An' how hot?'

'Just warm, for comfort's sake. And only a small bowlful. To help loosen this clotted blood.'

John handed the candle to Emma and, taking the rushlight over to the fire, peered into the pot and dipped his finger into it. 'Warm enough,' he said.

Ralph cried out as a spasm gripped his body, and Emma squeezed his hand. 'Simon'll make it right,' she said. But, when she raised her eyes to Simon's, she saw his were bleak, his lips pressed tight together. Holding back a sob, she leaned down towards her husband. 'Be brave,' she said again.

John carried over a bowlful of the water over and a rag.

'Thanks,' said Simon. 'I might need more.' Then he soaked the cloth and swabbed at the sticky blood. After a few moments, he gestured to Emma to try lifting the shirt and, gradually, with more swabbing, it began to come away.

'Bring the light closer,' said Simon, once the shirt had been pulled back. John came over to hold the candle, while Simon and Emma bent forward to inspect the uncovered wound. The stench was terrible, the sight of it horrifying, with the skin around the wound all red and shiny and puffed up, and inside a wet, green-brown slime.

Emma looked up at Simon. 'It's gone bad?' He nodded. 'How?'

He shook his head. 'I cleaned it well enough. Mebbe Matt's knife was dirty with summat? Who knows what, with him so—' He grimaced.

'Can you clean it up again?' Her voice was a whisper.

'I'll try,' he said, but his eyes were telling her the truth. She bent down and stroked Ralph's cheek. If he were to— But she couldn't bring herself to think it, and distracted herself by trying to say in her head the words of the shepherd's prayer. She couldn't remember much of it, only the bit about death's shadow.

Simon continued to clean the festering rupture in Ralph's belly, scraping the rot away with a knife. Emma was glad Ralph fainted at the first touch of the blade. When he'd finished scraping, Simon flushed the wound with water and smeared it with some honey. Then, taking from his bag a small wad of moss, he bade Emma hold it against the wound while he wrapped strips of linen tightly around Ralph's body to keep it in place.

Fingers of light were beginning to poke through the shutters as Simon packed away his things and got up to leave. Ralph was sleeping.

But Emma pulled a face. 'His breathing don't seem right. And he's so hot, no mind it's freezing cold in here.'

'His fever's raging. Not surprising with the rot.'

'Will he be well again?'

He bit his lip. 'I can't promise, Emma. If the blade had shit or summat on it, it might've gone inside him, and there's naught I can do to stop it.'

Emma whimpered. 'So he might die?'

Simon rubbed at his beard. 'I'm sorry.' He laid his hand on her arm. 'Ralph's a good man. We must trust in God.'

She nodded. 'I'll pray hard.'

John himself had raised the hue and cry.

When Emma awoke to find Ralph motionless and cold, she'd again sent Bea for John and, through his tears – shed, he said, for what he was about to lose as well as what she'd lost already – he'd cursed his brother for his wickedness.

'I'll defend him no longer,' he said, fighting to contain his sobs. 'I'll call out the constable, then I'll join the search.'

Despite her overwhelming misery, Emma was shocked at what John said. She touched his arm. 'Hunt down your own brother?'

'He's no brother o' mine,' said John, pulling away and pacing the floor. But, seeing Ralph, lying alone and unmoving, his eyelids closed, upon the pallet, he went to kneel at his cousin's side. He bent his head and touched Ralph's folded hands with his. He whispered a prayer and crossed himself, then got to his feet.

'Matt'll pay for this,' he said. 'Mebbe we come from the same dam's belly, but Matt don't deserve to call her Ma. She were a hard-working, God-fearing woman, Em, who tried to teach us right from wrong.' He shook his head. 'I dunno why or when Matt went astray, but he's betrayed her memory in his foulness. Jus' like 'e betrayed his Sarah...'

He bit his lip and hurried over to the door. 'I'll fetch the priest and Simon afore the constable,' he said, and then was gone.

Simon had come first and confirmed what he'd said might happen, that the poison in Ralph's body must have finally overwhelmed him.

The priest arrived soon afterwards and knelt, swaying slightly, by the bed to pray for Ralph's soul.

Meonbridge still didn't have a proper priest. The bishop had answered Sir Richard's request for a replacement for mad Hugo Garret by sending Godfrey Cuylter, an elderly curate, to conduct Saint Peter's affairs until a permanent priest could be found. But the old man seemed scarcely to understand the daily offices, and many folk complained of him dropping off to sleep when they were making their confessions.

Ralph had scratched at his head when Emma told him what she'd heard.

'It's still hard to find new priests,' he'd said. 'You remember it were eight weeks after Master Aelwyn died afore Hugo Garret came.'

'Might've been better if he'd never come.'

'But we were glad to have him at the time.'

'Anyway, that were years ago—'

Ralph had shaken his head. 'But it's not much better now, I've heard. Still not enough clerics to go round, when so many perished in the Death. We're lucky to have the old man now.'

But now she wondered if the old priest's mumbled prayers were powerful enough to reach God's ears.

When it seemed he'd prayed enough, he struggled to regain his feet and tottered over to her. 'He's already made his peace with God,' he said.

Despite her doubts about him, she'd asked Master Godfrey to come two days ago, when it was clear Ralph might not survive. He'd seemingly taken Ralph through the sacrament of confession, having to bring his ear close to Ralph's mouth, and mumbling his responses so feebly she worried Ralph might not be truly absolved. Then, when the old man tipped his little vial of holy oil and spilled much more than a drop of it onto Ralph's forehead, she hurried over with a cloth to mop up the excess, doubting the curate's ability to administer the Eucharist. Yet, though his hands shook uncontrollably, the wine did pass Ralph's lips without mishap. Nonetheless, she'd worried still that the priest's ineptitude might mean Ralph wasn't properly ready for his journey. But she could do naught about it.

Now, Master Godfrey laid his quivering hand upon Emma's head, then on each of the children's, and gave them all a muttered blessing before bidding them farewell. Emma stepped outside the door to watch the old man shuffle back towards the village and Saint Peter's, where he'd attempt, she assumed, to recite the Prime, the first office of the day. The old priest was kind enough, but she was fearful that, when the day came for her to bury her second love, the only cleric available to send him on his journey might just mumble, or say the words all wrong, and make a mockery of his passing.

Emma had to wait for the constable to come. She wanted to get on with the preparation of Ralph's body but, because his death was now a case of murder, she had to let Geoffrey see the body, so he could report back to Sir Richard.

Despite the early hour and the chilly morning air, Bea offered to take her sister and little brother outside for a walk. Emma almost wept with gratitude. How'd her little girl suddenly become so sensible of her mother's needs?

'You spend some time alone with Pa,' Bea said, and wrapped her arms round Emma's waist.

Then Emma lay down upon the bed, pressing her body close to Ralph's and putting her arm across his chest. The smell from his wound seemed to have lessened, or maybe she was just accustomed to it. But she no longer cared. She had only moments left to lie with her beloved husband, and she'd stay here till the constable arrived.

The weather matched her mood. Dark clouds filled the sky, and rain threatened. She remembered how bright and sunny the day had been when she buried Bart. She recalled thinking she might faint to watch his strong, handsome body being sewn inside a shroud; then remembered how she *did* faint, or almost so, at Hugo Garret's cruel denouncement of her beloved husband.

At least Master Godfrey had no cause to bring any accusation against Ralph. She tried to console herself with that.

Yet, when the carter arrived to take Ralph's body to the church, she wondered if she'd cope with the sight of it being lowered into the chilly ground. Folk lost loved ones all the time, but knowing that didn't make your own grief any easier to bear.

Both Eleanor and Will came to the cottage to walk with Emma and her children, following the cart as it trundled up through cottar Meonvale into the village centre and crossed the green to Saint Peter's church. Will offered to carry baby Bart, so Emma had a hand free for each of her girls.

As they walked, it seemed as if everyone in the village was joining the procession, just as they had for Bart. And, inside the church, the bier bearing Ralph's shrouded body was placed on the same table where Bart's had lain. Emma stood close by it, tightly clutching her daughters' hands, and shivered at the memory of that other dreadful day.

But, this time, Sir Richard and Lady de Bohun came – they'd not come for Bart. Those already gathered in the nave stared open-mouthed as their lord, her ladyship on his arm, strode between them, down towards the altar to take the church's only seats, set aside for them, though scarcely ever used.

Before she sat down, Lady de Bohun came across to Emma and touched her arm. 'Sir Richard and I are much saddened by Ralph's death. He was a good man.'

Emma bobbed a curtsey, but her ladyship grasped her hand and held it. 'Emma, come to see me when all this is over.' She smiled at Sir Richard, who inclined his head to Emma, his face bearing, she thought, an expression of genuine regret.

As Lady de Bohun took her place next to his lordship, Emma twisted around to see her neighbours still pushing into the little church. Though, really, it was hardly crowded. The church was never full these days – how could it be? She remembered how different it had been, long years before the Death, when she felt crushed by the throng of people standing in the nave on Easter Sunday. It'd never be like that again. Yet, a good crowd had come today to see Ralph on his way. Her ladyship was right. He was a good man, and well loved by his friends and neighbours.

Later, standing at the edge of the deep pit awaiting Ralph, Emma curled her arms around her daughters and tried to make her breathing slow and steady. Amice was trembling beside her and she clutched the girl more closely. She wanted to weep herself but was determined to keep dignified and brave.

'We commit his body to the ground,' said Master Godfrey, 'earth to earth, dust to dust, in certain hope of resurrection…' Emma raised her eyes to watch the men lower Ralph's shrouded body down into the grave.

Amice sobbed, and Emma couldn't help but shudder at the horror of it.

Yet, at least this time, she wasn't so fearful of the journey her loved one was about to take. When Bart was put into the ground, she'd thought his idleness and mutinous ways might mean his soul would stay in Purgatory forever. But God surely knew Ralph was a good man, and would soon raise him up to Paradise?

And, to her surprise and relief, Master Godfrey confirmed it. He had swayed a little as he stood high up on Hugo's platform, his rheumy eyes gazing across the congregation as he spoke of Ralph, his voice for once clear enough, if quiet. Emma was moved to find he'd troubled himself to learn about the man Ralph was, and was heartened when he assured those present that Ralph would soon be with God.

But it didn't ease the pain of seeing his dear body touch the damp, dark earth at the bottom of the pit.

At last, as the rest of the watchers moved away, and she heard Eleanor whisper to Beatrix and Amice that perhaps they might leave Ma and Pa alone a while, Emma allowed her tears to gather. Then, dropping to her knees beside the pit, she leaned forward, let the tears rain down to wet Ralph's shroud, and howled out her grief.

# 25

Eleanor crested the hill of Riverdown, a little out of breath from climbing with the chilly wind blowing in her face. Will was waiting for her, pacing back and forth outside his cottage. Seeing her arrive, he strode over, the dogs scampering beside him.

'You heard the news, missus?' His eyes were bright.

'I suppose not, as Hawisa let me break my fast in peace.' She gave him a thin smile.

Will grinned. 'She's a right one for gossip, ain't she?'

Eleanor nodded. 'So what *is* the news?'

'He's back, is what.'

Eleanor's heart began to pound. 'Walter?'

Will bit his lip and, ripping off his cap, ran his fingers through his hair. 'Ah, no— Sorry, missus— But no, not Walter…' Despite the cooling air, his face quickly reddened.

Her shoulders drooped but, a moment later, pulling herself together, she touched Will's arm. 'No, *I'm* sorry, for jumping to such a ridiculous conclusion.' She looked away, knowing her face too was flushed. 'So, who *is* back?'

'Matt. The constable's men found him at last and brought him home.'

'It's been six weeks since he ran off,' she said, her heart thumping once again, for quite a different reason. 'Do you know where they found him? Or how he is?'

'I dunno where, but they come back yestereve. After constable put him in the lockup, they all come back to Meonvale for a pot or three of ale. An' they were right glad of it, for they'd had none since they left a week ago, following a new scent.'

She shivered. 'Can we go inside the cottage if we're going to talk?'

''Course, missus. I've a fire still.'

Sitting in the warm, if dark and smoky, cottage, Eleanor felt better able to continue. 'So, how did they track him down?'

Will hooted. 'Did you know Luke went?' She shook her head. 'John said

Luke were bitter when Matt ran off and left him. And he'd a tale to tell about summat Matt did years ago, though John won't say what it were. But it's been paining Luke – an' 'im too, he said – a long while.'

'Whatever can it be?'

'Dunno but, whatever it is, Luke were so 'grieved about his Da, he joined the hunt for him. And, according to John, he knew where to look.'

'Goodness! Luke betrayed his father?' She was not sure how she did – or should – feel about that. It seemed a shocking thing for a son to do, yet Matthew was a very dangerous man.

Will scratched at his chin. 'But 'e deserved it.'

She pressed her lips together. 'He's not a good man—'

'An' a terrible father.'

'So what will happen?'

'He's in the lockup, and John said Sir Richard'll take him afore the Hundred court.'

She wrinkled her brow. 'Not the king's judges?'

'So he said. He wants Matt dealt with soon and proper, an' the Hundred bailiff'll be willing enough to do his bidding.'


In November's gloom, there was never much to do on Riverdown. The rams had been with the ewes a month, and they would stay together a little longer before being separated, leaving the dams in peace to grow their lambs. Eleanor and Will strolled through the flock, checking which ewes were in lamb, and how many seemed not yet tupped. Eleanor then left Will mending fences and made her way home again.

This was one of her days to call on Emma. Emma had not been up to Riverdown since she had buried Ralph. With so little work needing to be done, it seemed right to let Emma grieve and spend time with her children. But Eleanor liked to visit her often, to make sure she was coping.

Eleanor's heart still beat a little faster when she approached Emma's house. She thought she never would forget the sight of Matthew leaping over his wall and coming to assault her. But today, she knocked, and the door was opened by a smiling Beatrix.

'Come in, missus,' said the girl. 'Ma were just talking 'bout you.'

Eleanor stepped inside. She always marvelled at Emma's home. It was tiny, like other cottar cottages, with just one room for everything, the big pallet where they all slept together taking up much of the space beyond the fire. But Emma kept it so clean and neat that it seemed somehow bigger, and more comfortable, than it was.

Emma looked up. 'Good to see you, Elly. Warrant it's chilly up on Riverdown?'

'A cold wind. But at least it's dry. We have just checked the ewes again.'

'Are they all tupped?'

'Most, I think.'

Emma stirred the pottage she was making. 'You'll join us?'

Eleanor chewed her bottom lip a moment. She hated to think she might be taking food from the children's mouths. But Emma always offered, and she always expected her offer to be accepted. So, after her usual brief prevarication, Eleanor agreed. Despite everything, Emma was a good cook – better than Hawisa – and could turn the most unpromising ingredients into a tasty stew.

After dinner, the children played together on the pallet, while Eleanor and Emma stayed at the table.

'I've heard the news,' said Eleanor.

Emma's eyes were bleak. 'I'm glad he's caught, and John says Sir Richard'll see him hang.'

Eleanor closed her eyes. 'I suppose he did kill Ralph.'

'An' he should die for it.' Emma's voice was hard.

Eleanor could hardly be surprised if she was bitter. 'But when did we last see a hanging here?'

Emma tilted her head. 'Robert Tyler and Gilbert Fletcher would've hanged if they'd not died aforehand.'

'And Thomas Rolfe *was* hanged in Southampton,' said Eleanor. 'But we've not had many Matts in Meonbridge.'

'I've heard it's worse in other places.'

Eleanor took Emma's hand. 'The trial will be hard for you, having to relive poor Ralph's death.'

But Emma twisted her hand around and clasped Eleanor's in return. Her eyes were wet, and she wiped them with the hem of her apron. 'Hard for John, too. He says Luke's got summat shocking to tell, about his father.'

'Will told me that, but he didn't know what it was.'

'Me neither. John won't tell. He says it'll come out at the trial. And'll serve to prove Matt guilty.'

'Another murder, then?' said Eleanor. Who else could Matthew have killed?

'Mebbe. It'll be hard for poor Luke too,' said Emma. 'He's living with John now, did you know?'

'Perhaps, once the trial and all is over, John will be able to set Luke on the right path?'

'Mebbe,' said Emma once again. 'But I'll not hold my breath.'

*

Eleanor thought she'd had enough of courts, but she had to see this business with Matthew through to the end, however painful. She still felt somehow responsible for what had befallen Luke, though she could hardly be blamed for what Matthew had brought upon himself.

She was curious too about the Hundred court, for she had never attended one before. The court was held in a specially built hall, in the Hundred's most central village, only three miles or so from Meonbridge. She wondered if, being more local than the king's court at Winchester, it might be a more casual affair – the justice rougher, the jurors perhaps readier to convict? Yet the jurymen appeared respectable enough, and the judge, whom she took to be the Hundred bailiff, looked appropriately serious.

But it was clear that this court had been convened specially to try Matthew for murder, which in itself, she thought, was "casual". Murderers were surely supposed to face the king's justices, not a local court? Yet Will had said that Sir Richard wanted the matter settled quickly, and was not willing to wait months for the king's bench to return. He'd hinted too that the bailiff would ensure Sir Richard had the result he wanted.

Eleanor felt uncomfortable with it all, but there was nothing she could do to influence events. And, in truth, she *would* sleep easier for knowing that Matthew could no longer assault her, or murder one of her friends.

She had hired ponies and travelled to the court with Will and Emma. Both had been in a stonily merry humour, speaking with grim excitement of the prospects of Matthew hanging. Eleanor was queasy at the impropriety of their banter but, understanding why Emma, at least, was entitled to be bitter, she kept her counsel.

The trial took much the same course as Susanna's.

Matthew stood before the judge and jury, his hands bound, the Hundred gaoler at his side. Then Sir Richard put the case against him, that, in a fight, he had used a knife and stabbed his cousin Ralph, who died later of his wounds. His lordship then called some witnesses to confirm the story – first, William Mannering and two other men who had seen the fight. Eleanor wondered why Sir Richard had not asked either her or Emma to speak, but was glad enough that he had not. Then Simon reported that, although the wound was shallow, Matthew's knife must have been somehow contaminated, and poisoned Ralph's body.

Then it was Luke's turn to speak.

The court room was not large – not even as spacious as Sir Richard's hall – but so many Meonbridge folk had come along, eager to hear Luke's tale, that the air was already uncomfortably warm, despite the chill outside. Eleanor was glad she had come early enough to find one of the few seats available, for most folk were standing together in an uneasy, restive crush. And when John ushered his nephew forward, the throng of bodies surged, like a stand of saplings struck by a sudden wind, as folk jostled for position.

As Luke came forward, he sneered at his father standing only paces away, and placed himself so he was facing Sir Richard, his back towards the man whom he was, she assumed, about to accuse. She heard Matthew growl at his son, and saw Luke turn and glare at him over his shoulder. Yet fear was in his eyes.

If Eleanor had ever felt sorry for the Wards, she certainly did now pity Luke. She had thought him thin when she last saw him at the fight, but now he was even more so, his one strangely oversized hand seeming to unbalance him as he lifted it to rake at his strawy thatch.

And Luke seemed anything but eager to tell his story. He looked more like a rabbit caught out in the open by a barn owl than the savage young wolf he had been only months ago.

When he stayed silent, Sir Richard lunged forward and spoke to him in a low, urgent tone. Luke nodded but, when he wiped the sleeve of his shirt across his nose, Eleanor realised he must be crying and, despite herself, her heart went out to him. But Sir Richard seemed to have little sympathy, and cuffed him on the arm, urging him to speak. John then stepped forward and whispered to his lordship, who waved his hand, and John stood at Luke's side, his hand upon the boy's shoulder. 'Speak, lad,' Eleanor heard him say. And Luke gave a great sniff and then began.

'It were in the Death,' he said, starting in a quiet voice. 'I were twelve or thereabouts. It were just my two sisters got sick. Ma wore herself out caring for them, certain she could make them well. But Da just said the world were at an end and spent all his time and money in the ale-house.'

He let out a small sob. 'Ma told me to run away, hoping I'd not get it. But I couldn't leave her. Da allus beat her when he come home from the ale-house. He were always raging—' His eyes were wet. 'An', when he come home and found my sisters cold, he raged at Ma, much worse 'n usual. Calling her a slut, and a wicked whore, and a useless mother who'd *let* her daughters die—'

There were mutterings from the crowd.

'But how could she have?' cried Luke. '*She* were with 'em all the time, while he did naught to help.' He wiped his face against his sleeve. 'And then he 'it her. And he 'it her, and he 'it her—' He was sobbing. 'He hit her so hard, she fell and broke her head open on the hearthstone. And the blood were—'

He fell silent, as the crowd erupted into cries of 'Shame!".

'He's kept that terrible memory locked up inside him all these years,' Eleanor said to Emma, in a whisper.

'Mmm, poor boy,' Emma whispered back, though Eleanor was not sure if she meant it.

Sir Richard then stepped forward. 'Matthew always claimed that his wife, Sarah, died from the Mortality,' he said. 'He took *three* bodies to be buried in the common grave. And of course, no one then thought to question the truth of what he said.'

Then there was a scuffle and Matthew yelled at Sir Richard, 'My Sarah *did* perish in the Death. It's lies what Luke's been saying.'

But Luke spun round. 'You shuddup. *You're* the liar!'

The judge raised his eyebrows, and gestured to the gaoler to keep Matthew quiet.

'I were hiding an' Da found me,' Luke went on. 'He beat me wi' a leather strap. He said I weren't to tell no one what 'appened to Ma. She deserved to die, he said, 'cause she were so wicked.' He sniffed. 'I didn't believe him, but I'd no choice but throw my lot in wi' him, did I?'

John whispered something to Sir Richard, who nodded, and John stepped forward to face the judge. 'It weren't true, sir, what Matt said about his Sarah,' he said. 'She were a good woman, a good mother, married to a violent man. I didn't see it 'appen, but I warrant she did die at Matt's hand, just like young Luke said.'

It took the jury only moments to declare Matthew guilty of murder, of both his cousin Ralph and his wife Sarah. The judge said he would be hanged forthwith, and his body taken back to Meonbridge. Mayhem followed the announcement – the onlookers cheering their approval, Matthew screaming his innocence. Emma and Will crowed and hugged each other, Luke hung his head, and John sank onto a stool and wept.

The crowd shuffled from the courtroom. They were going to watch.

Emma touched Eleanor's elbow. 'You coming?'

'I've no wish to see Matthew die...'

She glanced across at Luke and John, sat together, John's arm around Luke's shoulder. Her heart ached for them both – for the mutilated and mistreated boy, and the man who now had to live with the shame of his brother's crimes.

'Mebbe you need to see his end?' said Emma, her voice a whisper. 'I do.'

Eleanor nodded. 'The unhappiness he brought me hardly compares with your grief.'

'Nonetheless...'

'We'll be with you, missus,' said Will. 'An' you can look away.'

She felt a little nauseous. There had been few executions in Meonbridge:

she couldn't remember the last time, perhaps when she was a child. Though Emma had been right that both Robert Tyler and Gilbert Fletcher would have hanged if they had been captured, and then there was Thomas Rolfe… But attending a hanging wasn't something her family had ever done, for her father had thought it unseemly to watch a man's demise. Yet most folk considered it a commonplace, a way of seeing justice done.

And that was, after all, what Emma wanted.

At length, Eleanor looked up at Will. 'In truth, I do not want to, but I'll come. To stand with Emma.' Wrapping her cloak about her shoulders, she fixed the clasp and pulled the hood up over her head. Then she took Emma's arm, and the three of them followed the crowd towards the gibbet that stood at the crossroads where the road led back to Meonbridge.

Eleanor had to brace herself for what was about to happen. The crowd continued to cheer and crow, as a cart trundled forward, carrying Matthew, held fast by the Hundred gaoler and his henchman. Matthew was still struggling against his captors, still protesting that he was not guilty. But his cries and weeping were ignored. A priest climbed up into the cart and intoned some words that Eleanor couldn't hear but presumed were the last rites. But Matthew wasn't listening: uselessly, he continued to kick out, refusing the priest's attempts to give him consolation. In one wild moment, Matthew wrested himself free enough to butt the priest in the face, striking the man's nose with his forehead. The priest let out a cry and, his hand pressed against his bleeding face, clambered down from the cart and hurried away.

It was already an unseemly spectacle.

But Matthew was doing himself no good. The gaoler gripped his arms more tightly, and the other man tied a rope around his wrists, before urging the pony forward a little to bring them all directly underneath the noose. Then he reached up and, grasping the loop, placed it over Matthew's head.

Eleanor looked away. Hearing it would be more than enough.

And what she heard would, she thought, live with her for ever. The sound of Matthew crying out, then the click of the gaoler's tongue, the clop of the pony's hooves and the grate of the cart's wheels against the rough surface of the road. Yet she was spared the noises she had dreaded most – the slump of Matthew's body as his feet slipped off the cart, his choking on the rope – for the watching crowd raised such a roar of approval that she couldn't hear those final moments of Matthew's life. Instead, she was able to take Emma's hand and squeeze it, knowing that, for her at least, she had witnessed retribution for the loss of her beloved Ralph.

*

In the weeks after Matthew's grisly death and ignominious burial, in some place unknown to everyone except the constable and his men, a pall of despondency hung over Meonbridge. Preparations for the Christmas celebration went ahead but with little merriment. Even the traditional feast provided at the manor threatened to be a subdued affair, though Eleanor knew that Margaret was making great efforts to bring light and joy to the occasion.

The horror of Matthew's hanging still weighed heavily on Eleanor's heart, although she was trying to put it behind her. So, when Margaret invited Eleanor to sit at the high table at the feast, although she might have preferred to spend the meal in Emma's company, and Will's, she could scarce refuse her ladyship's request, and decided to consider it as an opportunity to overcome her melancholy.

Hawisa fussed over her unmercifully at the news, insisting she order a new gown from a tailor in Winchester for the occasion. 'You got naught else to wear,' she cried, flapping at her apron.

Eleanor knew the claim to be ridiculous. Nonetheless, it *was* an honour to be invited to sit with the de Bohuns at such a public feast, and she did admit, to herself at least, that it would be lovely to have something new to wear. And, when the gown came, and Hawisa nearly fainted with excitement as she helped her try it on, Eleanor had to admit – this time to Hawisa – that she had never before thought herself even a little beautiful. But the new fine wool cotehardie, its colour such a lovely leafy green, seemed to look so well over the deep blue of her best kirtle.

She asked Hawisa to fetch the small, polished metal mirror that her father had bought years ago as a special gift for her mother. Hawisa held it up, and Eleanor could just see how well the low curve of the bodice top showed off her long, slim neck. It was disappointing that she could not see whether the tight fit of the bodice and wide flare of the skirt displayed her figure to advantage.

'How I wish I could see all of it,' she said.

Hawisa's eyes lit up. 'It looks very well on you, mistress.' Eleanor thought those eyes held something close to love, and was grateful for it, despite Hawisa's many irritations.

'It *is* very different from my dull working kirtles, and the old brown surcoat.' She loved the way the sleeves of the cotehardie ended in long tippets of decorated cloth. 'These would be so impractical with the sheep.'

Hawisa tilted her head. 'You'll have to be sure you don't dip them in your pottage, neither,' she said, with a chuckle.

'I can't think we'll be having *pottage* at the Christmas feast, Hawisa,' said Eleanor, giggling. 'But, yes, I'll try and keep my tippets off the table.'

*

It was icy cold in Eleanor's house. She awoke to find a heavy frost had settled overnight, cloaking the trees and hedgerows, and the unhappy leavings of her potager, with a fine white rime, overlaying the ground with a crust so thick it almost looked like snow. It had come suddenly, this icy whiteness, for the winter had so far been mild and a little damp, rather than bright and chill. Yet, this morning, the sun was shining in a clear blue sky, making the rime sparkle as if a giant had scattered jewels across the fields. Nonetheless, despite the beauty of what Eleanor saw when she opened the shutters, indoors the fire was unable to counter the sharp blasts of air surging beneath the door and through the windows. For, downstairs, she found Hawisa flapping at the fire, supposedly encouraging it to draw.

But it was the day of the Christmas feast and, drawing fire or no, they had to ready themselves to dine at Sext. Nathan's preparations would be few, so Hawisa fetched him from the scullery, demanding that he deal with the dratted chimney, as she put it. Eleanor and Nathan exchanged a grin, but then he sighed and knelt down at the hearth, while she and Hawisa went back up to the solar.

'Wi' a gown as fine as this one, you 'ave to dress your hair,' said Hawisa, clearly unwilling to consider any dissent.

She pinned Eleanor's usual braids into elegant coils, then covered them with a fine crespine net she had found amongst the few things of her mother's that Eleanor had kept. She topped it all off with a narrow silver fillet, another of her father's long-ago gifts. Eleanor was not sure she wanted the net and fillet, for fear she might look matronly. Indeed, perhaps it was wrong to be decking herself out like this at all, when the mood in Meonbridge seemed anything but festive? But, in the end, she let Hawisa have her way, wondering too how it was she knew how to dress her hair so well. And, seeing her reflection in the little mirror, she agreed that perhaps she was *almost* as beautiful as she remembered her mother had been on those occasions she and Papa had gone out to dine.

'Thank you, Hawisa,' she said, putting the mirror down. 'I hope I don't look out of place.'

'Nah, mistress. As fine as any other lady sat at the top table.' Hawisa's eyes were shining.

When all three of them were ready, Hawisa went outside to test the road. 'It's right icy underfoot, mistress. You'll have to wear your boots.'

Eleanor grimaced but could not help but join in Hawisa's giggles at the absurdity of wearing stout leather boots with such an elegant gown. 'I'll take my shoes with me in a bag,' she said, and Hawisa lumbered off upstairs to fetch them. Eleanor fastened her thickest cloak around her shoulders and pulled up the hood, then she and her servants linked arms and, together, they slipped and slithered to the manor.

Eleanor had dined with the de Bohuns before, but had not sat at their table for such a great feast. She had been placed between Margaret and Adam, the bailiff. She might have wished her long slim neck was not after all quite so much on display for, as she took her place, Adam's eyebrows shot up.

'Good Heavens, Mistress Titherige, is that truly you?' he said, his eyes alight.

She tried to respond with grace but, feeling a flush spread across the pale skin above her revealing bodice, then on up to her naked neck, she stumbled over her words.

But Adam must have seen he had embarrassed her, for he blushed too. 'My apologies, dear Eleanor. That was most ungallant of me. It's just, of course, that we do so often see you dressed for toil, rather than festivity.'

Eleanor flapped at her face. It was beginning to cool. 'I've already forgiven you, Master Wragge.' She smiled. 'In truth, I'm not accustomed to troubling much with my appearance.'

'Well, the result was certainly worth the trouble.'

A little warmth returned to her neck. 'I'm also somewhat unaccustomed to being complimented.'

'Shame!' said Adam, grinning broadly. 'I can't imagine what the young men of Meonbridge are thinking of.'

She laughed, but only moments later she noticed Nicholas, sitting a few paces away at a table arranged sideways on to hers. He was staring at her. Then, seeing that she had noticed him and sweeping his hands down across his chest in an effusive gesture, he grinned and bowed his head. She felt the flush blooming once again. She had heard that Nicholas had been courting other women in Meonbridge and beyond, Susanna amongst them. She was relieved, assuming – hoping – it meant that, despite his gesture, he had relinquished any thoughts of winning her. But it would be churlish not to accept his compliment, so she smiled and nodded, but was glad when Adam touched her arm and offered her some wine.

'Look, Eleanor,' he said, as he poured, 'the feast is about to begin.'

She looked behind her. Through the doors that led in from the buttery and the kitchens beyond came a small procession of manor servants bearing dishes, held in their hands before them or carried aloft upon a shoulder. One by one, the servants came to stand before Sir Richard and bowed their heads, then laid down the dishes along the length of the high table.

Eleanor turned back to Adam, grinning. 'What a splendid feast her ladyship's provided.'

Soon, there were coneys in wine, and little pies of venison, a brewet of beef in a thick spicy sauce, and hens stuffed and roasted and glazed with green. A wonderfully rich blend of smells, spicy and savoury, vinegary and sweet, tingled in her nostrils, enticing her to eat. But, today, gowned and bedecked as she was, she cautioned herself to ensure her behaviour matched her mien. She must wait patiently to be offered a morsel of this or a slice of that, and not help herself as she was accustomed to doing, simply needing to sate her hunger.

It was hard to restrain her eagerness to try at once all the appetising dishes laid out around her, but she contented herself with sipping wine and nibbling at the little white wheaten loaves, as she waited for her turn to come to be offered a rabbit leg and a few slices of roasted chicken. And then she ate with delicacy, picking at the morsels and lifting them to her lips with care, to save dropping any and soiling the bodice of her gown.

As the first dishes were being consumed, more followed, the most mag-nificent a whole roasted pig, its mouth stuffed with apples, borne in on a great platter, still hot and steaming, presented to Sir Richard, then placed on a serving table for carving into thick, succulent slices.

Eleanor had tasted a little of everything, for Adam was a most solicitous table companion, and had just accepted a second helping of the delicious brewet, when Margaret leaned in to her and touched her lightly on the arm.

'Master Ashdown,' she said, 'seems unable to take his eyes off you, my dear.'

Eleanor had already put a morsel of the meat into her mouth. She was glad that she had cut it small, for her ladyship's comment surprised her and she had to swallow before replying. 'I think he admires my new gown.'

Margaret hummed agreement. 'You do look lovely. The green goes so very well with your russet hair, and reflects the colour of your eyes.' Margaret took a sip of wine. 'Any man would be proud to call you his wife.'

Eleanor gulped, as she wiped a drop of spicy sauce from her lips. 'Wife?'

Margaret laughed lightly, and patted Eleanor's arm. 'I am not suggesting anything by it, my dear. Although—' Her eyes twinkled. 'Perhaps there *is* a young man whose wife you would like to be?'

Eleanor took several sips of the rich red Gascony wine. Of course there was. She remembered the first Christmas after the Mortality, when she had come to the manor feast on his arm, and had made John atte Wode so unhappy. She bit her lip. She had thought then that she and Walter were a couple. She had regretted hurting John but, despite the lowliness of Walter's status –

and the gossip that she knew would follow – he had just seemed right for her.

Some sweetmeats had been brought to the tables, for those who had had their fill of meat – dishes of pears in wine and plates of honey cakes, baked apples and sweet custard tarts. Eleanor accepted a little tart and stared at it. 'I wonder where he is?' she said out loud, not meaning to.

Margaret's eyes glinted a little. 'Who, dear? Or perhaps I do not need to ask, for only one man is not here.' She touched Eleanor's arm again. 'You miss him?'

Without warning, tears brimmed in Eleanor's eyes. 'And it's all my fault he's not here.'

'I know. Cecily has told me all about it.'

'Cecily?'

'Indeed,' said Margaret. 'I visit her from time to time. She is quite frail now, but ever alert, and fully aware of the – shall we say? – rift between you and her nephew.'

'It was so many months ago that he came back to see her, when she was ill.'

'She was. Although, despite her blindness, Cecily is very healthy for one so old.'

'I should visit her – her cottage is so close to home,' said Eleanor, wondering, not for the first time, why she'd not done so before.

'She would surely welcome it.'

Eleanor took a small bite from her tart and let the pastry crumble in her mouth. 'Does Mistress Nash know where Walter is?'

'She does.' Margaret pursed her lips, then opened them again to drink more wine. She set the goblet down upon the table. 'As do I.'

Eleanor gasped. 'You, my lady?'

'Cecily confided it to me so, if she needed him, I could arrange for a message to be sent. That is how it was he came back to Meonbridge last spring.'

This news took Eleanor's breath away. She felt betrayed. She had just bitten off another morsel of tart, and now she was choking as it caught in her throat.

Margaret handed her her goblet. 'Drink some wine, my dear, to wash it down.'

Eleanor tried but spluttered, and some droplets of red splashed onto the bodice of her gown. But she did not care about the gown. She glared at Margaret, all sense of propriety for the moment lost.

Her ladyship shook her head. 'My dear child, I realise that you think I have been cruel. But I had little choice. Walter made Cecily promise not to tell you where he had gone. So, when she confided in me, I had to do the same.' Eleanor nodded feebly. 'I could not betray the trust that Cecily had placed in me.'

'And you will not tell me now?'

'I cannot. But, if Cecily needs him to come again, I shall send a message.' She tilted her head. 'Perhaps, when you visit her, my dear, you could persuade her that she needs to see her nephew soon? She might not take much persuading, for she does have his – and your – best interests at heart.'

'You mean that she thinks Walter does care for me?'

'I cannot say for sure. And he *has* been gone from Meonbridge for many months.'

It was snowing heavily the day that Eleanor decided to put on her stout winter boots and thickest cloak, and follow the track to Upper Brooking. It was already January, many days since her ladyship had recommended that she visit Mistress Nash, and Eleanor wondered why it was today she chose to go, when the weather had turned so bad again. But, when she awoke this morning, she knew she had been dreaming of Walter, and in the few moments after waking, something – was it him? – was urging her to delay no longer.

It was not far, but it was an arduous trudge through knee-high snow, on a track whose boundaries were hard to mark. Slung across her shoulder she wore a scrip containing a loaf of bread, some cheese and a small flask of ale, in case the old lady was finding it too onerous to come into the village.

At the cottage, snow was banked up against the door and Eleanor had to lean hard against it to push it open. She fell inside, the piled snow tipping on to the floor behind her. The inside of the cottage was almost colder than the air outside. Once her eyes accustomed to the dark, she saw that the hearth was dead, and a few icicles hung from the rafters. Peering into the gloom, she saw a strangely towering bed in the corner of the room beyond the hearth and, at the same moment, she heard a faint groan.

'Mistress Nash?' she cried, hurrying forward. 'It's so cold in here.'

Piled high on the bed was a mound of cloaks and blankets. Eleanor took off her glove and, reaching out to touch the pile, found the top layer covered in thin ice. She began to brush it off and, as she did so, the mound stirred and slipped a little as the old woman's wizened face darted out from beneath the bottom blanket.

'Who's that?' she said, her tone querulous. 'And you leave be my drinking water.'

'It's Eleanor Titherige, Mistress Nash.' She touched Cecily's cheek lightly with her fingers. It was not quite as cold as she feared it might be. 'I'd thought to visit you in this dreadful weather. Would that I'd come sooner.'

Cecily nodded weakly. 'If you'd not come today, you might've found me dead.'

Her words echoed in Eleanor's head, and it took her only moments to recall Walter's words when she had found him, all those years ago, in his cottage, also alone and near to death.

'Are you sick, Mistress Nash?'

The old woman shook her head. 'Sick of being cold and hungry.' She tried a weak grin. ''Least I had the blanket to suck on.'

Eleanor's brow furrowed. 'Blanket?' Then she chuckled. 'Oh, I see, the ice. So how long have you been like this?'

'Not long...' She seemed to think a moment. 'Two days past it were I fell. Hurt my arm, an' couldn't do the fire.'

'So you took to your bed?'

'Naught else t' do. Had t' keep warm. And hope someone'd come.'

Eleanor bit her lip. 'I'm so sorry I didn't come before.'

Cecily seemed to shrug beneath her blankets. 'You weren't to know.'

'I'll go now to Lady de Bohun. She'll surely send someone to help you.' She moved towards the door. 'Is there anything I can give you before I go?'

She gave her some of the ale she had brought and a piece of the bread. In truth, she wondered how the old woman managed so well on her own, isolated as she was out here and with such poor eyesight. But now was not the time to ask.


Margaret insisted that Cecily be brought to the manor, to rest and recover from her injury. At the same time, she sent a message to Walter.

'Of course,' she said to Eleanor, 'there is no real need for him to come. I will tell him that his aunt is being cared for here.'

Eleanor nodded, yet her heart ached. Her ladyship surely *knew* how desperate she was to see Walter again, so why did she not insist that he return? Yet she could hardly criticise her decision.

'My dear,' said Margaret, tilting her head. 'We must leave it to Walter to decide. It will not help your cause if he feels he is being *pressed* into returning.' She took Eleanor's hand. 'Be patient.'

But Eleanor felt anything but patient.

# 26

## WINTER 1354

Susanna uttered a silent prayer. Snow had been falling more or less since Christmas, and even just going to the village was a treacherous journey. The path from the mill up to the village thoroughfare was sloping and had become almost as slippery as she imagined the track up to Riverdown must be. But, this morning, although the world outside her door was still covered in a clean white mantle, at least the sky was clear again. How she hoped it marked the beginning of a thaw.

The snowy scene looked pretty enough, but Susanna was bored with it now, wearied with finding every step outdoors a danger, and wishing the snow would just go away and let everyone get on with their lives.

Yet, if she found it tedious, the children seemed never to tire of snow.

Maud put on her angelic face and tilted her head, as she tweaked Susanna's skirts. 'Can we play by the river, Ma?'

'Your secret place?'

The child shook her curly head. 'Nah, proper river.'

'The meadows?'

Her eyes lit up. 'Tom says we can snowball there.'

Tom stopped chewing at his bread and grunted. 'More's the pity I can't come.'

Susanna laughed. 'You did want to work, Tom dear.'

He grunted again. 'I do. But it's boring with no customers. No one'll come, the path's so slippery. They all go to the village bakehouse.'

'I know, but mebbe it'll be better now the snow's stopped falling?'

He made a face. 'It'll be days afore it clears.'

Maud huffed and pulled on Susanna's sleeve. 'Stop *talking*,' she said, pouting. '*Can* we?'

'We'll go for a while later, after we've *all* done our jobs.' Maud pouted again, but briefly, then yelled so her cousin Francis could hear, 'Ma says aye!'

Between the river and the rise of Riverdown, where the rough meadow followed the meandering of the river, the snow was lying in a broad swathe, bright in the winter sunshine, though many tracks had already spoiled its pristine whiteness. The ceasing of the snowfall seemed to have brought everyone out to play. No men, of course – they'd use the opportunity of drier weather to check on their beasts or mend some fences. But many women came with their children – the chance to let them run free for a while, after being cooped up for days on end like pigeons, too good to miss. Families of every degree were drifting down, and scattering across the meadow.

Susanna was surprised to see Eleanor standing in the snow close to the riverbank, waving at her. She stepped down from the bridge onto the snow and trudged towards her, Joan balanced on her hip, though she was really too big now to carry, and Francis held firmly by the hand. Maud waded cheerfully alongside, sinking up to her knees with every step. Eleanor grinned as they approached. A fresh snowball was in her mittened hand, and she bent down to Maud.

'Shall I throw this at you, Maudie?'

Predictably, Maud squealed and tried to run away, but toppled over, face first, into the snow. Undaunted, she picked herself up and, laughing, scooped up handfuls of snow and threw them up into the air.

'What brings you here?' Susanna said to Eleanor.

'Hoping to see Maud, of course. I don't often have a chance to play with my goddaughter.'

'I see Emma's already here,' said Susanna, gesturing to where Emma was helping Amice make a snow man, a little further along the riverbank. 'Where's Beatrix?'

Eleanor pointed across the meadow towards the slope up to Riverdown, where some boys were sliding down the hill, a few on makeshift sledges, most just on their breeches. 'She insisted she was too old to make snow men.' She grinned. 'She wanted to be with the boys.'

Maud must've heard that, for she tottered forward and pulled at Susanna's skirts. 'Can I go play with Bea?'

Susanna squinted across the meadow in the bright sunlight. A lot of boys seemed to be on the slope, most, she suspected, nearer Bea's age than Maud's, or even older. The sounds of gleeful squealing carried easily on the still, cold air, but she saw too a good deal of jostling and scrapping. Then a boy was tumbling head over heels down the slope, wailing as he fell headfirst into a deep drift at the bottom.

'Those boys're too rough for you, Maudie,' she said, then pointed to where the snow man already had a body as tall as Amice. 'But Ami's having fun. Let's go and help her.'

Maud pouted. 'I wanna slide!' she cried. Susanna tried to take Maud's arm, but the girl wriggled from her grasp. Susanna shook her head at Eleanor, who tried the same and, at length, Maud let her godmother take her hand, and all of them trudged over to the snow man.

Susanna giggled. 'Look at little Bart!'

Emma grimaced. The boy was sitting in a deep patch of snow. 'He do love eating it. But he'll soon find hisself freezing cold.' Sighing, she went over and, hauling him to his feet, clutched the wet, protesting child underneath her arm.

Maud soon seemed to forget about sliding, and was happily scooping up snow in her little mittened hands, and patting it onto the snow man's body, while Amice had begun to roll some into a bigger and bigger ball.

The three women moved away, taking Joan and the boys with them, so that the bigger girls could play together undisturbed. But Francis tugged his hand out of Susanna's and, running a few yards off, just dashed about, throwing handfuls of snow up into the air and at the girls. Susanna grimaced but decided to let him be. It was struggle enough keeping Joan in check.

Moments later, she saw Agnes hastening across the bridge, with Geoffrey wriggling on her hip, and Stephen held fast by the hand. She was apparently pursuing Dickon, who was ploughing ahead towards Riverdown with Libby plunging at his side.

Susanna gestured towards Agnes with her chin. 'Poor Agnes,' she said to the others, 'she always looks so harassed.' She waved at Agnes, who looked up at that moment and nodded briefly, before calling out to Dickon and Libby to wait. She hurried on towards them, as best she could with the little ones in tow. Dickon stopped and turned to face his mother, and Susanna could see him scowling. Agnes said something to him, the agitation in her voice clear enough, if not the words. But, moments later, Dickon turned again and stomped off once more towards the hill, with Libby lumbering behind him. Agnes stood a while, her shoulders slumped, staring at her son's departing back. Then she shook her head and trudged towards Susanna and the others, with Stephen pulling on her hand and Geoffrey struggling to get down.

Susanna thought Agnes's eyes looked wet and, quickly handing Joan to Eleanor, took the writhing Geoffrey from his mother and set him on his feet, then bent down to Stephen. 'Why don't you help Maud and Amice with the snow man?'

Stephen pouted a moment, then seemed to change his mind. Plodding over to the snow man, he scooped up some snow and slapped it rather too forcefully onto its body, knocking some of it off onto the ground. Amice and Maud exchanged grimaces, but said nothing. However, Stephen quickly tired of snow man building and joined Francis in throwing snow about, laughing when it fell onto the heads of the two girls, who shouted at them to go away. But he just smirked and carried on until Agnes cuffed him around the ear and threatened to take him home. He pouted again, then told Francis to come and make their own snow man. 'A better one 'n *theirs*,' he said and sneered. Joan now also demanded to be put down and she and Geoffrey plodded after their older brothers.

Susanna touched Agnes's arm. 'Let's leave them on their own.' Agnes agreed, and they trudged back towards the bridge. And, for a while, there was peace, as the second snow man rose beside the first.

But it was short-lived, as the boys began to squabble. Agnes stared at Maud and Amice, and Susanna saw her eyes were glistening again. 'Agnes, aren't you well?'

Agnes wiped the heel of her hand across her eyes. 'I'm fine, Susy,' she whispered. 'I'm just so *hoping* this one'll be a girl.' She patted her belly, then gestured towards the snow builders. 'Look at the two girls, how happily they play together. No arguing or fighting. Whereas my boys, especially Dickon—' She waved her hand towards Riverdown.

'Boys'll be boys,' said Susanna. 'And your Dickon's certainly a lively one, no mind he's still so little.'

'And the village boys seem to like him, even the older ones,' said Agnes.

Susanna followed Agnes's eyes towards the Riverdown track. The jostling for position on the slope had become more vigorous, and boys struggling up the hill were being pushed back down. Sounds of wailing were as frequent as the squeals of glee.

'I should go and fetch him and Libby back,' said Agnes, but made no move. Her face was pale, Susanna thought, and it wasn't just the cold.

As Eleanor and Emma joined them on the bridge, Eleanor pointed to where a man was hurrying down the hill towards the boys. 'Look, is that Will?'

'Perhaps he's going to chide them,' said Agnes. 'I suppose I should go over.' And this time she set off, ploughing heavily through the snow towards the hill.

Susanna squinted across to Riverdown. 'He's not tall enough for Will.'

'Who is it, then?' said Eleanor but, a moment later, her face reddened a little, as the answer became obvious to them all.

Not stopping after all to reprimand the boys, the man strode on down the hill, as vigorously as if there was no snow to slow him. He seemed to acknowledge Agnes as he passed her, then, as he crossed the snowy meadow towards them, he hailed the three women standing on the bridge.

'Master Nash,' said Emma. 'You're back in Meonbridge. Only just arrived?'

'Yestereve. Staying at Mistress Rolfe's—'

'And how're Elly's sheep?' continued Emma.

He seemed to colour a little at the question, and paused before he answered. 'Ewes're in fine fettle,' he said at last. 'And Will's got the shepherd's cot right cosy.'

'You've not brought Dart with you?'

He shook his head. 'Left him with my master. The journey's difficult enough this time o' year.'

Susanna glanced at Eleanor, whose blush was still brightening her cheeks. She tried to catch her eye, but her friend seemed intent on staring into the distance. 'You seen your aunt yet, Master Nash?' she said. 'I hear she's much recovered from her fall.'

'On my way t' the manor now, Mistress Miller. I'm to have my dinner there.' He swept his hand across his body to indicate his fine wool surcoat, which Susanna presumed was new.

She smiled, then Emma asked about his journey, and Susanna enquired how long he planned to stay in Meonbridge. His answers were brief and vague, as they often were. Yet Susanna struggled on, willing Eleanor to speak to him too, but she still said nothing. Walter was looking over his shoulder towards the village, and Susanna could see her efforts were all in vain.

But then a child shrieked, and Susanna spun around. The shriek was followed by a great splash, and other screams. Glancing at the children huddled at the river's edge, she saw at once that Maud was not among them. She cried out and stumbled towards the riverbank, as fast as the snow would let her.

As she reached the bank where Maud had fallen in, Susanna could see her little head, hatless, bobbing beneath the flowing waters. Then she surfaced, let out a single cry and, gulping in some air, tried to clutch at the overhanging vegetation. But her mittened hands couldn't grip the soft, grassy stuff and she was drawn back into the river's current. Susanna's ears were ringing with Maud's cries, and her heart was pounding from the terror of it. *Her* little girl!

Susanna plunged into the water, and its coldness took her breath away. Her skirts at once were heavy, dragging at her legs. She could scarcely move, and the flailing Maud had already passed her by. Susanna panted out a cry of desperation, then heard another, louder, splash. Looking up, she saw Walter was waist-deep in the river, downstream of her, his arms spread wide. As Maud tumbled towards him, she bumped into his outstretched arms, and he grasped her tight. Then, lifting her up, he held her to his chest and waded the short distance to the bank.

Susanna struggled from the water and, still panting, ploughed through the snow towards them. Eleanor was already there, helping Walter to clamber out. Susanna took Maud from his arms, and hugged her close.

'As well the river weren't too deep or running fast,' Walter said, trying to catch his breath.

'She might have been swept away,' said Eleanor, a sob rising in her throat.

Walter picked up his abandoned cloak and wrapped it around Susanna and Maud, just as Emma caught them up.

'Let's take her to my house,' said Emma. 'It's closest.'

'You must dry off, too,' said Eleanor, touching Walter's arm. He was shuddering, his fine new clothes soaked through. She took off her own cloak and put it around his shoulders, fastening the clasp at his throat. He gave her a fleeting smile. 'I'll go to Mistress Rolfe's to change. I'll come to see the child later, Mistress Miller.'

Susanna still found it hard to catch her breath. 'Thank you, Master Nash,' she said, her voice hoarse, 'for saving my little Maud.'

He bowed his head and hurried away, back towards the bridge, and Susanna saw Eleanor stare at his retreating back. Then she gave a sudden shudder, and realised her clothes were as wet as Walter's.

Emma grasped her elbow. 'We must go too, Susy. The sooner you get yourself and Maudie dry—' Susanna nodded but, twisting her head, glanced across at Francis, throwing snow again with Agnes's boys, and at little Joan, crawling towards her brother, wailing.

Eleanor touched her arm. '*I'll* gather up the children.'

'Can you bring Ami too, and Bea?' said Emma, then drew Susanna and Maud away.

By the time Eleanor arrived with the other children, Maud had been stripped of her wet clothes, dried off and wrapped in blankets. Susanna too had changed her wet kirtle for an old threadbare one of Emma's and was sitting by the hearth, cradling Maud on her lap. She glanced across at Emma, admiring her quick efficiency at rekindling the fire and hanging a pot of broth beside the flames to warm.

She lifted her face as Eleanor struggled through the door, clasping Francis by the hand, and with a still wailing Joan in her arms. Beatrix had her arm around her sister, whose eyes were red. Agnes had come too, with Geoffrey in her arms, her two older boys and Libby all crowding into the little cottage behind her. Emma ran over and, taking Joan from Eleanor, bid everyone go sit by the fire and warm themselves.

251

But Agnes shook her head. 'We won't stay. Susanna, I just wanted to apologise for Stephen's behaviour.' She rolled her eyes. 'I think it was his fault Maud fell into the river. I'll take my boys home, then get Libby back up to the manor.'

Susanna nodded. It was very likely Stephen had *pushed* Maud hard enough for her to fall, but Agnes looked so desolate she couldn't bring herself to be vexed with her.

'Maud's fine, Agnes,' she said. 'It were an accident, I'm sure.' She gave a little grin. 'Mebbe it weren't such a good idea after all to go snow balling?'

Agnes's lips twitched a moment but then her face crumpled. 'Thank you, Susanna' was all she said before plunging back out through the door, the children shuffling after her.

Susanna and the others stared at the closing door, then she shook her head. 'Poor Agnes,' she said again. 'She always seems so unhappy.'

'It's those boys of hers,' said Emma. 'Dickon specially's so unruly.'

'Girls are easier,' said Susanna.

But Emma laughed. 'Not always.' She jerked her head towards Beatrix and Amice, sitting just behind her on the edge of the bed. Susanna saw Beatrix's face was gloomy, and she squinted at Emma, who lightly touched her daughter's cheek.

'Summat amiss, sweetheart?' she said, but Beatrix turned her face away.

Then Amice smirked at her mother. 'Missus Sawyer told her off.'

'Why, Bea?'

Beatrix glared at her sister. 'She said I were bullying Dickon an' Libby.' She huffed. 'More like them bullying me! Little tikes—'

'Bea!' cried Emma, but the girl pouted and rolled over on the bed to face the wall.

Emma grimaced, and Susanna blew out her lips in sympathy. But then she noticed Eleanor, hunched down on a stool some distance from the fire, was shuddering.

'Oh, Elly, you poor thing, you're freezing.'

Emma spun round and went to her. 'O' course, you gave up your cloak to Master Nash.'

'He'd more need of it than I,' said Eleanor, her teeth clicking together.

'Mebbe then, but look at you now.' She took her arm. 'Come and sit closer to the fire.' She found another blanket and wrapped it around Eleanor's shoulders. Then, ladling some of the hot broth into a pot, she put it into Eleanor's hands.

*

The warmth of the fire seemed to be making everyone drowsy. The children took to playing together on the bed and, after a few sips of broth, Maud fell fast asleep in Susanna's arms. The women were mostly quiet with their thoughts, chatting idly as the afternoon wore on.

Emma came to peer at the sleeping child. 'See how she's got her colour back. She's tough, is little Maud. Look how she fought through when she were a baby.'

Susanna nodded. 'Strong in body, and strong in spirit.' She stroked the little girl's curls.

'She was so brave when she was in the water,' said Eleanor, looking brighter now. 'Determined not to let the river take her.'

'But thank all the blessed saints that Walter were there to stop her being taken more downstream,' said Susanna.

'Like a knight errant,' said Eleanor and at once flushed pink. She bit her lip and stared down at her lap. 'How silly of me—'

'No, Elly, not silly.' Susanna gave Maud a hug. 'We might've lost our little girl if he'd not been there to save her.'

Moments later, Maud snuffled awake, and fixed her still-drowsy eyes on Susanna's. 'Home time?' said Susanna, and eased herself to her feet.

'I'll help you with the others,' said Eleanor, beginning to take Emma's blanket from her shoulders.

But Emma wrapped it round her again. 'Keep it, Elly. It's cold outside. Bring it back another day.'

It wasn't far to the mill cottage, but the road was treacherous underfoot, the snow still deep but now crisp and icy on the top, for the sun had long since disappeared and the late afternoon air was chilling fast. By the time she reached home, Susanna's legs were shaking from the effort, her arms aching from holding Maud, no longer small enough to make carrying her a pleasure.

'What I said were right,' she said, as they all fell through the door of the mill cottage in relief. 'It weren't at all a good idea to go the river meadow today.' Despite her pain, she couldn't help but laugh, though her merriment was fragile and might crumble easily into weeping, if she didn't hold herself in check.

Young Tom's face was grey as he sprang up from the pallet he slept on at night. 'Where've you *bin*, Ma?' he said, his voice both quavery and cross. 'I were so worried.' Then he saw Maud in Susanna's arms. 'Why—?'

Susanna gestured to him to follow, as she went into the small room with the big bed she used to share with Henry. She lay Maud upon it and covered her over with a blanket. 'There were an accident at the river,' she said in a whisper. 'Maudie fell in, but she's all right now.'

'What d'you mean, "fell in"?'

But Susanna cupped his face in her hands. 'Mebbe there were a bit of squabbling, an' Maudie were knocked over? Anyway, Master Nash were there and he got her out.'

'I should've bin there,' he said.

'Aye, Tom dear, you're the man of the family now.' She held his shoulders lightly. 'But she's fine. A strong little body.'

They went back into the hall, where Eleanor was hovering near the door.

'I should go home,' she said. 'I've put Joan into her cot and given Francie a hunk of bread.'

Susanna nodded her thanks, but didn't want Eleanor to go yet. She'd something important to say to her. 'Do you have to, Elly? Stay here tonight. I've pallets enough.'

Eleanor knit her brow. 'You know how Hawisa worries.'

'Just some supper, then? We've had naught all day but Emma's broth.'

As soon as supper was eaten, the two little ones fell asleep. Tom, seeming to recognise the pointed look Susanna gave him, sidled off into the room where Maud was sleeping, so she and Eleanor could have a few moments alone to talk.

Susanna poured her friend another pot of warmed ale, and sat beside her by the fire.

'Elly,' she said, taking her hand. 'I just want to say—' She hesitated, not wanting Eleanor to think her interfering. But it had to be said.

'Elly,' she said again, 'd'you remember how you gave me the heart to wed my Harry? I didn't love him then, but you said, despite that, it were the right thing to do, for the sake of baby Maud, and Tom, *and* me. And I were so happy when I first married him, then when we had Francie and little Joan—' She looked away a moment. 'I know in the end it turned out bad,' she whispered, 'but Harry *did* love me, and I soon enough loved him back. Just like with my Fran. I didn't love him neither when my Pa chose him for me. But he were a good man. An' so was Harry, till he got so ill…'

She drifted off, and Eleanor squeezed her hand. 'We've said before, the gloomy man who died was not the happy man you married.'

Susanna nodded. 'But that's not what I wanted to say.' She took a sip of ale. 'It's about grabbing the chance of happiness when it comes—' Eleanor tilted her head, but Susanna ploughed on. 'You've such a chance right now, dear Elly, but you're refusing to accept it.'

'Am I?' said Eleanor, lowering her eyes.

'It's obvious to anyone you love Walter.' She paused. 'An' that he loves you.'

'How can you say that, Susy, when he refuses to stay in Meonbridge?'

'He don't *refuse*, but he's a man of few words.' She took Eleanor's chin in her hand. 'I saw the look in his eyes when you gave him your cloak.'

'Gratitude?'

'Not only that. He's waiting – hoping – for a sign from you.'

Eleanor glanced away, and Susanna smiled to herself. She knew Eleanor was blushing again. She squeezed her friend's hand and opened her mouth to carry on, but at that moment there was a loud knock on the door. Opening it, she found Walter himself standing outside on the snowy track.

'Come to see how the child is,' he said, as she bid him enter and sit by the fire, offering him a stool directly facing Eleanor.

'I went first to Mistress Ward's,' Walter continued, 'thinking you'd still be there. But o' course, it's late—'

'We brought Maud home soon as she woke up,' Susanna said. 'She's sleeping again now, but seems recovered from her dip.' She bent over the pot hanging on the tripod at the edge of the hearth and stirred the contents, scraping up the tasty morsels sticking to the bottom. 'There's still a little stew left,' she said to Walter, 'if you'd like it.'

He declined. 'I ate heartily at the manor, despite arriving late.'

'You've seen your aunt?'

'She's very well. I told her and her ladyship what happened at the river. To explain why I'd come so late for dinner. Lady de Bohun said you must ask for help if you need it, Mistress Miller.'

'That's kind of her,' said Susanna, then glanced across at Eleanor, willing her – again! – to say something.

Instead, Eleanor half rose from her stool. 'Perhaps I should go now, Susy? Hawisa will be worrying.'

Walter leapt up and whisked off the cloak he was wearing. 'You must have your cloak back. My thanks for it.' He handed it to her. 'It's not quite dry, I'm afraid.'

Susanna saw warmth in the smile on his face, but Eleanor seemed not to notice it. 'No matter, Master Nash,' she said, 'Hawisa will get it fully dry—'

'And you must have yours,' said Susanna, hurrying over to the drying rack the other side of the hearth, and plucking off Walter's heavy cloak. 'It's almost dry, I think.' But then she bit her lip, vexed with herself for cutting in when Eleanor might've had more to say. She picked up the jug of warmed ale and, first pouring Walter a pot, she shuffled across and refilled Eleanor's. 'No need to go yet, surely?'

Walter shrugged and sat down again, sipping at his ale.

'Do tell us summat of your work in Sussex, Master Nash,' said Susanna.

He seemed pleased enough to do so, relaxing a little with the warmth of the cottage and the ale.

Susanna fixed her eyes on Eleanor's and let them widen. Her friend nodded, but seemed still unable to put the question Susanna knew she wanted answering.

'And, now you've seen your aunt, how long d'you think you'll stay in Meonbridge, Master Nash?' said Susanna.

He hesitated a few moments, then, in a low voice, almost as if he was saying it to himself, said, 'I'd rather not leave Meonbridge at all.'

Eleanor let out a small gasp.

'But your position in Sussex is too good to give up?' continued Susanna, glaring at Eleanor, who seemed more interested in the dark corner beyond the hearth.

'It's *very* good.' He stared into his pot of ale. 'Yet mebbe there are prospects here?' Again, his voice was so low, Susanna wasn't sure he intended her to hear.

She raised her own voice a little. 'And d'you have one such in mind?'

He cast his eyes at Eleanor, whose gaze had returned now to her lap, then let his shoulders fall. Deducing, perhaps, Susanna thought, with clenching teeth, that the prospect was unattainable?

He stood up then and, swinging his recovered cloak around his shoulders, fastened it. 'Shall I walk you home, Mistress Titherige?'

'Thank you, Master Nash, but there's no need.'

'But it's dark, and the roads are treacherous. You shouldn't be walking on your own.'

Eleanor put on her own cloak and drew the hood up over her head. Susanna managed to catch her eye, and nodded vigorously. Eleanor returned the nod, then smiled at Walter. 'You are right, of course, so, thank you.'

Susanna hugged herself as she bade them both farewell and, leaning against the closed door, sent up a small prayer to Saint Valentine. Perhaps Master Nash *wasn't* willing to give up his prospect after all?

Three weeks later, the snow had gone, and Meonbridge was on the move again. Goodwives returned to the mill for their flour *and* their bread, and a few even braved the still chilly air to get on with some of the outside tasks they'd put off during the two months of snow and ice. It was a relief too to be able to make visits to one's neighbours without risking a broken limb or, at the very least, a sodden cloak.

Susanna knew that, until lambing began in a month or so, Emma still spent most of her days at home, so she hurried down to Meonvale to share some news. But, when Emma opened the door, and Susanna saw the broad grin upon her face, she knew at once the news was not only hers to share.

'Have you heard Elly's news!' both women cried together, then fell into each other's arms.

'When did you hear?' said Emma.

'Elly told me yestereve. And you?'

'I've not seen her,' said Emma, 'but Will told me how Walter's been asking his advice.' She bit her lip.

'Will's told *you* about his private conversations with Walter?'

Emma laughed. 'Walter just wanted to be sure Elly wouldn't spurn him again if he told her how he felt.'

'Was that what he were doing up on Riverdown the day Maud fell in the river?'

'It were. And more since, once he decided to stay in Meonbridge.'

Susanna shook her head in amused disbelief. 'So *Will* were being matchmaker?'

Emma laughed again. 'Not exactly. But he's sharper 'n you might think. *Notices* things—' She tapped the side of her nose. 'Will knew how Elly *truly* felt, for all her blowing hot an' cold, and told Walter so.'

'So it were Will,' said Susanna, giggling, 'and not my prayers to Saint Valentine, that brought the two of them together.'

'At last!'

'D'you wish you was getting married too?' said Susanna, feeling wistful.

Emma shook her head. 'Will's been wooing me and he's a sweet man, but I'm not sure I want another husband.'

'I've always thought he carried a torch for you, Em.'

'Mebbe, but it's too soon to be thinking of loving another, when I've only just buried my Ralph.'

'I feel the same about Harry, despite it all.'

'But ain't Nick Ashdown courting you?'

Susanna cocked her head. 'Goodness, Em, how d'you know that?' Emma tapped her nose again. 'Well, aye, especially the past couple of weeks.'

'So ain't you interested?' It was Emma's turn to cock her head.

'After everything I used to say to Elly about what a good catch he was, you'd think I'd be keen. But I think mebbe I'll stay an unwed widow too, for a while at least.'

Emma laid her hand over Susanna's a moment and smiled. 'Actually,' she said, 'I'm thinking I might take up in business on my own. In Winchester. I've wanted to a while now, though Ralph weren't all that keen. But now, what's there to stop me?'

Susanna brought her hands up to her face. 'Goodness, Em, that's brave.'

'Meonbridge don't feel like a place I want to be no more.' Emma's eyes looked sad.

'Have you told Elly?'

Emma's lip wobbled and she closed her teeth over it. 'I won't say aught till after the wedding. I dread it. Elly's been so good to me, as a mistress and a friend. But she's going to have a new life with Walter. An' I need to find a new life of my own.'

# 27

Eleanor almost felt like slapping Hawisa, the fuss she was making over her. It was hardly surprising the woman was excited but, in the matter of what her mistress should wear for her wedding day, and how her hair should be dressed, and who should be invited to the bride ale, Eleanor thought she was capable of deciding for herself. Yet Hawisa had been working herself up into such a dither about it all that Eleanor was worried she might fall into a faint.

At least Hawisa was now content enough about what was going to happen later.

When Eleanor first announced that she and Walter had agreed to marry, her servant was so far from being pleased as to be affronted. And, being Hawisa, she made no attempt to hide the way she felt about her mistress's plans.

'Walter?' she'd cried. 'I thought it were Nick Ashdown.'

'Hawisa, you know very well it's months past since I spoke with Master Ashdown.'

'Knew naught 'bout that.' Hawisa huffed. 'Anyway, why *not* him, mistress? Better looking, more prosp'rous, *an'* a freeman. While Walter's the same as me and Nat, a cottar, with no land and hardly two beans to make a pottage.'

Eleanor was very fond of Hawisa and forgave her many foibles and irritations but, that evening, she'd come close to telling her servant to leave her house. But, of course, she stayed her tongue and, over the ensuing days, Hawisa continued to talk Nicholas up and Walter down, until Eleanor could not stop herself dissolving into tears.

By chance, Nathan, just come into the hall, saw the cloudburst. And, to Eleanor's astonishment, he grabbed his shrewish wife by the elbow and spun her round to face him. Then he slapped Hawisa hard across the mouth – something, Eleanor thought, he had maybe never done before in all their married life. Hawisa yelped and Eleanor gasped. Even for the mild-natured Nathan, it seemed his wife had gone too far.

'You're a wicked, interfering old besom!' he roared. 'Look how you've upset our missus. It ain't for *you* to say who she should and shouldn't wed. An', as for Walter, cottar or no, he's one o' the most honest, hard-working an' honourable men in Me'nbridge. And he's our lady's *choice*, so you shut your mouth about it, you hear?' Then he cuffed her on the shoulder and pushed her through the door back towards the passage and the scullery. 'Now, you go 'bout your *rightful* business, woman.'

Eleanor's tears had dried completely. She didn't think she had ever heard old Nathan say so many words one after the other, let alone in anger.

Once Hawisa had left the room, Nathan bowed his head to Eleanor. When he lifted it up again, his eyes were moist and his cheeks taut. 'I'm right sorry you 'ad to see that, missus. But I couldn't stand for it no longer—'

Eleanor got up and went to him. She touched his arm. 'She doesn't say it to be unkind.'

His shoulders heaved. 'You know her loves you like you was her daughter?' She nodded. 'We both do,' he went on, in a whisper. ''Cause we never 'ad none o' our own—'

'I do understand, Nathan. Don't be too hard on her. She *is* a bossy besom, I agree—' She giggled, and Nathan joined in, his face relaxing. 'But I know she has my best interests at heart. Though you are quite right that, in the matter of my choice of husband, it is most definitely *my* decision, and not hers, to make.' She giggled again and squeezed the old man's elbow.

He reddened slightly, perhaps at her unaccustomed familiarity, and turned to follow his wife back to the service rooms. But Eleanor pressed his elbow again. 'So, you do, at least, approve my choice?' she said, her head slightly tilted.

He reddened further. 'I didn't mean to speak out o' turn. But, aye, missus, I do. Walter's a fine man, for all his lowly start in life. Master Ashdown may be all the things her in there,' he cocked his head towards the scullery, 'said he were, but he ain't as honourable as he seems—'

'Goodness, Nathan, whatever do you mean?'

Perhaps poor Nathan already regretted speaking out against Nicholas, for he at once clamped his mouth shut.

But Eleanor was intrigued. 'Nathan?'

He shuffled from foot to foot, and pushed out his lips. 'Only what I 'eard, missus,' he mumbled. 'He's been paying court to other women in the village—'

Eleanor laughed. 'And why ever not? If he once thought he had a chance with me, it was long ago and now he knows for sure that chance is lost.'

'An' I'm right glad of it,' said Nathan, and gave her a toothless grin.

Since that evening, Hawisa had been uncommonly sweet-tongued, even admitting her own shock at Nathan's wrath, and asking Eleanor's forgiveness for her ill-spoken words.

But, today, with the wedding ceremony almost upon them, she was gossiping and chattering like an old mother duck. Whether or not Hawisa had changed her mind about Walter, Eleanor could not tell, but the woman was at least willing to admit it was obvious to anyone that Eleanor loved him, and that he loved her back.

'When all's said an' done, not many get to marry for love,' she said, as she helped Eleanor into her long-sleeved, dark blue kirtle. 'Take me an' Nat. He asked my Pa for me, but I didn't want him. He were old even then, an' an ugly fellow, always were. But Pa said I were hardly any beauty meself an' should be grateful *any* man were asking for me.' She tittered, as she laced the back of the kirtle. 'So that were that. I'd no choice in the matter. Not like you, eh, mistress?'

Eleanor gasped, at the tightness of the lacing and Hawisa's comment, but she decided to ignore them both. After all, the kirtle needed to be well fitting under the new cotehardie.

She had wanted to wear again the green cotehardie she wore to the Christmas feast. But, when she took it out of the chest, she noticed the red spots on the bodice, and remembered spraying wine on it when she choked at Margaret's surprising admission. Hawisa had tried to remove the spots but, although they had faded, somehow Eleanor felt it was not right to wear a soiled gown at her own wedding, and had ordered a new one, in the same colour and style. Hawisa was shocked at the extravagance, but agreed that her mistress should look her absolute best on her wedding day, even if the groom was nothing to admire.

'But you're happy with Nathan?' said Eleanor, as Hawisa picked up the new cotehardie and lifted it over Eleanor's head.

Hawisa huffed. 'He's good enough. Not got any better looking, mind. What wi' all his teeth falling out.' She paused a moment. 'An' no good in the getting of little 'uns neither. So I had to make do wi' looking after other women's children.'

Eleanor nodded from inside the cotehardie, as she fought to push her arms through the tight-fitting sleeves with their long dangling tippets. How did she know it was *Nathan* who could not make the babies? Maybe it was her? Who knew? And anyway, it hardly mattered now. Her head and arms emerged from the heavy woollen gown. 'Didn't you once work for the Tylers?'

Hawisa rolled her eyes. '*Long* years. Afore the bailiff lost his wits an' killed young Sir Philip. Mind you, Master Tyler never were the same after he lost Anne and their little lads in the Death.' She pulled at the laces in the bodice of the cotehardie, making Eleanor gasp again. But Hawisa just continued with her story. 'Did you know Anne were my cousin? Never took to being a high and mighty bailiff's wife. And her Margery took after her – what a misery she were – still is. But, as for young Matilda, a flibbertigibbet if ever I knew one. With her airs and graces, and fine clothes, and never doing a day's work— And look where it got her? Married to a rogue and left alone wi'out a penny an' a babe to care for.'

Eleanor had to smile, despite feeling a little breathless. Once you set Hawisa going, it was hard to stop her talking. 'Hawisa, can we concentrate on my getting ready? I'm to be married in an hour.' She took in a sharp breath. 'And can you *please* let out the lacing on the gown a little, else I think that I might faint at Walter's feet.'

Once Hawisa had eased the lacing so Eleanor no longer felt her chest was being crushed, it was time to dress her hair. Hawisa had wanted her to wear the net and fillet again but, this time, Eleanor had determined to have her own way, insisting her hair was not even braided but left hanging loose.

'In a few hours I will be a married woman,' she had said, 'and thereafter I'll be wearing my hair covered, out of doors at any rate. Today I am, at last, changing from a maid into a wife, and I want my hair to stand as a token of that change.'

And, to her astonishment, Hawisa had not even argued. Instead, she had sent Nathan out to find what flowers he might from along the hedgerows and in the woods, and he returned with pale primroses and a few shining golden celandines. She had put them all into a pot of water. 'I'll make a posy of them just afore you're ready to go, and fix them to your hair.'

Hawisa again showed surprising deftness as she fixed the flowers to the little silver fillet, then placed the fillet on top of Eleanor's brushed-out hair. She held up the little polished metal mirror, and Eleanor smiled at her reflection. Despite the hazy metal, she could see her hair was shining like fine copper strands, and she loved the crisping left by the unravelled braids, and the way the fillet wound with the yellow flowers sat atop her head like a little jewelled coronet. Then Hawisa lowered the mirror, and Eleanor saw how the low-cut bodice of the leaf-green cotehardie set off her pale neck and throat.

'It looks well?' she said.

'Very well, my *lady*.' Hawisa chuckled at her little jest. 'You look a lady for all you're marrying a—' She stopped, and put two fingers to her lips. 'He's marrying a *beauty*,' she said, and waggled her head.

'Hardly that, Hawisa,' said Eleanor, giggling, 'but I'm glad at least I look my best for my wedding day.'

*

At last, Eleanor was ready for the walk down to Saint Peter's, her best cloak around her shoulders. She was glad the day was dry, if cold, so she could wear shoes more suited to her lovely gown than the boots, incongruous but necessary, she had been obliged to wear at Christmas.

Hawisa was pacing up and down the hall, awaiting the arrival of the man who was to accompany Eleanor to the church, and present her to be married. Eleanor had not seen much of her stepbrother, Roger, in recent months, although they still occasionally dined together. As step-siblings, they were not close, but had become fond enough of each other. And, as Roger was Eleanor's only living male relative, she decided to ask him to stand in for her dead father, Edward.

Roger was wearing his best surcoat – of good quality, if not in the latest style – when he arrived at Eleanor's door, in good time for their walk to the church, despite Hawisa's fretting.

Susanna and Emma arrived at the same time, each accompanied by their children, and the little party, with Hawisa and Nathan too, set out together to walk down towards the village. At the end of the track that led from her house and joined with the main village thoroughfare, fifty yards or so down from the manor gate, to Eleanor's astonishment, Sir Richard and Lady de Bohun were awaiting them.

'My lady, your lordship!' she cried. 'I'm honoured that you should walk with us.'

Sir Richard screwed up his eyes. 'Margaret insisted,' he said, his whole face gloomy. But then the cloud lifted and his eyes recovered their usual twinkle. 'But the weather is clement enough this morning to warrant a short stroll before a feast.' He held out his hand and, taking hers, dropped a light kiss on it. 'Our good wishes on your happy day, dear Eleanor.'

Lady de Bohun then stepped forward and, taking Eleanor's hand, squeezed it, her face alight. 'I knew you would draw him back to you.' Then she and Sir Richard fell in immediately behind Eleanor and Roger, as the little procession continued on into the village and to the green.

The path that led across it to the church was edged with smiling people. Eleanor blushed at the sight of so many, presumably come to wish her and Walter well. All the village, perhaps, was here, for she thought not many more than a hundred or so folk lived in Meonbridge now. She chided herself for thinking of it at this happy time, but could not stop herself recalling how half of Meonbridge had died in the Mortality five years ago, including her little brothers and beloved father – the father who, despite Roger's kind support, she so wished was here to see her wed.

But, as she approached the church and saw Walter waiting for her, with Will standing at his side, gloomy memories flew away. Walter came forward to take Eleanor from her stepbrother. He bowed to Roger and, beaming to his bride, took her hand in his. She heard Hawisa let out a little whoop behind her.

'Oh my, he looks almost 'andsome,' said Hawisa, and the women around her giggled and agreed.

And so did Eleanor.

She knew Walter was not truly handsome but, in her eyes, he was the best-looking man in Meonbridge. Holding his hand, she stepped back a little and, holding him at arm's length, looked him up and down. Like her, he seemed to have invested in new clothes for the occasion, in his case, a short, and very fashionable, surcoat, in a darker shade of green than her cotehardie and also made of good wool. It looked expensive, so Hawisa must be wrong about the beans, she thought, delighted.

'You approve?' said Walter.

'And you, me?'

He raised his eyebrows. 'How could I not? You're the most beautiful woman in Meonbridge, mebbe in the whole of Hampshire.'

She laughed and squeezed his hand, and they walked forward to the church porch where the priest was waiting to conduct the exchange of marriage vows. Sire Raphael, as he liked to be called, had come only two weeks ago, to take Hugo Garret's place. Old Godfrey Cuylter stood just behind him. He had not been considered suitable by the bishop to take on the full responsibilities of priest but, despite his shaky start, had at length so endeared himself to the villagers with his kindness that Sir Richard recommended he stay on in Meonbridge, to see out his days as curate, and neither the bishop nor Sire Raphael raised any objection.

A hush fell on the gathering, as Sire Raphael asked Walter and Eleanor in turn to make their vows, and then to exchange the rings he had already blessed.

It was all over in a moment, or so it seemed. Eleanor was a married woman, and the man she loved was standing at her side. Walter took her hand and together they followed Sire Raphael into the church, where he would say the Mass and bestow a blessing on their union.

Margaret had surpassed herself, thought Eleanor, as she stepped through the great oak door from the bailey to the manor hall and saw what her ladyship had arranged for her and Walter's marriage feast. Eleanor had expected simply to hold a small celebration in her own house for her closest friends but, when Margaret heard of her plans, she had insisted that too many people would wish to share her happiness for that to be a practical consideration.

'No, my dear Eleanor,' she had said, 'let us hold your bride ale at the manor. It is years since I had the opportunity to arrange such a celebration, with Johanna deciding to become a bride of Christ rather than of Sir Giles Fitzpeyne.' She gave a feeble smile. 'Such a pity, yet my daughter does seem most content with her new life. She is the prioress's deputy – have I told you that?'

Eleanor chuckled to herself. Margaret was, despite her initial disappointment, very proud of her only daughter, now called Sister Dolorosa, and spoke of her more often than she realised. 'Indeed, you have,' said Eleanor, 'and I'm glad Lady Johanna has found such fulfilment at the priory.'

Now, as Eleanor gazed around the hall, delighting at the lavishness of the tables and the elegance of the decorations, Margaret touched her arm. 'It will be a wonderful feast,' she said, and Eleanor was alight with happiness.

Then Margaret took Eleanor's hand and led her towards the high table set on the dais at one end of the hall, where Walter was already waiting for her. Behind them, the folk of Meonbridge were pushing through the bailey door and taking up their places, allotted according to their status, at the tables lined up at right angles to the dais.

Eleanor thought the hall seemed as full as it had been at Christmas. She leaned to whisper in Walter's ear. 'How delightful it is that everyone wishes to share our happiness.'

'Of course they do, my love,' he said, his eyes twinkling. 'Who in Meonbridge'd turn down the offer of a free meal?'

She pouted at his pragmatism, then smiled. 'I suppose you're right. I'm too much of a romancer—'

'Then we complement each other well,' he said.

Eleanor blinked, and a small lump came to her throat. She looked up into Walter's face, and his eyes were bright, boring deep into hers. She blinked again, to stop her feelings spilling over into tears of happiness and, slipping her hand through his arm, she laced her fingers into his.

If the dishes her ladyship had provided for her wedding feast were delicious, Eleanor scarcely noticed. She picked at the morsels Walter offered her, while noting that he at least was tucking in, as all the other diners seemed to be. But Eleanor was too filled with wonder that this day had come at all, to be much interested in – or have need for – food, her heart too overwhelmed with love for the man beside her, the man she almost drove away.

Her eyes sought out Susanna and Emma, sitting together with their children, and, when they looked her way, she raised her goblet to them. Both women raised theirs in return and beamed. What gratitude Eleanor owed her friends for freeing her from her ridiculous obstinacy. What had made her become so stubborn? Pride, perhaps? Or fear that Walter might refuse to return to her?

As the feast progressed, with dish after dish presented, first to the high table, then to those on the main floor of the hall, musicians – none Eleanor knew, so presumably hired in for the occasion – played, to her ears, rather melancholy tunes and roundelays. Watching them, she wondered if this was to be her one disappointment in her ladyship's arrangements. She recalled Susanna's wedding four years ago, when the happiest part of the celebration had surely been the dancing on the village green, accompanied as it was by *Meonbridge* musicians, Alan Fuller on his fiddle, Nick Cook his pipe and Will his tambour, and, of course, Adam, now the sober and respected manor bailiff, with his fine lusty voice. The music and dancing had been a wonderful release from the horrors of the preceding months.

She was expecting any moment that the rather dull musicians would be joined by other hired entertainers, jugglers and jesters perhaps, such as those Margaret had brought in when Philip married Isabella de Courtney a few months before the Mortality came to Meonbridge. Such entertainers were not what Eleanor would have chosen but, in truth, if she had organised the celebration herself, any sort of entertainment would hardly have been a possibility inside her house.

But, as the meal drew to a close – unusually, for feasts at the manor invariably continued for many hours, with the menfolk becoming ever more inebriated – and no such entertainers appeared, Eleanor understood that she was not to be disappointed after all.

The manor hall was very large – at Christmas feasts before the Mortality, it had seated twice the number of Meonbridge people here today – and the far end, she realised, was free from tables. And, now, Alan and Nick and Will, all three, had risen from their places and were moving towards the open area, their instruments held aloft. The hired musicians then stopped their playing and, bowing low to Sir Richard and Lady de Bohun, left the hall.

Sir Richard rose and, coming over, held out his hand to Eleanor. 'Time to dance?' he said, and she blushed, as she stood and let him lead her down the hall, while the three Meonbridge musicians struck up a very merry tune.

Eleanor felt quickly giddy as his lordship whirled her around, the wine she had drunk with only a little food now having its effect. As she danced, other diners were leaving their tables and gathering close by, cups still in their hands. But then the tune came to an end and, while the onlookers were clapping, Sir

Richard led her to where Walter was now standing, a broad smile on his face.

His lordship held her hand out and placed it upon Walter's. 'Your lady, Master Nash,' he said. 'And, now, your turn, I think?'

Eleanor flashed a smile at Walter but, spotting a sudden flutter in his cheek, she knew at once that, in truth, he would not want to dance. She leaned forward, bringing her lips close to his ear. 'Can you not bear to dance with me?'

He grasped her hands in his. 'I can't bear you to think ill of me,' he said, his voice low. 'So I'll try, no matter if your toes're crushed in the attempt.'

She laughed lightly. 'Thank you, my love. Just one dance, then.' She led him to the middle of the floor. 'Follow my lead,' she said.

She gestured to the musicians, certain they would know what sort of tune to play, then stood face-to-face with her new husband, their clasped hands held out to the side. As the music started, Eleanor took a step forward, pulling Walter gently to her, then stepped back again.

'Now you,' she whispered, and he reprised the stepping forth and back. Then 'Twice more,' she said, and they mimed in dance again, and yet again, the bill and coo of lovers.

'Now, you stand still,' she whispered and, letting go his hands and stepping smoothly to the right, she grasped his left hand in hers, then returned to face him, then stepped again, this time to the left.

'Can you do the same?' she murmured. 'It represents the lovers' quarrel and reunion.'

'How apt.' His eyes twinkled a moment, but then he pouted. 'But don't be angry with me if I can't do it.'

But he did it, almost perfectly, treading upon her toes just once.

'Now, all the same steps once more?'

'Your toes can stand the pain of it?'

'Once more, I think they can.' She was so happy that sore toes scarcely mattered.

And when they had reprised the quarrel and reunion, and then again the bill and coo, amidst much clapping and merry laughter, other couples came to the floor and glided through the steps of the simple lovers' dance.

Adam then came forward to stand with the other players, still willing to sing, it seemed, despite his high status in the village. He whispered something in Alan's ear, and Alan nodded and struck up the tune of a familiar ballad, which Adam sang out loud and clear. Soon everyone was joining in the chorus, and Eleanor's heart was full.

After a few more songs from Adam, Alan's fiddle began a different sort of tune and, with much cheering, many folk ran forward. Adam stepped into the middle of the floor and couples – married, betrothed, or only just met – all joined hands, men and women alternately, forming a wide circle around him.

'Will you carole with me?' Eleanor said to Walter, her eyes alight.

He twisted his mouth into a pout. 'Must I?'

She pouted back. 'This is our wedding day, Walter. I promise I'll never ask you to dance again. But, please, just today?' She tilted her head to one side.

He rose slowly to his feet. 'Very well, Mistress Nash. I'll hold you to it, mind.'

Eleanor's heart fluttered at the first mention of her new name but, taking his hand, she pulled him into the circle, just as Adam began to sing. The dancers stamped their feet in unison and then, as one, all in the circle sidestepped to the left, then each brought the right foot to the other, tapping the two feet together. Then they did it again, and again, circling Adam as he sang.

'You see?' cried Eleanor to Walter. 'It's very simple.'

He grinned. 'Even for me.'

Shortly, Adam reached the song's refrain, and all those who knew the words joined in, making a glorious, joyful sound that rose up to the hall's high rafters.

After several verses of the carole, and several circuits of the floor, although the musicians continued playing, many dancers drifted back to the tables and benches, for another cup or two of wine or ale.

Eleanor and Walter separated and went to speak with their friends and neighbours, Eleanor first seeking out Lady de Bohun, wanting to thank her especially for permitting a dance at her wedding feast.

'I thought you would like it,' said Margaret, her eyes twinkling, 'and I can see that I was right. Although I am not so sure that Walter would quite agree?'

Eleanor laughed. 'I don't think he has ever danced in his life before. And he hates any sort of display.'

'But, for you, he danced, so he must love you.' Her ladyship actually winked.

Eleanor had noticed earlier that neither Emma nor Susanna had joined in the dancing, and were now still sitting together, apart from the rest of the company, like old maids with few expectations. But, when she gently upbraided them for not taking part, they just simpered.

'We've the children to mind,' Susanna said.

'Or perhaps we're feeling old,' said Emma.

'That's ridiculous,' said Eleanor. 'Neither of you is *old*. You'll have your chance again—'

But when her two friends exchanged knowing glances, it occurred to her that perhaps neither of them even *wanted* another husband. Though, when she said it, just in jest, Emma almost frowned.

'There're more chances for women these days,' said Emma, 'and we owe it to ourselves, women like me and Susy, to make the best of things.' She tilted her head at Eleanor. 'Just like you've done, Elly. You made the right choice. Walter's a good man, and a very good shepherd. Between the two of you, an' Will, you'll surely build the finest flock in Hampshire.'

At that moment, Nicholas Ashworth came over and, bowing to Susanna, asked her to dance. Emma signalled that she would happily mind the children, and Susanna smiled at Nicholas and took his hand. Two or three dances later, she returned, thanking Nicholas with grace, but insisting that Emma should now have her turn. And, almost at once, John Ward approached to take Emma's hand and, after a dance or two, they sat together talking.

But then, as she was talking to Walter's Aunt Cecily, Eleanor saw, from the corner of her eye, that Will had spotted John, perhaps intruding where he thought he had no right to. Abandoning his tambour, he strode over to where John and Emma were in conversation, and flung himself down upon the bench between them. Eleanor smiled to see John, red-faced now, at once jump up and, bowing, bid Emma a good night. At which Will poured more wine into Emma's cup and shuffled along the bench so he could wrap his arm around her waist. Emma offered no resistance, Eleanor noted. So was it possible that, despite what she had just said, Emma would find her future happiness with the kindly shepherd?

Despite all the pain that she had brought him, Eleanor felt obliged to talk to John atte Wode, who had brought his mother Alice, despite her frailty, to the feast. John still seemed wistful, Eleanor thought, for what might have been, but he had scant chance to say much, for his sister Agnes, and her husband Jack, came forward to offer Eleanor their good wishes. Their three boys, tired perhaps and over-excited, were running around like piglets escaped from the sty, upsetting benches and dragging cloths from tables, bringing cups and plates and flagons crashing to the floor. Agnes, while trying to express her happiness for Eleanor, seemed distracted, and left the conversation to her husband.

Not long after, Walter came to Eleanor and, enclosing her hand in his, whispered in her ear that maybe it was time to go. 'I want you to myself,' he said, wrapping his arm around her waist and drawing her close.

'I too,' she said. She tilted her head. 'Though I think we may have to accept that we'll be followed.'

He shrugged. 'Let's go withal.' He spun her around so they were breast to breast and, putting his hand upon her back, pulled her tight against his body. 'I've waited long enough for this, Mistress Nash.'

Eleanor felt a curious sensation inside her and bit her lip. Did it mean that she too was eager to be alone with Walter?

She was right that, once she and Walter had signalled to the company that they were leaving, a group of villagers, perhaps those most replete with wine and ale, would follow them back to the house.

'The sooner we go upstairs and snuff out the candle,' Walter said, once they were indoors, 'the sooner they'll go away.' He grinned, but Eleanor, despite her undoubted love for him, felt a sudden queasiness.

'Surely we don't have to hurry on their account,' she said, sitting down.

But Walter grasped her hand. 'Indeed not, but *I'm* in a hurry to share your bed, my lady.'

She blushed. 'Goodness, Walter, I never thought you'd be so eager.'

He laughed. 'I can't think why. Just because I've spent so long alone with your sheep—?'

'No, no, don't say it!' she cried. 'I was a fool even to think it.'

She sprang up and, moving round the room, blew out the candles and rushlights that Hawisa had left for them before she and Nathan had, apparently, bedded down in the scullery, to keep out of their way. Then, taking the best candlestick in one hand, she held out her other hand to Walter. 'Come, then, husband,' she said. 'Let us retire, and give those fellows out there something to cheer about.'

An hour or so after sunrise, one brisk but bright March morning, two weeks after Eleanor Titherige had become Mistress Nash, she and Walter took the track up to Riverdown, as they did most days, to check on the progress of the lambing ewes. One or two had already dropped their lambs and, although Will could cope easily enough alone with these early birthings, Eleanor had made it clear to him that she and Walter intended to continue working with him, just as they had done in the past.

The climb up to Riverdown was bracing, for a chilly wind was blowing across the track, and Eleanor was glad she had chosen still to wear her thickest cloak and hood. But the rising sun lent a cheerfulness to the day, and they were both singing as they neared the top of the hill.

But when they reached the shepherd's cottage, they found Will still indoors. They had sought him first amongst the nearest flock of ewes but, when there was neither sign of him nor the dogs, Eleanor returned to the cottage and knocked lightly on the door.

'Who is't?' came the mumbled reply, and Walter shoved open the door, still swollen from the winter rain and snow.

'Who d'you imagine it'd be?' said Walter, as he and Eleanor fell inside, heaving the door closed behind them.

It was gloomy inside the cottage. The shutters were still closed and no rushlights had been lit. Will was sitting by a feeble fire, a cup of something in his hands. He kept his head bowed as they came in.

'Mornin',' he said, still staring into his cup.

Eleanor went closer. 'Whatever is the matter, Will?' She touched his shoulder.

He raised his face then, and she thought she saw the glint of tears moistening his eyes.

'Will?' she said again. 'Is something amiss with the sheep?'

'No, missus, not the sheep.'

'What then?' said Walter, a slight impatience in his voice.

Eleanor took her husband's arm and squeezed it lightly. 'Tell us, Will.'

Will suddenly jumped up, as if he had realised his discourtesy, and bid Eleanor sit down on one of the two stools. He gestured Walter to the other, but Walter shook his head, and Will sat down again. He rolled the cup around between his hands, then pressed his lips together.

'It's Em,' he said, his voice a whisper. 'She's gone.'

'Gone?' repeated Eleanor. 'Whatever do you mean?'

'John come up here soon after first light. Dunno how or why, but he found out Em'd left Meonbridge afore dawn, while it were still dark, taking Bea and Ami and the baby with her. He said she went wi' a carter, on his way back to Winchester.'

'You mean she's gone to Winchester?' said Eleanor.

''S'pose so,' said Will, his face grey.

'Oh, Emma!' Eleanor felt a sudden tightness in her chest. That was what Emma meant when she talked of her and Walter and Will building the finest flock in Hampshire, but did not include herself. She knew *she* would not be here.

Eleanor let out a groan. 'Why didn't she tell me she was going to leave, Will?'

'I reckon she couldn't bear to, missus.' He wiped his sleeve across his face. 'She didn't tell me neither, though I knew she were thinking on it—'

'You knew?' cried Eleanor, feeling betrayed.

'Not exactly. She made it clear she didn't want another husband. Not even me—'

Eleanor then, understanding, bit her lip. 'Oh, I'm so sorry, Will. I hadn't realised you cared for her so much.'

He shrugged. 'It were foolish of me to imagine—'

'No, Will, not foolish,' said Eleanor. 'Emma did say, at the wedding feast, she needed to make the best of life without Ralph. I didn't understand then what it was she meant. But now we know.'

# EPILOGUE

## SPRING 1354

Arthur was wriggling, trying to get comfortable in his roost between the knobbly roots of one of the tall oaks at the woodland edge. So far, tonight, it had been quiet most of the time they'd been up here, watching over Mistress Titherige's sheep. All he could hear was the soft rasp of them nibbling at the new spring grass, or an occasional hushed bleat, as if the beasts were whispering to each other. So, when a long, piercing screech rent the air, it made him jump and set his heart thumping, as it always did. The sheep, too, must've heard the cry, for the nibbling stopped and their bleating became louder and more urgent. He could hear them jostling each other too, maybe trying to run away.

Arthur recalled the first time he'd heard that particular screeching sound up here. Then, he'd been so scared, thinking it was a demon, he'd almost wet his braies. But, these days, he knew it was just the barking of a fox, and knew too that, with only a couple of lambs birthed so far, the fox'd probably ignore them for now.

He settled back against the roughly fissured tree trunk. He wished Luke'd stop snoring and wake up. They were supposed to watch the sheep together.

Arthur wasn't scared of foxes any more, but some of the other noises of the night still made his belly twitch: the creak and groan of branches swaying in the breeze, the endless rustlings in the undergrowth. He knew the rustlings were just small creatures about their nightly search for food, but he thought some of them might bite him and he hated the idea of them slithering and jiggling inside his hose. Drawing his feet up close to his body, he wrapped his arms across his chest, wishing he was back at home, in bed.

It wasn't long before the bleating, jostling sheep seemed to settle back to cropping. Arthur peered into the gloom, but the sky was cloudy, and it was hard to see much beyond the animals closest to him. He shrugged to himself. He hoped the moon would come out in a while. Then he'd wake Luke up and they'd make a turn around the flock, like Master Nash had said they must.

*

Luke started awake, his heart racing. An unearthly shrieking had invaded his dream, goading him from sleep. But the noise wasn't, after all, coming from inside his dream.

Scrambling to his knees, he leaned across and thumped his cousin on the shoulder with his stump. 'Shuddup, you idiot! You'll set the sheep off.'

Arthur cried out, rubbing at his shoulder. 'I thought you was asleep.'

'I was till you started up wi' that un'oly row.' He punched him again. 'What were it this time?'

Arthur sniffled. 'That owl.' He wiped his sleeve across his face. 'It flew out the trees, y'know, like a great white ghost— I felt it riffling my hair—'

'But why d'you always 'ave to scream, you half-wit?'

'It made me jump.'

'"*It made me jump*",' mimicked Luke, rolling his eyes. 'God's bones, Art, when you gonna grow up?'

Arthur whimpered. 'I can't help jumping.'

Luke snorted, and rolled over, back to his own roost at the foot of the next tree.

'God's eyes, I'll lose my wits if I 'ave to watch these sheep much longer,' said Luke. He got to his feet and Arthur heard him stumble a few steps and piss into the undergrowth, before coming back and flopping down again.

'I like watching them,' said Arthur, smiling to himself. He liked the peace of it. Though he thought it'd be better without the rustlings and the owl and such.

'You're as stupid as them,' said Luke. 'Good for naught but eating and being afeared of foxes.'

'I ain't afeared o' foxes.' Arthur was affronted.

'You should be.' Luke sniggered. 'You wait till the lambs start dropping—'

Arthur bit his lip. 'What d'you mean?'

'Easy meat for foxes, little lambs.' Luke leaned across and flipped his hand at his cousin's shoulder. 'You'll have t' keep your wits about you then.'

'So we'll be guarding them, 'stead o' just watching?' said Arthur, thinking it sounded more important, as well as a bit scary.

Luke scoffed. 'Oh, yeah, I can just see you saving a lamb from out a fox's maw.'

'Maw?'

'Yeah, maw, you half-wit—'

Arthur put his hands up to his ears. Whatever Luke was saying about the fox's maw was too muffled for him to hear. Maybe it was enough withal just to *watch* the sheep.

\*

Luke blew out a long deep sigh. His whole body hurt from being hunched at the foot of the damned tree. Unable to find sleep again, he writhed and twitched, trying to ease the pain. Then, the familiar, *impossible*, pain started up, as it often did at night. In the dark and silence, or when he woke up from a doze, he could feel his missing hand, still there, tingling. Sometimes, the pain was sharper, like his flesh was being sliced through with a blade. And, sometimes, that made him cry. He kneaded at the stump, trying to quell the unearthly feeling and ease the pain. Then he wiped the heel of his hand roughly across his eyes, and leaned back against the oak's rough trunk. He'd told no one about these unnatural feelings, for fear that folk might think him brainsick.

'Lu?'

'What?' He snorted.

'We're s'posed to take a turn about the sheep.'

He sighed again, more fiercely. 'And what if we don't?'

'Lu, we can't *not*—'

'Who's to know?' Luke said. Though he knew it was a stupid question. Groaning, he struggled to his feet. He felt like a man three times his age. 'Come on, then, pillock, what you waiting for?'

Arthur scrambled up, then pointed to the sky. 'The moon's come out.'

Luke glanced up. The moon's light was hardly bright, still hidden behind a thin veil of cloud, but it was enough to let them see the sheep. They weren't to go amongst them, just make a wide circuit round, looking out for any problems, and for ewes seemingly about to drop their lambs. Luke thought it all a waste of time. It'd be more interesting if a fox did sneak in and cause a bit of havoc. But tonight, as usual, there was nothing to remark upon, and the boys went back to their trees.

'Sheep are boring,' said Luke, easing himself back down.

'Da says we should be grateful Missus Titherige took us on,' said Arthur.

'"*Da says, Da says*",' mocked Luke. 'It's a lousy job. Why'd anyone wanna be a shepherd?'

He thought back to earlier today, when he was struggling to hold fast to a ewe. It'd been hard enough when he had two hands. That time when he and Arthur had taken their first sheep, he'd almost lost his grip, with the damned thing bleating and flailing its legs, trying to get away. And now, with only one hand to hang on with, and the stump no use for aught, the job was nigh on impossible. Sometimes he wanted to weep with the frustration of it, but he refused to let himself seem weak in front of Will and Master Nash.

Sometimes he wished his uncle John hadn't agreed, when Walter Nash came to offer him a job as well as Arthur.

'My wife,' Master Nash had said, 'thinks your nephew deserves a second chance.' He tightened his lips. 'I disagree, but I'm willing to give it a go.'

His uncle had nodded his thanks, then scratched at his head. 'But, Walter – Master Nash – I don't see how the lad can work one-handed. Sheeps're brainless, obstinate creatures. Can try the patience of a fit man.'

Master Nash shrugged. 'I agree wi' you, but Eleanor reckons the lad's got to learn to live, one hand or no.'

''Tis true, and he's making a fair fist of it, wi' dressing an' eating an' such.'

'But he has to work too. You can't support him all his life, John.'

His uncle's shoulders slumped, and when he turned away from the shepherd, his face was crumpled.

'You're right, Master Nash, I can't. 'ard as I work, I can't keep us all.'

'So let him come to us. We'll teach him how to work with sheep. Learn him a trade. He'll get the hang of things, and work out how to do it wi' just the one set o' fingers.'

Luke had been sitting in the shadows, at the far end of the cottage, beneath the platform his uncle slept on. He got up and came forward.

'Like a 'prentice?' he said.

Master Nash's eyebrows had shot up. 'Didn't know you were hiding there.'

'Weren't hiding,' said Luke, 'just sitting.'

John put his hand upon Luke's shoulder. 'D'you agree, son?'

Luke had shrugged. He didn't have much choice.

'I like sheep,' said Arthur now.

'That's 'cause you're just like them – stupid.' Having to spend all night with his idiot cousin was getting on Luke's nerves. 'I'm not sticking this much longer.'

'But what else can you do?' said Arthur, scratching at his head.

At that, Luke lunged sideways and aimed his stump end at Arthur's chin. Arthur yelped, but Luke hit him again before slumping back against the tree. 'Why d'you 'ave to say that? I can do whatever I want.'

Luke's voice was hoarse and quavery, but Arthur didn't notice. He was snivelling and cradling his throbbing chin. 'No you can't!' he said. 'You can't be a carpenter or a blacksmith or even a proper labourer. You can't do nothin' much with only one hand.'

'You little prick!' Luke yelled, then lunged again, punching Arthur with his stump and slapping him with his hand.

Arthur let out a stream of wails and, amidst the uproar, the nearest sheep began to trot about and bleat. But then the boy seemed to find his strength and threw Luke off onto his back. 'You're frightening the sheep!' he cried. 'An', if we're not careful, Will'll come and we might lose our jobs.'

Luke sat up again, rubbing at his stump. 'What do I care? I don't want it anyway.'

When Arthur arrived up on Riverdown next Monday morning, he told Will that Luke would not be coming.

'He didn't come 'ome last night,' he said, chewing at his lip. 'He went t' the ale-house wi' his friends—'

'Didn't you go with him?' said Will.

'Nah,' said the boy. 'Lu never wants me with him now.' He chewed again. 'He says I'm a baby.'

'You think he's run off again?'

Arthur shrugged.

'Good riddance, if he has,' said Will.

Walter, who had just arrived and overheard the end of the conversation, agreed. But Eleanor, only a pace or two behind him, did not.

Walter grimaced. 'I was about to say to Will you'd not agree with us.'

'Of course I don't,' said Eleanor. 'The boy needs steady work and a firm master. There's no reason he can't learn.'

Walter shrugged. 'Not sure you're right, my love. But, have it your way. Will, you'd best go see John, find out what's going on. We'll mind things here till you get back.'

But Eleanor shook her head. 'I'll go. Poor John must be worried sick.' And she turned at once and hurried back down the hill to Meonbridge.

The two men shared a grin. 'Still a woman of resolve, then?' said Will, and Walter could not help but laugh.

When Eleanor knocked on John's door and opened it in answer to his muffled greeting, she found John pacing up and down his cramped, untidy hall.

'I don't know where he's gone,' John said, raking his fingers through his hair. 'An' I should. I'm responsible for him.'

'Do you think he's run away?' said Eleanor.

John shrugged. 'I dunno, missus. But I do know how melancholy he's become. He's suffered more than many in his young life. What wi' losing his sisters, then watching his Ma beat to death, an' getting thumped daily by his Da, an' not learning proper what's right and wrong—' He raked his hair again. 'I'd hoped to set him on the rightful path.' His eyes were wet.

'You can only do your best. It is hardly your fault if Luke isn't a willing learner.'

John slumped down on a stool, his head in his hands.

Eleanor stepped forward and touched John on the shoulder. 'Master Nash and I are willing to take Luke back if you can find him.' She pursed her lips. 'Well, in truth, Walter's not so keen… But I am certain, John, that if we can encourage Luke to apply himself in earnest, he *can* make something of his life. He's no fool, and he's strong, albeit he only has one hand.'

John looked up. 'But we 'ave to find 'im first.'

'And I will help you.'

'You?' John shook his head. 'No, missus, you don't 'ave to.'

'But I want to, and I will.'

Eleanor knew Walter would not approve of her plan but she was determined, if she could, to help John set his unhappy nephew back onto the right path.

'Why d'you want to, missus, after all he and my accursed brother've done to you?'

Eleanor drew John's other stool out from underneath the rough-hewn table and sat down. 'I recall what Luke said at the trial, about his mother. Despite all his bluster and bravado, Luke loved his mother. He stayed with her, even after she told him to leave, because he wanted to protect her from his father.'

John nodded, the corners of his eyes moist.

'Of course at length he was unable to protect her, for Matthew was too strong, too violent. But he tried. In that, he was good boy, a loving son. No one can deny that.'

'And 'cause of that, you think 'e's worth saving?'

She smiled. 'Yes, John, I do. I agree with all you said about how much Luke has suffered. He deserves a chance to have a better go at life.'

'Gen'rous of you to say so, missus.'

She stood up and pressed her hand upon his shoulder. 'So where do you think he might be hiding?'

Eleanor sent a message up to Walter to say she would see him at home for supper. She imagined the irritation her message would cause, but considered it a penalty worth paying if Luke Ward could be found and returned to his uncle's charge.

She wasn't quite sure why she cared so much about him. John was right that he and his father had caused her considerable grief, but also that Luke had suffered sorely at his father's hands. But her own father had taught her the importance of compassion to those less fortunate than herself, and she did have it in her power to help Luke show again the courage he'd shown as a boy, and make something of his life.

They searched the places where Luke and Arthur and, later, Tom, had hidden out. Eleanor let John scramble over the heaps of debris in the derelict crofts of Meonvale and hack his way through waist-high thickets of ivy, brambles and newly growing nettles, before she joined him at the entrance door. They must have tried a dozen cottages and barns without success. But then, in a cottage so decrepit she wondered if the boys had even considered it before, John seemed to sense something and knelt down on the floor, just by an upturned bench. He plucked some morsels from the blackened rushes, and looked across at Eleanor, waiting in the doorway.

'See here, crumbs of bread, an' cheese,' he said.

Then Eleanor heard the faintest rustling, and gestured to a dark corner of the cottage, beyond a broken table and the long-dead hearth. John nodded, and stood up.

'Luke,' he said quietly. 'We know you're here. Come out, son. Hiding won't do no good.' He stared into the gloom, his eyes trying to penetrate the darkness. Beyond the table, he could see a bed, quite a good bed for a cottar, with a wooden frame and thick straw mattress, albeit torn and leaking stalks. John wondered who'd once lived here to own such a bed. But it hardly mattered now.

Then, as John stared, Luke stood up from behind the bed.

'Nothing's no good,' said Luke.

John righted the bench and sat down on it. He gestured Luke to do the same. He crept forward and perched next to his uncle. John's heart turned over at the sight of his nephew's melancholy face.

He gestured towards Eleanor, still standing by the door. Luke started at the sight of her, but John put a reassuring hand upon his shoulder.

'The missus and me, we've both come to take you 'ome.'

Luke shrugged and tears leaked from his eyes. He held up his stump. 'What use am I wi' this?'

'I can't pretend life will not be hard for you, Luke,' said Eleanor, stepping forward a few steps, 'but folk *do* work it out.' And she told him the story of her father's servant, who lost his arm in the war. 'You can too, if you have a mind to.'

Luke sniffed. 'Not sure I 'ave.'

'But you 'ave to try,' said John. 'Do it for your Ma's sake. You loved your Ma. You tried to protect her, didn't you, even when you were a little lad? An' she were a good woman, Sarah. She jus' made a bad choice of husband, albeit he were my brother. An' it were her lot in life to suffer at his brutal hands. Yours too, lad, but you don't 'ave to follow your Da's example any more.'

Eleanor nodded. 'Luke, your mother never gave up trying to make the best of things, and she wanted you to live.'

Luke squinted then looked away, and John thought their words must have fallen on unwilling ears.

For long moments, Luke sat in silence, staring into the corner beyond the bed. But, at last, he got up slowly from the bench. He rubbed at his stump, and looked up at his uncle, then at Eleanor. John could see the boy's eyes were wet. He wanted to put his arm around his shoulders, but waited to hear what Luke would say.

Luke's shoulders heaved as a small sob escaped. But, at length, he nodded. 'For 'er sake, then,' he said, and moved towards the door.

# GLOSSARY

**Bailey** – A courtyard of a castle or fortified house, enclosed by an outer wall.

**Bailiff** – The lord's chief official on the manor.

**Braies** – The equivalent of men's underpants, braies were a loose garment, usually made of linen and held up by a belt, and which might hang below the knees or be short to mid-thigh.

**Brewet** – Generally, a sort of meat stew, which, in wealthy households, might be rich and spicy. In peasant households, a brewet was likely no different from a vegetable pottage (that is, it would have little or no meat).

**Bride ale** – A wedding feast.

**Barber-surgeon** – A medical practitioner who, unlike many physicians of the time (who were more interested in the imbalance of *humours*), carried out surgical operations, often on the battle field. Many had no formal training, and were often illiterate. Alongside surgery, the tasks they carried out included bloodletting, teeth extraction, performing enemas, treating all manner of ailments and selling medicines (as well as, presumably, cutting hair).

**Carole** – A dance with any number of participants who danced in a ring or chain, following a leader and singing the accompanying music, probably a well-known ballad.

**Choler** – See *Humours*.

**Cotehardie** – A fitted tunic worn by both men and women, the male version often quite short, the female's sometimes trailing on the ground. It was worn over an undergarment of some sort, a shirt for a man, perhaps a chemise and a thin kirtle for a woman.

**Cottar** – The tenant of a cottage, usually holding little or no land, on the bottom rung of village society.

**Crespine and fillet** – Elements of a headdress for a wealthier woman: a net, possibly made of wire, and a band of some sort to hold it in place.

**Croft** – The garden plot of a village house.

**Demesne** – The part of the lord's manorial lands reserved for his own use and not allocated to his tenants.

**Frankpledge** – A policing system by which every member of a tithing over the age of twelve was responsible for the conduct of every other member. See also *Tithing*.

**Freemen** – Free tenants were not only personally free, but had no obligation to do regular work on the demesne land of the lord.

**Heriot** – A death duty, usually the "best beast" or some other goods, paid to dead man's lord.

**Hue-and-cry** – A way of apprehending a criminal, in which everyone within earshot of a person calling out for help was required to give chase, and hopefully catch, any sort of malefactor.

**Humours** – Ancient medical theory held that the human body encompassed four humours, which needed to be kept in balance. Illness of whatever kind supposedly arose from an excess or deficit of one of the humours. The four humours were black bile, yellow bile, phlegm, and blood, and corresponded to the four "temperaments", respectively, melancholic, choleric, phlegmatic and sanguine. The physician's task was to attempt to correct any imbalance between the humours to restore a person to sound health.

**Hundred** – Administrative division of an English shire or county, in theory equalling one hundred hides though it rarely did. A hide was roughly four *virgates*. A Hundred usually held its own court, which met monthly to handle civil and criminal cases.

**Journeyman** – A craftsman who, having completed his apprenticeship must undergo a few years of practising his craft.

**Manor** – A small-holding, typically 1200-1800 acres, with its own court and probably its own hall, but not necessarily having a manor house. The manor as a unit of land was generally held by a knight or managed by a bailiff for some other holder.

**Megrim** – Migraine.

**Melancholy** – See *Humours*.

**Phlegm** – See *Humours*.

**Reeve** – A principal manorial official under the bailiff, and always a villein.

**Rouncey** – An ordinary, everyday sort of horse, generally used for riding.

**Rushlight** – A type of candle made by soaking the dried stem of a rush in some sort of fat, the cheapest, and commonest kind of light source used by medieval peasants.

**Sanguine** – See *Humours*.

**Sext, Nones, Terce** – The canonical hours were the specified times for prayer but also used to mark the times of day:

Matins: Midnight or sometime during the night.

Lauds: Dawn or 3 a.m.

Prime: The first hour, about 6 a.m.

Terce: The third hour, about 9 a.m.

Sext: The sixth hour, about noon.

Nones: The ninth hour, about 3 p.m.

Vespers: The "lighting of the lamps", about 6 p.m.

Compline: The last hour, just before retiring, around 9 p.m.

**Sheriff's tourn** – The circuit made by the sheriff of a county twice a year, in which he presided at the court in each Hundred of the county.

**Surcoat** – An outer garment, much like a sleeveless coat, worn by both men and women.

**Tippets** – The *cotehardie* sometimes had hanging sleeves, which, over time, became longer and narrower like a dangling streamer, and called a tippet.

**Tithing** – A unit of ten or twelve village men mutually responsible for each other's conduct. See also *Frankpledge*.

**Toft** – The yard of a village house.

**Villein** – The wealthiest class of peasant. Villeins usually cultivated 20-40 acres of land, often in isolated strips.

**Virgate** – A unit of land theoretically large enough to support a peasant family, varying between 18 and 32 acres.

# ACKNOWLEDGEMENTS

I am so grateful to the many people who have helped me along my writing journey, without whom I don't think I'd have had the confidence to make it this far.

For *A Woman's Lot*, I decided to ask a small group of what I called "beta readers" to have a first read of the manuscript, to identify any horrible glitches and what Jane Austen termed "infelicities" (I love that...). So, Claire, Alan, Rhonwen and David, thank you so much for your initial thoughts and suggestions – they were of enormous help.

Then of course I must thank my lovely editor, Hilary, who is so good at assuring me that my writing does actually have some merit, while not shying away from making recommendations for clarifying a character's motives, tightening up some woolly writing, or bringing a scene more vividly to life.

And of course I am grateful to the team at SilverWood Books, for producing, once again, such a stunning cover and beautifully presented book.

You can connect with me through my website and social media:

Website and blog: www.carolynhughesauthor.com
Goodreads: www.bit.ly/2hs2rrX
Facebook: CarolynHughesAuthor
Twitter: @writingcalliope

# AND FINALLY...

If you've enjoyed reading *A Woman's Lot*, please do consider leaving a brief review on your favourite site. Reviews are of enormous help to authors, both in terms of providing feedback and in building readership.

If you enjoy my writing, perhaps you'd like to join my supporters' team? Everybody needs a little moral support and authors need all the help they can get!

In return for your support, I will send you updates on my books, and periodically ask for your help or feedback. As a small "thank you" for joining the team, I will send you occasional unpublished short stories or novellas featuring some of the Meonbridge characters.

If you are interested, please go to my website (carolynhughesauthor.com) and select Subscribe to open the sign up form.

I hope you will enjoy the short read(s) while you wait for the next Meonbridge novel to be published.

I look forward to your company!

Lightning Source UK Ltd.
Milton Keynes UK
UKHW01f1811010718
325034UK00002B/85/P

9 781781 327883